SMALL FELONIES 2
BY BILL PRONZINI
AFTERWORD BY BARRY N. MALZBERG

Stark House Press • Eureka California

SMALL FELONIES 2

Published by Stark House Press
1315 H Street
Eureka, CA 95501, USA
griffinskye3@sbcglobal.net
www.starkhousepress.com

SMALL FELONIES 2
Copyright © 2022 by Bill Pronzini.
(See Acknowledgements for original copyright information.)

Published by arrangement with the author. All rights reserved under International and Pan-American Copyright Conventions.

"The Felicities of Fiction or The Heart of the Artichoke" copyright © 2022 by Barry N. Malzberg

ISBN: 978-1-951473-65-5

Book and cover design by Mark Shepard, shepgraphics.com

PUBLISHER'S NOTE
This is a work of fiction. Names, characters, places and incidents are either the products of the author's imagination or used fictionally, and any resemblance to actual persons, living or dead, events or locales, is entirely coincidental.

Without limiting the rights under copyright reserved above, no part of this publication may be reproduced, stored, or introduced into a retrieval system or transmitted in any form or by any means (electronic, mechanical, photocopying, recording or otherwise) without the prior written permission of both the copyright owner and the above publisher of the book.

First Stark House Press Edition: April 2022

CONTENTS

PREFACE 11
Trade Secret 13
Wishful Thinking 18
The Monster 24
Home is the Place Where (A "Nameless Detective" Story) 27
Night Walker (with Barry N. Malzberg) 32
Out Behind the Shed 37
Chip 42
Multiples (with Barry N. Malzberg) 48
The Being 52
Stroke of Luck 56
Betrayal 61
Shade Work 65
The Man Who Loved Mystery Stories (with Barry N. Malzberg) ...70
Lines 74
Wedding Day 79
Putting the Pieces Back 84
Birds of a Feather (with Barry N. Malzberg) 88
Where Am I? 92
The Shrew 98
Meadowlands Spike (with Barry N. Malzberg) 102
Angelique 107
Crazy 111
Demolition, Inc. (with Barry N. Malzberg) 114
The Last Laugh 119
Confession 123
The Tuesday Curse (with Barry N. Malzberg) 128
Bones 132
I Think I Will Not Hang Myself Today 137
A Matter of Survival (with Barry N. Malzberg) 142
Dago Red 146
Why Did You Do It? 151

Bomb Scare (A "Nameless Detective" Story)	155
What Kind of Person Are You? (with Barry N. Malzberg)	157
The Wind	160
Such Things as Nightmares Are Made Of	164
A Matter of Justice (with Barry N. Malzberg)	170
I Didn't Do It	175
Home	178
The Crack of Doom (with Barry N. Malzberg)	181
Do It Yourself	186
The Night, the River	191
Always Her Eyes (with Barry N. Malzberg)	196
I Know a Way	203
Neighbors	206
Final Exam (with Barry N. Malzberg)	211
Funeral Day	217
Caius (with Barry N. Malzberg)	220
The Space Killers	225
Free Durt	230
Zero Tolerance (A "Nameless Detective" Story)	236
AFTERWORD by Barry N. Malzberg	241
Bibliography	244

SMALL FELONIES 2

50 short-short stories told in first-person, third-person, present as well as past tense, and in epistolary format; tales of detection (three feature long-running series character, the "Nameless Detective"), psychological suspense, historical noir, light and dark fantasy, satirical humor, horror, the biter-bitten, the O. Henry twist, a shaggy dog story or two, even a shameless futuristic Hemingway pastiche.

The earliest entry, "I Know a Way," was published in 1971; the most recent, "Such Things As Nightmares Are Made Of," appears here for the first time. Fourteen were written in collaboration with Barry Malzberg. More than a score were first printed in *Ellery Queen's Mystery Magazine*; others in *Alfred Hitchcock Mystery Magazine, Mystery Scene, Cemetery Dance, The Strand Magazine, Analog Science Fiction, Mike Shayne Mystery Magazine*; the balance in anthologies.

50 crime stories… each a connoisseur's delight!

ACKNOWLEDGMENTS

"The Monster," "Home is the Place Where," "Stroke of Luck," "Betrayal," "Shade Work," "Wedding Day," "The Shrew," "The Last Laugh," "Confession," "The Tuesday Curse," "Bones," "I Think I Will Not Hang Myself Today," "Why Did You Do It?", "Bomb Scare," "The Wind," "Do It Yourself," "Always Her Eyes," "Neighbors," "Free Durt," "A Matter of Justice" were originally published in *Ellery Queen's Mystery Magazine*. Copyright © 1993, 1995, 1996, 2000, 2004, 2008, 2010, 2011, 2013, 2015, 2017, 2019, 2020, 2021 by Bill Pronzini; copyright © 2008, 2020 by Bill Pronzini and Barry N. Malzberg.

"Night Walker," "Birds of a Feather," "Putting the Pieces Back," "A Matter of Survival," "What Kind of Person Are You?", "The Crack of Doom," "Final Exam" were originally published in *Alfred Hitchcock's Mystery Magazine*. Copyright © 1976 by Bill Pronzini; copyright © 1976, 1977, 1978, 1979, 2016, 2018 by Bill Pronzini and Barry N. Malzberg.

"Lines" and "Crazy" were originally published in *Cemetery Dance*. Copyright © 2012, 2019 by Bill Pronzini.

"I Know a Way" and "Demolition, Inc." were originally published in *Mike Shayne Mystery Magazine*. Copyright © 1971 by Bill Pronzini; copyright © 1981 by Bill Pronzini and Barry N. Malzberg.

"Trade Secret" originally appeared in *Damn Near Dead II*. Copyright © 2011 by Bill Pronzini.

"Wishful Thinking" originally appeared in *Irreconcilable Differences*. Copyright © 1999 by Bill Pronzini.

"Out Behind the Shed" originally appeared in *Final Shadows*. Copyright © 1991 by Bill Pronzini.

"Chip" originally appeared in *Mystery Scene*. Copyright © 2001 by Bill Pronzini.

"Multiples" originally appeared in *Tricks and Treats*. Copyright © 1976 by Bill Pronzini and Barry N. Malzberg.

"The Being" originally appeared in *Analog Science Fiction*. Copyright © 2018 by Bill Pronzini.

"The Man Who Loved Mystery Stories" originally appeared in *The Strand Magazine*. Copyright © 2000 by Bill Pronzini and Barry N. Malzberg.

"Where Am I?" originally appeared in *Borderlands 7*. Copyright © 2020 by Bill Pronzini.

"Meadowlands Spike" originally appeared in *New Jersey Noir*. Copyright © 2011 by Bill Pronzini and Barry N. Malzberg.

"Angelique" originally appeared in *Horror Drive-In*. Copyright © 2010 by Bill Pronzini.

"Dago Red" originally appeared in *Measures of Poison*. Copyright © 2002 by Bill Pronzini.

"I Didn't Do It" originally appeared in *New Crimes 2*. Copyright © 1989 by Bill Pronzini.

"Home" originally appeared in *Night Freight*. Copyright © 2000 by Bill Pronzini.

"The Night, the River" originally appeared in *Quietly Now*. Copyright © 2004 by Bill Pronzini.

"Funeral Day" originally appeared in *New Crimes*. Copyright © 1989 by Bill Pronzini.

"Caius" originally appeared in *Blood and Other Cravings*. Copyright © 2011 by Bill Pronzini and Barry N. Malzberg.

"The Space Killers" originally appeared in *Beat to a Pulp II*. Copyright © 2012 by Bill Pronzini.

"Zero Tolerance" originally appeared in *Spadework*. Copyright © 1996 by Bill Pronzini.

"Such Things As Nightmares Are Made Of." Copyright © 2022 by Bill Pronzini.

SMALL FELONIES 2
50 SHORT SHORT STORIES
BY BILL PRONZINI

PREFACE

Most professional writers find the short-short story difficult to write. Fortunately, I'm not one of them. In fact I consider the short-short to be much easier to concoct than longer stories or full-length novels. One reason is that I enjoy the challenge of creating a story of 2,000 words or less that has all the necessary elements – plausible and unusual plot, believable characters, suspense, dramatic payoff – of good fiction in microcosm. Another reason is that I have a hyperactive and somewhat devious imagination. A third is that writing a short-short or vignette takes very little time and provides immediate gratification, if not always a quick sale.

I can't claim to have achieved the level of accomplishment of such masters of the form as Fredric Brown, Gerald Kersh, and Jack Ritchie, but I do believe I'm in the running for the most prolific purveyor past and present with close to 150 published. Fifty early tales were collected in the first *Small Felonies* (1988). Most of the fifty which comprise the present volume were written over the past thirty years. As the titles indicate, all stories in both books involve crime – directly or indirectly, to one degree or another.

The earliest entry, "I Know a Way," was published in 1971; the most recent, "Such Things As Nightmares Are Made Of," appears here for the first time. Fourteen were written in collaboration with Barry Malzberg. More than a score were first printed in *Ellery Queen's Mystery Magazine*; others in *Alfred Hitchcock Mystery Magazine, Mystery Scene, Cemetery Dance*, The Strand Magazine, *Analog Science Fiction, Mike Shayne Mystery Magazine*; the balance in anthologies.

In my preface to the first *Small Felonies*, I referred to the contents as "a slumgullion of short-shorts" – many disparate ingredients mixed together in the same kettle. That whimsical collective noun applies to *Small Felonies II* as well. The ingredients here are tales told first-person, third-person, present as well as past tense, and in epistolary format; tales of detection (three feature my long-running series character, the "Nameless Detective"), psychological suspense, historical noir, light and dark fantasy, satirical humor, horror, the biter-bitten, the O. Henry twist, a shaggy dog story or two, even a shameless futuristic Hemingway pastiche.

May this second slumgullion of mine provide a savory feast from first bite to last.

Bill Pronzini
Petaluma, California
June 2021

TRADE SECRET

I was sitting in one of the canvas chairs on the back deck, adjusting the drag on my Daiwa fishing reel, when I heard the car grinding uphill through the woods. My cabin is on a backcountry lake, pretty far off the beaten track, and the gate across the private road has a No Trespassing sign. The only visitors I get are occasional tradespeople from the little town a dozen miles away, by invitation only, and I wasn't expecting anybody today.

I got up, slow—now that the cool early fall weather had set in, my arthritis was acting up—and shuffled inside for my 30.06. Then I went out front to find out who it was. The car that rolled out of the pines was a shiny new silver Lincoln I'd never seen before. Illinois plates—that told me something right there. The driver was a man and he was alone; the angle of the sun let me see that much. But I didn't get a good look at his face until the Lincoln swung to a stop alongside my Jeep and he opened the door.

Surprise. Easy Ed Malachi.

He hadn't changed much. A little less of the dyed black hair, a few extra wrinkles in his jowly face and another ten pounds or so bulging his waistline. Dressed same as in the old days, like an Armani ad in a magazine—silk shirt, Bronzini tie, a suit that must've set him back at least three grand. But the outfit was all wrong for a trip into this wilderness country. That told me something, too.

Malachi was smiling when he got out, one of those ear to ear smiles of his that had always made me think of a shark. I leaned the rifle against the wall next to the stacked firewood, moved over to meet him when he came up onto the porch.

"Hey, Griff," he said, and grabbed my hand and pumped it a couple of times. Sunlight glinted off his gold baguette diamond ring, the platinum Philippe Patek watch on his left wrist. "Hope you don't mind me just showing up like this, but you're a hard man to get hold of. Long time, huh? Must be, what, six years?"

"More like seven and a half."

"Some place you got here. Middle of nowhere, not easy to find."

"That's the way I like it."

"Sure, you always were your own man. But I never figured you'd turn into a hermit."

"People change."

"Sure they do. Sure. You're looking good, though, fit as ever. Retirement agrees with you."

"You didn't come all the way up here to make small talk," I said. "What do you want, Ed?"

"How about a drink for starters? I been on the road five hours, I can use one. You still drinking Irish?"

"Now and then."

"Spare a double shot for an old friend?"

We'd never been friends, but there was no point in making an issue of it. I led him inside, poured his drink and a dollop for myself while he looked around at the knotty pine walls, the furniture and bookcases I'd built myself, the big native stone fireplace. "Some place," he said again.

"Suits me."

"You get cell phone reception up here?"

"No."

"Didn't think so. I couldn't find a number. But I see you got a landline."

"Unlisted and blocked. I don't use it much."

"What about TV reception? Pretty bad?"

"I wouldn't know. I don't have a television. Or want one."

"Yeah? So what do you do nights, winters?"

"Read, mostly. Work puzzles, listen to CB radio. Fall asleep in front of the fire."

"The quiet life." Malachi's expression said what he meant was boring life. He couldn't imagine himself living the way I did, without luxuries and all the glitz he was used to. "What about women?"

"What about them?"

"You always had one around in the old days."

"That was the old days. Now I like living alone."

"But you don't always sleep alone, right? I mean, you're not even seventy yet."

"One more year."

"Hell, sixty-nine's not old. I'm sixty-five and I still get my share." His laugh sounded forced. "Good old Viagra."

"Let's take our drinks out on the deck," I said.

We went out there. Malachi carried his glass over to the railing, stood looking down at the short wooden dock with my skiff tied up at the end, then out over the mile and a half of glass-smooth lake, the pine woods that hemmed it on three sides, the forested mountains in the near distance.

"Some view," he said. "Anybody else live on this lake?"

"No. Nearest neighbors are six miles from here and they're only around in the summer."

"You do a lot of fishing?"

"Fair amount. Mostly catch and release."

"No fun in that. What about deer? Catch and release them too?"

"I don't hunt as much as I used to."

"How come? Still got your eye, right?"

"My eye's fine. Arthritis is the problem."

"But you can still shoot? Your hand's still steady?"

"Steady enough. Why don't you get to the point, Ed, save us both some time?"

He took a swallow of his Irish, coughed, drank again. He was still smiling, but it looked as forced now as his laugh had been. "I got a problem," he said. "A big problem."

"You wouldn't be here if you didn't. And you wouldn't've come alone."

"I don't know who to trust anymore, that's the thing. I'm not even sure of my bodyguards, for Christ's sake. Things've gotten dicey in the business, Griff. Real dicey."

"Is that right?"

"Might as well tell you straight out. Me and Frank Carbone, we're on the outs. Big time."

"What happened?"

"Power struggle," Malachi said, "and it's none of my doing. Frank's gotten greedy in his old age, wants to expand operations, wants full control."

"Why come to me about it?"

"Why do you think? Do I have to spell it out?"

"Contract offer? After all these years?"

"Sure, a contract. Best one you ever had."

"I'm an old man. Why not bring in some young shooter from out of town? Detroit, Miami, L.A."

"I got to have somebody I know, somebody I can trust. I could always trust you, Griff. You never took sides, never rocked the boat. Just took the contracts we gave you and carried them out."

"That was a long time ago," I said. "I've been out of the business almost eight years."

"Not such a long time. I'm betting you're as good as you ever were. The best. Not one screw-up, not one miss. And you always had an angle nobody else thought of. Like the time the cops stashed that fink Jimmy Conlin in the safe house with half a dozen guards, and still you found a way to make the hit. How'd you manage it, anyway? I always wondered."

"Trade secret," I said.

Another forced laugh. He gulped the rest of his drink before he said, "Fifty K was the most you ever got in the old days, right? For Jimmy Conlin? I'll pay you seventy-five to hit Frank Carbone."

"I'm not interested."

"What? Why the hell not? Seventy-five's a lot of money."

"Sure it is. But I don't need it."

"Everybody needs money. Sooner or later."

Well, he was right about that. I was down to only a few thousand stashed in the strongbox under the bedroom floor, and the cabin could use a new roof, a new hot water heater. I could use a bigger skiff, too, with a more reliable outboard. But money and the things it could buy weren't important to me anymore. I could make do with what I had, make it last as many years as I had left.

"No sale, Ed."

"Come on, don't play hard to get. Seventy-five's all I can afford. Think what that much green'll buy you. Round the world cruise. Trips to Europe, South America, anywhere you want to go."

"There's no place I want to go," I said. "Everything I want is right here. I haven't been away from this wilderness in five years, not even for one day, and I don't intend to leave again for any reason or any amount of money. I'm staying put for the rest of my life."

"Bullshit, Griff. Can't you see how desperate I am?"

"I see it, but the answer is still no."

Malachi's fat face was a splotchy red now—anger, fear, the whiskey. "Goddamn you, I done plenty for you in the old days. Plenty. You owe me."

"No, I don't. I don't owe you or anybody else. I paid all my debts before I retired."

"You better take this contract," he said. He pointed an index finger at me, cocked his thumb over it. "You hear me? You know what's good for you, you take it and you do it right and fast."

"You threatening me, Ed? I don't like to be threatened."

"I don't care what you like. You got to do this for me, you got to hit Frank, that's all there is to it. If you don't and I have to take a chance on somebody else—"

"Then that somebody hits me too. That what you're saying?"

"Don't make me do this the hard way, that's what I'm saying. I like you, Griff, I always have, you know that. But you got to take this contract."

I gave him a long look. His words had been hard, but his eyes were pleading and he was sweating into the collar of his expensive silk shirt. I said, "I guess I don't have much choice."

"Neither of us has. So you'll take it?"

"Yeah. I'll take it."

"Good! Good man! I knew you'd come around." Malachi's big smile was back, crooked with relief. He used a monogrammed handkerchief to wipe off his sweat, then clapped me on the arm. "How about we have another drink," he said, "seal the bargain?"

I said that was fine with me and went inside to refill our glasses. Before I took them out to the deck, I made a quick detour into the bedroom.

"What's that you got there?" Malachi asked when I handed him his drink. He was looking at the wicker creel I'd slung over my shoulder.

"Creel. I'm going fishing after you leave. Let's take our drinks down to the dock."

"The dock? What for?"

"Nice by the water this time of day, good place to talk. There're a few things I'll need to know about Frank and his habits. Besides, there's something I want to show off, something I pulled out of the lake."

"Sure, okay, what the hell."

We went down the back steps, across to the dock, out along it to where the skiff was tied at the end.

Malachi said, "So what's this thing you want to show me?"

"Down there, in the skiff."

When he turned and bent to look, I took the silenced .38 out of the creel and shot him twice point blank. He fell over into the skiff's stern, just as I'd intended him to. Neat and clean like in the old days.

I climbed down and made sure he was dead. Then I stripped off his diamond ring and the Philippe Patek watch, put them in my pocket, and covered him up with the tarp. Later I'd run the body out to the middle of the lake and weight it and drop it overboard. I'd have to get rid of the Lincoln, too, but in rugged mountain country like this it wouldn't be too much of a chore, even for an old guy like me.

Back in the cabin, I put in a long distance call that got picked up right away. "I changed my mind," I said. "I'll take you up on that contract offer after all. But it'll cost you seventy-five."

"For you I don't argue," Frank Carbone said. "Seventy-five it is. But how come you changed your mind? You told me before you're never leaving that retirement place of yours."

I didn't have to, now. Didn't have to worry about having enough money to last me the rest of my life, either. But all I said was, "Send somebody up with the cash in a couple of days. I'll have proof the job's done in exchange."

"A couple of days? How you going to do it that quick?"

"That's my business."

"Sure, sure. Same old Griff. Trade secret, huh?"

"That's right," I said. "Trade secret."

WISHFUL THINKING

When I got home from work, a little after six as usual, Jerry Macklin was sitting slumped on his front porch. Head down, long arms hanging loose between his knees. Uh-oh, I thought. I put the car in the garage and walked back down the driveway and across the lawn strip onto the Macklins' property.

"Hi there, Jerry."

He looked up. "Oh, hello, Frank."

"Hot one again today."

"Hot," he said. "Yes, it's hot."

"Only June and already in the nineties every day. Looks like we're in for another blistering summer."

"I guess we are."

"How about coming over for a beer before supper?"

He waggled his head. He's long and loose, Jerry, with about twice as much neck as anybody else. When he shakes his big head, it's like watching a bulbous flower bob at the end of a stalk. As always these days, his expression was morose. He used to smile a lot, but not much since his accident. About a year ago he fell off a roof while on his job as a building inspector, damaged some vertebrae in his back, and was now on permanent disability.

"I killed Verna a little while ago," he said.

"Is that right?"

"She's in the kitchen. Dead on the floor."

"Uh-huh."

"We had another big fight and I went and got my old service pistol out of the attic. She didn't even notice when I came back down with it, just started ragging on me again. I shot her right after she called me a useless bum for the thousandth time."

"Well," I said. Then I said, "A gun's a good way to do it, I guess."

"The best way," Jerry said. "All the other ways, they're too uncertain."

"Well, I ought to be getting on home."

"I wonder if I should call the police."

"I wouldn't do that if I were you, Jerry."

"No?"

"Wouldn't be a good idea."

"Hot day like this, maybe I—"

"Jerry!" Verna's voice, from inside the house. Loud and demanding, but with a whiny note underneath. "How many times do I have to ask you to come in here and help me with supper? The potatoes need peeling."

"Damn," Jerry said.

Sweat was running on me; I mopped my face with my handkerchief. "If you feel like it," I said, "we can have that beer later on. I'll be in the yard after supper—come over any time."

"Sure, okay."

He got to his feet, wincing on account of his back, and shuffled into his house. I walked back across and into mine. Mary Ellen was in the kitchen, cutting up something small and green by the sink.

"I saw you through the window," she said. "What were you talking to Jerry about?"

"Three guesses."

"Oh, Lord. I suppose he killed Verna again."

"Yep. In the kitchen this time, with his service pistol."

"That man. Three times now, or is it four?"

"Four."

"Other people have normal neighbors. We have to have a crazy person living next door."

"Jerry's harmless, you know that. He was as normal as anybody else before he fell off that roof."

"Harmless," Mary Ellen said. "Famous last words."

I went over and kissed her damp neck. "What're you making there?"

"Ceviche."

"What's ceviche?"

"Cold fish soup, Mexican style."

"Sounds awful."

"It isn't. You've had it before."

"Did I like it?"

"You loved it."

"Sounds wonderful, then. I'm going to have a beer. You want one?"

"I don't think so." Pretty soon she said, "He really ought to see somebody."

"Jerry? You mean a head doctor?"

"Yes. Before he really does do something to Verna."

"Come on, honey. Jerry can't even bring himself to step on a bug. And Verna's enough to drive any man a little crazy. Either she's mired in one of her funks or on a rampage about something or other. And she's always telling him how worthless and lazy she thinks he is."

"She has a point," Mary Ellen said. "All he does all day is sit around drinking beer and staring at the tube."

"Well, with his back the way it is—"

"His back doesn't seem to bother him when he decides to work in his garden."

"Hey, I thought you liked Jerry."

"I do like Jerry. It's just that I can see Verna's side, the woman's side. He was no ball of fire before the accident, and he's never let her have children—"

"That's her story. He says he's sterile."

"Well, whatever. I still say she has some justification for being moody and short-tempered, especially in this heat. Anyhow, her moods don't give Jerry the right to keep pretending he's killed her. And I don't care how harmless he seems to be, he could snap someday. People who have violent fantasies often do. Every day you read about something like that in the papers or see it on the TV news."

" 'Violent fantasies' is too strong a term in Jerry's case."

"What else would you call them?"

"He doesn't sit around all day thinking about killing Verna. I got that much out of him after he scared hell out of me the first time. They have a fight and he goes out on the porch and sulks and that's when he imagines her dead. It's more like…wishful thinking."

"Even so," Mary Ellen said, "it's not healthy and potentially dangerous. I wonder if Verna knows."

"Probably not, or she'd be making his life even more miserable. We can hear most of what she yells at him all the way over here."

"Somebody ought to tell her."

"You're not thinking of doing it? You don't even like the woman." Which was true. Jerry and I were friendly enough, but the four of us had never done couples things.

"I might go over and talk to her," Mary Ellen said. "Express concern, if nothing else."

"I think it'd be a mistake."

"Do you? Well, you're probably right."

"So you're going to do it anyway."

"Not necessarily. I'll have to think about it."

Mary Ellen went over to talk to Verna two days later. It was a Saturday and Jerry'd gone off somewhere in their car. I was on the front porch fixing a loose shutter when she left, and still there when she came back less than ten minutes later.

"That was fast," I said.

"She didn't want to talk to me." Mary Ellen looked and sounded miffed. "She was barely even civil."

"Did you tell her about Jerry's wishful thinking?"

"No. I started to, but she cut me off and as much as told me to mind my own business."

"Well?" I said gently.

"Oh, all right. It's her life. And it'll be as much her fault as Jerry's if he suddenly decides to make his wish come true."

Jerry killed Verna three more times in July. Kitchen again, their bathroom, the backyard. Tenderizing mallet, clock radio, manual strangulation—so I guess he'd decided a gun wasn't the best way after all. He seemed to grow more and more morose as the summer wore on, while Verna grew more and more sullen and contentious. The heat wave we were suffering through didn't help matters any. The temperatures were up around a hundred degrees most days that month.

Jerry came over one evening in early August while Mary Ellen and I were sitting under the big elm in our yard. He had a six-pack under one arm and a look on his face that was half-hunted, half-depressed.

"Verna's on another rampage," he said. "I had to get out of there. Okay if I sit with you folks for a while?"

"Pull up a chair," I said. At least he wasn't going to tell us he'd killed her again.

He sat and opened a can of beer and drank half at a gulp. It wasn't his first of the day by any means.

"I don't know how much more of that woman I can take," he said. "Morning, noon, and night—she never gives me a minute's peace anymore."

Mary Ellen said, "Well, there's a simple solution, Jerry."

"Divorce? She won't give me one. Doesn't believe in divorce. Till death do us part—that's what she believes in."

"So what're you going to do?" I asked him.

"Man, I just don't know. I'm at my wits' end." He drank the rest of the beer in broody silence. Then he unfolded, wincing, to his feet. "Think I'll go back home now. Have a look in the attic."

"The attic?"

"See if I can find my old service pistol. A gun really is the best way to do it."

After he was gone Mary Ellen said, "I don't like this, Frank. He's getting crazier all the time."

"Oh, come on."

"He'll go through with it one of these days. You mark my words."

When I came home the next evening, one of the Macklins was sitting slumped on their front porch. Not Jerry—Verna. Head down, hands hanging between her knees. It surprised me so much I nearly swerved the car off onto our lawn. Verna almost never sat out there, alone or otherwise. She preferred the glassed-in back porch because it was air-conditioned.

The day had been another scorcher, and I was tired and soggy and I wanted a shower and a cold drink. But Verna sitting on the porch puzzled me enough to draw me over there.

She looked up when I said hello. Her round, plain face was red with prickly heat and her colorless hair hung limp and sweat-plastered to her skin. There was a funny look in her eyes, a look that made me feel uneasy.

"Frank," she said. "Lord, it's hot."

"And no relief in sight. Where's Jerry?"

"In the house. But you can't talk to him."

"No? How come?"

"He's dead."

"What?"

"Dead," she said. "I killed him."

I wasn't hot anymore; it was as if I'd been doused with ice water. "Killed him? Jesus, Verna—"

"We had a fight and I went and got his service pistol and shot him in the back of the head while he was watching TV."

"When?" It was all I could think of to say.

"Little while ago."

"The police ... have you called the police?"

"No."

"Then I'd better—"

The screen door popped open with a sudden creaking sound. I jerked my gaze that way, and Jerry was standing there. "Hey, Frank," he said.

I gaped at him with my mouth hanging open.

"How about a cold one? Look like you could use it."

"... No. No, thanks."

He shrugged, wagged his bulbous head. Without looking at his wife, he went back into the house and the screen door banged shut.

Verna was still sitting in the same posture, head down, staring at the steps with that funny look on her face. "I know about him killing me all the time," she said. "Did you think I didn't know, didn't hear him saying it?"

There were no words in my head. I closed my mouth.

"I wanted to see how it felt to kill him the same way," Verna said. "And you know what? It felt good."

I backed down the steps, started to turn away. But I was still looking at her and I saw her head come up, I saw the odd little smile that changed the shape of her mouth.

"Good," she said, "but not good enough."

I went home. Mary Ellen was upstairs, taking a shower. When she came out I told her what had just happened.

"My God, Frank. The heat's made her as crazy as he is. They're two of a kind."

"No," I said, "they're not. They're not the same at all."

"What do you mean?"

I didn't tell her what I meant. I didn't have to, because just then in the hot, dead stillness we heard the crack of the pistol shot from next door.

THE MONSTER

He was after the children.

Meg knew it, all at once, as soon as he was inside the house. She couldn't have said exactly how she knew. He was pleasant enough on the surface, smiling, friendly. Big and shaggy-haired in his uniform, hairy all over like a bear. But behind his smile and underneath his fur there was menace, evil. She felt it, intuited it—a mother's instinct for danger. He was after Kate and Bobby. One of those monsters who preyed on little children, hurt them, did unspeakable things to them

"Downstairs or upstairs?" he said.

"... What?"

"The stopped-up drain. Downstairs here or upstairs?"

A feeling of desperation was growing in her, spreading toward panic. She didn't know what to do. "I think you'd better leave." The words were out before she realized what she was saying.

"Huh? I just got here, Mrs. Thompson. Your husband said you got a stopped-up drain—that's right, isn't it?"

Why did I let him in? she thought. Just because he said Philip sent him, that doesn't make it so. And even if Philip did send him ... Oh God, why *him*, of all the plumbers in this city?

"No," she said. "No, it ... it's all right now. It's working again, there's nothing wrong with it."

He wasn't smiling anymore. "You kidding me?"

"Why would I do that?"

"Yeah, why? Over at the door you said you been expecting me, come on in and fix the drain."

"I didn't—"

"You did, lady. Look, I haven't got time to play games. And it's gonna cost you sixty-five bucks whether I do any work or not so you might as well let me take a look."

"It's all right now, I tell you."

"Okay, maybe it is. But if it was stopped-up once today, it could happen again. You never know with the pipes in these old houses. So where is it, up or down?"

"Please ..."

"Upstairs, right? Yeah, now I think of it, your husband said it was in the upstairs bathroom."

No! The word was like a scream in her mind. The upstairs bathroom was between their room, hers and Philip's, and the nursery. Baby Kate in her crib, not even a year old, and Bobby, just two, napping in his bed so innocent and helpless ... and this man, this beast—

He moved past her to the stairs, hefting his tool kit in one huge, scab-knuckled hand. "You want to show me where it is?"

"No!" She cried it aloud this time.

"Hey," he said, "you don't have to bust my eardrums." He shook his head the way Philip did sometimes when he was vexed with her. "Well, I can find it myself. Can't hide a bathroom from an old hand like me."

He started up the stairs.

She stood paralyzed, staring in horror as he climbed. She tried to shriek at him to stop, go away, don't hurt the babies, but her voice had frozen in her throat. If any harm came to Kate and Bobby, she could never forgive herself—she would shrivel up and

die. So many childless years, all the doctors who'd told her and Philip that she could never conceive, and then the sudden miracle of her first pregnancy and Bobby's birth, the second miracle that was Kate.... If she let either of them be hurt she would be as much of a monster as the one climbing the stairs

Stop him!

The paralysis left her as abruptly as it had come on; her legs pumped, carried her headlong into the kitchen. A knife, the big butcher knife ... She grabbed it out of the rack, raced back to the stairs.

He was already on the second floor. She couldn't see him, but she could hear his heavy menacing tread in the hallway, going down the hallway.

Toward the nursery.

Toward Kate and Bobby.

She rushed upward, clutching the knife, her terror so immense now it felt as though her head would burst. She ran into the hallway, saw him again—and her heart skipped a beat, the fear ripped inside her like an animal trying to claw its way out of a cage.

He was standing in the nursery doorway, looking in at the children.

She lunged at him with the knife upraised. He turned just before she reached him, and his mouth shaped startled words. But the only sound he made was an explosive grunt when she plunged the knife into his chest.

His mouth flew open; his eyes bulged so wide she thought for an instant they would pop out like seeds from a squeezed orange. One scarred hand plucked at the knife handle. The other groped in her direction, as if to catch and crush her. She leapt back against the far wall, stood huddled against it as he staggered away, still grunting and plucking at the knife handle.

She saw him fall once, lurch upright again, finally reach the top of the stairs; then the grunting ended in a long heaving sigh and he sagged and toppled forward. The sounds he made rolling and bouncing down the stairs were as loud and terrible as the thunder that had terrified her as a child, that still frightened her sometimes on storm-heavy nights.

The noises stopped at last and there was silence.

Meg pushed away from the wall, hurried into the nursery. Bobby, incredibly, was still asleep; he had the face of a golden-haired angel, lying pooched on his side with his tiny arms outstretched. Kate was awake and fussing. Meg picked her up, held her tight, soothed and rocked and murmured to her until the fussing stopped and her tears dried. When the baby was tucked up asleep in her crib, Meg steeled herself and then made her way slowly out to the stairs and down.

The evil one lay crumpled and smeared with red at the bottom. His eyes still bulged, wide open and staring. Dead.

And that was good, it was *good*, because it meant that the children were safe again.

She stepped over him, shuddering, and went to the phone in the kitchen. She called the police first, then Philip at his office to ask him to please come home right away.

A detective sergeant and two uniformed officers arrived first. Meg explained to the detective what had happened, and he seemed very sympathetic. But he was still asking questions when Philip came.

Philip put his strong arms around her, held her; she leaned close to him as always, because he was the only person since her daddy died who had ever made her feel safe. He didn't ask her any questions. He made her sit down in the living room, went with the detective to look at what lay under the sheet at the foot of the stairs.

"... don't understand it," Philip was saying. "He was highly recommended to me by a friend. Reliable, honest, trustworthy—the best plumber in town."

"Then you did send him over to fix a stopped-up drain."

"Yes. I told my wife I was going to. I just don't understand. Did he try to attack her? Is that why she stabbed him?"

"Not her, no. She said he was after your children. Upstairs in the nursery where they're asleep."

"Oh my God," Philip said.

He must have sensed her standing there because he turned to look at her. I had to do it, Philip, she told him with her eyes. He was a monster and I had to protect the children. Our wonderful son Bobby, sweet baby Kate ... I'm their mother, I couldn't let them be hurt, could I?

But he didn't believe her. She saw the disbelief in his face before he turned away again, and then she heard him lie to the detective. He lied, he lied, Philip lied—

"We don't have any children," he said.

HOME IS THE PLACE WHERE
A "Nameless Detective" Story

It was one of those little crossroad places you still find occasionally in the California backcountry. Relics of another era; old dying things, with precious little time left before they crumble into dust. Weathered wooden store, gas pumps, a detached service garage that also housed restrooms, four warped tourist cabins clustered close behind, a couple of junk-car husks and a stand of dusty cottonwoods. This one was down in the central part of the state, southeast of San Juan Bautista. The name on the pocked metal store sign was *Benson's Oasis*.

No other cars sat on the apron in front when I pulled in at a few minutes past two. Nor were there any vehicles back by the cabins. The only spot to hide one was in the detached garage. Maybe something in that, maybe not.

Heat hammered at me when I got out, thick and deep-summer dry. In the distance, haze blurred the brown hills of the Diablo range. It was flat here, and dust-blown, and quiet. The feeling you had was of isolation, emptiness, displacement in time. I wasn't bothered by it. I like the past a hell of a lot better than I like the present or the prospects for the future.

It was even hotter inside the store. An old-fashioned ceiling fan stirred the air in a way that made me think of a ladle stirring bouillon. The old man perched on a stool behind the counter at the rear was studying a book of some kind. A bell had tinkled to announce my arrival but at first he didn't look up. He turned a page as I crossed the room; it made a dry rustling sound. The page was black, with what looked to be photographs and paper items affixed to it. A scrapbook.

When I reached him he shut the book. It had a brown simulated leather cover, the word *Memories* embossed on it in gilt. The gilt had flaked and faded and the ersatz leather was cracked. The book was almost as old as he was. Over seventy, I judged. Thin, stoop-shouldered, white hair as fine as rabbit fur. Heavily seamed face. Bent left arm that was also knobbed and crooked at the wrist, as if had been badly broken once and hadn't healed well.

"What can I do for you?" he asked.

"You're the owner? Everett Benson?"

"I am."

"I'm looking for your son, Mr. Benson."

No reaction.

"Have you seen him, heard from him, in the past two days?"

Still nothing for several seconds. Then, "I have no son."

"Stephen Arthur Benson. He's in trouble. Serious trouble."

Face like a chunk of eroded limestone, eyes like cloudy agates. "I have no son," he said again.

I took out one of my business cards, tried to give it to him. He wouldn't take it. Finally I laid it on the counter in front of him. "Stephen was in jail in San Francisco," I said, "on a charge of selling amphetamines and crack cocaine. Did you know that?"

Silence.

"He talked the woman he was living with into bailing him out. His trial date was yesterday. Two nights ago he stole some money from the woman, and her car, and jumped bail."

More silence. "The bondsman hired me to find him and bring him back," I said. "I think he came here. You're his only living relative, and he needs more money than he's got to keep running."

Benson pushed off his stool, laid the scrapbook on a shelf behind him. Several books lined the rest of the shelf, all of them old and evidently well read.

"Aiding and abetting a fugitive is a felony," I said to his back, "even if the fugitive is your own son. You don't want to get yourself in trouble with the law, Mr. Benson."

He said again, without turning, "I have no son."

For the moment I'd taken the argument as far as it would go. I left him and went out into the midday glare. And straight over to the closed-up service garage.

There were two windows along the near side, both speckled with ground-in dirt, but I could see clearly enough through the first. Sufficient daylight penetrated the gloom so I could identify the two vehicles parked in there. One was a thirty-year-old Ford pickup, no doubt the old man's. The other was a newish red Mitsubishi. I didn't have to see the license plate to know that the Mitsubishi belonged to Stephen Arthur Benson's girlfriend.

I went to my car and unclipped the short-barreled .38 revolver from under the dash and slid it into the pocket of my suit jacket. Maybe I'd need the gun and maybe I wouldn't, but I felt better armed. Stephen Benson was something of a hardcase, and for all I knew he was armed himself.

The stand of cottonwoods grew along the far side of the parking area. I moved over into them, made my way behind the two cabins on the south side. Both had blank rear walls and uncurtained side windows. Their interiors were empty.

The farthest of the north-side cabins was also empty. The near one showed signs of occupancy, but there wasn't anybody in it. The old man's living quarters, I thought.

Nothing to do now but to go back inside and brace him again. When I entered the store he was on his stool, eating a Milky Way in little nibbling bites.

"Where is he, Mr. Benson?"

No response. The cloudy agate eyes regarded me with the same lack of expression as before.

"I saw the car in the garage," I said. "It's the one he stole from the woman in San Francisco. Either he's somewhere around here or you gave him money and another car and he's on the road again. Which is it?"

He chewed his candy bar; he didn't speak.

"All right then. We'll have to do this the hard way. I'll call the county police and report the stolen car, and you'll be charged with aiding and abetting and harboring stolen property." I turned and started out.

Benson let me get halfway to the door before he said, "You win, mister," in a dull, empty voice. "He didn't go anywhere. I'll take you to him."

I came back to the counter. "Now you're being smart. Just tell me where he is."

"No. I'll take you there."

Might be better at that, I thought, if his son was close by. Easier, less chance for trouble, with the old man along. I said, "All right," and Benson came out from behind the counter. He put a Closed sign in the front window, then we went out and he locked up.

I asked him, "How far do we have to go?"

"Not far."

"I'll drive, you tell me where."

We got into the car. He directed me east on the county road that intersected the main highway. We rode in silence for about a mile. Benson sat stiff-backed, his knobbed hand gripping his knee, eyes straight ahead.

Abruptly he said, " 'Home is the place where.' "

"... How's that again?"

" 'Home is the place where, when you have to go there, they have to take you in.' Lines from a poem by Robert Frost. 'The Death of the Hired Man,' I think. You read Frost?"

"No."

"I like him. Makes sense to me, more than a lot of them."

A rural storekeeper who read poetry and admired Robert Frost. Well, why not?

Home is the place where, when you have to go there, they have to take you in. The words ran around inside my head. Now I knew something more about Everett Benson and the nature of his relationship with his son.

Another couple of silent miles through sun-struck farmland. Alfalfa and wine grapes, mostly. A private farm road came up on the right; Benson told me to turn there. It had once been a good road, well-graded, but that had been a long time ago. Rutted and not much used these days. It led along the shoulder of a sere hill, then up to the crest. From there I could see where it ended.

Benson's Oasis was a dying place; the farm down below was already dead—years dead. It had been built alongside a shallow creek where willows and cottonwoods grew: farmhouse, barn, chicken coops. Skeletons now, broken and half-hidden by high grass and tangles of wild berry vines.

"Your property?" I asked Benson.

"Built it all with my own hands. Raised chickens, alfalfa, apples. Moved out eight years ago, when my wife died. Couldn't bear to live here anymore without her. Couldn't bear to sell the place, either." He paused, drew a heavy breath, let it out slowly. "Don't come out here much anymore. Just a couple of times a year to visit her grave."

There were no other cars in sight, but I could make out where one had angled off the roadway and mashed down an irregular swath of the summer-dead grass. I followed the same route to where the swath ended near what was left of the farmhouse front porch.

There was no sign of life anywhere. I had my window rolled down but there was nothing to hear, either.

I said, "Is he inside the house?"

"Around back."

"Where around back?"

"There's a beat-down path. Just follow that."

"You don't want to come along?"

"No need."

I gave him a long look. There was no tension in him, no guilt; not much emotion of any kind, it seemed.

I got out, taking the keys from the ignition. Before I shut the door I drew the .38; then I leaned back in to look at Benson, holding the gun down low so he couldn't see it.

"Just wait quiet," I said. "Don't do anything foolish like blowing the horn."

"I won't."

The path was off to the right. I walked it slowly through the tangled vegetation. Near where the stunted remains of an apple orchard began, the path veered off toward a big weeping willow that grew on the creek bank.

And under the willow was where it ended—at the grave of Benson's wife, marked by a marble headstone etched with the words *Beloved Elizabeth* and her birth and death dates. But hers was not the only grave there. Next to it was a second, a new one, the earth so freshly turned some of the clods were still moist. That one bore no marker of any kind.

I hurried back to the car. Benson was out of it now, standing a few feet away looking at the house. He turned when he heard me coming, faced me squarely.

"Now you know," he said. "I didn't lie to you, mister. I have no son."

"Why didn't you tell me he was dead?"

"Wanted you to see the grave for yourself."

"How did he die?"

"I shot him. Last night, about ten o'clock."

"Why? What happened?"

"He brought me trouble, just like before. He was bad, Stephen was. Mean clear through, even as a boy. Stealing things, breaking up property. Hurting his mother." Benson held up his crooked left arm. "Hurting me too."

"He did that do you?"

"When he was eighteen. Broke my arm in three places when I wouldn't give him money he wanted. I told him before he ran off, don't ever come back. And he didn't, not until last night at the Oasis."

"He wanted money again, is that it? Tried to hurt you again when you wouldn't give it to him?"

"Punched me in the belly," Benson said, "threatened to break my other arm. So I went and got my pistol and shot him, twice through the heart. Then I brought him out here and buried him."

"Why did you do that?"

"I told you before. 'Home is the place where.' I had to take him in, didn't I? For the last time?"

Neither of us had anything more to say on the heat-soaked drive back to Benson's Oasis. He asked then, "You going to call the sheriff now?" Matter of factly, not as if he cared.

"No."

"How come?"

Old and dying like his crossroads store, with precious little time left. Where was the sense—or the justice—in forcing him to suffer any more than he already had?

"No reason to," I said. "There's no crime in an act of self defense."

Benson had nothing more to say. He lifted himself out of the car, walked in a slow stooped gait to the store. I waited until he disappeared into the dimness within, then I drove out onto the highway and headed north. To San Francisco. To my office and my flat and Kerry, the woman I loved.

Home is the place where.

NIGHT WALKER
(With Barry N. Malzberg)

For the past three months I have been a creature of the night.

During the daylight hours I exist in a state of stasis in my empty house, waiting like a vampire in its coffin for the darkness to come. I live for the darkness, seem to come alive only after nightfall. No matter what the weather, I leave the house well before midnight and do not return until near dawn. I walk alone through parks, along dark streets, alleys, byways—anywhere there is little or no light. I do not like the light.

Once I, Henry Boyd, was like millions of other men in the mid-strata of society. I had a family, a job with an income that admirably suited our needs. I had friends, though none close enough to be considered a confidante. Twice a month I played golf with the same threesome, once a month penny-ante poker with a group of co-workers at Shepherd Electronics. I pursued my hobby of woodworking with a certain zeal and pride of craftsmanship. I attended concerts and films and went on picnics and camping trips with my wife and son. I was content because the future seemed secure.

That part of my life ended the moment the lives of Doris and Andrew ended—on a bright sunny day on our way to the beach, when I distractedly, unconscionably ran the red light and the SUV slammed into the passenger side of our small Honda. My wife and son were destroyed on impact. I survived with relatively minor injuries that required only a brief hospital stay.

My grief, my guilt knew no bounds. I expected to be prosecuted and imprisoned for manslaughter, and welcomed the prospect, but this did not happen. The authorities and the judge at my trial decided, given my previously exemplary driving record and my great remorse, that the loss of my driving privileges and a large fine were sufficient punishment. I wept openly when the verdict was given. With resentment, as well as sorrow and shame.

When I returned home, I found that I could not leave the house in the daylight hours. I had lost all interest in my former pursuits, all hope for the future. I was unable to deal with people on any conscious level; as a result I soon lost my job, my friends and acquaintances. Each day I took to my bed and slept ten, eleven, twelve hours, often from dawn to dusk. And relived the horror of the accident over and over in sweat-soaked nightmares.

That was when I began to embrace the darkness.

That was when I became a night walker.

During the day the house is a fortress, all doors and windows locked and shuttered so that as little light as possible intrudes. I must obtain food, or I would not have the strength to continue my shadow walking. I have it delivered by a neighborhood market, pay them and my few remaining bills by computer-arranged bank transfer. These matters require an hour or two of daylight effort, a necessary but difficult activity.

I do not turn on the lights at any time, nor do I cook my tasteless food; I eat sparingly, only at night and quickly before I leave the house. Other than the telephone my one concession to what most would consider normal living is use of the furnace during the day when the weather requires it. No matter how windy, foggy, rain-wet the night is I am never cold once the darkness descends and I have embarked on my night walks.

At first I told myself my outings had no purpose, that I was merely wandering aimlessly, but I knew even then that this was not true. What I am doing is making myself available to those other creatures of the night, the wicked ones who prowl with weapons seeking prey—a search for the punishment I deserve for the three lives cut short by my criminal carelessness. I do not have the courage to mete out the extreme penalty to myself, therefore I must rely on someone else, a stranger or strangers, to act as my executioner.

Yet to my chagrin, this has not yet happened. Only once have I been accosted on my nocturnal ventures, by a scruffy young man in a leather jacket and low-billed cap in the depths of Municipal Park five blocks from my home. He showed me a large knife and demanded I gave him my wallet, wristwatch, wedding ring. Instead I attacked him in the hope that he would he carry out his threat to kill me. But he did not. He was so surprised, so frightened by my aggressive reaction, that he dropped his weapon and fled.

Some of the other individuals I have encountered seemed at first to be threatening, but turned out not to be. The nonthreatening ones—men on their way to or from work, drunks, insomniacs, homeless people, night walkers like myself perhaps—I take pains to avoid. The only person I wish to have to contact with, the only one I am looking for, is my executioner.

He will cross my path eventually. Or they will, for predators also roam in twos, threes, packs. And so I keep wandering the dark and lonely places, thinking of Doris and Andrew, waiting, hoping each night will be my last.

It has occurred to me that I may have been seeking that final darkness for most of my life. An unconscious search for some equipoise, some balance to justify my existence. But no, that isn't so. The death wish has existed in me only since Doris and Andrew were effectively slain by my hand. I embraced life before that terrible day. My search is for justice and absolution, nothing more.

On the night of November 8th I leave the house once again, shortly before ten o'clock as usual. A heavy overcast blots out moon and stars, and there is a wind whose chill I do not feel. I walk, first, to Municipal Park, for it has the deserved reputation of being the most dangerous place in the city in the dark hours. Not for me in the past, however, except for that one incident, and not for me again tonight. I encounter no one, and not for the first time I think bitterly that the gods must be toying with me, granting me temporary protection that I do not want so as to increase my suffering.

I traverse the tunnels and tree-shadowed pathways for two hours without seeing another person. Then I leave the park, make my way to the slum section known as the Tenderloin. There are furtive figures on the streets there, but none of the sort I am seeking. I move on to the old warehouse district. Except for a few tawdry saloons, this section is mostly deserted after dark. Two drunks emerge from one as I pass, but they pay no attention to me and so I none to them.

It is late, after two o'clock, when I skirt the edge of the nightclub district. The clubs are closed now, but their neon brightness remains a stain on the night. The street is dark, deserted. I start to cross it to avoid the pale nightlights in a parking lot just ahead.

Someone screams.

A woman, her shriek one of mortal terror.

The cries come from inside the lot, not far away. I stop, stand staring into the gloom that shrouds the handful of parked cars. The woman screams again, and as the echoes fade I hear other sounds—the crack of flesh on flesh, a thumping noise that cuts off a third scream. I can tell where they're coming from now, make out the shapes of two figures next to one of the cars, a man clutching the limp form of a woman while he opens its passenger side door.

I don't hesitate. Without thinking I rush headlong into the lot.

The man is shoving the woman into the car when I reach them. He hears me, releases her and spins around. In the pale glow of the inside dome light I see his face, his mouth twisted into an animal grimace. His hands are empty, he has no weapon. But the hands are big, strangler's hands. I lunge at him, clutch at his coat with my head up to expose my throat.

He does not take advantage of the opening presented to him. He claws at my hands, tears himself free of my grasp. And runs away. Another coward like the young mugger in the park.

My first reaction is disappointment. Then I realize that the woman, lying half in and half out of the car with her skirt pulled up over her thighs, is not moving. A half forgotten feeling of compassion seizes me and I tug the skirt down, then lean in to look at her. Her coat has been pulled off her shoulders, her blouse torn. She is alive but unconscious, her breath coming in little choked gasps. Gently I lift her into a sitting position so I can see more clearly if she is injured. There is a bloody gash on one cheek, finger marks on the pallid skin of her throat.

As I peer at her face framed by a tangle of blond hair, I feel a sense of shock. For I know her.

Her name is Margaret Lopez. She works as a hostess in one of the nearby nightclubs, lives less than a mile from me. And she was an acquaintance of my poor late wife.

She moans but does not regain consciousness as I loosen my grip on her arms. When I step back from the car, my foot brushes against something that makes a faint jingling sound. Keys, a ring of keys. And close by on the ground, I see then, is a leather purse. This car must be Margaret's, the assault coming just after she unlocked the door.

The lot, the street are still deserted. I pick up the items, put the keys inside the purse, start to close it. A thought occurs to me then, and I rummage blindly through the contents until my fingers trace the outlines of a cell phone.

I walk quickly around the car, look closely at its logo and the license plate. Then I switch on the phone and place a 911 call.

An assault and probable attempted rape has occurred in the parking lot at the corner of Ninth and DeSoto, I say. The assailant has been driven off and the injured victim is now safe inside a late model Mazda, presumably her vehicle. I give the operator the license number. When she tells me to remain at the scene until the police arrive and asks for my name, I disconnect.

I return the cell phone to the purse, place the purse on the seat beside Margaret, close the door. I wait beside the car, keeping careful watch, until I hear sirens in the distance, then I hurry through the lot to its far end and away onto the shadowed streets.

It is not until I have gone several blocks that the significance of what has just happened comes to me. My search for an end to my life has led me to the prevention of what might well have been the end of Margaret Lopez's; she is alive because my wife and son are dead and because I wish to join them. I am an unwitting surrogate of justice. It is something very much like what I once called providence. Or is it? It may also be nothing more than coincidence, randomness.

I don't know. What I do know is that the incident changed everything for Margaret and nothing for me.

I am still looking for my executioner.

That was what I believed then. It is not what I believe now.

Two weeks have passed since that momentous night. I continue to walk the dark hours, but the walks have become progressively shorter. I no longer prowl the recesses of Municipal Park, or the meaner of the city's streets and byways. And I am more attuned to my surroundings, less vulnerable, more watchful.

I have begun to understand that what I did for Margaret Lopez may have changed me after all. That it was not merely an impulsive act of human kindness, but an act of atonement. That providence may in fact be responsible and I have been kept from harm not only to save Margaret but to save myself.

That I am no longer walking in and toward darkness, but through it back to the light.

OUT BEHIND THE SHED

There was a dead guy behind the parts shed. I went out there to get a Ford oil pan for Barney and I saw him lying on his back in the weedy grass. He didn't have a face. There was blood and bone and pulp and black scorch marks where his face used to be. I couldn't even guess if he was anybody I knew.

I stood there shivering. It was cold ... Jesus, it was cold for late March. The sky was all glary, like the sun coming off a sheet-metal roof. Only there wasn't any sun. Just a shiny silver overcast, so cold-hot bright it hurt your eyes to look at it. The wind was big and gusty, the kind that burns right through clothing and puts a rash like frostbite on your skin. No matter what I'd done all day I couldn't seem to get warm.

I'd known right off, as soon as I got out of bed, that it was going to be a bad day. The cold and the funny bright sky was one thing. Another was Madge. She'd started in on me about money again even before she made the coffee. How we were barely making ends meet and couldn't even afford to get the TV fixed, and why couldn't I find a better-paying job or let her go to work part-time or at least take a second job myself, nights, to bring in a little extra. The same old song and dance. The only old tune she hadn't played was the one about how much she ached for another kid before she got too old, as if two wasn't enough.

Then I came in here to work and Barney was in a grumpy mood on account of a head cold and the fact that we hadn't had three new repair jobs in a week. Maybe he'd have to do some retrenching if things didn't pick up pretty soon, he said. That was the word he used, retrenching. Laying me off was what he meant. I'd been working for him five years, steady, never missed a day sick, never screwed up on a single job, and he was thinking about firing me. What would I do then? Thirty-six years old, wife and two kids, house mortgaged to the hilt, no skills except auto mechanic and nobody hiring mechanics right now. What the hell would I do?

Oh, it was a bad day, all right. I hadn't thought it could get much worse, but now I knew that it could.

Now there was this dead guy out here behind the shed.

I ran back inside the shop. Barney was still banging away under old Mrs. Cassell's Ford, with his legs sticking out over the end of the roller cart. I yelled at him to slide out. He did and I said, "Barney ... Barney, there's a dead guy out by the parts shed."

He said, "You trying to be funny?"

"No," I said. "No kidding and no lie. He's out there in the grass behind the shed."

"Another of them derelicts come in on the freights, I suppose. You sure he's dead? Maybe he's just passed out."

"*Dead*, Barney. I know a dead guy when I see one."

He hauled up on his feet. He was a big Swede, five inches and fifty pounds bigger than me, and he had a way of looming over you that made you feel even smaller. He looked down into my face and then scowled and said in a different voice, "Froze to death?"

"No," I said. "He hasn't got a face anymore. His face is all blown away."

"Jesus. Somebody killed him, you mean?"

"Somebody must of. Who'd do a thing like that, Barney? Out behind our shed?"

He shook his head and cracked one of his big gnarly knuckles. The sound echoed like a gunshot in the cold garage. Then, without saying anything else, he swung around and fast-walked out through the rear door.

I didn't go with him. I went over and stood in front of the wall heater. But I still couldn't get warm. My shoulders kept hunching up and down inside my overalls and I couldn't feel my nose or ears or the tips of my fingers, as if they weren't there anymore. When I looked at my hands they were all red and chapped, like Madge's hands after she's been washing clothes or dishes. They twitched a little, too; the tendons were like worms wiggling under a handkerchief.

Pretty soon Barney came back. He had a funny look on his moon face but it wasn't the same kind he'd had when he went out. He said, "What the hell, Joe? I got no time for games and neither do you."

"Games?"

"There's nobody behind the shed," he said.

I stared at him. Then I said, "In the grass, not ten feet past the far corner."

"I looked in the grass," Barney said. His nose was running from the cold. He wiped it off on the sleeve of his overalls. "I looked all over. There's no dead guy. There's nobody."

"But I saw him. I swear to God."

"Well, he's not there now."

"Somebody must of come and dragged him off, then."

"Who'd do that?"

"Same one who killed him."

"There's no blood or nothing," Barney said. He was back to being grumpy. His voice had that hard edge and his eyes had a squeezed look. "None of the grass is even flattened down. You been seeing things, Joe."

"I tell you, it was the real thing."

"And I tell *you*, it wasn't. Go out and take another look, see for yourself. Then get that oil pan out of the shed and your ass back to work. I promised old lady Cassell we'd have her car ready by five-thirty."

I went outside again. The wind had picked up a couple of notches, turned even colder; it was like fire against my bare skin. The hills east of town were all shimmery with haze, like in one of those desert mirages. There was a tree smell in the air but it wasn't the usual good pine-and-spruce kind. It was a eucalyptus smell, even though there weren't any eucalyptus trees within two miles of here. It made me think of cat piss.

I put my head down and walked slow over to the parts shed. And stopped just as I reached it to draw in a long breath. And then went on to where I could see past the far corner.

The dead guy was there in the grass. Lying right where I'd seen him before, laid out on his back with one leg drawn up and his face blown away.

The wind gusted just then, and when it did it made sounds like howls and moans. I wanted to cover my ears. Cover my eyes, too, to keep from seeing what was in the grass. But I didn't do either one. All I did was stand there shivering with my eyes wide open, trying to blink away some of the shimmery haze that seemed to have crawled in behind them. Nothing much was clear now, inside or out—nothing except the dead guy.

"Joe!"

Barney, somewhere behind me. I didn't turn around but I did back up a couple of steps. Then I backed up some more, until I was past the corner and couldn't see the dead guy anymore, Then I swung around and ran to where Barney was in the shop doorway. "He's there, Barney, he's there, he's there—"

He gave me a hard crack on the shoulder. It didn't hurt; only the cold hurt where it touched my face and hands. He said, "Get hold of yourself, man."

"I *swear* it," I said, "right where I saw him before."

"All right, take it easy."

"I don't know how you missed seeing him," I said. I pulled at his arm. "I'll show you, come on."

I kept tugging on him and finally he came along, grumbling. I led the way out behind the shed. The dead guy was still there, all right. I blew out the breath I'd been holding and said, "Didn't I tell you? Didn't I?"

Barney stared down at the dead guy. Then he stared at me with his mouth open a little and his nose dripping snot. He said, "I don't see anything."

"You don't ... what?"

"Grass, just grass."

"What's the matter with you? You're looking right at him!"

"The hell I am. The only two people out here are you and me."

I blinked and blinked and shook my head and blinked some more but the dead guy didn't go away. He was *there*. I started to bend over and touch him, to make absolutely sure, but I couldn't do it. He'd be cold, as cold as the wind—colder. I couldn't stand to touch anything that cold and dead.

"I've had enough of this," Barney said.

I made myself look at him instead of the dead guy. The cat-piss smell had gotten so strong I felt like gagging.

"He's there," I said, pleading. "Oh God, Barney, can't you see him?"

"There's nobody there. How many times do I have to say it? You better go on inside, Joe. Both of us better. It's freezing out here." He put a hand on my arm but I shook it off. That made him mad. "All right," he said, "if that's the way you want it. How about if I call Madge? Or maybe Doc Kiley?"

"No," I said.

"Then quit acting like a damn fool. Get a grip on yourself, get back to work. I mean it, Joe. Any more of this crap and you'll regret it."

"No," I said again. "You're lying to me. That's it, isn't it? You're lying to me."

"Why would I lie to you?"

"I don't know, but that's what you're doing. Why don't you want me to believe he's there?"

"Goddamn it, *there's nobody there!*"

Things just kept happening today—bad things one right after another, things that made no sense. The cold, Madge, Barney, the dead guy, the haze, the cat-piss smell, Barney again—and now a cold wind chilling me inside as well as out, as if icy gusts had blown right in through my flesh and were howling and prowling around my heart. I'd never felt like this before. I'd never been this cold or this scared or this frantic.

I pulled away from Barney and ran back into the shop and into the office and unlocked the closet and took out the duck gun he lets me keep in there because Madge don't like guns in the house. When I got back to the shed, Barney was just coming out with a Ford oil pan in his gnarly hands. His mouth pinched up tight and his eyes got squinty when he saw me.

He said, "What the hell's the idea bringing that shotgun out here?"

"Something's going on," I said, "something crazy. You see that dead guy there or don't you?"

"You're the one who's crazy, Joe. Give me that thing before somebody gets hurt."

He took a step toward me. I backed up and leveled the duck gun at him. "Tell me the truth," I said, desperate now, "tell me you see him lying there!"

He didn't tell me. Instead he gave a sudden lunge and got one hand on the barrel and tried to yank the gun away and oh Jesus him pulling on it like that made me jerk the trigger. The load of birdshot hit him full on and he screamed and the wind screamed with him and then he stopped but the wind didn't. Inside and out, the wind kept right on screaming.

I stood looking down at him lying in the grass with one leg drawn up and his face blown away. I could see him clear, even through that shimmery haze. Just him down there. Nobody else.

Just Barney.

CHIP

John Valarian felt as he always did when he came to St. Ives Academy—a little awkward and uncomfortable, as if he didn't really belong in a place like this. St. Ives was one of the most exclusive, expensive boys' schools on the east coast, but that wasn't the reason; he'd picked it out himself, over Andrea's objections, when Peter reached his eighth birthday two years ago. The wooded country setting and hundred-year-old stone buildings weren't the reason, either. It was what the school represented, the atmosphere you felt as soon as you entered the grounds. Knowledge. Good breeding. Status. Class.

Well, maybe he *didn't* belong here. He'd come out of the city slums, had to fight for every rung on his way up the ladder. He hadn't had much schooling, still had trouble reading. And he'd never been able to polish off all his rough edges. That was one of the reasons he was determined to give his son the best education money could buy.

He climbed the worn stone steps of the administration building, gave his name to the lobby receptionist. She directed him up another flight of stairs to the headmaster's office. He'd been there once before, on the day he'd brought Peter here for enrollment, but he didn't remember much about it except that he'd been deeply impressed. This was only his third visit to St. Ives in three years—just two short ones before today. It made him feel bad, neglectful, thinking about it now. He'd intended to come more often, particularly for the father-son days, but some business matter always got in the way. Business ruled him. He didn't like it sometimes, but that was the way it was. Some things you couldn't change no matter what.

The headmaster kept him waiting less than five minutes. His name was Locklear. Late fifties, silver-haired, looked exactly like you'd expect the head of St. Ives Academy to look. When they were alone in his private office, Locklear shook hands gravely and said, "Thank you for coming, Mr. Valarian. Please sit down."

He perched on the edge of a maroon leather chair, now tense and on guard as well as uncomfortable. The way he'd felt when he got sent to the principal's office in public school. He didn't know what to do with his hands, finally slid them down tight over his knees. His gaze roamed the office. Nice. Books everywhere, a big illuminated globe on a wooden stand, a desk that had to be pure Philippine mahogany, a bank of windows that looked out over the central quadrangle and rolling lawns beyond. Impressive, all right. He wouldn't mind having a desk like that one himself.

He waited until Locklear was seated behind it before he said, "This trouble with my son. It must be pretty serious if you couldn't talk about it on the phone."

"I'm afraid it is. Quite serious."

"Bad grades or what?"

"No. Chip is extremely bright, and his grades—"

"Peter."

"Ah, yes, of course."

"His mother calls him Chip. I don't."

"He seems to prefer it."

"His name is Peter. Chip sounds ... ordinary."

"Your son is anything but ordinary, Mr. Valarian."

The way the headmaster said that tightened him up even more. "What's going on here?" he demanded. "What's Peter done?"

"We're not absolutely certain he's responsible for any of the ... incidents. I should make that clear at the outset. However, the circumstantial evidence is considerable and points to no one else."

Incidents. Circumstantial evidence. "Get to the point, Mr. Locklear. What do you *think* he did?"

The headmaster leaned forward, made a steeple of his fingertips. He seemed to be hiding behind it as he said, "There have been a series of thefts in Chip's ... in Peter's dormitory, beginning several weeks ago. Small amounts of cash taken from the rooms of nearly a dozen different boys."

"My son's not a thief."

"I sincerely hope that's so. But as I said, the circumstantial evidence—"

"Why would he steal money? He's got plenty of his own—I send him more than he can spend every month."

"I can't answer your question. I wish I could."

"You ask him about the thefts?"

"Yes."

"And?"

"He denies taking any money."

"All right then," Valarian said. "If he says he didn't do it, then he didn't do it."

"Two of the victims saw him coming out of their rooms immediately before they discovered missing sums."

"And you believe these kids over my son."

"Given the other circumstances, we have no choice."

"What other circumstances?"

"Chip has been involved in—"

"Peter."

"I'm sorry, yes, Peter. He has been involved in several physical altercations recently. Last week one of the boys he attacked suffered a broken nose."

"Attacked? How do you know he did the attacking?"

"There were witnesses," Locklear said. "To that assault and to the others. In each case, they swore Peter was the aggressor."

The office seemed to have grown too warm; Valarian could feel himself starting to sweat. "He's a little aggressive, I admit that. Always has been. A lot of kids his age—"

"His behavior goes beyond simple aggression, I'm afraid. I can only describe it as bullying to the point of terrorizing."

"Come on, now. I don't believe that."

"Nevertheless, it's true. If you'd care to talk to his teachers, his classmates ..."

Valarian shook his head. After a time he said, "If this has been going on for a while, why didn't you let me know before?"

"At first the incidents were isolated, and without proof that Peter was responsible for the thefts ... well, we try to give our young men the benefit of the doubt whenever possible. But as they grew more frequent, more violent, I *did* inform you of the problem. Twice by letter, once in a message when I couldn't reach you by phone at your office."

He stared at the headmaster, but it was only a few seconds before his disbelief faded and he lowered his gaze. Two letters, one phone call. Dimly he remembered getting one of the letters, reading it, dismissing it as unimportant because he was in the middle of a big transaction with the Chicago office. The other letter ... misplaced, inadvertently thrown out or filed. The phone call ... dozens came in every day, he had two secretaries screening them and taking messages, and sometimes the messages didn't get delivered.

He didn't know what to say. He sat there sweating, feeling like a fool.

"Last evening there was another occurrence," Locklear said, "the most serious of all. That is why I called this morning and insisted on speaking to you in person. We can't prove that your son is responsible, but given what we do know we can hardly come to another conclusion."

"What occurrence? What happened last night?"

"Someone," Locklear said carefully, "set fire to our gymnasium."

"Set fire— My God."

"Fortunately it was discovered in time to prevent it from burning out of control and destroying the entire facility, but it did cause several thousand dollars' damage."

"What makes you think Peter set it?"

"He had an argument with his physical education instructor yesterday afternoon. He became quite abusive and made thinly veiled threats. It was in the instructor's office that kerosene was poured and the fire set."

Valarian opened his mouth, clicked it shut again. He couldn't seem to think clearly now. Too damn quiet in there; he could hear a clock ticking somewhere. He broke the silence in a voice that sounded like a stranger's.

"What're you going to do? Expel him? Is that why you got me up here?"

"Believe me, Mr. Valarian, it pains me to say this, but yes, that is the board's decision. For the welfare of St. Ives Academy and the other students. Surely you can understand."

"Oh, I understand," Valarian said bitterly "You bet I understand."

"Peter will be permitted to remain here until the end of the week, under supervision, if you require time to make other arrangements for him. Of course, if you'd rather he leave with you this afternoon ..."

Valarian got jerkily to his feet. "I want to talk to my son. Now."

"Yes, naturally. I sent for him earlier and he's waiting in one of the rooms just down the hall."

He had to fight his anger as he followed the headmaster to where Peter was waiting. He felt like hitting something or somebody. Not the boy, he'd never laid a hand on him and never would. Not Locklear, either. Somebody. Himself, maybe.

Locklear stopped before a closed door. He said somberly, "I'll await you in my office, Mr. Valarian," and left him there alone.

He hesitated before going in, to calm down and work out how he was going to handle this. All right. He took a couple of heavy breaths and opened the door.

The boy was sitting on a straightback chair—not doing anything, just sitting there like a statue. When he saw his father he got slowly to his feet and stood with his arms down at his sides. No smile, nothing but a blank stare. He looked older than ten. Big for his age, lean but wide through the shoulders. *He looks like I did at that age*, Valarian thought. *He looks just like me.*

"Hello, Peter."

"Chip," the boy said in a voice as blank as his stare. "You know I prefer Chip, Papa."

"Your name is Peter. I prefer Peter."

Valarian crossed the room to him. The boy put out his hand, but on impulse Valarian bent and caught his shoulders and hugged him. It was like hugging a piece of stone. Valarian let go of him, stepped back.

"I just had a long talk with your headmaster," he said. "Those thefts, the fire yesterday ... he says it was you."

"I know."

"Well? Was it?"

"No, Papa."

"Don't lie to me. If you did all that ..."

"I didn't. I didn't do anything."

"They're kicking you out of St. Ives. They wouldn't do that if they weren't sure it was you."

"I don't care."

"You don't care you're being expelled?"

"I don't like it here anymore. I don't care what the headmaster or the teachers or the other kids think. I don't care what anybody thinks about me." Funny little smile. "Except you, Papa."

"All right," Valarian said. "Look me in the eyes and tell me the truth. *Did you steal money, set that fire?*"

"I already told you I didn't."

"In my eyes. Up close."

The boy stepped forward and looked at him squarely. "No, Papa, I didn't," he said.

In the car on the way back to the city he kept seeing Peter's eyes staring into his. He couldn't get them out of his mind. What he'd seen there shining deep and dark ... it must've been there all along. How could he have missed it before? It had made him feel cold all over; made him want nothing more to do with his son today, tell Locklear he'd send somebody to pick up the boy at the end of the week and then get out of there fast. Now, remembering, it made him shudder.

Lugo was looking at him in the rear view mirror. "Something wrong, Mr. Valarian?"

At any other time he'd have said no and let it go at that. But now he heard himself say, "It's my son. He got into some trouble. That's why I had to go to the school."

"All taken care of now?"

"No. They're throwing him out."

"No kidding? That's too bad."

"Is it?" Then he said, "His name's Peter, but his mother calls him Chip. She says he's like me, a chip off the same block. He likes the name, he thinks it fits him too. But I don't like it."

"How come?"

"I don't want him to be like me, I wanted him to grow up better than me. Better in every way. That's why I sent him to St. Ives. You understand?"

Lugo said, "Yes, sir," but they were just words. Lugo was his driver, his bodyguard, his strongarm man; all Lugo understood was how to steer a limo, how to serve the mob with muscle or a gun.

"I don't want him in my business," Valarian said. "I don't want him to be another John Valarian."

"But now you think maybe he will be?"

"No, that's not what I think." Valarian crossed himself, picturing those bright, cold eyes. "I think he's gonna be a hell of a lot worse."

MULTIPLES
(With Barry N. Malzberg)

Kenner murdered his wife for the tenth time on the evening of July 28, in the kitchen of their New York apartment. Or perhaps it was July 29. One day is much the same as another, and I cannot seem to keep dates clearly delineated in my head. He did it for the usual reasons: because she had dominated him for fourteen years of marriage (fifteen? sixteen?), and openly and regularly ridiculed him, and sapped all his energy and drive, and, oh I simply could not stand it any more.

He did not try to be elaborately clever as to method and execution. The simpler the better—that was the way he liked to do it. So he poisoned her with ten capsules of potassium, I mean nitrous oxide, disguised as saccharine tablets, which he neatly placed in her coffee with a twist of the wrist like a kiss. Nothing amiss.

She assumed almost at once the characteristic attitude of oxide poisoning, turning a faint green as she bent into the crockery on the table. A cigarette still smoldered unevenly beside her. She drank twenty cups of coffee every day and smoked approximately four packages of cigarettes, despite repeated warnings from her doctor. Kenner found it amusing to think that her last sensations were composed of acridity, need, and lung-filling inhalation. It was even possible that she believed, as death majestically overtook her, that the *cigarette* had done her in.

Kenner, a forty-five-year-old social worker of mundane background, few friends, and full civil service tenure (but nevertheless in grave trouble with his superiors, who had recently found him to be "insufficiently motivated"), then made all efforts to arrange the scene in what he thought to be a natural manner: adjusting the corpse in a comfortable position, cleaning the unused pellets of cyanide from the table, letting the damned cat out, and so forth. Immediately afterward, he went to a movie theater; that is, he went immediately after shutting off all the lights and locking all the doors. Windows were left open in the kitchen, however, to better dispense what he thought of as "the stench of death."

What Kenner did at the movie theater was to sit through a double feature. The price he paid for admission and what films he saw or did not really see are not known at the time of this writing. Furthermore, what he hoped to gain by leaving the scene of the crime only to reenter at a "safer" time remains in doubt. I must have been crazy. Also, Kenner's usual punctiliousness and sense of order did not control his actions during this tragic series of events. I was too excited.

After emerging from the theater, Kenner purchased an ice cream cone from a nearby stand and ate it slowly while walking back to his apartment. As he turned in a westerly direction, he was accosted by two co-workers at the Welfare Unit where he was employed. They greeted him and asked the whereabouts of his wife. Kenner responded that she had had a severe headache and, since she suffered from a mild heart condition complicated by diabetes, wanted to restrain her activities to the minimum. I suppose Kenner was attempting with this tactic to lay the groundwork for a "death by natural causes" verdict, but I'm not quite sure. I do know that one of the co-workers, commenting on Kenner's appearance, said that he looked "ghastly."

Once parted from his colleagues, Kenner continued west and eventually re-entered his apartment at 10:51 p.m. It was frightening in the dark. Turning on the lights, he went into the livingroom and found his wife waiting there for him—sitting under a small lamp, reading and drinking coffee and smoking five cigarettes in various stages of completion. Much perturbed, he was unable to account for the fact that she was still alive. I felt as if I were dreaming.

There was a brief exchange of dialogue between Kenner and his wife, the substance of which I cannot recall, and then he proceeded to his own room. He wanted to lock the door behind him but could not, owing to the fact that his wife—saying that separate bedrooms or not, she wanted to know what the "little fool" was doing at all times—had forbidden him a bolt. On the way he noticed that the plates had been removed from the kitchen table and heaped as always to fester in the sink, and that there was no sign of the violence he was *sure* had taken place earlier.

Immediately after closing his door, Kenner seized his journal and began to record the evening's curious events in his usual style. I could have been a published writer if only I had worked at it. He was hopeful that the documentation would help him to understand matters, but I was wrong, this was never the answer.

He was interrupted midway through his writing by his wife's customarily unannounced entrance into his room. She told him that his strange state of excitation this evening had upset her, and therefore agitated her mild heart condition (she had one, all right, although she did not have diabetes). She said she thought I was "breaking down," and went on to say that she knew the "impulse to murder her" had long been uppermost in Kenner's mind but he "didn't have the guts to do it." She further stated that Kenner was no doubt "dreaming all the time of ways and means and you probably fill that damned journal of yours with all your raving imaginations; I've never cared enough to bother reading it, but it's sure to be *full* of lunatic fantasies."

Kenner responded that he was a mature person and thus not prey to hostile thoughts. He begged her to leave the room so that he could continue his entries. I told her I was writing a novel, but she didn't believe me. She knows everything.

She laughed at him and dared him to make her leave the room. Kenner stared at her mutely, whereupon she laughed again and said if looks could kill, she'd certainly be dead right now. Then she said, "But if I were dead, you'd be completely lost; you'd fall apart altogether. You need me and you don't really want me dead, you know, even though as I'm talking to you you're probably filling up pages with more vicious fantasies. I'll bet I even know what you're writing this very minute. You're imagining me dead, aren't you? You're writing down right this minute that I'm dead."

She's dead.
She's dead.
She—is—dead!

Kenner murdered his wife for the eleventh time on July 29 or July 30, in her bedroom in their New York apartment. He did it for the usual reasons, and he did not attempt to be elaborately clever as to method and execution. In fact, he chose to repeat the procedure of the previous evening. While she lounged in bed as was her custom on weekends (this was either Saturday or Sunday), I made her breakfast and poisoned her coffee with eleven capsules of nitrous oxide.

When Kenner took the tray into her bedroom, she was sitting up in bed and there were three cigarettes burning on the nightstand. She smiled at him maliciously as she lifted her cup, and asked if he had "put in a few drops of arsenic or something to sweeten the taste." After which she laughed in her diabolical way and drank some of the coffee.

With clinical curiosity, Kenner watched the cup slip from her fingers and spill the rest of the liquid over the bedclothes; watched her expression alter and her face and body once more assume the characteristic attitude of oxide poisoning as she fell back against the headboard. The faint green color looked quite well on her, he concluded.

This time Kenner did not arrange the scene in what he thought to be a natural manner. He also did not open the windows. He simply left the apartment and took a subway to Times Square, where he consumed a breakfast of indeterminate nature in a restaurant or perhaps a cafeteria. Once finished he browsed through a bookstore, purchased a candy bar, and finally took the subway home again. Upon entering his apartment, I think the time was 10:51 a.m., he proceeded directly to his wife's bedroom.

She was still lying in bed, and she was still quite surprisingly dead. The scene, however, had after all been changed in certain ways. The coffee which he was *sure* had been spilled across the bedclothes had not been spilled at all; the cup, in point of fact, rested empty on the breakfast tray. Her color was not greenish, but rather a violent purple. The three cigarettes had become four, and each had burned down to skeletal fingers of gray ash. Her hands were clutched somewhat pathetically at her breast.

Kenner stared at her for a long time, after which scrutiny he went to his room and attempted to write in his journal. I could not seem to think, I knew I would have to wait until later. Returning to his wife's bedroom once more, he paused to study the empty coffee cup and the remains of the cigarettes. It was then that he understood the truth.

The *cigarettes* and the *coffee*, not Kenner, had done her in.

What he did next is not clear. Very little is clear even now, many hours later. He does seem to have telephoned his wife's doctor, since the physician arrived eventually and pronounced her dead of a heart attack. Two or three interns also came with a stretcher and took her away. As I write this I can still smell the after-shave lotion one of them was wearing.

One thing, therefore, is quite clear: she's dead.

Damn her, she really is dead and gone forever.

What am I going to do *now?*

Kenner murdered his dead wife for the first time on August 1, or possibly August 6, in the bathroom of their New York apartment ...

THE BEING

I was on duty in Exobiology when Sam Meisner, head of Isolation Unit security, called me. "I hate to be the one to break this to you, Doc," he said, sounding breathless, "but it got out."

"What? You don't mean—"

"I'm afraid so."

"When? How?"

"Fifteen minutes ago, about. The tech, Hiller, was supposed to put it back in its cage after giving it its nutrition injections, but he…well, he was laughing so hard at the thing's screwball antics he got the hiccups and dropped its tether. It danced out before he could stop it."

I slammed my free hand down on the desktop. "Of all the stupid—! Your people were warned over and over to be extra careful when the being was let out. It is still in the complex?"

"No way it could've got out, but—"

"But what?"

"We haven't been able to find it yet. We started looking as soon as Hiller sounded the alarm, but it had a two-minute jump on us and you know how fast it moves. It's gotta be here somewhere."

"Then find it and re-cage it—quick."

The fact that the being had gotten loose was disturbing in the extreme. It seemed to be completely harmless, a fascinating scientific conundrum, but I couldn't help feeling that it presented an amorphous threat of some sort. The feeling was so strong at the moment that I almost wished the military patrol hadn't discovered it capering around in the Nevada desert three and a half weeks ago.

Rather than fidgeting in my office waiting for Meisner to get back to me, I headed down to Isolation. It took me ten minutes to get there via elevator and the maze of corridors in the complex's nether regions. And when I did the unit was in a state of turmoil, security personnel and techs scurrying every which way. I didn't see Meisner among them, but one of the other security officers, Fred Goldman, was there talking into the radio mic Velcro-ed to the shoulder of his uniform. One look at his face was enough to tell me the worst-case scenario had happened.

He said in harried tones, "I was just trying to contact you, Doc."

"The being got all the way out, didn't it."

"Yes, sir. There's no way it could have, yet somehow it did."

"Christ! Where's Meisner?"

"He and three others chased out after it a few minutes ago, as soon as he got word."

"What word?"

"Where the thing went," Goldman said. "Over to the intersection of Fourth and Ainsley. He just radioed that it's still there."

"Have they captured it yet?"

"No, sir. Him and the others can't get through."

"Through? Through what?"

"The crowds. It's got traffic all jammed up and drawing people like a magnet. The whole area's already packed solid."

"What is it doing?"

"The same thing it does in its cage," Goldman said, "all it knows how to do. Put on a crazy show."

I got down to the Fourth and Ainsley area as fast as I could. The sector was swarming by then, traffic backed up for blocks—I had to half run on foot the last four—and I couldn't get anywhere close to the intersection where the being was.

There must have been a few thousand people jammed together on the streets and sidewalks, dozens more hanging out of windows, and still more arriving singly and in bunches every second; the ones who could see it in the intersection kept raising a tumult of laughter and cheers of encouragement. At least one mobile TV news van was on the scene—it gave me a chill when I spotted it and the cameraman atop its roof—and there were bound to be others. There were several police cars, too, and blue uniformed patrolmen making an effort at crowd control, but the mob was just too large and merrily unruly. Flashes from God knows how many cell phone cameras painted the gray afternoon with bursts of light.

I had made radio contact with Meisner on the way and he'd given me his location. But it took me fifteen minutes of pushing and shoving through the melee to get to where he and the other security officers were grouped together at the perimeter.

"You see how bad it is, Doc," he said, "and getting worse all the time. We tried more than once to get through, waving badges and brandishing weapons, but all that did was threaten to turn the crowd ugly. If we'd started knocking heads, there would've been a full-scale riot. We had no choice but to back off."

Another wave of hysterical cheering went up. I did not have to see the creature to know what it was doing. Capering, frolicking, rolling its big orange eyes, waving its soft-furred appendages, contorting its strangely elastic features into all sorts of bizarre shapes, and all the while making those weird burbling noises that may or may not have been alien speech. Putting on a crazy show, as Meisner had said. A crazy show that could be and often was amusing; it had even made me laugh in the beginning.

"I notified Command Center," Meisner said. "They're calling out the National Guard. Once the troops get here, we shouldn't have any trouble recapturing the thing. And this time we'll make sure it's locked up in an escapeproof cage."

"It won't matter then," I said. "It's already too late."

"You mean because it got loose and all the hoopla it's causing?"

"Yes. The secret is no longer highly classified, it's out in the open now." The words were bitter in my mouth, the next ones even more so. "The Pentagon, the N.S.A., Homeland Security ... they're as much to blame as that idiot tech who let the being escape. We kept telling them it was a bad idea to bring it here to the city, that it should have been kept hidden away in Area 51, but they wouldn't listen."

"They had to bring it, didn't they? Because of the advanced testing facilities in the complex here?"

"No, dammit, they didn't. The testing facilities in Area 51 are more than adequate. And the security a hell of a lot tighter," I added pointedly.

One of the other officers said, "Well, at least the thing's harmless."

"Harmless? You think so?"

"You mean it isn't? The tests you and the other scientists have been conducting..."

"None of which have told us anything except that the being has no measurable intelligence and is not of this earth."

"And completely non-aggressive, right?"

"From all indications, yes, but aggression isn't the only danger it presents."

"Hell," Meisner said, "all it is is a ... I don't know, a clown, a court jester, one of those animated characters in a kids' TV show."

"Is it? We have no idea where it came from, or how it got here or why," I said. "We haven't enough data to make even an educated guess as to what it *is*—its DNA is like none science has ever encountered before. For all we know there are other such beings scattered around the world that haven't been found yet or are being held in government isolation like this one was. Or that more will come."

"So what are you saying, sir?"

That the seeds had been sown and the damage done, whether by alien or cosmic design or a monstrous twist of fate. That the danger was real and all of us, all of us everywhere, were in jeopardy. But all I said aloud was, "There'll be hell to pay now."

"How do you figure that?"

"Thousands of people have already seen it," I said. "Video-taped it, photographed it, live-streamed its image on television and the Internet. By tonight the country, the entire world will know of its existence."

"And have a fine time laughing at its silly antics."

"For now, yes. For now."

"What do you mean?"

"What do you suppose will happen when the novelty wears off and the fun subsides? People are going to start asking questions, hard questions that we don't have answers to. Then what? Paranoia. Panic, maybe."

"Come on, Doc, you're overdramatizing. Things won't get that bad—"

Shouts rose suddenly from the packed humanity closest to Fourth and Ainsley, excited cries repeating the same words or variations of them. *"Look, now it's dancing off down the street! Where's it headed, what's it going to do? Come on, come on, let's follow it, let's find out!"* The throng surged forward, broke apart into running, jostling figures, their raised voices and their pounding feet creating rolling waves of sound as loud as thunder. Watching the spectacle, I couldn't help thinking of the legend of Hamelin Town.

"Oh, yes, they will," I said, but no one was listening.

STROKE OF LUCK

I was tending to the floribunda roses in my garden when the car pulled up to the curb in front. I barely noticed it at first, my attention on the application of Miracle-Gro and aphid spray to the largest of the Tuscan Sun bushes. It was a warm spring day and my arthritis was not bothering me nearly as much as it did in cooler weather. Not that it would have mattered if it had been bothering me. At 79, with decade number nine just around the corner, a person learns to tolerate the various discomforts of aging, particularly when there is a task that needs doing.

The sound of the front gate opening brought my head up. A smiling young man dressed in a suit and tie and carrying a briefcase stepped through, closed the gate behind him, waved toward where I was perched on my gardening stool, and proceeded along the flagstone path. I had never seen him before. Uh-oh, I thought, a salesman—either the persistent kind or one who can't read plain English. I got to my feet with only a couple of minor joint twinges and looked past him at his car, a nondescript gray Ford. It didn't tell me what he might be selling.

"Mrs. Dalworth?" he called cheerfully. "Mrs. Ellen Marie Dalworth?"

"The sign on the gate means what it says."

"Sign?"

" 'No Solicitors.' "

"Oh, I'm not a solicitor. No, ma'am, on the contrary. My name is Crown, James Crown. I'm with the County Assessor's Office."

Frowning, I crossed to where he stood on the flagstones. He was about thirty, poochy-cheeked but not fat, with a mop of curly brown hair and a neatly trimmed mustache. His smile testified to the fact that he had good dental hygiene. The photo ID badge he showed me had the county seal and stated that he was a representative of the office's Appraisal Support Unit.

"What does the County Assessor want with me?" I asked. "My property taxes are all paid up."

"Oh, yes, certainly," he said. "But property taxes are nonetheless an essential reason why I've come to see you. The fact is, Mrs. Dalworth, you're one of several Bay City homeowners who have had a stroke of luck. Very good luck."

"Is that right?"

"Yes, indeed. Your property has been deemed worthy of reassessment at a lower value. The new figure, I'm pleased to report, will reduce your annual tax burden by a considerable margin."

"Oh? How considerable?"

"I'm sure you'll be pleased when you see the particulars. I have the paperwork right here." He patted his briefcase. "May we go over them inside where it's more comfortable?"

"All right. Just let me fetch my gardening tools."

"I'll fetch them for you, if you like."

"That's not necessary."

I went back to the floribundas, put my trowel and gloves and the Miracle-Gro and aphid spray into the gardening basket, picked up the stool, and returned to the path along the front fence. James Crown had turned his back and was looking at the house in an admiring way.

"You have a lovely home, Mrs. Dalworth," he said when I joined him. "Beautifully kept up, house and garden both."

"Thank you. I take pride in my surroundings."

"Indeed you must, and have for quite a long time. Our records show you've resided here forty-four years."

"Forty-four ... yes, that's right. My late husband and I bought the property in 1976."

"An admirable long-term investment, to say the least. You're currently the only occupant, correct?"

"Ever since my husband died seven years ago. I have no intention of going anywhere else as long as my health permits."

"You seem very fit, if I may say so."

"I am, and you may."

He chuckled as if I'd said something funny.

We went up onto the porch. I set the basket and stool down there and then led him inside to the front parlor. Living room, Harold called it, but I prefer the old-fashioned term my grandmother always used.

"Have a seat, Mr. Crown. Anywhere you like."

He perched on the chintz-covered sofa. When I sat in my walnut rocker across from him, he laid his briefcase on the coffee table between us, opened it, and shuffled through a stack of papers inside. "Here we are. Twenty-nine ten Carlsbad Lane."

I put on my reading glasses. All the documents bore the letterhead of the County Assessor's Office. One set contained data on the property at 2910 Carlsbad Lane owned by Ellen Marie Dalworth and valued at $122,000—the assigned parcel number, the size of the lot, the date the house was built, the date Harold and I purchased it and the price we paid, the number and size of the rooms. Another document, this one signed by Marvin Fletcher, the county assessor, confirmed that the property was due for immediate reassessment, and listed the new appraised value as $103,000. At that figure, the annual tax bite would be some $1,500 less than I was currently paying. There was also a legal form that required my signature.

"Do you have any questions, Mrs. Dalworth?" James Crown asked when I finished reading.

I held up the legal form. "This says I have to pay a fee of $700 in order to get the reassessment."

"Yes, a required processing fee. But as the form states, there are no additional fees."

"So I see."

"The fee is agreeable to you, I trust?"

"Is it payable immediately?"

"Immediately upon signing the agreement, yes."

I nibbled my lower lip. "Well, I don't know. Seven hundred dollars is a lot of money."

"It is, but not when compared to the annual tax savings. The amount of your first year savings more than covers the fee."

"Could I pay it in installments, over a period of time?"

"I'm afraid not," he said. His smile was sympathetic now. "Office policy doesn't permit it. Would it be a hardship for you to pay the full amount now?"

"Well ... no, not really. I suppose I could write a check. I've written enough of them to the County Assessor, God knows."

"Payable to C.A. is sufficient," he said. "With a notation of your parcel number, of course."

"But still ... seven hundred dollars. I'd like to think about it for a few minutes."

"By all means. Meanwhile, on the likelihood that you'll decide favorably and with your permission, I'll take the required measurements."

"Measurements?"

"Of each room, to verify that no renovations to the house have been made since the previous assessment."

"Is that necessary? None have, I assure you."

"Necessary, yes, but it's a mere formality. You have no objection?"

"I suppose not."

"Excellent." From inside his briefcase he produced a black and red object about the size of a cell phone. He held it up for my inspection, identifying it as a 120-foot laser measuring tape. "Makes the task quick and easy," he said. "Shouldn't take me more than twenty minutes. If you'll be so good as to show me the other rooms, I'll measure each in turn and finish up in here."

I conducted him through the house. On the back porch he said, "Do you mind waiting in the living room, Mrs. Dalworth? I'll be as quick as I can, then hopefully we can finish our business."

"Very well. I believe I'll make some iced tea while I do my thinking. Would you like a glass, Mr. Crown?"

His smile brightened. "Why, yes, I would, if it's not too much trouble."

"No trouble at all."

In the kitchen I filled and put on the teakettle, then proceeded to the parlor. Almost exactly twenty minutes had passed when he reappeared.

"All done except for this room," he said.

"The iced tea isn't ready yet, I'm afraid."

"Quite all right. Have you come to a decision?"

"I have. We will definitely be doing business."

"Excellent."

The kettle whistled. I went in to the kitchen to turn it off, but I didn't stay there long.

James Crown had his back to me, flashing that laser measuring gadget of his along one wall, when I reentered the parlor. When he turned around, he was not looking at a glass of iced tea—he was looking into the muzzle of a .38 revolver.

"All right, you son of a bitch," I said. "Don't make any sudden moves."

The combination of pointed gun and epithet stunned him. He gawped at me goggle-eyed and open-mouthed.

"I may be seventy-nine," I said, "but my hand is still steady and I won't hesitate to shoot you if you force me to. Sit down on the sofa and keep your hands where I can see them. Go on, do as you're told."

He was too shocked and confused to argue. And not the aggressive type anyway, evidently. He did as he was told, saying in a sputtery voice, "I ... I don't understand ..."

"Oh, yes you do. You're no more an employee of the County Assessor's Office than I am, Crown or whatever your name is. County employees drive cars with the county seal on the doors and yours has none. Home reassessments are almost always increased in appraised value, not decreased, and if there were to be one on this property I would have received official notification by mail well in advance of any visit. And I wouldn't have been asked to pay a processing fee, or to make out a check to 'C.A.' that could be cashed by a person with a dummy business bank account using those initials. Your photo ID and the documents full of easily obtainable public information are computer forgeries, as phony as that wig and mustache you're wearing. All part of a plot to swindle me, and no doubt other senior homeowners, out of money we can ill afford to lose. Yes, and not incidentally to gain access to my house."

He shook his head, not once but three times, as if he still couldn't quite grasp what he was seeing and hearing.

"You're not only a lowlife scam artist preying on the elderly," I said, "you're also a sneak thief. You thought an old lady wouldn't miss a few expensive items, at least not until you were long gone, so you rifled my jewelry case when you were alone in the bedroom. I know because I checked the case when I went to get this gun just now. Four pieces missing, including the emerald pendant my late husband gave me on our twenty-fifth anniversary." I made a slight angry gesture with the revolver. "Put them and anything else you may have swiped on the coffee table. And make sure that's all you take out of your pocket."

He hesitated, but only briefly, before he obeyed. The four pieces of jewelry were all that he'd stolen. He hadn't come across the gun because I kept it well hidden under my mattress.

"That nonsense about needing to take room measurements told me what else you were up," I said. "If your game had been just a reassessment swindle, I would have paid the bogus fee, let you leave, and called my bank and the police after you'd left. You wouldn't have gotten far; when I retrieved my gardening tools I detoured along the fence so I could memorize the license plate on your car. Scammers are bad enough, one who's also a thief is twice as despicable."

There was a kind of grudging awe in his gaze now. "How … how did you figure it all out so fast—?"

"It wasn't difficult. Vermin like you think all seniors are borderline senile, but the truth is most of us are as sharp-witted as we ever were. I've never forgotten any of my training and experience."

"Training? Experience?"

"Your biggest mistake was not bothering to find out just whom you were dealing with—a stroke of *bad* luck for you." I had my cell phone in hand now and I tapped 911 with my left thumb. "I was a Bay City policewoman for forty years, retired with honors and the rank of sergeant."

BETRAYAL

Nick sits on the bench watching the old man feed bread crumbs to a gaggle of pigeons. The day is warm, the trees and shrubbery starting to bud, the lawns turning a bright green. The kind of day, after a long winter, that makes the world seem like a more peaceful place than it is.

"How come you sat down here with me?" the old man asks him. "Most younger guys, strangers, they don't want nothing to do with somebody my age."

"You looked like you could use some company. Other than those birds, I mean."

"They ain't company. Feeding 'em helps pass the time, that's all. Fattening 'em up for a good stew." He chuckles at his joke, then sobers. "Good to have somebody to talk to for a change," he says. "Got no friends around here, no friends at all anymore."

"What about family?"

"Gone. All gone. What'd you say your name was again?"

"Nick."

"Mine's Charlie. Don't think I've seen you here before."

"Well, I don't come as often as I'd like. I work long hours, don't get much time off."

"I know how that is. I used to put in long hours, too. What kind of work you do?"

"I'm a cop," Nick says.

Charlie's rheumy eyes brighten. "No kidding? Now ain't that a hell of a coincidence. I used to be on the job myself."

"Is that right?"

"Worked out of the Forty-eighth. Which precinct you in?"

"The Seventy-ninth."

"Uptown."

"No, it's downtown."

"Right. Downtown. Uniform or plain clothes?"

"Plain clothes the past four years."

"What rank?"

"Detective third-grade."

"I was a sergeant. Took me twenty years, but I finally made it. Figured I had it made, too." The brightness fades in the rheumy eyes. "I sure as hell was wrong about that."

"Were you?"

"The bastards threw me off the force, right before I was due for my pension. You want to know why?"

"Why?"

At the old man's feet the pigeons coo and burble. One of them tries to peck at his blue-veined hand; he swats it away, then throws crumbs at it. "Claimed I was dirty, that's why. On the take, and worse—a thief. You remember the Hollis Transport holdup?"

Nick shakes his head.

"Happened back in ... I don't remember exactly," Charlie says. "A while back. Two armed robbers shot a guard, made off with seventy-five large in cash. Me and my partner, Pete Decker, got a tip on where the perps were holed up, this abandoned warehouse on the east side. We went in after 'em, just the two of us. Brass said we should've waited for backup, but we had other ideas. There was a lot of shooting, bullets flying all over the goddamn place, only time I ever fired my service weapon except on the pistol range. When it was all over the two perps were dead and Pete had a slug in his arm. Department reprimanded us for not following procedure. That's all Pete got, the reprimand. I got the shaft."

Charlie gazes off into the distance for a time, a light breeze ruffling his wispy white hair. Two people walk slowly along the cinder path, but he isn't watching them. Focused on the distant past.

Pretty soon he says, "No sign of the seventy-five thousand in the warehouse. No sign of it anywhere. Department figured maybe I snagged it, or Pete did, or both of us. Big investigation. Never found out what happened to the money, no proof of wrongdoing on our part. Case closed. Except that it wasn't. You want to know what happened?"

"If you want to tell me."

"They had to have a scapegoat, so they phonied up a bunch of graft charges against me. Claimed I was taking payoffs from bookies, the racket boys that controlled numbers and prostitution in the precinct. Pete, he got off clean, no charges against *him*." Charlie scratches at a stubble of gray whiskers on his chin. "You know Pete Decker?"

"Heard of him."

"He still on the job?"

"Still at the Forty-eighth," Nick says. "He's a captain now."

"Sure, that figures. He gets promoted up the line, I get thrown out on my ass. It ain't right. It's damn unfair."

"Yes, it is."

"*Damn* unfair. He should've got the same treatment."

"Why, if he was innocent too?"

"Who says he was innocent?"

"You mean he wasn't?"

"Dirty as hell. Guilty as sin."

"Pete Decker was on the take?"

"Now and then, before that day. Big-time dirty then."

"... Are you saying he stole the seventy-five thousand?"

Charlie winks at him. "Hell of a big pile of cash."

"Did you see him take it?"

"I was there, wasn't I? I just told you."

"Why didn't you turn him in, Charlie?"

"Couldn't. Had to keep my mouth shut, didn't have no other choice. They'd have prosecuted me right along with him."

"No, they wouldn't. You didn't take the money."

The old man is silent for a time, looking off into the distance again. Then he jerks as if coming out of a doze, sighs heavily. "Like hell I didn't," he says.

"What?"

"Like hell I didn't take that money. It was right there in the warehouse in a suitcase. Me and Pete grabbed it, hid it, split it up later."

Nick sits staring at him. "Jesus, Charlie, you're not serious—"

"I'm serious, all right. Better believe it."

"You betrayed your badge, you and Pete Decker?"

"Wasn't the first time. Those graft charges I told you about, they wasn't phonied up. I was on the take, all right, and IAD found out about it."

"But for God's sake ... why admit it now, to me?"

"I'm sick of telling the same lies over and over. Got to stop sometime, might as well be now. Don't make no difference you're a detective. I ain't gonna to be around much longer anyway."

"Dirty. A dirty cop."

"Hell, I'm not proud of it."

"Then why—?"

"Why do you think? Long hours, lousy pay, bills piling up. You're on the job, you understand how it is. You keep getting tempted, and finally one day you say the hell with it and start taking a little here and there—"

"I don't," Nick says. "Not once, ever."

"How long you been on the force?"

"Fifteen years."

"Married?"

"Once. Not any more."

"Kids?"

"No."

"Be different if you had the obligations I did."

"No, it wouldn't. No."

"Never even been tempted, eh?"

"Never."

"Bet you would've been if you'd stumbled on more green than you ever saw before or will ever see again. Bet you'd've grabbed it, just like Pete and me did."

Nick says thinly, "He talked you into it?"

"Other way around." Charlie makes a humorless cackling sound. "Didn't take much talking, either."

"What happened to your share?"

"I spent it, same as I spent the rest of the graft. Some before I got thrown off the force, some after. Bills, clothes, second car, new TV, house repairs. Department couldn't prosecute me because they couldn't prove none of it, the payoffs were all under the table and I was real careful about where I hid the Hollis money and how I spent it. *Real* careful. All they could do was kick me out, screw me out of my pension."

The old man's bitter, self-serving confession makes Nick feel sick. He gets to his feet. "I've heard enough. I'm leaving now."

Another cackle, this one ending in a phlegmy cough. "Guess you won't be coming back, eh?"

Nick doesn't answer, just walks away.

The old man's story weighs on Nick all the way back to his apartment. Is it true? It must be, even though he doesn't want to believe it. Charlie's account of those past events was sharp, too sharp to be delusional; his crimes, his betrayal must have been festering in him for a long time. And the look on his face …

Inside the small, cramped apartment, Nick pours himself a large whiskey. There's nothing he can do about Charlie or Pete Decker now— and the old man knew it. The Hollis money is long gone, there's no evidence to back up the confession, and the statute of limitations on the theft has run out besides. He'll only stir up a hornet's nest if he goes to the brass with it, and he'll be the one to get stung.

He takes a long pull of whiskey, but it does nothing to relieve the cold emptiness inside him. The old man's image is vivid in his mind.

Why did it have to be me you unburdened yourself to after all these years? he thinks. Why did you have to be so lost in the past, today of all days, you didn't know me up there on the care facility grounds?

Ah, Pop, why couldn't you let me go on believing I'm not the only honest cop in the family?

SHADE WORK

Johnny Shade blew into San Francisco on the first day of summer. He went there every year, when he had the finances; it was a good place to find action on account of the heavy convention business. Usually he went a little later in the summer, around mid-July, when there were fifteen or twenty thousand conventioneers on the loose, a high percentage of them with money in their pockets and a willingness to lay some of it down on a poker table. You could take your time picking your vic.

But this year was different. This year he couldn't afford to take his time. He had three thousand in his kick that he'd scored in Denver, and he needed to parlay that into ten grand—fast. Ten grand would buy him into a big-store con Elk Tracy was setting up in Louisville. Elk needed a string of twenty and a nut of two hundred K to set it up right; that was the reason for the ten grand buy-in. The guaranteed net was a cool million. Ten grand buys you fifty, minimum. Johnny Shade had been a card mechanic for nearly two decades and he'd never held that much cash in his hands at one time.

He was a small-time grifter, a single-o traveling around the country on his own looking for action wherever he would find it. Stud and draw games in hotel rooms with marks who never seemed to want to lose more than a few hundred at a sitting. He wasn't a good enough mechanic to play in even a medium-stakes game and hope to get away with crimps or hops or overhand run-ups or Greek-deals or hand-mucks or any of the other shuffling and dealing cheats. So he relied on his specialty, shade work.

Shade work was fine in small games. Most amateurs never thought to examine or riffle-test a deck when he ran a fresh one in, because it was always in its cellophane wrapper with the manufacturer's seal unbroken. The few who did check the cards didn't spot the gaff on account of they were looking for blisters, shaved edges, blockout or cutout work—the most common methods of marking a deck.

He had the shade gaff down to a science. He diluted blue and red aniline dye with alcohol until he had the lightest possible tint, then used a camel's hair brush to wash over a small section of the back pattern of each card in a Bee or Bicycle deck. The dye wouldn't show on the red or blue portion, but it tinted the white part just lightly enough so you could see it if you knew what to look for. He could spot his shade work on a vic's cards across the table in poor light without even squinting.

But the high-rollers knew about shade work, just as they knew about every other scam a professional hustler could come up with. You couldn't fool them. So if you were Johnny Shade, you had to content yourself with making pocket and traveling cash instead of the big score.

He was tired of the grift, that was the thing. He'd been at it too long. He wanted a slice of the good life. With fifty K he could travel first-class, wine and dine and bed first-class woman, maybe even find a partner and work one of the fancier short cons.

First, though, he had to parlay his Denver three K into ten K. Then he could hop a plane for Louisville. Ten days ... that was all the time he had before Elk Tracy closed out his string. Ten days to pick the right vics.

He found the first set his first night in Frisco. That was a good omen. His luck was going to change; he could feel it.

Most weeks in the summer there was a convention going on at the Hotel Nob Hill, off Union Square. He walked in there on this night, and the first thing he saw was a banner that said WELCOME FIDDLERS in great big letters. Hick musicians, or maybe some kind of organization for people who were into cornball music. Just his type of crowd.

He hung out in the bar, nursing a beer, circulating, keeping his ears open. When he heard one of four guys in a booth say the word "poker," he sidled closer and saw they were all wearing badges with FIDDLER on them and their names and the cities they were from written underneath. They were talking stud poker, bragging about how good they were at it. Ripe meat. All he had to do was finagle his way among them, and he was good at finagling. He had the gift of gab, a face like a Baptist preacher's, and a winning smile.

First he sat at a table near their booth. Then he contrived to bump into a waitress and spill a fresh round of beers she was bringing to them. He insisted on paying for the drinks, flashed his wallet so they could see that he was flush. He laid on the oil about being in town for a convention himself, and that got him an invitation to join them.

Dave from Cleveland, Mitch from Los Angeles, Verne from Cedar Rapids, Harry from Bayonne. And Johnny from Denver. He didn't even have to maneuver the talk back to cards. Mitch from L.A. brought up the subject.

"We're thinking about getting up a game," he said. "You play poker, Johnny?"

Johnny said he did—five-stud and draw. No wild card games, none of that crap; he was a purist.

"So are we," Harry from Bayonne said. "You feel like sitting in with us?"

"I guess I wouldn't mind," Johnny said. "Depending on the stakes. Nothing too rich for my blood." He showed them his best smile. "Then again, nothing too small, either. Poker's no good unless you make it interesting, right?"

If they'd insisted on penny-ante or buck-limit, he'd have backed out and gone looking elsewhere. But they were sports: table stakes, ten-buck limit per bet, no limit on raises. They looked like they could afford that kind of action. Fiddle-music jerks, maybe, but reasonably well heeled. Might be as much as four or five grand among the four of them.

Verne from Cedar Rapids said he had a deck of cards in his room, they could play there. Johnny said, "Sounds good. How about we go buy a couple more decks in the gift shop? Nothing like the feel of a new deck after a while."

They all thought that was a good idea. Everybody drank up and they went together to the gift shop. All Johnny had to do was make sure the cards they bought were Bicycle blue-backs; he had two shaded blue-back Bicycle decks in his pocket. Then they all rode upstairs to Verne from Cedar Rapids's room and got down to business.

Johnny played it straight for a while, card-counting, making conservative bets, getting a feel for the way the marks played. Only one of them was reckless: Mitch from L.A., the one with the fattest wallet. He'd have liked two or three of that type, but one was all he needed.

After an hour and a half he was ahead about fifty and Mitch from L.A. was the big winner, betting hard, bluffing at least part of the time. Better and better. Time to bring in one of his shaded decks. That was easy, too. They'd let him hold the decks they'd bought downstairs; simple for him to bring out one of his own instead.

He didn't open it himself. You always let one of the marks do that, so the mark could look it over and see that it was still sealed in cellophane with the manufacturer's stamp on top intact. The stamp was the main thing to the mark, the one thing you never touched when you were fixing a deck. The way you did it was to carefully open the cellophane wrapper along the bottom and slide out the card box. Then you opened the box along one side, prying the glued flaps apart with a razor blade. Once you'd shaded the cards, you resealed the box with rubber cement, slipped it back into the cellophane sleeve, refolded the sleeve ends along the original creases, and resealed them with a drop of glue.

The light was pretty good in there; Johnny could read his shade work easily as the cards were dealt out. He took a couple of medium-sized pots, worked his winnings up to around two hundred, biding his time until both he and Mitch from L.A. drew big hands on the same deal. It finally happened about 10:30, on a hand of jacks-or-better. Harry from Bayonne was dealing; Johnny was on his left. Mitch from L.A. drew a pat full house, aces over fives. Johnny scored trip deuces. The top card on the rest of the deck—his card on the draw—was the fourth deuce. Beautiful.

Mitch from L.A. bet ten and Johnny raised him and Mitch raised back. Dave from Cleveland stayed while the other two dropped. Dave owned four high diamonds in sequence and was gambling on a one-card draw to fill a straight flush. But he was not going to get it because Mitch had his diamond ace and Johnny had his diamond ten.

Johnny raised again, and Mitch raised back; Dave hung in stubborn. There was nearly a grand in the pot when Mitch finally called the last raise. Johnny took just one card on the draw, to make the others think he was betting two pair. Mitch would think that even if Johnny caught a full boat, his would be higher because he had aces up; so he'd bet heavy. Which he did. Dave from Cleveland had caught a spade flush and hung in for a while, driving the pot even higher, until he finally realized his flush wasn't going to beat what Johnny and Mitch were holding; then he dropped. Mitch kept right on working his full boat, raising each time Johnny raised, until he was forced to call when his cash pile ran down to a lone tenspot. That last ten lifted the total in the pot to $1,800.

Johnny fanned out his four deuces face up. Mitch from L.A. didn't say a word, just dropped his cards. Johnny grinned and said, "My lucky night, gents," and reached for the pot.

Reaching for it was as far as he got.

Harry from Bayonne closed a big paw over his right wrist; Verne from Cedar Rapids did the same with his left wrist. They held him like that, his hands imprisoned flat on the table.

"What the hell's the idea?" Johnny said.

Nobody answered him. Mitch from L.A. swept the cards together and then began to examine them closely, one at a time.

Dave from Cleveland said, "What is it, shade work?"

"Right. Real professional job."

"Thought so. I'm pretty good at spotting blockout and cutout work. And I didn't feel any blisters or edge or sand work."

"Nice resealing on that card box, Johnny," Harry from Bayonne said. "If I hadn't known it was a gimmicked deck, I might not have spotted the gaff."

Johnny gawped. "You knew? You all *knew?*"

"Oh sure," Mitch from L.A. said. "As soon as you moved in on us down in the bar. We wanted to see what kind of hustler you were, how you worked your scam. You might call it professional curiosity."

"Christ. Who are you guys?"

They told him. And Johnny Shade groaned and put his head in his hands. He knew then that his luck had changed, all right—all for the worst. And that once word of this got out, and these four guys would see that it did, his grifting days were numbered; he'd be a laughingstock from coast to coast.

They didn't belong to some hick music group. They weren't fiddlers; they were FIDDLERS, part of a newly formed nationwide professional organization. Fraud Identification Detectives, Domestic Law Enforcement Ranks.

Vice cops. He'd tried to run a gambling scam at a convention of vice cops...

THE MAN WHO LOVED MYSTERY STORIES
(with Barry N. Malzberg)

"And so," the Colonel said, flourishing his walking stick before the assembled guests, "we come to the simple, the inevitable explanation of this baffling case. An explanation so obvious, dear people, and yet so clouded by subterfuge that you will be amazed when it is revealed to you." He paused, touched his mustaches, smoothed them to a fine and dangerous sheen. "I am talking of the little anomaly of the Ganges Goblet. The supposedly missing Ganges Goblet. The Ganges Goblet that was, in fact, never there at all—was it, Mr. Jensen?"

There was a shout from the back of the room, a thin scream as a red-faced Christopher Jensen pushed his fiancée aside and ran frantically for the door. But before he could make good his escape, the Colonel's huge hands had halted him, gathered him into a fierce embrace.

"Now, lad," the Colonel said, "you know it's too late for that. The game's up. You may as well tell us what you've done with the Goblet."

"Leave me alone!" Jensen shouted. He seemed outraged, but beneath the anger and pose of bravado was defeat. He struggled briefly against the detective, then slumped all at once and was still in the Colonel's powerful grasp.

Martha leaned over him, crying, "Oh, Christopher, you can't be guilty, you can't be! There must be some other explanation!"

"I am afraid not, madam," the Colonel said gently. "Yer almost-betrothed is a thief and a murderer."

I have always been enticed, passionately so, by the mystery novel in all its forms and alternatives. For nearly a quarter of a century I have read at least six per week, more if I have had extended free time. According to my wife, this should be a focus of shame for me. A man of my education, Felicia has told me time and again, of my stature in society—I am the president of a small bank—should find his diversion in more respectable and intellectual pursuits. If I am to read other than the classics of our literature, she says, contemporary philosophy and political writings would best suit my profession, my education, my position in the community. At the beginning of our marriage, she was more amused than annoyed by my obsession, but that has changed as she has changed over the past twenty years.

Perhaps, as Edmund Wilson said and Felicia has reiterated, the mystery story is best suited to the emotionally inert or those seeking intellectuality on the cheap, but I do not believe this. I am an intelligent and thoughtful man and I, as I'm sure is the case with so many others like me, respond to the mystery as to no other product of human endeavor ... the sharp pieties which underlie the genre, the struggle toward order, the assumption—as is no longer possible in our daily lives and experiences—that order can be achieved, life made to be rational; that out of a welter of conflicting data, order through expurgation can emerge. I find this very comforting in an era where heads of state commit acts of betrayal, where random murders have neither rational motive nor explanation, when the very fabric and constancy of our way of life seems to have become uncontrollable. It is possible for the duration of a mystery novel to believe that insight and deductive reasoning can produce truths, that consequences can be made predictable by their actions, that a beneficent outcome awaits the innocent and swift justice the guilty.

"No," Devereaux said, "it wasn't that way at all. You never wanted the money. The money was nothing more than a smoke screen. You wanted Doreen. You wanted her life."

"Yeah, sure," Harper said. "You keep right on talking, Devereaux. Talk and talk all you want." He shifted his gaze to the others. "This guy is crazy," he sneered. "Only a crazy man would say that I wanted a harpy like Doreen."

"I didn't say you wanted Doreen, I said you wanted her life. You wanted her out of the way because she knew the truth about you, things no one else knew because of your past association with her, and she hated you enough to have used her entire $50,000 savings to find a way to destroy you. Instead you destroyed her first, so she could never reveal your true name and the real reason you came to this country."

"I don't know what you're talking about," Harper said. But his hands were trembling as he raised the glass of Scotch to his weak lips. Again he appealed to the others. "Why don't we put an end to this crazy charade?"

"Doreen was once your fiancée," Devereaux went on inexorably. "You believed she was still in England, perhaps even dead, and when you chanced to see her at the charity benefit, you had no choice but to act swiftly to protect your career and your freedom. You're the only one who could have put the poison into her drink, Harper, and I can prove it—"

"Bastard!" Harper screamed, a gun suddenly appearing in his hand. "I'll kill you for this, I'll kill anybody who gets in my way!"

"No, you won't," Devereaux told him. "I found that pistol in your overcoat pocket when we were together in your apartment earlier. There are no bullets in it now—I emptied all the chambers while you were in the bathroom."

Occasionally, my love for the mystery has embarrassed me ... condescending looks when I exposed the gaudy cover of an old paperback edition while eating in a restaurant, a loan almost thrown into default when I told the buyer that Hercule Poirot would never have lent money to a man with shoes so scuffed or pants so shiny. For the most part, however, I have been able to privatize my obsession and concerns; would have had an easier time doing so if it were not for Felicia, who constantly chastises me—her once sweet tongue has turned to acid—and who now and then, out of spite, comments on my "disgusting habit" in the company of others.

I console myself with the knowledge that the mystery novel, in the decades since I began reading this most rewarding fare, has gained a measure of respectability—become the darling of a small but growing coterie of academics, been the diversion of heads of state, achieved lofty status on the national bestseller lists. Even so, Felicia refuses to be swayed. If she knew how deeply read I am in the form, how often I have slipped away from my desk at the bank and locked myself in a bathroom stall to finish a particularly intriguing book, how often I have compared the fictional triumphs of order and justice to the horrors of contemporary existence and wished that I could somehow exchange my outer, my observed life for a complete immersion in those clean and illusory entertainments ... if she knew how little most of my life interests me, how little *she* interests me, she would be even more vituperative than she is.

On many a night, when Felicia was still permitting me the occasional pleasure of marital intimacy, I was unable to turn off the light and take her in my arms until I had finished the novel in progress. Thus she blames me for our childless marriage, another source of her bitterness toward me. I have never told her this, but I am relieved by the fact that we did not become parents. Children would only have been a further distraction, an additional obstacle in the pursuit of my one true passion.

"Oh, you're tough, all right," I said. "You're a real tough guy—the kind that strangles a cripple with his bare hands, then bludgeons the widow to death with a poker."

"No," he whimpered, "no, please ..."

"Yes," I said remorselessly, "oh yes, Smith. Then you arranged their apartment so that the murders would look like the work of an intruder. That took real toughness, too, with all the blood splashed around. You're so tough that here you are on all fours, begging for your life like the sniveling coward you really are. Well, listen to this, tough guy. I'm going to show you just as much mercy as you showed Joe and Gloria."

"Please, Hardman, please, you can't just kill me in cold blood!"

"Can't I?" I said.
The gun was huge in my hand.

Sometimes, in half-sleep, I contemplate the possibilities of my own life, had I been a policeman, amateur sleuth or avenging private eye. I think of prowling through the night, hunting clues, fighting off predators, searching for the missing valuables, the kidnapped victim, the last elusive piece of the puzzle, while others—the innocent and the guilty both—await my return, my explanation, my wisdom. I think of returning the stolen goods, unmasking the murderer, bringing light to darkness, restoring faith and hope to those who have lost their way. I think of the awed smiles, the murmurings of gratitude, the adulate eyes as I raise my walking stick, my umbrella, my pistol, my hand, and give them that which I alone can give.

I think of this often, and each time it saddens me. For I know that even if I were given the chance, I could never be such a man as those fictional giants—I could never be the hero.

If I were thrust into the world of the mystery story, were it to become my reality rather than my fantasy, I would fail miserably in the role of detective. I lack the mathematical brain, the imagination and ratiocinative skills of a Queen, a Poirot, a Dr. Fell. Not once, in all the years I have been reading mysteries, have I arrived at the solution before it was revealed or indeed anticipated any of the major clues. I lack, too, the dogged determination of a Steve Carella or an Inspector Wexford, the physical prowess and unswerving moral dedication of a Philip Marlowe. It is simply not in my nature to be a righter of wrongs, a champion of the downtrodden.

Nor would I be well-suited to the part of victim. I am capable of strong emotion, I have the capacity to hate deeply and profoundly, but I do not engender such virulent feelings in others. I am a mild man, with mild tastes, leading a mild and unfulfilled life. I have no enemies; not even Felicia would consider doing me in.

Nor would I fare well as one of the secondary characters. For one reason and another I am unfit for duty as bit player, false suspect, comic foil.

Only one role could be mine, only one role for which I am emotionally and psychologically suited. I know this now, with utter certainty. The fact does not disturb me as once it would have, nor am I frightened by the understanding that there can be only one just outcome of such a role. It is perhaps a matter of destiny that I, a man who loves mystery stories above all else, play the vitally important part of the one unmasked, the slumped figure in powerful hands, the trapped schemer, the sniveling coward begging for his life, the broken, the defeated, the lost.

"You must understand," I say to Felicia, "that what is about to happen is both inevitable and appropriate. I am the ideal murderer, and you of course are the ideal victim."

The gun is huge in my hand.

LINES

It was a wide spot on a secondary road in a corner of the Nevada desert. Line, it was called. Some name for a town, Hood thought as he drove in. Maybe whoever founded it had called it that because the road ran line-straight through it from one long section of sun-blasted wasteland into another. Or maybe it was because of the dozen or so old-fashioned western-style buildings that faced each other across the road like sagging blocks stretched out along a plumb line.

Dry, dusty, deserted except for an old man sitting in the shade in front of one of the storefronts. A dead town. A nowhere place.

Fitting, though, name and town both. Just right. He was in Line to cross a line, to make Line the end of the line for Teresa and the drifter, Kincaid, she'd run off with three months ago.

Hood had done a lot of things in his life. Boosted cars when he was a kid in East L.A. Committed a couple of burglaries, sold some meth, worked as a bagman for a gambling outfit, busted a few heads for money. But he'd never killed anybody. Until now. That was the line he was here to cross.

He'd tracked Teresa and Kincaid from L.A. to Phoenix to Vegas to Tonopah. Kincaid worked different jobs when he could get them but jobs were scarce these days and he hadn't worked much in those three months. Mostly they were living off the two thousand of Hood's money Teresa had stolen from him the night before they ran off. Traveling here and there in no definite pattern, spending their nights in cheap motels or holed up in Kincaid's car. Not easy to track, but not too difficult, either—not when you had enough hate driving you.

Nobody ran out on Joe Hood. Nobody took what belonged to Joe Hood and got away with it. Nobody.

The two of them had spent last night in Tonopah. So from there Hood had driven north, the direction he figured they'd taken, and when he came to the secondary road leading to Line he knew that was where he'd find them. Knew it for certain, as if somebody had suddenly opened up his head and dumped in the knowledge.

It was late afternoon when he drove into Line. There was a crumbling, six-unit motel on the outskirts, but he didn't stop there. On a blistering hot day like this, Teresa and Kincaid would be sitting in a bar sucking down ice-cold beer, Teresa's second favorite pastime.

Heat shimmers gave the false-front buildings a wavery look. The sun-glare off white walls and sheet metal roofs was so bright it struck fiery glints off the windshield and created blind spots; Hood didn't see the drunk come lurching out into the road until it was almost too late. He stood on the brakes, cramped the wheel, and the grill and left front fender just missed a collision.

"Watch where you're going, you stupid son of a bitch!" Hood yelled through the open driver's window.

The drunk stood staring and blinking stupidly, then wiped his mouth and shambled across on the street and disappeared into an alleyway between two of the storefronts.

The building the drunk had come out of had a sign on the front wall: *Buckhorn Tavern*. Hood drove ahead to the far end of town, going slow. There wasn't another car in sight, not even one parked in front of the buildings. And no other bars besides the Buckhorn. He made a U-turn and parked across from the tavern.

He unlocked the glove box, unwrapped the chamois cloth from around the 9mm Glock. The piece was loaded, but he jacked the clip out, checked it, then checked the action before he slammed the clip home again. He flipped off the safety, stuck the gun in the waistband of his pants, and got out of the car. The sun's heat seared him as he crossed the road, but he wasn't even sweating when he walked into the tavern.

It was dark inside, cooled a little by a couple of whirring ceiling fans. Hood stood for a couple of seconds just inside the door, looking around. A fat bartender slouched behind the long bar on the left. A beefy guy in a pearl-button shirt sat on a stool with a schooner of draft beer in front of him.

And in one of the low-backed booths on the right, heads together over bottles of Bud, there they were—Teresa and a man that had to be Kincaid.

They didn't see Hood at first. Too wrapped up in each other. Teresa didn't look much different than the last time he'd seen her, big, sweet-faced, her feathery black hair heat-limp. Kincaid was long and lean, with a bald spot on the crown of his head. It was the first time Hood had set eyes on the man. What did Teresa see in a blue-collar jerk like him? Hung like a horse, probably. Size mattered to her, all right. Anything that had to do with sex mattered to her.

Nothing mattered to Hood, not anymore.

He walked over to the booth, taking the Glock out of his waistband on the way. "Hello, Teresa," he said.

The look of shocked disbelief on her face was almost comical. She started up out of the booth. So did Kincaid. Hood shot Kincaid first, to get him out of the way—a clean kill shot that took off part of the right side of his head. The sound of the gun going off was deafening.

Teresa screamed, her eyes bulging wide, her hands clawing at the edge of the table.

"I told you," Hood said. "I warned you what would happen if you ran out on me."

"Oh God, Joe, no! Don't!"

"Goodbye, baby."

She threw up a hand, and he shot her right through it. Big round hole in her palm, big round hole in the middle of her forehead. And down she went, sliding off the seat and under the table.

The echoes faded. Quiet in there, then. Quiet as death.

Hood took one last look, then turned and walked back out into the heat.

Hood was sitting sleepily in the shade in front of the hardware store when his rheumy old eyes saw the car roll past and almost hit the drunk. Close but no cigar, he thought, and cackled to himself as the drunk staggered off. The car rolled on slow to the end of town, U-turned, came back and slid to the curb. The man who got out and went across into the Buckhorn was nobody Hood had ever seen before.

A little while later, when he heard the gunshots, he got up as quick as his tired old bones would let him and went inside the store. He didn't want any part of what was going on over in the tavern.

Hood lurched out of the Buckhorn and into the street. He was pie-eyed drunk, drunker than anybody had a right to be in the middle of the day. But when it was this damn hot, what else was there to do but wrap yourself around a bucket of cold beer? The sun dazzled his already blurred vision so that he didn't see the car until it almost hit him.

"Watch we're you're going, you stupid son of a bitch!" the driver yelled at him.

Hood blinked at the man, didn't recognize him. He wiped his mouth and staggered over into the alley between the feed store and café. In the shade there, he leaned over and puked until he felt better. Then he thought about having another beer or two.

From where he slouched behind the bar, Hood watched the stranger come in, stand for a few seconds, then walk over to the booth where the gangly guy and the girl were sitting. He didn't spot the gun until it appeared in the stranger's hand. At first he was so shocked that he just stood there staring. But then, when the shooting started and he saw the gangly guy's head fly apart, Hood dropped and flattened himself on the planks and lay there shaking with his hands covering his head.

Hood was just lifting the schooner to his mouth when the stranger walked in. Big guy, tough looking. Better not be looking for trouble, Hood thought because the heat was making him feel mean. Anybody messes with me on a hell-hot day like this, I'll kick a lung out of him.

He took a long draught of beer as the stranger walked over to the only occupied booth. Next thing he knew, the big bastard had a gun in his hand and it went off like a cannon and the blood, oh Jesus the blood—

Hood moved so fast the schooner went flying one way and the stool the other. He ran straight down the aisle between the crappers and out the back door and didn't stop until he was a block and a half away.

In the booth Hood was sitting with Teresa's hand in his, watching her and thinking about how much he liked screwing her and wishing it wasn't so damn hot so he could take her back to the motel and screw her again right now. Maybe he would anyway. Beer in the afternoon always made him horny.

He didn't pay any attention when the door opened and somebody came in. But then he heard steps, hard steps, and when he looked up a big, stone-faced man was standing there looking at him. He knew right away who it was. Knew it before he heard Teresa's gasp. Knew it with a kind of sick disbelief even before he heard the words, "Hello, Teresa," and saw the gun.

Hood started up out of the booth, knowing there wasn't time to do anything, that he was a dead man. The last thing he saw was the automatic's muzzle swinging up toward his head.

In the booth Hood hung on tight to Kincaid's hand. Five bottles of Bud had given her a buzz and she was feeling free and easy, the way she had ever since she'd let Kincaid talk her into taking the two thousand dollars and running off with him. Oh, sure, she'd been afraid there for a while, but she wasn't anymore. It'd been three months now and they were a long way from L.A., out in the middle of nowhere with their tracks all covered behind them. Safe.

She didn't much care for the nowhere part, but that would change. Kincaid would find some way to make money, and when they had enough they'd head east and south to Miami. She'd always wanted to go to Miami...

"Hello, Teresa."

Hood looked up, blinked, gasped. Incredibly Hood was standing right there looking down at her, big as life, big as death. The first moment of shocked disbelief gave way to terror when her eyes focused on the gun in his hand. Jerkily she started to stand up her. Across from her Kincaid was doing the same—but before he got all the way up there was a deafening roar and his head exploded in a burst of bright red.

Hood screamed, her eyes bulging wide, her hands clutching at the edge of the table.

"I told you. I warned you what would happen if you ran out on me."

"Oh God, Joe, no! Don't!"

"Goodbye, baby."

Hood threw up her hand, as if a hand could stop a bullet.

Hood walked slow out of the Buckhorn, crossed the deserted road again, and got into his car. The seat and the steering wheel were fire hot. He knew he should get out of Line as fast as he could, but he didn't do it. He had nowhere to go, nothing left to do. Now that Teresa and Kincaid were dead, he just didn't care anymore.

End of the line for them. End of the line for him, too.

The Glock was still in his hand. After a time, all in one motion, he lifted it and put the muzzle into his mouth and pulled the trigger.

It was a wide spot on a secondary road in a corner of the Nevada desert. Line, it was called. Some name for a town, Hood thought as he drove in. Maybe whoever founded it had called it that because the road ran line-straight through it from one section of sun-blasted wasteland into another. Or maybe it was because of the dozen or so old-fashioned western-style buildings that faced each other across the road like sagging blocks stretched out along a plumb line.

Dry, dusty, deserted except for an old man sitting in the shade in front of one of the storefronts. A dead town. A nowhere place....

WEDDING DAY

Lucia awoke slowly, smiling, clinging to the gauzy remnants of the dream. She and David already on their honeymoon at Lake Tahoe, lying close together in a king-size bed in a suite with large windows that overlooked the blue blend of water and sky, the towering snow-capped Sierras. A beautiful dream that would soon become reality. Had David been able to reserve such an elegant suite for them? Well, of course he had. He'd found that marvelous inn in Carmel, hadn't he?

She peered drowsily at the clock on the bedside table. The time surprised her: 8:20. She'd slept later than usual by more than an hour. But that was all right. She wasn't scheduled to meet David until noon; there was plenty of time to pack and dress. So why not pamper herself a little at the beginning of this day, this special day.

Her wedding day.

The phrase echoed through her mind; she formed the words silently with her lips, then spoke them aloud, and their taste was the sweetest she'd ever known. Her wedding day. *My* wedding day. I, Lucia Trent, soon to be Mrs. David Kincaid. Lucia Kincaid. That, too, tasted sweet on her tongue. Just right, perfect.

Thirty-seven years old and unmarried until today.

Thirty-seven years old and still a virgin until this past weekend.

She lay with her eyes closed, thinking of the blissful two days in Carmel. Her blood raced and her face grew warm as she replayed portions of them in her mind. Mother, so strict and old-fashioned, would have been scandalized. Naughty Lucia, jumping the gun without a moment's regret! But Mother had been gone five months now, and she had no one to answer to anymore except herself. And David, of course. Dear David.

How fortunate she was that he'd stopped into Treasures From the Past that day three weeks ago. Browsing on his lunch hour; the offices of the insurance company he worked for were nearby. The small collection of Mayan stone artifacts were what interested him most, but when he saw the price tags he smiled ruefully and said, "Way out of my price range, I'm sorry to say." He had such a nice, infectious smile. And he was so good-looking with his curly black hair and soft brown eyes. She felt an almost instant rapport, but hadn't dared to think that he might find her as attractive as she found him. She'd been completely astonished when he invited her to have a drink with him when the shop closed.

And so unsure of herself, as always, that she had automatically and politely turned him down. She hadn't had many dates in her life, and none in nearly a year. It wasn't that she avoided men or they avoided her; her strict upbringing, her shy nature and awkwardness in social situations, and of course Mother's invalidism and declining health, were the reasons for her cloistered lifestyle. And Mother's death five months ago, expected though it was, had had a lingering emotional effect that narrowed her world even more.

David, thankfully, hadn't taken no for an answer. He kept asking in his charming, offhand way until finally she relented and accepted the invitation. She'd been very nervous that first evening, her mind drawing blanks at first, words seeming to stick in her throat. She seldom drank, but one glass of wine relaxed her and a second opened inner floodgates in a way she wouldn't have thought possible with a man she barely knew. David was such pleasant company, such a good listener, that she found herself confiding all sorts of things about herself and her life, the years spent caring for Mother, her reclusiveness since the funeral; she even hinted at her virginity.

Afterward she was afraid she'd been too forthcoming, too personal, but the contrary was true; the evening's intimacy served to strengthen the rapport between them. He asked her out again the next day, to dinner at a restaurant in Ghirardelli Square. More wine that night, more confidences—on his part, too. His unhappy childhood in a succession of foster homes after his parents were killed in an accident, his work and a pending promotion, places he'd visited and hoped to visit again—New York, Las Vegas, the Yucatan Peninsula.

Each subsequent date drew them closer, and when he suggested they spend the weekend together in Carmel, she hesitated only briefly before saying yes. She felt no shame then, no shame after their first night together at the inn. And after the second night, she knew beyond any doubt that what they shared was true love. She hadn't been a bit surprised when he proposed to her on the drive home; hadn't hesitated a moment before saying yes.

Ever since, she had been in what Mother would have called "a pink fog." Lucia Trent soon-to-be Kincaid. She could scarcely believe it, even now. David was only three years older than she, but so much more worldly. He could have had his pick of more attractive women her age and younger—he'd never spoken of past affairs but surely he'd had a few, for like her he'd never been married—and yet it was she he'd chosen to share the rest of his life with.

Not that she was an ugly duckling, but she had always considered herself rather plain and lacking in sex appeal. Her features too angular, her body too thin and not very well endowed above the waist. Her best feature was her eyes, lovely brown eyes Mother always said. And she'd always paid careful attention to her appearance. Dressed fashionably, used a minimum of makeup, kept her chestnut hair perfectly styled for the shape of her face. If it hadn't been for Mother's illness and her own shortcomings, she might have found a life partner before now. But if she had, she wouldn't have met David, and no man could possibly have captured her heart the way he had.

Lucia stretched and glanced again at the bedside clock. 8:35. Enough self-indulgent reverie. Time to get up and get busy.

Bathroom first, to brush her teeth. Kitchen to put on coffee. Back into the bathroom to shower. She almost never sang in the shower, but this was her wedding day and so she gave voice to as much of "Oh Promise Me" as she could remember. Lucia, she thought as he dried herself, you're giddy as a teenager. She smiled at her image in the full-length mirror behind the bathroom door, then dropped the towel and inspected her nakedness front and back. Too thin, yes, but David didn't mind. Her freshly scrubbed skin had a youthful glow this morning. Tonight...

No, mustn't think of tonight yet. Focus on the wedding day first, then on the wedding night.

Coffee, orange juice, a piece of buttered toast. Her usual breakfast. She would have to learn to prepare larger breakfasts, though, to satisfy David's healthy appetite. He'd eaten ravenously both mornings in Carmel.

What should she wear? She put on undergarments and then looked through her closet. Nothing white, of course; it wouldn't be appropriate now. Something David hadn't seen her in yet ... her pale blue suit or her dark green dress. The suit would be better for the drive to Lake Tahoe; the dress would wrinkle. She would take it along, though, to wear later on their honeymoon.

Her short dark hair was easy to manage, but she spent several minutes combing and recombing before she was satisfied. And several more minutes applying just the right amount of blush and eye shadow and the light-colored lipstick David liked. It was 10:30 when she finished in the bathroom, 10:45 when the packing was done, 10:55 when she slipped on her best pair of shoes to compliment the blue suit. Right on schedule.

She called for a taxi. David couldn't pick her up because he had things to attend to this morning, so they'd agreed to meet in the lobby at the St. Francis. The drive from San Francisco to Lake Tahoe wouldn't take more than four hours, the weather being as mild as it was, and David would have a wedding chapel on the Nevada side of Stateline all picked out. By five at the latest, she would be Mrs. David Kincaid.

Lucia tidied up while she waited for the taxi, then took one last look around the apartment she'd shared with Mother. So many memories here, but only a few of them cherished. She knew she wouldn't miss it once she moved into David's larger, more comfortable apartment and began her married life. She would return here just once more, to pack up her personal belongings and arrange for disposal of the furniture and the rest of Mother's things.

It was 11:50 when the taxi deposited her at the St. Francis. No, she wasn't checking in, she told the porter who tried to take her suitcase, this was her wedding day and she was only here to meet her betrothed. He tipped his cap and offered congratulations.

In the lobby, she sat on a comfortable chair with her suitcase beside her and eagerly watched the entrance for David's arrival.

Noon came, but he didn't. That was strange. He was always so punctual.

12:15. His errands must have taken longer than he'd expected. Or perhaps he'd gotten caught in the noon hour traffic. But why hadn't he called to tell her he'd be late?

12:30. Still no David, still no word from him.

12:45. Lucia called his apartment. No answer. A call to his cell phone went to voice mail. "David, where are you?" she said. "I've been at the St. Francis forty-five minutes now and I'm starting to worry. Please call and tell me when you'll be here."

1:00. Why didn't he come? Where was he?

1:15. The waiting, the not knowing, had put a strain on her nerves, brought on a tension headache. She couldn't sit still; she paced around the lobby, back and forth, back and forth, alternately watching the entrance and her suitcase by the chair. People came in, alone and in groups, a constant stream, but none of them was David.

1:45. Another call to his apartment; still no answer. Another call to his cell; voice mail again.

2:00. Two hours late now. David, where are you!

2:15. Something must have happened to delay him this long, to keep him from phoning. Her imagination conjured up all sorts of dire possibilities. The headache had worsened; she felt sick to her stomach.

2:25. She couldn't bear any more passive waiting. She had to do something, go somewhere. David's apartment? It was the only place she could think of. He *could* be there, hurt, ill, unable to use the phone. She spoke to the concierge and then the door porter, telling them who she was and where she was going in case David finally came to the hotel, and tipped them well so they'd remember.

Another taxi ride, perched on the edge of the rear seat with her suitcase beside her and her temples pounding. O'Farrell Street. David's building. Up the stairs to his apartment on the second floor.

Be here, David, please be here!

She rang the bell. No answer. Rang it again, again, again.

If only she had a key. But he hadn't given her one and the door was surely locked. Wasn't it? She reached down to try the knob. No, it wasn't. She drew a shaky breath, opened the door, stepped inside calling his name.

The living room was dark, the window drapes drawn. She felt for the light switch, flicked it on, and started across the room.

David!

He was here, he'd been here all the time. Sprawled alongside the sofa, crusty red spilled over the front of his white shirt, crusty red staining the carpet under his head, crusty red in the gaping wound in his neck and on the weapon nearby.

Lucia stared down at him, her mouth open in a soundless scream. And there was a sudden sensation like a flash of fire across her mind. And she remembered.

Last night, when she came to him with her wedding day hopes and plans and he laughed at her and said all those cruel, hateful things ... *where'd you get the crazy idea I'd marry you ... two-night stand, that's all it was ... wouldn't have bothered with you if you hadn't been a virgin ... probably the only lover you'll ever have only lover you'll ever have only lover you'll ever have....*

Last night, when she silenced him forever with the antique Mayan dagger she'd brought him as a wedding present.

PUTTING THE PIECES BACK

You wouldn't think a man could change completely in four months—but when Kaprelian saw Fred DeBeque come walking into the Drop Back Inn, he had living proof that it could happen. He was so startled, in fact, that he just stood there behind the plank and stared with his mouth hanging open.

It had been a rainy off-Monday exactly like this one the last time he'd seen DeBeque, and that night the guy had been about as low as you could get and carrying a load big enough for two. Now he was dressed in a nice tailored suit, looking sober and normal as though he'd never been through any heavy personal tragedy. Kaprelian felt this funny sense of flashback come over him, like the entire last seven months hadn't even existed.

He didn't much care for feelings like that, and he shook it off. Then he smiled kind of sadly as DeBeque walked over and took his old stool, the one he'd sat on every night for the three months after he had come home from work late one afternoon and found his wife bludgeoned to death.

Actually, Kaprelian was glad to see the change in him.

He hadn't known DeBeque or DeBeque's wife very well before the murder; they were just people who lived in the neighborhood and dropped in once in a while for a drink. He'd liked them both though, and he'd gotten to know Fred pretty well afterward, while he was doing that boozing. That was why the change surprised him as much as it did. He'd been sure DeBeque would turn into a Skid Row bum or a corpse, the way he put down the sauce; a man couldn't drink like that more than maybe a year without ending up one or the other.

The thing was, DeBeque and his wife really loved each other. He'd been crazy for her, worshipped the ground she walked on—Kaprelian had never loved anybody that way, so he couldn't really understand it. Anyhow, when she'd been murdered DeBeque had gone all to pieces. Without her, he'd told Kaprelian a few times, he didn't want to go on living himself; but he didn't have the courage to kill himself either. Except with the bottle.

There was another reason why he couldn't kill himself, DeBeque said, and that was because he wanted to see the murderer punished and the police hadn't yet caught him. They'd sniffed around DeBeque himself at first, but he had an alibi and, anyway, all his and her friends told them how much the two of them were in love. So then, even though nobody had seen any suspicious types in the neighborhood the day it happened, the cops had worked around with the theory that it was either a junkie who'd forced his way into the DeBeque apartment or a sneak thief that she'd surprised. The place had been ransacked and there was some jewelry and mad money missing. Her skull had been crushed with a lamp, and the cops figured she had tried to put up a fight.

So DeBeque kept coming to the Drop Back Inn every night and getting drunk and waiting for the cops to find his wife's killer. After three months went by, they still hadn't found the guy. The way it looked to Kaprelian then—and so far that was the way it had turned out—they never would. The last night he'd seen DeBeque, Fred had admitted that same thing for the first time and then he had walked out into the rain and vanished. Until just now.

Kaprelian said, "Fred, it's good to see you. I been wondering what happened to you, you disappeared so sudden four months ago."

"I guess you never expected I'd show up again, did you, Harry?"

"You want the truth, I sure didn't. But you really look great. Where you been all this time?"

"Putting the pieces back together again," DeBeque said. "Finding new meaning in life."

Kaprelian nodded. "You know, I thought you were headed for Skid Row or an early grave, you don't mind my saying so."

"No, I don't mind. You're absolutely right, Harry."

"Well—can I get you a drink?"

"Ginger ale," DeBeque said. "I'm off alcohol now."

Kaprelian was even more surprised. There are some guys, some drinkers, you don't ever figure can quit, and that was how DeBeque had struck him at the tag end of those three bad months. He said, "Me being a bar owner, I shouldn't say this, but I'm glad to hear that too. If there's one thing I learned after twenty years in this business, you can't drown your troubles or your sorrows in the juice. I seen hundreds try and not one succeed."

"You tried to tell me that a dozen times, as I recall," DeBeque said. "Fortunately, I realized you were right in time to do something about it."

Kaprelian scooped ice into a glass and filled it with ginger ale from the automatic hand dispenser. When he set the glass on the bar, one of the two workers down at the other end—the only other customers in the place—called to him for another beer. He drew it and took it down and then came back to lean on the bar in front of DeBeque.

"So where'd you go after you left four months ago?" he asked. "I mean, did you stay here in the city or what? I know you moved out of the neighborhood."

"No, I didn't stay here." DeBeque sipped his ginger ale. "It's funny the way insights come to a man, Harry—and funny how long it takes sometimes. I spent three months not caring about anything, drinking myself to death, drowning in self-pity; then one morning I just woke up knowing I couldn't go on that way any longer. I wasn't sure why, but I knew I had to straighten myself out. I went upstate and dried out in a rented cabin in the mountains. The rest of the insight came there: I knew why I'd stopped drinking, what it was I had to do."

"What was that, Fred?"

"Find the man who murdered Karen."

Kaprelian had been listening with rapt attention. What DeBeque had turned into wasn't a bum or a corpse but the kind of comeback hero you see in television crime dramas and don't believe for a minute. When you heard it like this, though, in real life and straight from the gut, you knew it had to be the truth—and it made you feel good.

Still, it wasn't the most sensible decision DeBeque could have reached, not in real life, and Kaprelian said, "I don't know, Fred, if the cops couldn't find the guy—"

DeBeque nodded. "I went through all the objections myself," he said, "but I knew I still had to try. So I came back here to the city and I started looking. I spent a lot of time in the Tenderloin bars, and I got to know a few street people, got in with them, was more or less accepted by them. After a while I started asking questions and getting answers."

"You mean," Kaprelian said, astonished, "you actually got a line on the guy who did it?"

Smiling, DeBeque said, "No. All the answers I got were negative. No, Harry, I learned absolutely nothing—except that the police were wrong about the man who killed Karen. He wasn't a junkie or a sneak thief or a street criminal of any kind."

"Then who was he?"

"Someone who knew her, someone she trusted. Someone she would let in the apartment."

"Makes sense, I guess," Kaprelian said. "You have any idea who this someone could be?"

"Not at first. But after I did some discreet investigating, after I visited the neighborhood again a few times, it all came together like the answer to a mathematical equation. There was only one person it could be."

"Who?" Kaprelian asked.

"The mailman."

"The mailman?"

"Of course. Think about it, Harry. Who else would have easy access to our apartment? Who else could even be seen entering the apartment by neighbors without them thinking anything of it, or even remembering it later? The mailman."

"Well, what did you do?"

"I found out his name and I went to see him one night last week. I confronted him with knowledge of his guilt. He denied it, naturally; he kept right on denying it to the end."

"The end?"

"When I killed him," DeBeque said.

Kaprelian's neck went cold. "Killed him? Fred, you can't be serious! You didn't actually *kill* him—"

"Don't sound so shocked," DeBeque said. "What else could I do? I had no evidence, I couldn't take him to the police. But neither could I allow him to get away with what he'd done to Karen. You understand that, don't you? I had no choice. I took out the gun I'd picked up in a pawnshop, and I shot him with it—right through the heart."

"Jeez," Kaprelian said. "Jeez."

DeBeque stopped smiling then and frowned down into his ginger ale; he was silent, kind of moody all of a sudden.

Kaprelian became aware of how quiet it was and flipped on the TV. While he was doing that the two workers got up from their stools at the other end of the bar, waved at him, and went on out.

DeBeque said suddenly, "Only then I realized he couldn't have been the one."

Kaprelian turned from the TV. "What?"

"It couldn't have been the mailman," DeBeque said. "He was left-handed, and the police established that the killer was probably right-handed. Something about the angle of the blow that killed Karen. So I started thinking who else it could have been, and then I knew: the grocery delivery boy. Except we used two groceries, two delivery boys, and it turned out both of them were right-handed. I talked to the first and I was sure he was the one. I shot him. Then I knew I'd been wrong, it was the other one. I shot him too."

"Hey," Kaprelian said. "Hey, Fred, what're you saying?"

"But it wasn't the delivery boys either." DeBeque's eyes were very bright. "Who, then? Somebody else from the neighborhood ... and it came to me, I knew who it had to be."

Kaprelian still didn't quite grasp what he was hearing. It was all coming too fast. "Who?" he said.

"You," DeBeque said, and it wasn't until he pulled the gun that Kaprelian finally understood what was happening, what DeBeque had really turned into after those three grieving, alcoholic months. Only by then it was too late.

The last thing he heard was voices on the television—a crime drama, one of those where the guy's wife is murdered and he goes out and finds the real killer and ends up a hero in time for the last commercial....

BIRDS OF A FEATHER
(With Barry N. Malzberg)

August 16

Dear Marjorie:
As always, I was enchanted by your letter. Thanks to the Miss Emma Social Club, I have finally found a woman who understands me, and I hope you feel the same about me. We are truly birds of a feather, for we care a great deal about each other even though we have never met face to face. Someday soon, we shall.

I am writing this once again in my office at State Unemployment. Through the door I can see the passage of the colorless little people who are my fellow workers. None of them have, as do you, the soul to comprehend the real Walter Taylor, the difficult joys, sorrows, and passions which govern me.

No, none of them know me. None of them know how I go to bars alone at night and watch sports telecasts, how I sit alone in my apartment and watch the endless small torments of city life below—none know of my humanity, or even that they are human. They barely sense that they are alive.

But I have plans.
I tell you, Marjorie, I have plans.

August 18

Dear Walter:
I know what you mean about us being birds of a feather. We really are, aren't we?

I have plans too, but sometimes I wonder if I'll ever get to do any of them. I have my sick aunt, about whom I have told you too much already, to take care of all the time. Then there's my job in the beauty parlor. Between the two, my aunt and the job, it's too much for me to bear sometimes.

Take yesterday, for instance. This woman, this blonde who must be about 43, came into the salon. She was wearing false eyelashes and tight pants, and trying to look eighteen. She was ridiculous. She says to me, "I want bangs, Marjorie. Give me bangs." I wanted to say to her, "Listen, with bangs they'll put you in a cage in the zoo downtown," but she's a good customer. She comes in once a week and always tips me two dollars. The average here is about fifty cents. So that's very good. So I only said, "Look,

Mrs. Blodgett, the youthful look is not for people of your mature years."

Well, the look she gave me! And then she insisted that I give her bangs anyway. So I did it because you just cannot reason with people like that, and she went out looking sixty-five instead of forty-three. People just don't know what they look like to others.

The same is true of my aunt. I mean here she is, she looks like a hundred years old, and yet she always wears a ton-and-a-half of makeup, like she's going to a masquerade or something. She has arthritis and water on the knee and a lot of other things too disgusting to talk about, and all she does is make demands on me. Marjorie-do-this and Marjorie-do-that. Hand and foot I have to wait on her. Sometimes I can't stand it so bad I want to just walk out and leave her alone, But I can't because she's my only living relative and me hers, and when she dies I'll inherit all her money and the house and stuff It isn't much really, but it's better than nothing. Which is what I would have if I walked out. How could I walk out, Walter?

August 21

Dear Marjorie:
You're right of course that people don't know what they look like. One's internal image is not the same as what one presents to the world.

There is a big mirror in the bank where I cash my check every other Thursday, for instance, and plenty of time for me to look at myself on the line, as I happened to be doing just this morning. I saw a handsome man, I thought, a man in his early fifties with a certain *je ne sais quoi*, rather like an aging movie star. And yet inside I do not feel handsome because I am being smothered by the emptiness of my job and my life, all of my humanity draining away.

I would do anything to break free of the ties that bind me. But what can I do? I have nothing but your letters, it seems. Are they enough? Sometimes I believe they are. Other times—

Other times, Marjorie, I know I must find a way to alter my life. There is so much more in this world than this small little corner.

But how? This is the question that plagues me, as the poet said.
How?

August 23

Dear Walter:
I just don't know what I'm going to do about my aunt. Things are getting out of hand. Now she says she's got back pains and can't get out

of bed. The doctor says there's nothing wrong with her, but she won't get out of bed. She makes me wait on her hand and foot. Last night I had to run bedpans and bring her hot water bottles and all kinds of pills and stuff. I didn't get any sleep at all—not even one hour—can you imagine that?

Well, anyway, I think your letters are wonderful, and I'm glad we have each other to talk to like this, even if it isn't talking face to face. There's nobody else I can talk to, nobody else I can get it all off my chest to, you know?

August 26

Dear Marjorie:
You have to take risks in order to achieve the goals that really matter. This is what I have come to understand. I took a risk in joining the Miss Emma Social Club, in daring to write you so openly and freely, and in return I have found someone who understands me as no one ever has—someone with whom I often feel I could share my life. That was a great risk because despite my handsome appearance I am a rather shy man and I find it hard to open up and express my feelings. But the risk was worth taking, for what I have found teaches a lesson that I have come to learn: if one would get anywhere in this world one must extend oneself. The alternative is to be like those who surround you.

One must *dare!*

August 30

Dear Walter:
I got fired from the salon today. Can you believe that? They actually *fired* me because I said something to fat old Mrs. Landers when she wanted to have her hair dyed jet black. "You're too old to have jet-black hair, Mrs. Landers," I said to her. "It'll make you look like one of those women down on the waterfront who try to pick up sailors." I couldn't help myself. It was the truth, and I just had to say it. Mrs. Landers screamed to Monsieur Jacques and he fired me. After six years on the job, he fired me on the spot. Can you imagine?

Then I came home and tried to tell my aunt what had happened, and all she could talk about was her back, her arthritis, her water on the knee, and the other stuff. I can't stand much more of it. Yet now that I'm fired I'll have to stay home all day and listen to her complaining and ordering me around. I won't even be able to look forward to getting *out.*

I don't know what to do, Walter. I mean, I just don't know what to do!

September 10

Dear Marjorie:
I'm sorry for the delay in writing but things have not gone at all well for me in the past few days.

I took the risk I was telling you about, Marjorie, and I failed.

The risk, you see, was an idea that came to me as I was standing in line at the bank last time, looking at myself in the mirror. I thought about all the money in the cash drawers, and how that money would buy me escape and freedom and a new existence. I thought and thought about robbing the bank and finally, last Friday, I went ahead and did it. But I was caught and am now in jail awaiting arraignment.

Don't think badly of me, Marjorie. I was compelled—I had to go through with it. I just had to!

Please write and say you understand. I need to hear from you now more than ever.

September 10

Dear Walter:
I should have written earlier but I haven't been up to writing letters the past couple of days. I mean, I'm in jail and you don't feel like writing letters in jail. But you'll get worried if you don't hear from me, and you would have no way of knowing.

I guess you're going to hate me, but I tried to poison my aunt, Walter. I gave her a whole bottle of sleeping pills. Only she didn't die, she just got sick and screamed. When they took her to the hospital and found the pills in her stomach, they arrested me for attempted murder.

It was really stupid, I admit it. But I just couldn't help myself.

Walter, please don't stop writing to me, no matter what happens. Your letters, your strength, are all I ever had.

WHERE AM I?

I don't know where I am.
Or how I got to this place.
Or why I'm here.

I'm walking down a street in what appears to be a large urban center, on a warm evening not long past nightfall. Tall buildings, crowded sidewalks, traffic-clogged streets, multi-colored neon signs advertising restaurants, bars, theatres, nightclubs. Like Times Square in New York City, except that it isn't Times Square because there are no huge jumbotrons and LED signs—I've been there and I know what it looks like. This isn't anywhere I've ever been. None of the buildings or names on the signs is remotely familiar.

I have an odd, disoriented feeling as I walk along. As if I might be in the midst of a dream. But dream images and actions are distorted, surreal, and everything here is perfectly symmetrical, perfectly clear. I look at the people as I pass among them. They're not simulacra, they're flesh-and-blood individuals like one sees in any city—adult men and women, but no children; white, black, brown, Asian. A young blond woman standing by the door to a restaurant with a French name catches my eye, then looks away. An old man jostles my arm and says distractedly, more to himself than to me, "I must be more careful."

No, this is not a dreamscape.

And yet there's a strangeness to the people that makes me uneasy. There doesn't seem to be any purpose to their movements. Almost everyone appears to be walking without haste, as if out for an aimless evening stroll. Even the pace of the stop-and-go flow of cars, taxis, buses seems somehow desultory.

I don't remember coming here. The last thing I remember is ... what? I'm not sure. My memory has always been good, but it's hazy now. I don't understand why that should be.

I ask one of the men walking near me, "Where am I?"

"You're here," he says.

"Where is here?"

"Where you are."

"But where is that?"

"The same place I am."

"*Where?*"

"Here," he says, and edges away into the throng.

A taxi glides to the curb just ahead and a woman wearing a fur wrap gets out. A man immediately takes her place and the cab pulls back into traffic. I approach the woman. "Excuse me," I say, "but I seem to be lost. What city is this?"

"Mustn't ask questions," she says.

"But I don't know why I'm here."

"Don't ask, don't tell."

"Please, I need to know—"

"Taxi!" she says, waving a hand.

Another cab responds to her hail, swings to the curb. The woman gets in and the driver takes her away.

I keep walking. One block, two blocks, three blocks. The names on the blazing neon signs all seem to be the same. Abruptly I turn to the entrance to one of the tall buildings, step through automatic doors. The lobby is empty, its floors and walls lacking adornments of any kind. Street noises penetrate, but in here there are no sounds except the hollow echo of my footsteps. A sudden claustrophobic feeling seizes me and I hurry back outside.

I can use a drink to steady my nerves. One of the flashing bar signs beckons—Crystal Cave. I go inside, find a free spot at a long mahogany bar.

"Wild Turkey on the rocks," I say to the bartender.

"No Wild Turkey," he says.

"Jack Daniel's, then."

"No Jack Daniel's."

"What kind of bourbon have you got?"

"No bourbon."

"All right," I say, "make it scotch."

"No scotch."

"Gin."

"No gin."

"Vodka."

"No vodka."

"Beer."

"No beer."

I wave an exasperated hand at the spigots and gleaming array of bottles arranged on the backbar. "What's in all of those, then? Water?"

"No water."

"No— What kind of tavern is this?"

"The Crystal Cave," he says.

I start to make an angry remark, but then I realize that none of the other customers at the bar have drinks in front of them. They're just sitting or standing, a few talking to one another in low voices, the rest not doing anything except staring at their images in the backbar mirrors.

Quickly I leave the Crystal Cave, and when I emerge I nearly collide with the same blond woman who caught my eye earlier. I grasp her arm.

"Remember me?" I say. "You were about to enter the French restaurant a few minutes ago, and you—"

"*Voulez-vous coucher avec moi.*"

"What? No, I'm not trying to pick you up—"

"Restaurant? I have no reason to go there."

"Miss, I'm just trying to understand what's happening here."

"No reason at all."

"Please give me a straight answer. I have to know—"

She draws away from me. Before I can move, before I can even blink, she's gone.

I enter an Italian restaurant called La Fortezza. Men and women occupy tables and booths, but none of them is eating. There are no cooking smells, nor is anyone serving food.

It's the same in another restaurant I look into. A nightclub, then. No music, no one in the bandstand, no performers on the stage. Customers with nothing in front of them.

What's the reason for all these establishments? Why do people go into them, stay in them? How can they survive here without food or drink?

Shaken, I rejoin the moving masses. On the next corner there is a news vendor's stand. I stop and look at the newspapers on the counter, the periodicals on the rack behind the vendor. But I can't read any of the mastheads or headlines, any of the magazine titles. They're all blurred, as if a film has come down over my eyes. Yet when I look away at the crowd and the passing vehicles and up at the neon signs, I see them all as clearly as before.

"Which papers are these?" I ask the vendor. "Which magazines?"

"Only the latest, only the best."

"Then why can't I read them?"

"No charge for good customers."

"For God's sake, man, what is this place? Why am I here?"

"Paper, mister?"

I stumble on. Fantastic, all of this. Buildings with bare, empty lobbies. Bars and nightclubs that don't serve drinks, restaurants that don't serve food. Unreadable newspapers and magazines. People who answer direct questions with erratic non sequiturs, who wander or sit aimlessly, who don't seem to have normal emotional responses. As if—

Pod people? Aliens? Me an alien abductee, and this some massive segment of a spaceship or a freakish alien world? Preposterous. Irrational. My God, I must be losing my mind to even think of such foolishness.

Maybe I've already lost my mind.

Maybe none of this is actually happening and this place is some sort of intricate, dementia-induced hallucination.

No. That's not the answer, either. I'm not an unstable person, I'm an ordinary man with an ordinary job living an ordinary life. Nor do I have much imagination, certainly not the kind necessary to conjure up such a strange environment, such a weird set of circumstances.

I'm sane. Whatever this place I've been thrust into, it's real enough.

A side street beckons ahead. I veer into it, but there is no light of any kind here, only darkness, and after a dozen steps a high brick wall bars my way. Alarmed, I back away from it. My foot comes down on something hard that pitches me off balance, nearly turns my ankle. On impulse I reach down, pick up the object, take it with me back onto the sidewalk. In the neon blaze I see that it's a broken piece of brick.

I also see that I'm standing before a jewelry store with a glittering display behind its plate glass window. On impulse again, I hurl the brick fragment through the window. An alarm sounds, but hardly anyone seems to notice. There is none of the usual excited shouting and finger-pointing among the passers-by.

The urge to flee is strong, but my legs refuse to obey. I stand waiting, the crowd of people breaking around me like ocean waves around a rock.

A siren heralds the arrival of a police cruiser. Two uniformed officers emerge, take hold of me without asking if I'm the one who threw the brick, handcuff me, and put me into the rear seat.

"I broke that window because I don't want to be here," I say to them. "I want to leave, I want to go home."

"Nice night," one of them says.

"Why won't you talk to me? Why won't anybody listen?"

"They're all nice," the other one says.

I expect them to take me to a police station, but they don't. Instead I'm driven to one of the high-rise buildings, then marched across another empty, barren lobby and into an elevator. On the tenth floor the elevator stops and they usher me down a hallway to an unmarked door. The room beyond is vacant except for a plain wooden chair. They remove my handcuffs, sit me down in the chair, and immediately leave. All of this without another word being spoken by them.

I sit unmoving in the chair for a time, listening to the silence. Then I get up, go to the only window, stand with my face close to the glass. Bright blend of colors shimmering on darkness, but no moon, no stars. And far below, the wandering clusters and the endless stream of traffic.

I walk across to the door. It isn't locked. I open it, look out, see no one in the hallway. The elevator is waiting for me with its doors open. I ride down, cross the deserted lobby, exit onto the teeming sidewalk.

Senseless. All of it, senseless.

I lean against the wall of a movie theater, peer up at an illuminated marquee. The words appear smeared, indecipherable. And another disturbing thought occurs to me.

What if I'm dead?

What if I had a coronary or a stroke or a fatal accident, and this is some sort of purgatory?

I don't believe that, either. The dead don't walk around in their corporeal bodies, or sit in bars or ride in taxis or make pointless comments. The idea of a neon-lit, traffic-snarled purgatory is ludicrous.

So is the notion that this is the Netherworld, a corner of Hell. As absurd as the cartoon images of little devils with pitchforks and horned tails and a leering Satan seated on a fiery throne. I've led a good clean life, done nothing to warrant consignment to either a temporary place of suffering and misery or one of eternal damnation.

I'm not dead any more than I'm insane.

This is neither Purgatory nor Hell.

Then what is it? Why am I here?

I begin walking again, more quickly than before, through the light-spattered darkness, along the clogged sidewalks. Unlike those who surround me, I have a purpose.

An indeterminate length of time passes. I should be exhausted from the constant walking, but I'm not—I'm not tired at all.

How long before night gives way to day? Or is it always auroral night here?

On and on, on and on. Side streets lead nowhere. Each of the high-rise buildings I enter is empty. Few of the people on the sidewalks and in the bars and restaurants will talk to me, and those who do refuse to acknowledge my pleas.

All except one, a little man with sad eyes sitting in a booth in the Hideaway Club. When I repeat the same haunting questions to him, he peers up at me and says, "It doesn't matter."

"But it does. I have to know the answers!"

"There are no answers."

He slides out of the booth, makes his way to the entrance. I hurry after him. I'm right behind him as he steps outside, but somehow he eludes me and vanishes into the packed humanity.

Sudden panic grips me and I break into a run, dodging among the other pedestrians, through the stop-and-go street traffic. No one tries to halt my wild flight. No one pays any attention to me at all.

And the belated realization comes that I'm passing the same

intersections, the same signs and buildings, the same vehicles, the same people; that I have been all along. Running like a caged animal on a treadmill. Going nowhere.

I understand then, completely and irrevocably, what the little man and all the others understand. I stop running. The purpose is gone now, and so is the panic.

I walk again.

And walk and walk and walk.

Near the Crystal Cave a woman I haven't seen before clutches at me, her face gray with fright. "Help me," she cries, "help me. What place is this? Where am I?"

"You're here."

"Yes, but where?"

"Where we are."

"Please! I can't bear not knowing why or how—"

"There's no way out," I say, and I turn from her and walk on.

THE SHREW

Vera is in a nasty mood tonight as usual. Carping, complaining, criticizing in that shrill, acid-tongued voice of hers that always sets my nerves on edge.

"Why haven't you put on a clean shirt?" she says.

"This is a clean shirt."

"No, it's not. There's a stain on it."

"Where?"

"Right there, near the pocket. So you slopped food on yourself again."

"It's only a small spot of marinara sauce—"

"Why didn't you sponge it off?"

"I didn't notice it before."

"Are you going blind along with all your other failings? A red spot on a white shirt. How could you *not* notice it?"

"I just didn't, that's all."

"You ought to wear a baby's bib when you eat."

"I'll be more careful in the future—"

"No, you won't. You can't eat a mouthful of anything without spilling some of it on your clothes. Or even brush your teeth without drooling toothpaste on yourself. You're a slob, Howard. A pitiful slob."

And you're a shrew, Vera. "An ill-tempered, scolding woman," that's the dictionary definition of the word. Virago, termagent, fishwife, harpy, bitch, she-devil—shrew.

Relentless, merciless. Day after day, night after night, never letting me have a moment's peace. Do the dishes and get them clean for a change. Don't spill the garbage when you take it out. Wash the windows, vacuum the rugs, polish the floor, dust the furniture. Don't dawdle when you're buying the groceries. Wipe your feet, don't track dirt in the house. Close the door, were you born in a barn? Stop mumbling, speak up. You eat too much, you're getting fat. You're a poor provider, an inept lover. You snore like a pig. You're spineless, gutless, incompetent, childish, silly, stupid, useless, careless, sloppy, a sorry excuse for a man and a husband.

And it's been like that from the first, even before the honeymoon ended.

I don't know why I've stayed with her for ... what is it now, thirteen years? Yes, thirteen long, torturous years. Oh, but I do know why. I'm what she keeps saying I am—spineless, gutless. As angry as she makes me sometimes, as much as I want to leave her, now more than ever, I can't bring myself to do it. I haven't always been this weak, have I? Or have I? I don't know. I don't know anything any more ...

"Howard. Are you listening to me?"

"Yes, of course."

"Then what did I just say?"

"I ... didn't hear it clearly."

"Conveniently deaf as well as half blind. Why don't you buy yourself a hearing aid?"

"I'm sorry, Vera, I—"

"I *said* I'm sick and tired of this house, I want us to move somewhere else."

"Don't start that again. You know we can't afford to move."

"We could if you'd find yourself a better job," Vera says. "Or at least show some gumption and pressure that old skinflint you toady for to pay you a decent wage."

"I don't toady for Mr. Selkirk, I keep his firm's books."

"Oh, yes, I know. A low-salaried bookkeeper, that's all you are or ever will be. All those big plans you had of owning your own accounting firm—Howard Sheldon and Associates, Certified Public Accountants. Hah! Howard Sheldon, Certified Public Toady. Certified Public *Wimp*."

"Vera, please—"

"No ambition, no drive, no backbone. Working six days a week for next to nothing, without a single raise in fifteen years."

"That's not true. I had one raise four years ago and Mr. Selkirk promised me another soon. I told you that."

"When? Next year? And it'll be a paltry few dollars a month unless you demand more and do it right away. Which knowing you, you won't."

"My current salary is enough to pay the bills and buy everything we need," I say. "And we don't have to worry about a mortgage payment every month. This house is free and clear except for taxes, thanks to Uncle Alec—"

"Uncle Alec. That senile old fool. He left his niece a hundred thousand dollars in cash, or have you forgotten?"

"No, I haven't forgotten. But she took care of him in his last years—"

"And all you got is this drafty, falling-down old relic out in the middle of nowhere, no neighbors within a mile."

"This isn't the middle of nowhere, it's only a short drive to and from the city. And the house isn't falling down, it's in good repair—"

Her laugh is almost as piercing as her voice. "Good repair. What a joke *that* is. There's always something that needs fixing in this mausoleum, the plumbing more often than anything else."

"I make all the necessary repairs, don't I?"

"Not very well. None of the fixes stay fixed for long."

"That's not true. You know I'm good with my hands."

"Are you?" She laughs again, nastily. "Are you really?"

"Vera—"

"Are we going to sell this wreck and move to the city, or not?"

"Not. I keep telling you we can't, we just can't."

"That's right, deny me again. That's all you've ever done, deny me my few needs and pleasures, leave me nothing to look forward to."

"I've never denied you anything we could afford—"

"No friends, either. Another comfort you've denied me."

That's another lie. If anyone has been denied friends, it's me. How could I have any, with her for a wife?

"When are you going to wash the living room windows?"

"What?"

"You heard me, unless you really are going deaf. Well?"

"I washed the windows last week."

"Do it again. You did a poor job."

"No, I didn't. They're spotless."

"Don't argue with me," Vera snaps. "Wash them again. And vacuum the rugs again, too, all of them—they're filthy."

The rugs, like the windows, are clean. But I say, "All right."

"And don't set foot in public wearing that stained shirt. Try to look halfway decent for a change when you go to that crappy job of yours."

"Yes, all right, I'll try."

"It's about time you had your hair cut, too. And why can't you learn to shave that homely face of yours without leaving whisker-stubble all over your chin?"

I run fingertips along my jawline. There is no whisker-stubble, not even a stray bristle.

"You're a disgrace, that's what you are," Vera says. "The way you dress, the way you look, the way you move ... all of it disgraceful. Stop slouching and stand up straight. Don't shuffle your feet when you walk. Can't you do anything right?"

"That's enough, Vera."

"What did you just say to me?"

"I said that's enough, I've had enough for one evening."

"Oh, no, you haven't. I'm not through with you yet, not by a long shot—Howard! Don't you dare turn and walk away from me. Come back here, you stupid, spineless, worthless—"

I clamp my hands over my ears to shut out the vicious words, the terrible sound of that voice. I can't stand to listen to any more of her venom, not now, not tonight.

But there'll be more of the same tomorrow. And the next day after that. And the next and the next and the next.

Damn you, Vera. Damn you.

It's been more than a year now since I strangled you and put you down here in the cellar.

Why can't you finally shut up and leave me in peace!

MEADOWLANDS SPIKE
(with Barry N. Malzberg)

Listen to me. Please listen. Everything I'm about to tell you is the gospel truth.

I can't live with this terrible secret any longer. It's been thirty-five years, but I've never stopped thinking about what I did. Not for a single day. It's all there, every detail burned into the walls of my mind. It could've happened yesterday, that's how clear it is.

I see him alive, not just that night before the bullets tore into him, but the way he was when he had the power. Big man, bigger than life, bigger than death everybody thought, shouting words and slogans, promises and lies in his giant's voice. King of Labor, King of the Long Labor Con. The job action. The sitdown strike. The secondary boycott. The sick-in. All of that and so much more until they threw him in the slammer for jury-tampering.

James Earl Hoffa, that's right.

And then came the Nixon pardon that set him up for another run at the Union presidency. He should've known it wasn't going to happen. No one was stupid enough other than Brother James Earl himself to think he'd get the deal past his successors, as hard-nosed a bunch as he was. Should've known they'd take him out by any means necessary.

I was the means.

I picked him up that night in my car. Just me and him, nobody else. He thought we were going to a secret hush-hush meeting with some bigwigs in Rutherford

Sure, I know he was last seen in the Detroit area, but that was the day *before*.

They set him up by calling him back to Jersey on the QT. Nobody but Big Billy and me and a couple of others knew that the only meeting he was going to was with God or the Devil.

So anyhow, I drove him to the closed-up garage I owned. That's where I emptied my Colt automatic into him, six shots grouped in his chest like it was a bull's-eye target.

Then I put on overalls and gloves, dragged his body down into the grease pit, and dismembered it with a hatchet and a hacksaw. Awful job. Awful. But that was the way the big boys uptown wanted it done, don't ask me why.

I can still see him lying there dead after I put those six rounds into his chest. Still see the pieces of him after the butchering was done, all the bloody pieces, all the King's parts: legs, arms, torso, head—my last view of the Great Man before I stuffed the pieces into six separate plastic bags and put the bags into the trunk of my Buick.

Jimmy H. alive, Jimmy H. dead, Jimmy H. in pieces. Nothing left but chopped-up clay, the torso weighted with lead pellets, bouncing and thudding in the trunk as I raced along the Turnpike to the new Meadowlands stadium.

That's what I said, the Meadowlands.

How did I get in? I had a key to the gate, that's how. Back then I had connections, guys who'd do me a favor without asking questions and then keep their mouths shut. The refineries five miles to the south would have made quicker work of the remains, but butchering him was bad enough, I couldn't burn him up too. The Meadowlands was better. Home base. Burial instead of cremation.

The State of New Jersey is where America comes to die. You don't think so? Remember Paul Simon? The cars on the New Jersey Turnpike, each filled with people in search of America. I was one of them that night, in a Buick with a dismembered slab of America in my trunk and the rising yellow clouds from the refineries staining the night around me.

Oh, I remember, all right. Every detail after three and a half decades. Arriving at the deserted stadium site. Opening the Buick's trunk in the moonlit dark to get the shovel. Digging six holes all across the south end zone—

Don't laugh. It's not funny. I'm telling you just what I did: dug six holes, six little graves for the six pieces of Jimmy H.

If New Jersey is where America comes to die, then the end zone was the perfect burial spot for Brother James Earl. Hell, it would have been perfect for the Wobblies, Mother Jones, the '37 Ford strikers, hundreds of others like them. You see what I mean?

Once the bags were planted, the holes covered up and smoothed out, I stood leaning on the shovel, gasping in the cold, like an exhausted actor taking an involuntary crooked bow after a command performance. Thinking that the whole business hadn't been so bad, that I'd gotten it all done pretty quick. A speed run from the killing to the cutting up to the driving to the burying. Thinking that was the end of it.

But it wasn't. Not for me. I should have known it wouldn't be because even then I could see the pieces spread out deep under the end zone turf, as if I had X-ray vision. The flesh that would decay in summer heat and winter ice. The scattered bones that would crumble to dust.

I didn't stay there long. It was almost dawn and the almost finished stadium was glowing in the restless early light. Soon there'd be workers, traffic. I couldn't afford to be seen in the area.

I drove the Buick straight back to the garage, backed it inside, and took care of the clean-up. Washed the blood down the grease pit drain with a hose. Used some solvent to remove a couple of stains in the trunk. Burned the overalls and gloves and my filthy clothes in the incinerator out back. When I was done, there wasn't a trace left.

My house was half a mile from station. Jane was waiting for me when I got there.

Where were you all night? she said.

Never mind, I said. It's none of your business.

You look terrible, she said. What have you been doing?

Nothing, I said. What else could I have said to her? Oh, nothing much, babe, just out murdering the boss, cutting up the boss, burying the boss.

I walked past her, heading toward the shower. This is a filthy place, I said then. It's always filthy. Why don't you ever clean it up?

She didn't like that. She hadn't liked anything about me for a long time. Even thirty-five years later I can feel her contempt, her suspicion. I guess I can't blame her. Living jammed close together in that little house, not just her and me but the kid too, none of us getting along with each other, fearing Big Billy and the uptown boys, torn apart by secrets. She left me not long after that night, you know, just as soon as the kid got out of high school, and for all I know she's dead now. The kid, too—I haven't seen or heard from him in twenty years.

But I'm getting off track. After I had my shower and put on some of my better threads I drove into the city to report to Big Billy.

Disposing of Jimmy H. was the nasty part of the assignment, but facing Big Billy wasn't much better. You remember him? Sure. He's long gone now, most of the uptown boys are long gone, but back then he was a force. I did a lot of jobs for him before that night, but none like the one with Brother James Earl. None that was even close.

An hour later I was standing in Big Billy's office, surrounded by concrete, his hard little eyes boring into mine.

I dumped him, I said. It's finished business.

Don't tell me dumped, Big Billy said. Don't tell me finished business. Where did you put the fucker?

You really want to know? I said. You told me handle it any way I want, just make him disappear. So that's what I did.

I got to know, he said, so I can tell them uptown.

Well, they didn't want to know uptown, he'd told me that before. He wanted the information only for himself. But if you didn't want to end up like Jimmy H., you did what Big Billy told you to. And you never lied to him.

So I told him the truth. I put him where they'll never find him, I said.

The Meadowlands Stadium. Under the south end zone.

I thought he'd say that was a perfect spot, I couldn't have come up with a better one. I thought he'd say Good job, you'll get a bonus.

Get the fuck out of here, he said, and don't come around no more.

That was the last I ever saw of him. But that was all right with me. I didn't want any part of his operation after that night, any more than he wanted me to be part of it. I'm still above ground, so he must not have talked to the boys uptown. Or if he did, they decided I'd done the job right even if Big Billy didn't think so. Nothing ever happened to me because I was right: they never found Jimmy H.

It seems simple when you look at it that way. But it's not simple. New Jersey is not a state of simplicity, the sinkhole town of Rutherford not a site of easy answers. New Jersey is a place of secrets, complex, rotten with tangled branching vines and rivers of ancient, heaving blood. Somebody said that to me once, I don't remember who.

Well, anyhow, that's about it. They tore the stadium down after thirty-some years and still they didn't find what was left of Brother James, that's how good a planting job I did. I don't know how they could've missed finding the skull, some of the bones, but I guess they were in a hurry and careless with the demolition.

If it didn't make me sick now, thinking about it, I'd have to laugh about the turf wars between the Giants and all those other teams right there in the shadow of that end zone, in the end zone itself, players after they scored a touchdown spiking the ball down hard right above where the boss's head was buried—

What's that you said?

No, I sure as hell didn't make all of this up. You got no right to say that. I told you before, it's the gospel truth. Give me a Bible and I'll swear on it.

What do you mean, New Jersey is full of mooks like me, little guys with big ideas? I was never a little guy, I had connections, I knew secrets. That's how I got the job to take out the boss. One of the biggest jobs ever, horrible as it was, and my disposal idea was just as big. Smart. I couldn't have got away with it for thirty-five years if it wasn't big and smart.

Yeah, I got away with it, but I couldn't get away *from* it. You cops can't imagine what a burden it's been on me all that time—not the Meadowlands part, the killing and butchering part. How much of a toll it's taken. That's why I'm here now, that's what I been trying to get across to you. I can't live with it anymore. The nightmares, the awful bloody images

What? No! This isn't another false confession. It's my one true confession. Don't you see, don't you get it? Those previous confessions of mine ...

substitutes, surrogates. I couldn't make myself tell what I did to the boss, so I copped to other murders, other crimes instead.

I was trying to pay my debt with phony claims so I could finally have some peace. But now I know the only way to stop the haunting and the hurting is to reveal my secret, New Jersey's secret, America's secret—

What're you doing, Lieutenant? Who're you calling?

Oh Christ, no, you can't send me back to the Pines. I don't belong in that place. I'm not crazy any more than John the Baptist was crazy.

Please, you have to believe me! I shot Jimmy H., I dismembered his body, I buried the pieces in the end zone at the Meadowlands Stadium. I did, I did!

ANGELIQUE

She comes to me in the night, naked in the night.

The first time I believed her to be a dream image, a figment born of my passionate worship. I had dreamed of her often before then, more than once as she looked in the erotic nude scenes in her films, but not once had I imagined her there with me in my bed. My desire for her was intense, yet I never allowed it to become more than the wishful, respectful, unattainable kind one feels for a goddess.

On that first night when I heard the rustle of the sheets, smelled the alluring scent of her perfume, felt the velvety perfection of her body against mine, I thought: Don't wake up, not yet! But I was already awake. When I was sure of it, I reached out to turn on the bedside lamp. I cannot describe the awe, the rapture I felt when I saw her there naked beside me.

"You can't be real," I said to her. "You can't be Angelique."

"Oh, but I am," she said.

"How? Why? You don't know me."

"But I do know you. I know that you want me, I know that I want you."

"A woman like you, a man like me? It isn't possible."

"I came because you love me. Anything is possible when love and need are strong enough."

"I'm imagining this. You can't be real ..."

She took my hand. "Touch me here ... is this real? And here. Ah, and here. Is all of it real?"

"Yes. Oh, yes."

"And this?" she said as she lifted her body onto mine, as the soft wetness of her engulfed me like a fire that did not burn. "Is this real?"

"Yes!"

"Say my name."

"Angelique."

"Say it again."

"Angelique. Angelique. Angelique."

I am neither a handsome nor a successful man. Small, mild, nondescript, with a mundane job to match. No family left, no close friends. Lonely, yes, yet the real world often frightens and bewilders me. And so by design and inclination, as a form of self-defense, I've become an escapist.

I have always loved films of all types. A great deal of my free time is spent in darkened movie theaters, in front of television and computer screens in my modest apartment. By a conservative estimate I watch perhaps one hundred films new and old each month, and I have the capacity to lose myself in every one, to become part of whatever story is being told no matter how good or bad. In that respect, and this too I freely admit, I am an emotional sponge.

But I am not given to Walter Mitty-like flights of fancy. I do not see people who aren't there. I have no fantasy life beyond my involvement in the films I watch. I have not masturbated in thirty-three years, since the age of fourteen.

I did not and do not imagine that Angelique comes to me in the night, naked in the night, and mounts me, and gives me the greatest sexual pleasure I have ever known. She is not a dream or a figment. Not an astral projection or anything of that fantastic nature. She is real, flesh and blood real, and for some strange and wondrous reason which she refuses to divulge, she chose me, Harold Brenner, out of all her millions of admirers, to be her new lover. I did not doubt it that first night, I did not doubt it in the cold light of morning after she was gone, I do not doubt it now. I simply accept it on faith.

And I feel blessed.

Angelique has always been my favorite actress. And not just mine—the favorite of countless others world-wide. She is the brightest star in the firmament of Hollywood stars, as Venus at dusk is the brightest in the heavens. No matter what role she plays, her talent shines so much more radiantly than that of anyone around her. Even Meryl Streep and Nicole Kidman pale into insignificance alongside Angelique. Her luminous eyes, the golden fall of her hair, the sweetness of her smile and the grace of her movements are unparalleled. The critics might not agree with this assessment, but what do critics know?

I have seen all forty-two of her films at least a dozen times each, and I never tire of watching her perform. I could watch each one five hundred times and I would never tire of her. Perhaps the extent and magnitude of my adoration is the reason why she chose me.

Angelique came again two nights later, and the second night after that, and the next after that. Our bodies joined and rejoined ... again, again, again. And each time the level of my ecstasy intensified until it became nearly unbearable and I cried her name, cried out my love for her. Not once did she speak my name, nor tell me how much she loved me, but I don't fault her for this. She comes to me, she's real, she's mine for as long as she'll have me. That is all that matters.

Now she comes every night, and stays until just before dawn. Three, four, six, as many as eight times we merge and writhe and achieve simultaneous release. I think I can't possibly accommodate her so often, I am a middle-aged man with so little sexual experience, but no matter how many times we have made love, she has only to touch me, lightly, and again I become like stone.

Once, in our second week together, I said to her, "You're wearing me out, Angelique. Taking all my precious bodily fluids."

"Yes. Isn't it wonderful?"

She seemed not to have understood the small joke I'd made. Was it possible she was not as well versed as I in Hollywood film lore? "Precious bodily fluids," I said again. "General Jack D. Ripper's phrase in *Dr. Strangelove*. He felt it necessary to deny women his essence in order to remain pure."

Angelique bathed me in the glow of her smile. "But you'll never deny me yours."

"No. Never."

Again she touched me and again I was stone.

Every night, all night long, we revel in each other. That is all we do; she prefers not to talk about herself, me, anything at all. Again and again, again and again, with only short periods of rest between each coupling. Neither of us slept much in the beginning; now we hardly sleep at all. I am so tired each morning after she leaves that I can barely drag myself out of bed.

As much as I love and desire her, I must have a respite now and then—a night off to recharge my batteries, as it were. Tonight when she comes I'll ask her to grant me this small favor, for both our benefits.

Her answer was no. A sweet and gentle no.

"I can't get enough of you," she said. "Don't you feel the same about me anymore?"

"Of course I do."

"Then don't deny me. If you deny me, I might not come to you again."

"Don't say that! I couldn't bear it."

She gathers me to her again. And once more I drown in her warm soft wetness.

So tired now. Weak. I need sleep desperately, but even in the daytime I can't seem to do more than doze for a few minutes. Can't seem to eat anything, either; I have no appetite. My body looks and feels shrunken, shriveled, like that of a very old man.

I could not get out of bed at all yesterday or this morning. I can only lie here wide awake and wait for the night.

All day I found myself hoping Angelique would not come. But of course she does. And it seems not to matter to her that when she slips naked into my bed, she finds herself clutching a desiccated shell of a man.

"Not tonight," I say to her in a voice that croaks like a frog's, "please, not again tonight," but she only laughs and reaches out her hand to touch me. I try to will myself not to respond, but I have no resistance. Her seductive powers are amazing. In an instant I am as ready for her as I was the first night.

When she joins her body to mine she laughs again, but this time the laughter is neither soft nor throaty with passion. It's strange, shrill, a kind of hideous triumphant sound that fills me with ice instead of heat, terror instead of love. And I realize that I am not blessed but cursed.

"Lie still," she says. "I'm almost done."

I have no choice—I lie still.

"Now turn on the lamp. I want you to see me this last time."

I have just enough strength left to turn on the lamp. In its pale glow as she writhes above me, the flawless beauty of her face shimmers, fragments, falls away like a crumbling mask, and when I see what lies beneath I scream ... I scream ... I scream ... but my screams have no voice.

Quickly, hungrily, the thing that is not and never was Angelique finishes draining me dry.

CRAZY

You know how people are always saying something drives them crazy? It's almost always little things that make them say it. Words or actions from a spouse, an acquaintance, a stranger. Inconsiderate drivers, lying politicians, stupid mistakes by incompetents, squalling children, TV commercials, leaf blowers, back-up beepers, yapping dogs, robo phone calls, snotty clerks, badly designed gadgets, cell phone babblers in public places, a thousand and one other annoyances.

Well, an accumulation of all those little furies *can* drive you crazy. They truly can. I know because it happened to me.

I'm quite serious, Doctor Graber. I was one of those who often said this or that drives me crazy, so often that all of those little things finally combined to send me off the beam, over the edge, around the bend. I woke up one morning, went into the bathroom, looked at myself in the mirror, and realized that I was no longer sane. Not gibbering, run amok crazy, you understand. Oh, no. Nothing so overt, not yet anyway.

Just ... crazy.

Quietly and completely wacko.

They say that if you think you're insane, you're really not. Do you subscribe to that belief, Doctor? Yes, I understand it's what I believe that's at issue here, I was simply wondering—

Well, then. That popular conception is false. At least in my case it is. Arthur Allan Hopgood is living proof that you can be quite mad and fully aware of the fact. And that a crazy person can, even after realizing he is one, go about his daily activities in what passes for a normal fashion, so that no one who is acquainted with him has so much as a glimmer that he is nuttier than the proverbial fruitcake.

What makes me think I'm no longer *compos mentis*? Oh, Doctor, I don't think it, I know it beyond the slightest shadow of a doubt. How do I know it? By my actions since the understanding came to me that recent morning, of course. No sane person could have done what I have in the past few weeks.

Yes, certainly I'll explain.

To begin with, I shoplifted an expensive blue blazer from Denton's Department Store, the first time in my life that I ever stole anything. I didn't plan to do it, didn't know I was going to until I saw the blazer and decided to try it on. I found it to be a perfect fit, and simply walked out of the store wearing it with no one the wiser.

I realize that one impulsive act doesn't prove that I've lost my marbles.

Ah, but the theft of the blazer was only the beginning. My first misstep, a baby misstep you might say.

Three days later I stole a car.

It wasn't a new car, or even a very attractive one. A pea green Toyota, a color and make I dislike. I was walking home from Trilby and Bender, CPAs, where I'm employed as an accountant—

Didn't I inform you of that before? Oh, I told your secretary I was a law clerk at Houseman Associates when I made the appointment, did I? I have no explanation of why I should have made such a fabrication. Except, that is, for the fact that I'm off my rocker.

No, Doctor Graber, I assure you I am not attempting to be facetious. Or to mislead you in any way. If you say I told your secretary I was a law clerk, then I must have done so. I have no recollection of it. But I'm not employed by Houseman Associates. I am, as I have just said, an accountant with Trilby and Bender, CPAs.

Yes, of course my name is Arthur Hopgood. What could I possibly gain by providing a false name? If you'd care to see my driver's license—

I'll continue, then, if I may. Thank you.

The woman who owned the pea green Toyota parked it in front of a dry cleaning establishment and left the engine running while she hurried inside, presumably to pick up clothing. I happened to be passing by at the time; in her haste she nearly collided with me on the sidewalk. Without thinking about what I was doing, I stepped around the car, slipped in beneath the wheel, and drove away. I drove approximately eight blocks, at which point I abandoned the vehicle and walked to the nearest bus stop.

That was the second episode. The third, the following week, involved an attractive young woman in Mission Park—

No, Doctor, I certainly did not attack her. Not in the way you seem to have inferred. I merely followed her a short distance and then snatched her purse when no one else was in sight. *That* was a premeditated act—premeditated from the moment I saw her, I should say. I intended to steal a woman's purse and I did. Fortunately for her, she neither struggled nor tried to scream. I had no difficulty making my escape.

Would I have harmed her if she had struggled or screamed? Honestly, I don't know. I might have. Then again, I might not. All I can say for certain is that I was relieved when she gave me no cause to do so.

Three days later I decided to rob a bank.

I have no idea why. I went into my branch uptown to deposit my paycheck, and while I was there the urge came over me to commit a bank robbery. Not of my branch, but that of a trust company in another part of the city. A more lengthy premeditation was required in that case. First I had to choose the bank, then "case" it as the saying goes, then plan when and how to accomplish the theft with the minimum amount of risk.

Did I go through with it? Oh, yes. Absolutely. I not only went through with it, I succeeded with no difficulty whatsoever. I walked into the bank, undisguised in any way, handed a woman teller the note I had written—also undisguised—and she obeyed its instructions without hesitation or fuss. I then walked out with seven hundred and twelve dollars, entered an adjacent office building, passed through it to an exit on another street to where I'd left my car, and drove home.

No, I wasn't at all afraid the police would identify me and place me under arrest. Which did not happen, obviously. I simply didn't care, then or now. I still have the money, by the way. I considered spending it, but there is nothing I wanted to buy that I can't steal instead—

What's that, Doctor? Compulsive thievery, while an indication of mental imbalance, is not necessarily one of derangement? Well, perhaps not. But stealing isn't all I've done. There are a number of other things as well. Strange and wonderful things. Would you like me to describe some of them? No?

Ah, I understand. Our session is almost over.

I have no doubt you would like to see me again. Because you believe you can help me come to terms with my fear of madness and my fantasies, isn't that so? Oh, Doctor! I assure you that I am not prone to fantasies.

I'm so sorry, but another session won't be possible. Not for either of us. Why isn't it possible, you ask?

This is the answer.

Oh, yes, it's a real pistol, fully loaded. The same one I carried when I held up the bank.

You believed I made this appointment because I decided to seek help from an eminent psychiatrist, but you were quite wrong.

I'm here because I decided to kill one.

Why?

Why not? I really am crazy, you know.

DEMOLITION, INC.
(with Barry N. Malzberg)

Daniels was crossing the empty street, making his way from the diner to his car after finishing an early dinner, when the gray sedan with mud-covered plates tried to run him down.

He saw the dark shape of it just in time and flung himself out of the way; hit the street on his right shoulder and rolled up over the curb, bruising his left cheekbone on a sharp piece of concrete. The sedan swept by so close that he could feel the wind of its passage. Then there was a squeal of brakes, a flash of taillights as Daniels scrambled up into a kneeling position, and in the next moment the car vanished around the far corner.

Daniels got slowly and painfully to his feet and stood staring at the dark intersection for several seconds, muttering savage words under his breath. He slapped at his clothing, then went back across the street. Inside his car he rolled up the windows, locked the door, and sat there trembling.

Smith, he thought angrily. Smith again.

This hadn't been the first attempt on his life in the past few days. First there had been the concrete block dislodged from the roof of the Bristol Building which had missed him by a fraction; then there was the failure of the brakes on his car three days ago, the near-fatal accident on Old Canyon Road, and the subsequent discovery that the brake lining *might* have been tampered with. One or two close calls could have been accidents. Three close calls left no more doubt that it was intended homicide.

And there was only one person who could be out to get him: Ivan Smith.

The whole thing was crazy, that was what it was: Daniels still couldn't believe it was happening to him. The accidental death of Smith's brother wasn't *his* fault. How could it be? All he'd done was to show up at the condemned Harcourt Building at eleven a.m. two weeks ago, as he and Demolition, Inc., had been hired to do, and plant explosives inside it and set them off under police sanction.

How could he have guessed that the night watchman was an alcoholic and still inside the building, lying passed out behind some crates in a rear storeroom? How could he be held responsible for the man being demolished along with the rest of the building?

Well, *Smith* held him responsible and that was all that counted now. First, he'd tried to get Daniels' license revoked by the city for negligence. Then, when that failed, he'd tried to discredit Demolition, Inc., and Daniels' character by dredging up that old business from three years ago, the one about Daniels paying kickbacks to city officials for certain special contracts. And when that didn't work, the attempts on Daniels' life had started.

Smith was a nut case, all right, Daniels thought as he sat waiting for his hands to stop shaking. A real homicidal lunatic, like you read about in the papers from time to time. He was also inept, just like his drunken brother, the night watchman, but the law of averages was in his favor: sooner or later, if he was allowed to keep on trying, he was bound to succeed.

Daniels did some ruminating. He could go to the police, of course, but he didn't have any evidence—no eyewitnesses to any of the attempts, nothing at all—that Smith was out to get him. A falling block of concrete? Possibly gimmicked brake lines on his car? An attempted vehicular homicide by a gray sedan with muddied license plates? It all sounded pretty thin, even to Daniels. And that meant the police were likely as not to label him as some kind of paranoid nut himself.

Besides, too much publicity and too much police attention were things he didn't care to have, not with the kind of moonlighting activities in which he was involved. The secret work of Demolition, Inc., such as supplying quantities of explosives to representatives of foreign governments and certain private individuals, could be very embarrassing to Daniels if they ever came out into the open.

So he was left with only one choice, as far as he could see: he would have to do something himself about Smith.

Which meant killing Smith before Smith killed him.

Daniels lit a cigarette and thought about that. He thought about it for several minutes, with a good deal of calculation. Murder was a chancy business, no question about that. But if he was careful, if he took great pains to do just what Smith was trying to do—make the murder look like a simple accident—then it seemed a good bet he could get away with it. Contrary to what the police would have you believe, there were large numbers of unsolved crimes in this country every year; and murder was the most prominent among them. All it would require was cunning, caution, and a certain amount of ingenuity.

All right, Daniels thought, and nodded to himself. His hands were steady now. But just how was he going to do it? In murder, as in the demolition business, you couldn't afford to play odds that were any less than one hundred percent. Both required a precise, exacting discipline ...

It took him ten minutes of further ruminating to come up with a plan that satisfied him. At the end of that time he nodded once more, smiled grimly in the darkness, and then started his car and headed it crosstown toward the small building which comprised the office and warehouse space of Demolition, Inc.

When he got there he entered and took a small amount of plastic explosive—the kind that was illegal to possess in the United States—from the hidden storage room in back. He put on a dark sweater he kept in the shop area, filled his pockets with half a dozen selected tools. Then he returned to the car and drove north, toward the suburb where Smith lived.

He had done a little research on Smith when the man first started to harass him. Smith was a salesman with some sort of supply company, unmarried, living alone in a small house on a quiet cul-de-sac; his nearest neighbor was a hundred yards away. His hobby was reading books—things like encyclopedias and "how-to" books on just about any subject you could name. That was all Daniels had been able to find out, except that Smith apparently had an obsessive mind on some subjects. Like the death of his drunken brother. Like murder.

It was too bad all this had to happen, Daniels thought as he drove. For some reason—a beginning release of tension, maybe—he felt philosophical. The interconnections between men who should be strangers, the painful collision of personalities due to accidents, always bothered him. In different circumstances he and Smith might have gotten along well or not at all; it was only coincidence which had drawn their lives together. He sure hadn't *meant* the man's brother to be on the scene during the demolition of the Harcourt Building. A more careful sweep of the premises might have turned him up, but Daniels had been working on a tight schedule; he'd had a meeting planned for that afternoon with a couple of prospective explosives buyers from Central America, on a deal that hadn't worked out too well through no fault of his. He'd been as surprised as anyone when the watchman's body was found in the wreckage.

Yes, it was too bad—but what could you do? Protect yourself, that was all. Self-defense. Not murder, just simple self-defense.

He drove to within a block of Smith's house, parked his car in the shadows cast by two large oak trees growing inside a parklike lot, and made his way to the house on foot. From behind another oak tree he studied the place. Dark, empty-looking. It didn't seem likely that Smith had gone to bed yet; the time was only eight-thirty. Which meant that he hadn't returned yet and the house was as deserted as it looked.

Perfect.

Daniels left the shadows and crossed to the front porch. There were lights on in the nearest of the neighboring houses, but trees screened the properties; the odds against anyone seeing him were all in Daniels' favor. Just to be sure that Smith wasn't home, he crept up onto the porch, rang the bell and then jumped down into the bushes to watch and wait. Nothing happened, inside or out. The house remained dark and silent.

Daniels waited another couple of minutes before he went around to the rear. The back door was locked, as was the small window beside it; but the latch on the window yielded to one of the tools in his pocket. He slid up the sash and climbed over the sill into heavy darkness.

Using his pencil flash to guide him, he made his way through the house and down into the basement area where the furnace and hot-water heater were located. Then he took the plastic explosive from his pocket and moved up to the water heater.

Five minutes later, Daniels retraced his steps through the house and eased out through the rear window, shutting it after him. When he got back into the trees bordering Smith's property he checked his watch. The time was 8:55. He settled down against one of the trees to wait.

Smith returned at 9:20. The gray sedan came prowling up the hill, parking lights on, and stopped in front of the attached garage. The license plates, Daniels noticed, were now clean and visible. Smith got out of the car to open the garage door—an ungraceful, portly man in his fifties, who looked neither obsessive nor homicidal. Another few seconds and both Smith and the car had vanished inside the garage and the door had been secured from within.

Daniels stood and watched the house with a good deal of intensity. Five more minutes passed. Ten. Twelve—

Even though he was waiting for it, the explosion was startlingly loud. The flash seemed to light up the entire house and most of the surrounding neighborhood; the windows burst outward, pieces of debris sprayed the night. Flames began to soar and flicker inside the demolished house.

Quickly, but with the same caution as before, Daniels made his way back to where he had parked his car. There was a good deal of activity in the neighborhood—voices shouting, people running toward Smith's house; no one paid attention to him. And he would be long gone before the police arrived.

As he drove away, staying within the legal speed limit, he found himself thinking—philosophically again—of the irrationality, the unreasonable nature of life. If there was anyone at fault for all of this, it was Smith's late alcoholic brother. The fool should have been out of the Harcourt Building by eleven a.m. that morning; he'd been told of the demolition proceedings but must have forgotten in his stupor.

Daniels shook his head. The truly guilty, he thought, never pay. Which was part of the further irrationality of life.

When he reached his own house, on the far side of the city, he used the automatic opener clipped to the sun visor to lift the garage door, then drove inside. He shut off the engine, the headlights. As he got out of the car, he reached back inside to automatically close the door again.

Something moved in the bushes alongside the garage entrance.

Daniels stiffened, staring over there. Before he could do anything else two dark shapes glided into the garage and converged on him, one of them holding a blackjack upraised in one hand.

Daniels tried to run then but it was too late, much too late. The blackjack descended, struck him a glancing blow that knocked him sprawling to the concrete. Dimly he heard one of the men say in Spanish-accented English, "Start the car. We will make it seem an accident, just as before. Carbon monoxide poisoning."

The last thought Daniels had before he slid away into darkness was that life could *really* be irrational and unreasonable sometimes.

It hadn't been Smith who wanted to demolish him.

It was the people from Central America ...

THE LAST LAUGH

All my life people been telling me I'm not very smart. "You need a diagram to tie your shoes," Ma said to me once. And about six other times she said, "You got two brain cells, Bernie, and one of them's asleep half the time. That's why you keep getting yourself in trouble." My own mother.

I been in trouble a little, sure, but it was all minor stuff. Couple of car-theft raps, couple for shoplifting, a B&E. Three convictions and some jail time that wasn't too bad, except they worked my tail off on the honor farm. But it ain't because I'm stupid that I kept getting caught. Stupid's not the reason I can't seem to hang onto the jobs Ma and my probation officer get for me, neither. It's bad luck. I mean, I'm just about the unluckiest guy you'll ever meet.

Like for instance, when I was working for the A&P as a stock clerk, one of the best jobs I ever had, and the manager caught me sacked out on a pallet of fifty-pound sacks of dog food and fired me on the spot. It was plain lousy luck I happened to fall asleep right there in the open part of the warehouse instead of in the little storage closet behind the freezer where I usually hid out to catch some z's.

Or the night I busted into a brand-new Cadillac and stole a fur coat and some other stuff that was lying on the backseat, on account of I was broke and out of work and didn't have nothing else to do. Wouldn't you know a cop'd be driving by just as I was heading off with the bundle in my arms. I told him I found the coat and the other stuff in a trash bin, but he didn't believe it, probably because there wasn't no trash bin around there. Neither did the judge that sent me to the slam for a year and a half, my longest stretch.

Another cop that busted me, the time I broke into Klausmeyer's Novelty Store and set off a burglar alarm I didn't even know they had, he said I was a typical dumb criminal. I heard that from some other people, too, including Ma. Always made me mad, and hurt me, too, on account of it's not true. A dumb criminal is one like this guy I heard about swiped some jewelery from a store down in L.A., and he's on his way home when the cops pick him up and they find the stuff in his pants pockets. What do you think he says to the cops? "I didn't know it was in there," he says. "These ain't even my pants."

Now that's *real* stupid. I'm a lot smarter than that guy.

If I had any luck, I'd sure be better off than I am. I'd have a place of my own, maybe a nice apartment over by Greenbriar Park, instead of having to keep on living in my old room in Ma's house where she can nag at me all the time. I'd have cash for the flicks and the chicks, and for drinks at Fogarty's Saloon and eight-ball matches at the House of Billiards and all the other good things in life.

But the most cash I ever had all at once was a hundred and twenty dollars, the time I sold the iPod I boosted from Dennison's Department Store to a guy I met at Fogarty's. But I didn't have it long, on account of the guy turned out to be an undercover cop and he busted me for selling stolen property. That's another example of how bad my luck is.

I kept thinking how good things'd be if I could make one big score. A pile of cash to spend on a new car and some decent threads and a couple of girls I liked but who wouldn't have nothing to do with a dude who was broke all the time. But how was I gonna get it?

That was when I come up with the plan to rob Ma's bank.

I mean the bank where Ma has her checking account. She don't have a bank of her own, she's only a clerk at Klausmeyer's Novelty Store. But not the branch she uses, downtown—heisting that one wouldn't've been smart at all. The one over in the Eagle Ridge Shopping Center, in the other direction.

Robbing a bank was a pretty big step up from shoplifting and boosting a car now and then, but where else was I gonna get some real money? That's where you find all the real money, right? In a bank? Besides, my plan was a good one, if I say it myself. It even had a ace in the hole in case I got caught. I worked on it three weeks before I had it foolproof.

First thing I did then was write the note I was gonna give the teller. I didn't have no paper in my room so I waited until Ma went off to work at Klausmeyer's and then found some in her desk. It had printing on one side, but I didn't care about that. I was only gonna use the blank side.

I worked on that note awhile, getting it just right. When I had it all printed in big black letters, it said: **DONT SAY NOTHING. GUN IN MY POCKET. PUT ALL BIG BILLS IN BAG.** Short and sweet.

The next day I went downtown to this costume place and boosted one of them fake beards that look like real ones. I tried it on after I got back home and it sure changed how I looked. And when I put on one of my old sweatshirts that had a hood on it and tied the hood tight around my head and under my chin, I didn't look like myself at all. It was a real good disguise.

Next day after that, I was ready to go. After Ma left, I put on my disguise and took one of the big grocery bags she keeps under the sink and stuffed it inside my sweatshirt. Then I went out to the garage and got my old bicycle.

The bike was the beauty part of the plan, along with my ace in the hole. Almost every guy that robs a bank, he makes his getaway in a car or maybe on a motorcycle. Nobody was gonna expect a getaway on a kid's bike, right? Besides, I didn't have no car—the last old piece of junk I had got repossessed.

So I hopped on the bike and rode over to the Eagle Ridge Shopping Center. It was about ten-thirty when I got there. There was a walkway along one side of the bank and that was where I left the bike, propped up against the bank wall right around the corner where I could grab it quick afterward.

Two tellers' windows was open and only one customer when I went in. I didn't see no point in waiting around for the customer to leave, so I went right up to the open window and handed the woman teller the note. Her mouth dropped open when she read it. When she looked at me again I put on a mean look to show her I meant business.

Well, it went off without a hitch. Or it did until I come outside and around the corner with the bagful of money in my hand, and seen that some damn crook had stole my bike.

I didn't have no choice then, I had to make my getaway on foot. You can do that all right but you got to be lucky, and for a change I had some luck on my side. I started running, fast, straight on out of the Eagle Ridge Shopping Center. People looked at me but none of 'em tried to get in my way and wasn't nobody chasing me when I come out on 49th Street. I ducked into a alley and yanked off the fake beard and my sweatshirt and pitched them into a trash barrel. Then I went over a block to Mission, where I would've got on a bus back to my neighborhood except that I didn't have no change and only a dumb criminal would open up the bag and start hauling out some of the bank money in broad daylight on a crowded bus.

By the time I got home I was tired from the long walk and still a little shaky, but the shakiness went away soon as I dumped the money out on my bed. All that beautiful green. I figured there must be ten, fifteen grand there, easy, but I was wrong. It was more, a lot more.

$26,000 and change.

Man, oh man!

After I counted it again—it was even more that time, $27K—I put it back into the bag and hid the bag in my sock drawer. Ma never looks in my sock drawer.

Then I went to the kitchen and cracked a brew to celebrate. I was feeling good, the best I'd felt since the time Chuck Potter and me went joyriding in a '65 Mustang we boosted at Greenbriar Park and then picked up two girls who liked to party.

I was on my third beer, just kicking back and thinking about all that cash and what I was gonna do with it, when the doorbell rang. I thought it was probably some salesman, or maybe one of the neighbors. But it wasn't.

It was the cops.

City heat, a whole bunch of 'em in and out of uniform. Couple of FBI agents, too—I never seen a FBI badge before and man, it's really something, big and shiny, not like them cheap badges the city cops carry. They had a search warrant, so there wasn't nothing I could do but let 'em in and let 'em search and they found the $27K right away in my sock drawer. I could've told them I never seen it before, like that mook down south who said his pants wasn't his, but I got more smarts and more pride than that. I didn't say nothing, except for one question I just had to ask.

"How'd you find me so quick? Somebody see me running away from the bank?"

One of the FBI guys said it was the note I give the teller.

"The note? What about it?"

"Don't you know what you wrote it on?"

"Just a piece of paper I found ... wasn't it?"

"Not just any piece of paper," he said. "One of your mother's bank statements with her name and address on it."

Well, I should've looked closer at the printing on the other side of that paper, but I'd been too busy trying to get the words in the note down just right. You can't think of everything.

See what I mean about lousy luck?

So they read me my rights and hustled me down to police headquarters and stuck me in one of them interrogation rooms. I was scared, but not too scared. I mean, I knew I wasn't gonna get off with no slap on the wrist this time, but it wasn't as bad as it could've been. I still had my ace in the hole.

Two city detectives and one of the FBI agents come in and asked me did I want a lawyer present during questioning, and I said no on account of I never did like lawyers much. None of the public defenders I had ever made no real effort to keep me out of jail. Then they asked me to tell about my plan to rob the bank, then they told me to write it all down and that took awhile. When I got done I asked the FBI slick how long I was gonna have to spend in prison.

"Depends on the judge," he said. "Ten to fifteen years, with time off for good behavior."

"Well, that's not too bad," I said. "It'll be worth it."

"Why do you say that?"

So then I showed my ace. "On account of the money when I get out."

"What money?"

"From the bank," I said. "It's mine now, right? I sure as hell earned it."

The FBI slick and the two detectives all of a sudden bust out laughing. They laughed so hard one of the cops had tears in his eyes. I didn't see what was so funny, but I didn't care. When I get out of the slam and start spending that $27K, it'll be me that has the last laugh.

CONFESSION

The night is dark up here on the cliffs above Bodega Head, moonless, the stars hidden behind scudding clouds. Three a.m. dark, Fitzgerald's dark night of the soul. The sea wind whipping across the deserted parking lot is fierce; it buffets the car, howls and whistles at the windows. In the blackness hundreds of feet below, I can hear the gale frothing the sea and hurling high waves in a constant pounding roar against the rocks.

Dark. Cold. But no darker or colder than it is inside the shell of Lewis Everett.

Yet as I sit here recording this confession, my voice is calm and I'm no longer afraid. This night has been coming for a long time, though I never expected it would happen on our anniversary, Alicia's and mine. I bought the recorder on a whim some time ago, but it really wasn't a whim at all. In the back of my mind I've known all along what I would use it for.

My mind is empty now of all except dull resolve. And an awareness of one simple truth, a lesson learned too late. Much, much too late.

You can't get away with murder. Sooner or later, one way or another, you have to pay.

In the beginning I thought you could. I believed that if you planned carefully enough, took all the right precautions, you could create the perfect crime. So did Alicia. The two of us laboring under the same delusion, reinforcing it in each other.

But we were different people then. Arrogant, selfish, convinced that we were invincible. All things seem possible when you're in love, or believe you are, and hungry enough and bold enough to take the necessary risks.

I remember as vividly as if it had happened yesterday the afternoon we first talked about killing Alicia's husband, Jack Maitland. We were in bed together in an Inverness motel, lying close after a half hour's frenzied passion had been spent.

"We can't go on like this," I said. "He's bound to find out, and when he does there's no telling what he'll do."

"Beat me up, beat you up, maybe even kill us both," she said. "He's capable of it, Lew."

"I know," I said. "I've had a taste of his temper."

"I've had whole meals," she said, "and I don't want any more."

"All right, then. There's only one thing we can do if we want to have a life together. It's what we've both been thinking."

"Yes," she said.

"Do you hate him enough to go through with it?"

"More than enough. More."

"You're sure his will leaves everything to you, no other bequests?"

"Positive. He has no relatives and he's never given a dime to charity. It'll all be mine."

"Ours," I said.

"Yes," she said, "ours. But how can we do it without getting caught?"

"I've already thought of a way. A foolproof way, if we're careful."

"When? How soon?"

"As soon as we can arrange it," I said. "Then we'll have each other and everything we ever wanted."

Each other and everything we ever wanted.

Jack Maitland was a big man in Los Alegres. Owned the only luxury car dealership in the area, served one term on the city council, knew everybody of any importance. Worth better than half a million by Alicia's estimate—his business, a two-story Spanish style home in the best neighborhood, a portfolio of blue-chip stocks, cash in a pair of bank accounts and more cash that he hadn't declared to the IRS squirreled away in a private safe.

Alicia was ten years younger than Maitland, a red-haired beauty by anybody's standards. Bitter and full of hate for him because of his abusive ways, restless for the good things in life because he kept her on a short financial leash. I was her age, good-looking enough and smooth enough to attract her, and just as restless, just as hungry. Working as one of Maitland's salesmen for a small salary plus commissions, a dead-end job.

Maitland had two passions. One was making money, the other was driving back country roads at high speeds in his favorite of the three cars he owned, a souped-up Porsche 356. The race-car driver mentality. He had insomnia and did his joyriding late at night. And always alone.

A perfect set-up, the way I figured it, for the perfect crime.

All Alicia and I had to do was turn the Porsche into a death trap.

It wasn't difficult to accomplish once I had the logistics of the plan worked out. Maitland kept the Porsche locked up in his garage when he wasn't out joyriding; he drove a Buick to work and around town because Buicks and Lincolns were what he sold. It was too much of a risk for me to try to get into the garage and doctor the Porsche myself, so the first step in the plan was Alicia's.

She knew a little about cars and how they operate, enough so that when I showed her a schematic of the Porsche's engine in a repair manual and explained to her what to do, she understood right away. It was a simple matter of replacing the condenser on the distributor with a faulty unit I'd picked up at a car dismantler's in another town. The distributors are out in the open on a 356, easy to get at, and it doesn't take a mechanic's skill to make the switch.

She managed it with no trouble while Maitland was away from the house. What the faulty condenser did was to let the Porsche run okay at idle and low speeds—a problem that can drive even the best mechanics crazy trying to figure out the cause. When the engine started acting up, Maitland had no choice but to put the Porsche into the shop for repairs. I knew he'd pick the one at the dealership because his head mechanic had worked on the car before and it wouldn't cost him anything.

I made sure I was hanging around when he told the mechanic about the engine trouble, and like a good employee I stepped in and offered to pick the Porsche up at his house and run it in for him. I was pretty sure he'd agree because Alicia told me he had a full schedule that day, and he did right away. To make sure the Porsche stayed in the shop overnight, I stalled around before bringing it in until it was too late in the afternoon for an engine check and the repair work to get done.

As one of the salesmen I had a key to the lot gates, and it was easy enough to filch one of the spare keys for the shop when no one was looking. That night after midnight I slipped in and gimmicked the brakes. Porsche 356's have master cylinders tied to all four brake lines, so one defective line affects the whole system. Cut the line outright and there'd be no pressure almost immediately; but puncture any one line with the tip of an icepick, just a tiny hole, and the brakes will hold at low speeds and a light touch on the pedal, while hard pumps at high speed will cause the line to rupture. When you're traveling at seventy or more on winding country roads at night, the gearbox alone isn't enough for even an experienced driver to maintain control.

We didn't have long to wait once the faulty condenser had been replaced. Two nights later, the night of May 12, Maitland wrapped the Porsche around a tree on Chileno Valley Road, traveling at a speed estimated at eighty when the brakes went out. Dead on impact, his body so badly mangled he had to be buried in a closed casket.

Alicia and I waited six months before we started seeing each other openly. Us dating didn't raise any eyebrows; nobody suspected a thing. After two months, we went to Reno and got married. And then we had each other and Maitland's business and Maitland's house and Maitland's money—everything we'd ever wanted.

Only it didn't last very long. Not very long at all.

The money just seemed to evaporate. Expensive sailboat, expensive clothes, expensive jewelry, expensive gadgets. Trips to Las Vegas, New York, Hawaii. Catered parties at home, lavish meals in the best restaurants in San Francisco. And I took a flyer on a stock that had just gone public and lost a bundle.

Maitland's blue chips went next, at a loss in a buyer's market. It wasn't long before the money from that ran out, too. And then we lost the business because of poor management and a lousy economy that kept people from buying luxury cars. I didn't know or care anything about running a large dealership and the man I hired as manager proved to be incompetent.

The bankruptcy forced us to sell the house, and we didn't get anywhere near what it was worth. When the money from that was gone, we were right back where we'd started. Or rather I was. I had to go back to work as a used-car salesman to pay the bills, and at that we almost went under. Would have if Alicia hadn't reluctantly taken a job selling cosmetics.

That was when I knew for sure that there's no such thing as a perfect crime. That there are other kinds of punishments besides prison and the death penalty. That you can pay and keep on paying in installments, a little at a time over a period as long as a jail sentence.

I don't know why Alicia and I stayed together after we lost the house and the last of the good life disappeared. It wasn't love; that was long gone. Or sex; we quit sleeping together early on. Guilt had something to do with it. So did the subconscious desire to hurt and be hurt. But the main reason was the fear that if we split up, one of us would take revenge on the other, no matter what the cost.

I thought of ways of permanently cutting the cord that tied us together. So did Alicia, I'm sure. But we were too beaten down, too scared, too dependent, too gutless to do anything about it. We just went on and on in the mire of our shared misery.

Until tonight.

Until our anniversary.

We fought constantly after everything went to hell. Verbal battles, mostly, but every now and then things erupted into violence. She'd slap me, I'd slap her back. Once in the heat of rage she tried to stab me with a paring knife. I knocked her down and just barely managed to stop myself from beating her bloody.

The fight tonight started because I made the mistake of mentioning the anniversary, I don't know why except that I've always had a good memory for dates. It set her off on an immediate tirade, an endless rehash of what crap our life together had turned out to be, how it was all my fault. She wouldn't stop, the words growing uglier and uglier until my nerves were raw wounds and I ... I don't know, I guess I snapped. Finally snapped.

I have only a vague memory of rushing into the bedroom for my revolver, coming back into the living room shouting "Shut up, shut up!" and pointing the gun at Alicia and pulling the trigger. Shutting her up forever.

Murder number two.

If I'd had the courage then, I might have turned the gun on myself. But I didn't; my hand was shaking so badly I couldn't even hold onto it. I staggered out to the car and drove around going nowhere until I calmed down enough to think clearly. Then I drove straight here to Bodega Head.

The wind is louder now, the noises it makes like the screaming voice of a woman. Like Alicia's voice, just before I killed her.

No, you can't get away with murder. Sooner or later, one way or another, you have to pay.

My confession is nearly finished. In a minute or so I'll get out of the car and walk to the cliff edge and then step off into the dark—make the final payment for my two murders.

The one I committed on May 12, 1971.

And the one I committed tonight, on the fiftieth anniversary of the first.

THE TUESDAY CURSE
(with Barry N. Malzberg)

Bloom hated Tuesdays. In a lifetime of small catastrophes, almost all of them happened on a Tuesday.

This one started with a dull, throbbing headache. He took three aspirin before leaving his west-side bachelor apartment and walking to his bus stop, arriving just in time to catch a face full of exhaust fumes as the bus departed. He waited fifteen minutes for the next, and when it came it was so crowded he had to put up with standing room only. He amused himself on the way by surreptitiously stroking a strange girl's hip. He should have known better, this being a Tuesday. She not only caught and swore at him but threatened to have him arrested for sexual harassment, which forced him into a hasty exit five blocks before his usual stop. Mumbling imprecations, he walked the rest of the way to Bloom Novelties, Inc.

The latest in his long string of secretaries gave him a nervous smile when he passed her desk in the outer office. What was her name? Frobish, that was it. Stupid name, Frobish. Stupid name for a stupid woman.

"Good morning, Mr. Bloom."

He glared at her without replying. She was middle-aged, mousy, timorous—the kind he preferred to hire. They were all inept, but the young, attractive ones were even worse. He'd made the mistake of hiring one of those in the beginning. When he tried to kiss her at the end of her third day on the job, she slapped his face, called him an obnoxious pig, and quit before he could fire her.

In the slightly larger adjoining room that functioned as his private office, Bloom stood looking at the Tuesday morning clutter atop his desk with a familiar combination of indifference and muted dread. No worthwhile business, nothing good, ever came on this miserable day. It was as if the rhythm of his workweek was subject to a taunting, malevolent force—as if he were the victim of some sort of Tuesday curse.

This Tuesday was no different. In fact it was worse than usual. What lay atop the stack was a threatening letter from the Amalgamated Collection Agency demanding payment for a shipment of adult party supplies from Funnytimes Manufacturing. Bloom stared at the letter, his stomach quivering with rage. Three months past due. Remit full amount immediately or else. Bastards!

He picked up the phone and called Funnytimes' chief accountant, Haber, a repulsive specimen with fingernails the color of mustard and the bulging eyes of a frog. "What's the idea of siccing a collection agency on me?" he demanded. "You know damn well I returned that shipment of defective naked lady swizzle sticks and x-rated cartoon napkins. I don't owe you a dime for them."

"The items were *not* defective," Haber said, "and ten percent of the shipment was *not* returned. By contract you owe us the full amount of the invoice."

It was true that Bloom had shorted them the ten percent, having unloaded a small number of the party favors to one of his customers, but those crooks at Funnytimes had shorted *him* more than once and turnaround was fair play. "I won't pay it!" he shouted. "You hear me, Haber? I won't pay it!"

"Your account is already on temporary hold. If you fail to remit the full amount owed within thirty days, we will be forced to make the hold permanent and instruct the Amalgamated agency to take appropriate legal measures—"

Bloom slammed the phone down. Then in a still furious voice he summoned the Frobish woman.

She came in wearing an expression of controlled terror. "Yes, sir?"

"Why did you put this on my desk?" Bloom said, waving the Amalgamated letter at her.

"It was addressed to you personally, Mr. Bloom. You told me to open everything addressed that way—"

"I also told you that if it was a demand for money, to throw it out. Why didn't you throw this one out?"

"I ... I thought surely you would want to see it because it threatens legal action. Forewarned is forearmed, isn't that so?"

Bloom decided it was time to fire her. He was sick of the woman—they all turned into whining incompetents sooner or later, and he relished berating and firing them. He had little enough power otherwise, and little enough sources of pleasure these days; disposing of secretaries was a satisfying form of entertainment. Especially on Tuesdays.

"I don't care what it threatens!" he bellowed. "You spoiled my day!"

"I'm sorry, I—"

"Stupid cow!"

Frobish emitted a weak gasp. "You have no right to call me names, Mr. Bloom."

"I'll call you anything I damn well please."

Which he proceeded to do, not stinting on the profanity. She cringed away from him, and burst into tears when he sacked her at the end of his tirade. He wrote out a check, docking her for today and as usual including no amount of severance, and sent her packing. Number 5 in the past six months, number 9 for the year, number 15 since Bloom Novelties, Inc.

opened for business.

He felt better when she was gone. Getting rid of her made the rest of Tuesday more tolerable.

The new secretary had a Scandinavian name that Bloom couldn't pronounce, much less remember. Cut from the same cloth as the rest, if somewhat more efficient. He had to admit that she helped him in dealing with the growing pile of dunning letters and unpaid invoices, so he put off the pleasure of firing her.

But she wasn't smart enough to keep the Amalgamated Collection Agency off his neck. If they'd sent any more threatening letters she'd thrown them out, and also followed instructions by not putting through any phone calls. But then she brainlessly allowed one of their representatives to sneak past her into Bloom's office to deliver an in-person ultimatum: pay what he owed Funnytimes Manufacturing on the spot or face immediate legal action. He couldn't afford to fight Funnytimes in court so he had no choice but to pay the money.

After the bloodsucker left, Bloom spent ten minutes heaping epithets on the Swede or Norwegian or whatever she was before dumping her. He was so upset he didn't get any pleasure at all out of it this time.

The next two weeks Bloom hired and fired two more secretaries. He was getting them from newspaper ads now, instead of through one of the agencies. The ads were cheaper, and with the increased turnover and the shaky state of his finances, he had to cut corners wherever he could. Most of the agencies wouldn't have anything more to do with him, anyway.

He disposed of the first one for refusing to work overtime without extra pay, the other for making a slight mistake on a customer invoice. The second one gave him a sob story about needing the job desperately on account of her invalid son's medical bills, but he didn't believe it; they were all liars as well as incompetents. Besides, he had more important problems of his own.

Tuesday again. Bloom planned to spend this one alone, figuring ways to keep his business out of the red by robbing Peter to pay Paul, but no. He hadn't been in his office more than five minutes when the woman showed up. How had she known he was in the market for a new secretary? He hadn't had time to put a new ad in the paper on Monday, had intended to do that today. Not that it mattered how she'd found out. Some of them had an annoying knack for nosing out employment opportunities.

This one was like all the rest. Plain, middle-aged, and probably stupid. The only difference between her and the others who came to be interviewed was that she carried a briefcase. Her name was Smith, she said, Ms. Smith. Ms. Another one of *those*.

Bloom considered chasing her out, but there'd only be another like her to interview later. Might as well get the disagreeable process over and done with now. Hire her if she was qualified, get rid of her in a week or two.

He ushered her into his private office. "Sit down, *Ms.* Smith," he said, making the Ms. sound like a nasty word.

She didn't seem to notice. She sat primly with her knees together, the briefcase in her lap.

"Experience?" Bloom said. "References?"

"I beg your pardon?"

"Are you hard of hearing? I can't be expected to hire secretaries without a resume and references."

"I am not here to apply for a secretarial position, Mr. Bloom."

He scowled at her. "Then why are you here? What do you want?"

"I represent the following: Deborah Finkel, Amanda Horowitz, Christine Bellamy, Elena Rodriguez, Lucia Rizzuto, Margaret Hunter, Robin Levitsky, Claudia Frobish, Helga Nyqvist, Doris Reilly, and Marilyn Peabody."

"Who the hell are they? I don't know any of those people."

"Yes, you do. They are all former secretaries of yours—women you overworked, underpaid, harassed and verbally abused, fired without just cause, and gave poor references to, thereby inflicting grievous mental anguish and damaging their careers."

"So that's it. A female shyster and a ridiculous class-action lawsuit." Bloom was furious. Damn women! Damn Tuesdays! "Well, it won't work, Smith. You can't prove any of those bogus charges in court. You'll never get a penny out of me—"

"You misunderstand, Mr. Bloom. I am not an attorney."

"No? Then what the devil are you?"

From inside her briefcase Ms. Smith produced a large silenced revolver. "An instrument of justice," she said, and shot dumbfounded, Tuesday-cursed Bloom squarely between the eyes.

BONES

I was sitting on the farmhouse porch, as I sometimes do after supper in good weather, when Charlie Linderman showed up with the news.

It was a warm late summer night, the crickets and tree frogs in full voice, the scent of honeysuckle in the air. Peaceful. Lonesome, too. Twenty-two years now since the cancer took Mary Anne. And seventeen years since Marine Corporal Clayton Drivas Junior, our only offspring, died in Iraq. I've been alone ever since. I don't make friends easy, keep mostly to myself, but an old man gets lonely. Often enough on evenings like this one.

So I wasn't sorry to see Charlie's old Ford come rumbling up the drive, just a little surprised that he'd come calling this late in the day. He's about the only friend I have. Used to deliver mail out here in the country, which is how I got to know him. He's retired now, but I still work the farm so my free time is limited. Mostly we get together one or two Sunday afternoons a month to sip a beer or two and play cribbage.

He slewed the Ford to a stop in the farmyard and came hurrying up onto the porch. He's a skinny little guy, about half my size and weight, and when he's excited he gets red in the face and jumps around like a bantam rooster. Thing about Charlie is, he's a born gossip. When he knows something or other nobody else does, he swells up with it and just has to share.

"I got news, Clay," he said. "Big news. Figured you'd want to hear it right away."

"Must be big for you to come all the way out here."

"Tell you over a beer, if you got one to spare."

I went into the kitchen, opened a bottle of Budweiser and brought it out to him. He took a long swig, wiped off a foam mustache with the back of his hand. His eyes were bright in the slow-gathering dusk.

"That long missing girl's finally been found," he said then. "Leastways they're pretty sure it's her. Don't see how it could be anybody else."

"What girl? I didn't know anybody was lost."

"Not lost. Killed, just like everybody figured."

"Slow down, Charlie. Who're you talking about?"

"The Hansen girl, Lynne Hansen. Been dead all along, prob'ly right from the time she disappeared. You remember, Clay—the disappearance caused a hell of a flap at the time."

It was a few seconds before I said, "I remember. That was a lot of years ago."

"Nearly twenty. Never thought she'd be found, nobody did. Just pure luck she was."

"Found where?"

"A few miles from here, up on the side of Bald Mountain. Whoever killed her stuck her body in a little cave hid by rocks and brush. Couple of rockhounds stumbled on it by accident, looked inside, and there she was, what was left of her. Nothing but bones now."

"Bones," I said.

"And some rotted pieces of canvas that she must've been wrapped up in," Charlie said. "That's one way they know she was took in there dead, murdered. Another is the way the skeleton looked, head all bent, hyoid bone damaged and first cervical vertebra snapped. That's what happens when a person gets choked and her neck broke."

"How do you know all this?"

"Heard it from my nephew. So it's straight goods."

His nephew, Tony Peters, was a Cullum County deputy sheriff. "How can they be sure it was Lynne Hansen?"

"Well, they're not absolutely sure yet. Taking the bones to the state capitol for forensic tests and a dental check. But it's her, all right. Couldn't hardly be anybody else."

"I suppose not."

"Maybe the forensic experts will find some evidence to identify her killer, but it don't seem likely. Don't seem likely we'll ever know who did it. Too many years gone by, too many men it could've been." Charlie rested a knobby hip on the porch railing, oiled his voice box with another swig of beer. "Real pretty, she was, with all that blond hair. Gold blond—isn't that what the newspapers said?"

"I don't recall."

"Sure, gold blond. Face like an angel but a hellion underneath, young as she was. Morals of an alley cat. Took up with anybody in pants and money to spend—young or old, didn't matter to her. Wasn't above breaking the law to get what she wanted, neither. Two theft complaints against her, one that got her fired from the grocery where she worked. Yessir, a real hellion. Whoever killed her probably did the world a favor."

"Nobody deserves to be murdered, Charlie."

"Well, maybe not," he admitted. "Anyhow, old Sheriff Hoskins must've questioned a dozen men that'd had relations with her after she disappeared and couldn't pin a thing on any of 'em. Wouldn't be surprised if the one who did it was dead himself by this time."

"Does it really matter?" I said.

"Does what really matter?"

"Who killed her and why, all those years ago."

"Sure it matters. Nothing much happens around here, you know that.

Finding what was left of her in that cave is the biggest thing since ... well, since she disappeared and all that come out about the kind she was. Don't tell me you're not interested."

"All right, I won't."

He shook his head as if he were disappointed in me and my reaction to the news. He emptied the bottle, set it on the railing, and said he'd better be getting on back to town. I didn't try to change his mind.

Twilight had come by the time Charlie left. I kept on sitting there as the sky darkened from deep purple to black—remembering. The thrumming of the crickets and tree frogs seemed a long way off now, the honeysuckle scent sickly sweet. In the distance I could see the dark shape of Bald Mountain outlined against the star-bright sky.

It had been a night just like this one that it happened, except that it was later and the moon had been up and nearly full. All I had to do was shut my eyes and I could see her plain as day lying on the grassy riverbank, her face mottled and pale in the bright white moonshine, the fingermarks on her throat, the crooked angle of her head in the fan of golden hair.

So young, so pretty, so wicked. So dead.

After a little while I got up and went into the house and vomited my dinner into the toilet. Then I rinsed my mouth, washed my hands and face, and went back outside. But I didn't sit again. I walked down off the porch and across the farmyard past the barn and then down the dirt road alongside the alfalfa field. Not by choice—as if I was being pulled against my will by some irresistible force. It had happened like that before, more than once, but not in a long time.

When I got to the intersection with the farm road that branches in from the county highway, I crossed over and climbed the knoll on the far side. You could see a quarter of a mile in both directions from the top of it, the wide snakelike curves of the river, the willows lining the opposite shore. The moon was on the rise now, just a sickle tonight that laid silvery shimmers on the river's surface but didn't cast enough light to whiten the place on the bank where Lynne Hansen died. It was all shadows down there.

I made my way to the benchlike jut of rock halfway down. Sat on the cold stone and tried not to look at the shadowed place below. But memory images came into my mind again anyway, this time with my eyes wide open. A ragged series of them like clips from a silent movie.

I watched myself picking her up with gloved hands, wrapping the piece of old tarp around the body. Lifting the bundle and carrying it to the bed of my pickup. Driving away on the farm road, on the county highway, on the old fire trail that curled up along the flank of Bald Mountain. Hunting with a shielded flashlight for the entrance to the cave I'd found when I was a kid. Laying the bundle inside the dark, narrow space when I finally located it, then piling up rocks to hide the entrance. Driving again, the long drive home …

I don't know how long I sat there on the stone bench. It must have been a while because the moon was higher in the night sky when the flap and cry of an owl jerked me aware. The night was still warm, but I was cold now—cold enough to bring shivers. I walked fast back to the house.

I've never been much of a drinking man, but in the kitchen I took the bottle of Jim Beam out of the cabinet, poured a jelly glass half full, drank it all in three swallows. The liquor stopped the shivers but it didn't warm me. I told myself to take a hot shower, as hot as I could stand it. Instead I went into the front parlor, to the old cherrywood sideboard—drawn there as I had been drawn to the riverbank.

The framed photograph was on the sideboard, next to the one of Mary Anne in her wedding finery. I took it down, held it in both hands. Clayton Junior's high school graduation photo. Big and strong like me. Handsome, smiling, the future bright ahead of him.

And then the image dimmed and was replaced by another with the smile turned upside down, the features sweat-damp and distorted with panic—the way he'd looked that night when he came rushing into the house calling my name. The panic had been in his voice, too. I could hear the breathless rush of words once more, plainly, like echoes across the span of years.

"Dad, oh God, Dad, I picked up this girl tonight, took her out to the river … afterward she said she was only seventeen and if I didn't give her money she'd have me arrested for statutory rape … I slapped her and she started kicking and scratching and I … I grabbed her by the throat … I didn't mean to hurt her but I must've twisted her head somehow, I heard a pop and she went limp … she's dead, Dad, I killed her … oh God, you've got to help me, I don't know what to do!"

There was only one thing to do, as I saw it then, only one way to help him. And so I went and did what I did. He was my son, he was all I had left in this world.

Only I didn't have him for long.

Six weeks after that night, he left home sudden without a word to me and joined the Marine Corps. And less than a year later a casualty notification officer came to tell me he'd been killed by enemy fire while trying to aid a wounded fellow soldier.

When I was done grieving, I thought about driving into town and confessing the truth to the county sheriff. I might have if Lynne Hansen had had any close relatives, but she hadn't—just an uncle somewhere back east who hadn't wanted anything to do with her. So I hadn't confessed then, and I couldn't do it now or ever. Not because I was afraid of what would happen to me, but because Clayton Junior had died a hero in the service of his country. I couldn't bring myself to publicly dishonor his name and his memory.

Was it patriotism that made him join the military? Or was it shame, guilt? And was his act of battlefield bravery an attempt to atone for his crime? I don't know—I'll never know.

But I do know this: he didn't go unpunished.

And neither have I.

Lynne Hansen wasn't alone in that cave the past eighteen years. I put a part of myself in with her that night, and my bones will still be there on judgment day.

I THINK I WILL NOT HANG MYSELF TODAY

The leaves on the trees were dying.

She had noted that before, of course; neither her mind nor her powers of observation had been eroded by the passing years. But this morning, seen from her bedroom window, it seemed somehow a sudden thing, as if the maples and Japanese elms had changed color overnight, from bright green to red and brittle gold. Just yesterday it had been summer, now all at once it was autumn.

John had been taken from her on an October afternoon. It would be fitting if autumn were her time too.

Perhaps today, she thought. Why not today?

For a while longer, Miranda stood looking out at the cold morning, the sky more gray than blue. Wind rattled the frail leaves, now and then tore one loose and swirled it to the ground. Even from a distance, the maple leaves resembled withered hands, their veins and skeletal bone structure clearly visible. The wind, blowing from the east, sent the fallen ones skittering across the lawn, piled them in heaps along the wall of the old barn.

Looking at the barn this morning filled her with sadness. Once, when John was alive, the skirling whine of his power saws and the fine, fresh smells of sawdust and wood stain and lemon oil made the barn seem alive, as sturdy and indestructible as the beautiful furniture that came from his workshop. Now it was a sagging shell, a lonely place of drafts and shadows and ghosts, its high center beam like the crosspiece of a gallows.

So little left, she thought as she turned from the window. John gone these many years. Moira gone—no family left at all. Lord Byron gone six months, and as much as she missed the little Sealyham's companionship, she hadn't the heart to replace him with another pet. Gone, too, were most of her friends. And the pleasures of teaching grammar and classic English literature, the satisfaction that came from helping to shape young minds. ("We're sorry, Mrs. Halliday, but you know the mandatory retirement age in our district is 65.") County library setbacks had ended her volunteer work at the local branch. The arthritis made it all but impossible for her to continue her sewing projects for homeless children. Even Mrs. Boyer in the next block had found someone younger to babysit her two preschoolers.

The loneliness had been endurable when she was needed. Being able to help others had given some meaning and purpose to her life. Now, she had become the needy one, requiring help with the cleaning, the yardwork, her weekly grocery shopping. All too soon she would be totally dependent on others ...

No, that mustn't happen. I'm sorry, John, but it mustn't.

She thought again of the old barn, his workshop, the long, high rafter beam. When it had become clear what she must one day do, there had never been any question as to the method. Mr. Gilbert Chesterton had seen to that. She had bought the rope that very day, and it was still out there waiting, the noose tied. Climbing the ladder would not be an easy task, but she would manage. She had always managed, hadn't she? Supremely capable, John had called her. That, and the most determined woman he had ever known.

Chesterton's lines ran through her mind again:

The strangest whim has seized me...
After all I think I will not hang myself today.

She had first come across "A Ballade of Suicide," one of his minor works, when she was a college student, and there had been something so haunting in those lines that she had never forgotten them. One day, she would alter the last of the lines by deleting the word "not." This day, perhaps. Why not this day?

Miranda bathed and dressed. Downstairs in the kitchen she ate her usual breakfast of tea and toast. Then she entered the living room.

John had built every stick of furniture in there, of cherrywood and walnut. Tables, chairs, sofa and loveseat, sideboard, the tall cabinet that contained his collection of rifles and handguns. An artist with wood, John Halliday. She had loved to watch him work, to help him in his shop and to learn from him some of the finer points of his craft.

The photograph of John in his Navy uniform was centered on the fireplace mantel. She picked it up, looked at it until his lean, dark face began to blur, then replaced it. Her gaze passed over the other photos there. Mother, so slender and fragile, the black velvet-banded cameo she'd always worn at her throat. Father in his cap and gown at one of his college graduation ceremonies. Moira and herself at ages four and seven, and wasn't it odd how much prettier she had been as a child, when it was Moira who had grown into such a beautiful woman? Gone, all gone. Dust. Memories and dust.

The phone was ringing. Miranda sighed and went to answer it.

"Miranda, dear, how are you?"

"Oh, hello, Patrice."

"You sound a bit melancholy this morning. Is everything all right?"

"Yes. You mustn't worry about me."

"But I do. You know I do."

Miranda knew it all too well. Patrice was one of her oldest friends, but their closeness was neither deep nor confiding. Patrice's life had been one long, smooth sail, empty of tragedy; she had never needed anyone outside her immediate family.

"I called to invite you to lunch tomorrow," Patrice said. "You need to get out more, and lunch at the Shady Grove Inn is just the ticket. My treat."

"That's good of you, but I don't believe I'll be able to make it. I ... may not be here tomorrow."

"Oh? Going away somewhere?"

"I'd rather not say."

"Talking about something in advance really doesn't prevent it from happening, you know."

"It can," Miranda said. "Sometimes it can."

"Well, you must tell me all about it afterward."

"It won't be a secret, Patrice. I can promise you that."

It seemed quite cold in the house now, despite the fact that she had turned up the heat when she came downstairs. She put on the gas-log flame in the fireplace and sat in front of it with a copy of Oscar Wilde's *The Importance of Being Earnest* open on her lap and tried to read. She couldn't seem to concentrate.

Outside, the wind gusted noisily and rattled shingles and shutters. Inside, the house was very quiet. And still unwarm. And so empty.

I wish I had something to do, she thought, something useful and important.

Well, she thought then, there is something, isn't there? Out in the barn?

She stood, went into her sewing room, and removed the letter—three pages, carefully folded—from the bottom drawer of her desk. She had written it quite a long time ago, but she could have quoted it verbatim. In the front hall, she took her heavy wool coat and a pair of fleece-lined gloves from the closet. She had the coat over her shoulders, the letter tucked into one of the pockets, when the phone rang again.

"Mrs. Halliday? This is Sally Boyer."

"Yes, Mrs. Boyer."

"I wonder if I could ask a big favor? I know it's short notice and I haven't been in touch in a while, but if you could help us out I'd really appreciate it."

"Help you in what way?"

"Babysit for us tonight. My husband has a business dinner, a client and his wife from Los Angeles, and our regular sitter isn't available."

"I'm afraid I have another commitment," Miranda said.

"You do? You couldn't possibly break it?"

"I don't see how I can, now."

"But I thought you, of all people ... I mean ..."

"Yes, Mrs. Boyer, I understand. And I'm sorry."

"I don't know who else to call," Mrs. Boyer said. "Can you think of anyone? You must know someone, some other elder ... some other person?"

"I don't know anyone," Miranda said. "No one at all."

She said goodbye and replaced the receiver. She buttoned her coat, worked her gnarled fingers into the gloves, then crossed the rear porch and stepped outside.

The wind was blustery and very cold, but she didn't hurry. It would not do to hurry at a time like this. She walked at a measured pace across the leaf-strewn yard to the barn.

The front half was mostly a dusty catchall storage area, as it had been when John was alive. On the right side was a cleared section just large enough for the car she no longer drove. She made her way along the passenger side of the car to the doorway in the center partition; opened it and passed through into John's workshop.

His last few woodworking projects, finished and unfinished, were bulky mounds under dustcloths she had placed over them. His workbench, lathe, table saws, and such were also shrouded. The bench was where the rope lay, but Miranda did not go in that direction. Nor did she glance up at the ceiling beam in the shadows above.

At the workshop's far end, more shadows crowded the alcove where John had kept his cot and tiny refrigerator. On those long ago summer nights when he had been deep into one of his projects, he had slept out here to avoid disturbing her. Now there was nothing inside the alcove, only the bare wood floor over packed earth.

Miranda knelt and raised the hidden hinged section. Underneath, the flowers she had placed there last week were already withered and crumbling, dust and petals scattered across the pair of old graves.

So many years since she'd found John and Moira together here that night. So many years since the strangest whim had seized her -and she'd done what she felt she must—shot them both with one of John's handguns. So many years since she had, in her supremely capable fashion, dug for each of them a final resting place and then, using the woodworking skills John had taught her, rebuilt the flooring to cover the graves.

No one had ever suspected. John Halliday had run off with his wife's beautiful younger sister—that was what everyone believed. Such a terrible tragedy for poor Miranda, they all said. But no one but her could know how terrible it really was to be left all alone with nobody to love except a little dog and fewer and fewer ways in which to atone for her sin.

It would be quite a shock when the citizens of Shady Grove learned the truth. And learn it they must; she had kept the secret too long and she could not carry it with her to her own grave, that "fine and private place." She had explained everything in the three-page letter; it would be her final act of atonement.

John and Moira knew all about the rope and the letter. Over and over she had told them that one day she must again do what she felt was necessary. Yet they were so reluctant to let her go. Selfish. Even in death, they cared only for themselves.

"John," she said, "this is the proper day. Can't you understand how I feel?"

The wind mourned outside.

"Moira? We've hurt each other enough. Isn't it time we were together again?"

The earth seemed to tremble, as if there were stirrings within. As if they were beseeching and mocking her, saying quite clearly, "You can't leave us, Miranda. Who will tend to us once you're gone? Who will bring flowers? We need you, Miranda. We need you."

She did not argue; it never did any good to argue. She sighed and got slowly to her feet. "After all," she said, "I think I will not hang myself today."

She lowered the hinged section, thinking that she must buy fresh flowers to replace the withered ones because it was autumn and there were none left in the garden. But before she called the florist, she would ring up Mrs. Boyer and tell her she would be able to babysit tonight after all.

A MATTER OF SURVIVAL
(with Barry N. Malzberg)

Midway through the cocktail party—another of the dull, pointless affairs Victoria regularly insisted on having—Broome and Cutting went out onto the penthouse terrace to continue their discussion.

It was a warm night, and this high up, fifteen stories above the city pavement, you could not smell the pollution. The air was scented with lilac from the bushes Victoria had planted in boxes all around the stone floor. Drinks in hand, they stood near the wall at the far end and spoke in intense tones.

"We've *got* to go through with a merger," Broome said. "It's a simple matter of survival. Why in hell can't you see that, George?"

"Oh, I see a certain validity in it, all right," Cutting said. He could not hold his liquor very well and was somewhat drunk already. "The point is, I don't like you, Roger. I don't like you at all as a person, and I'd no doubt learn to loathe you as a partner."

"The feeling is mutual," Broome told him acidly. "But it's irrelevant."

"Is it?"

"You know it is. The development of that new type of circuitry back East and the cutbacks in government subsidy have created a buyer's market. Only one company can survive—"

"Exactly," Cutting said. "Mine."

"Don't be a fool. As long as I keep Broome Electronics afloat, you'll keep losing money—and vice versa." Broome spread his hands in a gesture that was half angry, half imploring. "Look, between us we've got the best engineers in the country. Team them up, streamline operations by eliminating unnecessary personnel, equipment and space, and we could start showing considerable profits inside of a year. Profits, man—black ink instead of red."

"I don't like the idea of sharing profits with you."

"No?" Broome studied him for a moment. "I don't see why it should bother you. After all, you haven't seemed to mind sharing Victoria with me these past few months."

Cutting had not expected this. He jerked in surprise, averted his eyes, and took a swallow from his glass. Broome watched him calmly, waiting. Party noises drifted out through the closed terrace doors.

"I don't think that's very funny," Cutting said finally.

"Oh, come on, George," Broome said, "I've known all about it from the beginning."

"You don't know anything. There's nothing to know."

"Have it your way."

Broome shrugged and fell silent, staring out over the lights of the city. He was conscious of Cutting's eyes on him, and he smiled to himself. Cutting was not the kind of man who could endure silence, particularly on a subject as volatile as this one.

Half a minute went by before Cutting said, "Broome—if you suspected something between Victoria and me, why the hell didn't you say so long before this?"

"I saw no point in it. You're not her first lover, you know—not by any stretch of the imagination."

Cutting scowled. "That's a damn lie."

"No, I'm afraid it isn't."

"She's not that kind of woman—"

"She is that kind of woman and a whole lot more. You don't know her like I do, George."

"I still don't believe you."

"All right," Broome said. "Don't."

This time fifteen seconds passed before Cutting spoke. "Why haven't you divorced her if what you say is true?"

"And let her have half my assets? This is a no-fault, community property state, remember. Besides, she enjoys tormenting me, even if she denies it."

"You make her sound like some kind of ..." Cutting let the sentence trail off.

"Some kind of what, George?"

A headshake.

"Well," Broome said, "how about 'predator'? Metaphorically speaking, that's an apt description of Victoria."

Cutting stared at him. His expression told Broome the words had touched a nerve.

"She's got her hooks in you deep by now," Broome said, "and it's costing you plenty. I'll bet you've already tried to end the affair before your wife finds out. But she won't let you do it, will she? Not until she's good and ready to end it herself. That's the way she operates."

Another nerve struck. Cutting passed a hand over his face.

Broome said, "You remember Chuck Ames, don't you?"

"Ames?"

"A young engineer I hired a couple of years ago. He drove his car into a utility pole one night, blind drunk, at seventy miles an hour. Remember now?"

"Yes."

"Why do you think he was drinking so heavily?"

"If you're going to say it was because of Victoria—"

"That's exactly what I'm going to say. Another of her conquests, but weaker and less stable than most of us. He went downhill fast when she dumped him. For all I know he drove into that utility pole on purpose."

Despite the night's warmth, Cutting seemed to shiver. "Why are you telling me this? If you think it's a way to get back at me ..."

"Not at all," Broome said. "I'm telling you for one reason only. The merger. You're holding back on it because of Victoria, that's obvious. She's against a merger for sly reasons of her own, and she's certainly communicated that to you just as she has to me."

Cutting was silent.

"You see how tightly she's got you wrapped up?" Broome said. "Because of her, you're willing to throw away the only hope you have of forestalling a business disaster—"

Broome stopped talking. At the periphery of his vision he saw Victoria approaching from the direction of the terrace doors. He glanced at Cutting, saw the other man stiffen, then returned his gaze to his wife. She wore a blue evening gown, and the pale light from the moon gave her blond hair a frosty tint, put an almost iridescent sheen on her bare shoulders.

"Well," she said, "I thought I might find you both out here. Talking merger again, I suppose."

"Yes," Broome said. "Among other things."

"I still think it's a mistake. Don't you agree, George?"

"I'm not sure," Cutting said without looking at her. She was standing closer to him than to Broome.

"Of course it is," she said. "You two are hardly partnership material." She laughed softly, a sound that made the hairs on Broome's neck prickle. "You have nothing at all in common."

The hell we don't, Broome thought. "A merger is the only answer," he said.

"Nonsense." She moved closer to Cutting, her bare shoulder against his arm.

"It's the only hope for us," Broome insisted, but he was talking to Cutting now. "A matter of survival, pure and simple."

Victoria laughed again.

Broome said, "You do see what I mean, don't you, George?"

"Yes," Cutting sighed, "I see what you mean."

They looked at each other, and then at Victoria standing between them with her back to the terrace wall.

-

The police accepted their explanation that Victoria's fall was a freak accident. There was no reason to believe otherwise; no one inside the apartment had seen or heard anything. If it had been a dull party, it had also been a noisy one.

When the authorities and the shocked guests had gone, Broome poured Cutting and himself a nightcap. "We'll go ahead with the merger on Monday," he said.

"The sooner the better," Cutting agreed solemnly.

They raised their glasses and drank to survival.

DAGO RED

Fog thick as pasta sauce stirred all along the Embarcadero. Headlights crawled through it, made yellow ghost shapes out of the gray coils and threads. Out on the Bay, the foghorns sounded like women moaning in the night.

I went down the alley behind Balducci's Produce. The cobblestones were shiny-wet, empty—it was too early for Paolo to show up with the Packard touring car. There was a doorway in the building on the near side of the alley, catercorner to the one in the produce warehouse. It was deep, full of shadows. You couldn't be seen in there even on a clear night.

I'd been waiting twenty minutes when the touring car turned into the alley behind me. I drew back tight against the wall. Paolo pulled up just beyond the warehouse door, same as he always did, and left the motor running and the lights on. Little puffs of exhaust mixed with the mist. The fog churned, seemed to glow around and in front of the Packard.

The warehouse door opened and Little Jack came out. He had his hand inside his coat, but he wasn't expecting any trouble. He looked around, then made a gesture and Balducci came out. The two of them started for the touring car. I could see them plain in the glowing mist.

I stepped out and shot Little Jack first. It was a clean body shot and he went down fast. Balducci stood frozen for a second or two, his head flopping from side to side. Then he started to run back toward the warehouse door. I put a bullet in his hip just before he got there. As soon as he dropped, the Packard jumped forward and went yawing crazily down the alley into the wall of fog. That was Paolo for you. He didn't have the guts of a rabbit.

Balducci was writhing around on the cobblestones, moaning. Little Jack hadn't moved and never would again. I made sure of that before I stepped over to Balducci. I kicked him in the belly and the groin three or four times. His body jerked into a tight, cramped C and he lay there clutching himself and moaning. I could smell his breath when I leaned forward. It stank of Dago Red. I kicked him in the face, hard, but not hard enough so he'd pass out.

I said, "Two choices, Balducci. You can take it lying down or you can get up on your feet and take it like a man."

He thought he had a third choice. His body straightened out and then he heaved up on his knees and started crying and begging, his words making little spitting bubbles through the blood on his mouth. It made me want to puke. I shot him once in the head to shut him up. Then I leaned down and shot him twice more, left eye, right eye, to make sure.

It was dark in the apartment. Through the big bay window I could make out a couple of streetlamps like eyes in the fog. On a clear night you'd be able to see the lights on Alcatraz out in the Bay. It was a fancy apartment, high up on Russian Hill—thick carpets, expensive furniture. It must've cost Balducci two hundred a month, easy.

A key scraped in the lock and the front door opened. Gina stood there, backlit by the wall sconces in the hallway. "Al? Why've you got the lights off?"

I sat quiet, waiting.

She walked on in, shut the door behind her. "Al?" Then the ceiling globe came on.

I said, "Al's not home."

"Joey!"

"He's not coming home. Not tonight, not ever."

"Oh my God!" Her face was white as milk, her eyes wide, scared.

"You shouldn't've done it, Gina."

"It's not what you think, I—"

"It's just what I think. I know all about it. So does Renzo."

"Joey ... please, you have to listen—"

"Why should I?"

She took a step toward me. Expensive perfume and expensive liquor came off her in waves. She was wearing the sable coat Renzo had given her. She'd dyed her hair a lighter blonde and had it marceled—the light from the ceiling globe made it look varnished. She looked expensive and cheap at the same time, like one of the women in Fat Leona's high-class bawdy house.

"Joey, please ... I couldn't help it, it wasn't my fault. I had to do something, I was going crazy. Renzo ... you think he's a swell guy but he's not. You don't know how mean he can be. He knocks me around, he—"

I said, "You shouldn't have done it," and got up on my feet.

She saw the gun for the first time and said, "Oh God, no, you can't, you wouldn't!" in a low moany voice. "Not you, not you!"

"You shouldn'eve done it, Gina."

She sucked in air and her red mouth opened wide.

I stopped her before she could start screaming. One clean shot was all it took.

The fog was even thicker down by Islais Creek. I had to grope my way around to the back of the Bay Area Distributors warehouse. The third time I knocked on the door, the peephole slid back and Mac looked out. He said,

"Hey, Joey, you're late. Where you been?" He didn't know about Balducci and Gina. Nobody knew except Renzo and me.

"Things to do," I said. "Hurry up, it's cold out here."

The locks rattled and he let me in. He had a Thompson gun in the crook of his left arm. Guido and Tony and a bunch of others were grouped around the big canvas-sided trucks, a Graham and two new Macks they'd brought over from Friendly's Garage. Some of them had choppers, too. A ship was down from Canada, anchored beyond the three-mile limit off the Sonoma County coast, and we had a two A.M. meet with the fishing boats that ran the whiskey in to one of the beaches south of Bodega Bay. We'd haul the cases back here in the trucks, get them ready for distribution. The fix was in with the county sheriff and the city coppers. We never had any trouble with them. You always had to worry about the Feds, but Balducci's crowd was the reason for all the extra heat.

I said to Mac, "Where's Renzo?"

"Waiting upstairs."

The stairs were at the far wall, the only break in the stacks of wine barrels, sacks of sugar, crates of jackass brandy and bonded Canadian hooch. You could smell the wine in there. It was good, pre-Prohibition Burgundy from the counties up north, but it still smelled sour to me—no better than Dago Red. You couldn't smell it from outside. The walls were thick concrete with wood facing. The place was like a fortress.

Renzo was behind the desk in his office. He had a glass of whiskey in one hand, a Toscanelli stogie in the other. He didn't look good. His long face was white, sweaty, and his eyes had a funny glass shine when he looked up at me. Like a dead man's eyes.

I said, "It's done."

"Both of them?"

"Both of them."

Renzo said, "Christ," and sucked hard on his Toscanelli. He was always smoking those stinking tule roots. I couldn't stand them myself. You had to drag hard just to get smoke from one end to the other and you couldn't get enough to inhale.

I said, "What time do we move out tonight?"

"Midnight. You don't need to go along."

"I don't mind. I'll ride shotgun with Guido in the Graham."

He gave me a long look. Then he got up and wandered around and stopped at the back wall, stood staring at the calendar hanging there. It was a San Francisco Chamber of Commerce calendar, with a picture of Cliff House and February 1930 showing.

He said, "How bad was it?" softly.

"Gina? Not as bad as I thought it'd be."

"You did it quick? She didn't suffer?"

"No."

"Balducci?"

"Not so quick. He took it on his knees, begging."

"Yeah? Begging? Good."

"Little Jack's dead too."

Renzo said, "That don't break my heart," and came back to his desk sucking on that tule root. He still looked sick. He tossed off what was left in his glass, poured it half full again. "Pour yourself one, Joey."

I got a glass, splashed in two fingers, tasted it. Canadian Club. Nothing but the best for Renzo. I took the glass over to where the calendar hung, tore off the February page. Today's date was Thursday, March 5. He never did pay any attention to little things like that.

"Christ, I wish it hadn't had to be like this," he said. "I loved her. You know that, Joey."

"Sure, I know it."

"A lush, a *scopona*. A traitor. Doublecrossing me with Balducci, that was bad enough. But those hijacks down the Peninsula, up north ... how'd Balducci know where to jump the trucks if he didn't get it from Gina? Nobody else knew, just you and me—not even Guido and Mac, the last time. It had to be Gina. In bed, bed talk. He screws her, then he screws us."

"Not any more."

"No, by Christ, not any more. *Noi sono levato Balducci nostro coglioni, eh?*"

"*Si. Per sempre.*"

Renzo swallowed more Canadian Club, fast, as if it was water. "She was like a bad barrel of wine," he said. Soft again, almost like he was talking to himself. "Fine Burgundy, young, sweet, then all of a sudden she went bad. Like maybe a bung worked loose in her head, too much air got in."

He'd said all of this before, last night. But if he wanted to say it again, that was all right with me.

"We had to do it," he said. "She might've gone to the Feds when she heard about Balducci. We had to do it, Joey."

"That's right. We didn't have any choice."

"I wish it could've been somebody besides you, but who else could I trust to do it right, Balducci and her both?"

"There wasn't anybody else," I said. "Just me."

The old lady was in the kitchen, drinking wine and reading the Bible, when I came into the house in North Beach. She'd been crying. Wet glistened like little rivers in the seams and lines of her face.

"You hear, Guiseppe? You know about poor Gina?"

"I heard."

"*Atroce!* Somebody kill her, shoot her like a dog. Why, why?"

"Maybe she doublecrossed somebody."

"Bah!" She made the sign of the cross. "Poor Gina, she's a nice girl, she never hurt nobody."

"She hurt plenty of people," I said.

"I don't believe it, not my Gina. What'sa matter with you? No tears, no sadness in your face. You don't care she's gone, she's killed? Your little sister?"

"She was no good, Mama."

The old bitch gave me the evil eye. She said, *"Silenzio! Tu parla pisciano legalline!"* and reached for the wine bottle. Dago Red. All she ever drinks is that goddamn Dago Red.

WHY DID YOU DO IT?

"Why did you do it?"

That question has been asked of me more times than I can count. The first person to ask it was the detective lieutenant who interrogated me at police headquarters, hours after I was arrested during the commission of my eighth holdup. He was a large, ponderous man with a keenly inquisitive manner.

"You've been cooperative and forthcoming, Mr. Barella," he said when I had made a full confession. "Except for one significant detail. You admit to eight armed robberies in less than three months, seven completed and one attempted, but you have yet to reveal what set you off on such a foolishly dangerous crime spree. Why did you do it?"

I avoided the question by saying, "I harmed no one at any time, and made no attempt to resist the arresting officers. You have the pistol I carried, you know it was unloaded and has a broken firing pin."

"Your victims didn't know it," he said. "And one of them might have had a loaded weapon and shot *you*."

"But none did."

"The point is, armed robbery is a Class A felony—eight separate Class A felonies in your case, the combination of which carries a stiff legal penalty. You do understand that?"

"Yes, I understand."

"From all indications you were a model citizen until three months ago. No police record, not even so much as a ticket for jaywalking. You're obviously an intelligent man, an educated man. So I ask you again: why did you do it? What turned a seventy-two-year-old retired librarian into the semi-notorious Graybeard Bandit?"

"Does it really matter?"

"It might, if it's relevant. It does to me in any case."

"I had my reasons," I said.

"What reasons?"

"I would rather not say."

"No? Why not?"

"They're personal and private."

"Was it because of your circumstances?" he persisted. "The fact that you've been living just above poverty level in a two-room apartment with no income other than minimum social security?"

"It didn't take you long to find that out," I said mildly.

"No, it didn't. We're very quick and very thorough in cases like yours.

Well? Is indigence why you chose to become a serial armed robber?"

"I would rather not say."

"Stubborn, aren't you, Mr. Barella?"

"On this particular issue, yes, I am."

He was silent for a time—ruminating, evidently. At length he said, "It wasn't just for the money, was it? I don't see how it could have been. You only robbed convenience stores and small neighborhood businesses, only netted a little more than a thousand dollars total from the first seven thefts. You could have gotten that much by holding up just one bank or savings and loan."

"I suppose I could have."

"Then why didn't you? Why eight small businesses for minor sums instead?"

"I would rather not say."

"Utilizing the same M.O. eight straight times with only a minimal attempt at disguise is about as high risk as it gets. You didn't think you could go on doing it indefinitely, did you? You must have known you'd be caught sooner or later."

"I suppose I did."

"And it didn't bother you? You didn't care?"

"I cared. Of course I cared."

"Yet you kept right on doing it. Was it because you wanted to be caught?"

"'Stop me before I rob again'? No, Lieutenant, it wasn't like that at all."

"What was it like?"

"I would rather not say."

He made an exasperated noise. "I don't understand why you won't come clean. It might go easier on you if you do."

"I have come clean," I said. "I've given you a full confession."

"Excluding even a partial answer to the question of why."

"Excluding that, yes."

There was another brief silence. "All right, let's try a different tack. We found what appears to be the aggregate amount of money you stole, one thousand and seventy-nine dollars, hidden in your apartment. What were you planning to do with it?"

"I wasn't planning to do anything with it."

"Why didn't you spend any of it?"

"I did. A few dollars for necessities."

"Why only a few dollars? Why not more?"

"I would rather not say."

"For personal and private reasons," he said with heavy sarcasm.

"That's correct."

"Have you confided to anyone what those reasons are? Relatives, friends?"

"No. I have no family. My wife passed away four years ago, we were childless, and neither of us has any living relatives."

"Friends, then?"

"What few friends I had have either died or moved away."

"So you were not only living a poor life but a lonely one," the lieutenant said. "Is that why you committed those robberies, Mr. Barella? Because you were starved for attention as well as money?"

"No."

"A desire for notoriety?"

"No."

"Excitement, the thrill of danger?"

"No."

"A bucket list thing, maybe? Breaking the law something you'd always secretly wanted to do?"

"No. You're grasping at straws, Lieutenant."

"How about sudden uncontrollable urges?"

"If you're implying that I'm not in my right mind," I said, "you're mistaken. I may be seventy-two, but my mental acuity is undiminished. I am in full possession of my faculties."

"If that's true, then each of the robberies must have been premeditated."

"Yes, I admit I planned them in advance. And carried them out without a hitch until today."

He leaned forward to stare into my eyes. "One more time, Mr. Barella. Why did you do it? *Why?*"

"I'm not going to tell you," I said, matching his stare with an unblinking one of my own, "so you may as well stop asking …"

The lieutenant did stop asking eventually, but others posed the question at every opportunity. The judges at my arraignment and my trial, my court-appointed public defender, the two psychiatrists who examined me, the newspaper reporter who had dubbed me the Graybeard Bandit, several individuals who shared my incarceration. I stonewalled all of them, too, in the same fashion.

My lawyer tried to convince me to plead diminished capacity at my trial, but I refused to allow it. I was guilty as charged of eight counts of armed robbery, and once I was pronounced mentally sound by the head doctors, I insisted that guilty be my plea. Nor would I agree to testify on my own behalf, or allow him to make a case for leniency with the trial judge after the jury convicted me. As prescribed by law, I was sentenced to prison for my crimes—a sentence of twenty years, which at my age is a life sentence. Naturally, given the extenuating circumstances, the institution to which

I was remanded was Sandhurst Prison, this state's only minimum security lockup.

I have been here over a year now. My cell is quite comfortable, the grounds well suited to exercise, the food not at all bad, the health care adequate, and there are a well-stocked library which I oversee, television privileges, and weekly films. I have made several friends among the other inmates, for Nicholas Barella, the Graybeard Bandit who steadfastly refuses to divulge to anyone his motive for committing eight robberies at the age of 72, is accorded a not inconsiderable amount of respect by the prison populace.

Yes, Sandhurst is everything I expected, everything my careful pre-crime spree research indicated it was. A poor, elderly man of modest needs could not ask for a more satisfactory place to spend his remaining years.

And that is the answer, you see.

That is why I did it.

BOMB SCARE
A "Nameless Detective" Story

He was a hypertensive little man with overlarge ears and buck teeth—Brer Rabbit dressed up in a threadbare brown suit and sunglasses. In his left hand he carried a briefcase with a broken catch; it was held closed by a frayed strap that looked as though it might pop loose at any second. And inside the briefcase—

"A bomb," he kept announcing in a shrill voice. "I've got a remote-controlled bomb in here. Do what I tell you, don't come near me, or I'll blow us all up."

Nobody in the branch office of the San Francisco Trust Bank was anywhere near him. Lawrence Metaxa, the manager, and the other bank employees were frozen behind the row of tellers' cages. The four customers, me included, stood in a cluster out front. None of us was doing anything except waiting tensely for the little rabbit to quit hopping around and get down to business.

It took him another few seconds. Then, with his free hand, he dragged a cloth sack from his coat and threw it at one of the tellers. "Put all the money in there. Stay away from the silent alarm or I'll set off the bomb, I mean it."

Metaxa assured him in a shaky voice that they would do whatever he asked.

"Hurry up, then." The rabbit waved his empty right hand in the air, jerkily, as if he were directing some sort of mad symphony. "Hurry up, hurry up!"

The tellers got busy. While they hurriedly emptied cash drawers, the little man produced a second cloth sack and moved in my direction. The other customers shrank back. I stayed where I was, so he pitched the sack to me.

"Put your wallet in there," he said in a voice like glass cracking. "All your valuables. Then get everybody else's."

I said, "I don't think so."

"What? What?" He hopped on one foot, then the other, making the briefcase dance. "What's the matter with you? Do what I told you!"

When he'd first come in and started yelling about his bomb, I'd thought that I couldn't have picked a worse time to take care of my bank deposits. Now I was thinking that I couldn't have picked a better time. I took a measured step toward him. Somebody behind me gasped. I took another step.

"Stay back!" the little guy shouted. "I'll push the button, I'll blow us up!"

I said, "No, you won't," and rushed him and yanked the briefcase out of his hand.

More gasps, a cry, the sounds of customers and employees scrambling for cover. But nothing happened, except that the little guy tried to run away. I caught him by the collar and dragged him back. His struggles were brief and half-hearted; he'd gambled and lost and he knew when he was licked.

Scared faces peered over counters and around corners. I held the briefcase up so they could all see it. "No bomb in here, folks. You can relax now, it's all over."

It took a couple of minutes to restore order, during which time I marched the little man around to Metaxa's desk and pushed him into a chair. He sat slumped, twitching and muttering. "Lost my job, so many debts ... must've been crazy to do a thing like this—I'm sorry, I'm sorry...." Poor little rabbit. He wasn't half as sorry now as he was going to be later.

I opened the case while Metaxa called the police. The only thing inside was a city telephone directory for weight.

When Metaxa hung up he said to me, "You took a crazy risk, grabbing the briefcase like that. If he really had had a bomb in there ..."

"I knew he didn't."

"*Knew* he didn't? How could you?"

"I'm a detective, remember? Three reasons. One: Bombs are delicate mechanisms and people who build them are cautious by necessity. They don't put explosives in a cheap case with a busted catch and just a frayed strap holding it together, not unless they're suicidal. Two: He claimed it was remote-controlled. But the hand he kept waving was empty and all he had in the other one was the case. Where was the remote control? In one of his pockets, where he couldn't get at it easily? No. A real bomber would've had it out in plain sight to back up his threat."

"Still," Metaxa said, "you *could've* been wrong on both counts. Neither is an absolute certainty."

"No, but the third reason is as close to one as you can get."

"Yes?"

"It takes more than just skill to make a bomb. It takes nerve, coolness, patience, and a very steady hand. Look at our friend here. He doesn't have any of those attributes; he's the chronically nervous type, as jumpy as six cats. He could no more manufacture an explosive device than you or I could fly. If he'd ever tried, he'd have blown himself up in two minutes flat."

WHAT KIND OF PERSON ARE YOU?
(with Barry N. Malzberg)

I arrived at Quality Supermarkets' Fairfield branch promptly at nine o'clock Monday morning and went immediately into the office to check the weekend receipts. A roving district manager with twelve stores and nearly one hundred employees to monitor cannot afford to waste time; I work on a very tight schedule.

At 9:40 I stood and walked into the store proper, to where Franklin was working at Register Three, his regular post. I waited until he finished serving a customer and then motioned for him to close down and join me. When he had done that, I took him back into the office and told him to sit down.

He sat poised on the edge of the chair, hands picking nervously at each other; he was about twenty-four, red-haired and gangly, and he reminded me somewhat of my son Ronald. I did not say anything for a time, watching him. He fidgeted under my scrutiny, eyes meeting mine, flicking away, flicking back. But he always seemed to be nervous in my presence; I had a reputation as a stern and uncompromising supervisor.

"I'll get directly to the point, Franklin," I said. "I have just been over the weekend receipts and register slips, and you're seventy dollars short—fifty on Saturday and twenty on Sunday."

His eyes grew wide and his face paled. "Seventy dollars?" he said.

"Exactly seventy dollars. That is a considerable amount, as I'm sure you realize."

"Are you certain, Mr. Adams? I mean, couldn't you have made a mistake..."

"I do not make mistakes," I said. "The mistake here, if that is what it is, rests squarely on your shoulders."

"I ... I don't know what to say. I've never been short before, I'm always careful—"

"Indeed?"

"I haven't been off a penny in the two months I've been working here. You know that, sir."

"I do know it, yes, but the fact remains that you are seventy dollars short for this past weekend—exactly seventy dollars, not a cent more or less. The question now, Franklin, is what kind of person are you?"

"Sir?"

"What kind of person are you?" I repeated. "An honest and fallible one, whose only crime is making careless errors? Or a foolish and culpable one who succumbed to the obvious temptation?"

His mouth opened, as though in shock, and he blinked several times. "Mr. Adams, you don't think I *stole* that money?"

"Did you?"

"No. No!"

I held up a hand. "I am not accusing you of anything, I am merely trying to ascertain the truth of the situation here."

"I'm not a thief," he said. "I don't know how I could have made mistakes like that but that's all it was—mistakes."

"I would like to believe that."

"You've *got* to believe it," he said. "It's the truth."

"Embezzlement of even a small amount is a serious offense, you know. I could have you arrested."

"Please, Mr. Adams—I swear I didn't steal that money!"

I picked up my pencil and tapped the eraser on the sheaf of papers spread out in front of me. "Have you ever been in trouble before? Any kind of trouble?"

"No, sir, never. Never."

"Very well, then. I am not a harsh man, and I have a son about your age; I see no reason not to give you the benefit of the doubt, in view of your prior work record. If you're willing to replace the seventy dollars, and assuming something like this does not happen again, I am willing to drop the matter entirely."

Relief made him slump on the chair. "I'll replace the money, sure," he said, "I know I'm responsible for it. I don't have as much as seventy dollars on me right now, but I can borrow it from my father and have it tomorrow—"

"It won't be necessary to involve your father," I said. "Do you have ten dollars?"

"Ten? Yes, I think so."

"I will accept that now and ten dollars per week for the next six weeks, assuming again that there are no further shortages and you continue to do your job properly."

"Oh, I will," he said, "I'll be extra careful. It'll never happen again, I promise you that."

"For your sake, see that you keep that promise."

He wasted no time producing his wallet. I took the ten-dollar bill he handed me and laid it on the desk. "You can go back to work now," I told him.

"Yes sir. Thank you, Mr. Adams."

When he was gone I sat for a moment looking at the branch's financial records. Then I finished my work, put Franklin's ten-dollar bill into my own wallet, and left the store to continue my rounds.

I arrived at the Essex branch at precisely noon and spent an hour checking the weekend receipts. At 12:50 I went out into the store proper and brought Trowbridge—another young man in his early twenties, tall and thin like Ronald—back to the office and told him to sit down.

"I have just been going over the weekend receipts," I said, "and you are seventy dollars short—fifty on Saturday and twenty on Sunday."

He stared at me incredulously.

"The question now is," I said, "what kind of person are you?"

At 8:00 the following Friday night, I arrived at the Dunes Motel on the outskirts of the city, knocked on the door of Unit 6, and was admitted.

"Right on time," Cobb said.

"I am always punctual." I opened my wallet and laid two hundred and fifty dollars on the bed.

He picked it up and counted it, twice. "Okay, Adams," he said. "That takes care of the first installment. Six more weeks and Ronnie and I will be square." He chuckled. "Unless he decides to borrow another thousand to pay off some more gambling debts."

"Ronald will never borrow another dime from you," I said, "I'll see to that. And he is not gambling any more."

Cobb smiled wisely. "Sure—whatever you say. Just make sure you're here with the second installment next Friday. I'd hate to have to send one of my boys out to pay Ronnie a visit."

A sudden rush of anger made me clench my fists. "What kind of person are you to prey on decent people this way? What kind of *monster* are you?"

Cobb's laughter rang in my ears all the way out to the car and all the way home to my son.

THE WIND

I don't know why I'm writing this.

It wasn't a conscious decision. Nor even a sudden whim. I was sitting in front of the fire in the living room, drinking 40-year-old scotch and trying not to listen to the wind. The next thing I knew I was here in the study, with the computer booted up and my fingers on the keyboard.

The wind is gale-force strong tonight, much worse than we usually get up here on the hilltop. A wild wind full of moans, wails, banshee screeches. It lashes the nearby trees, scrapes branches against the walls of the house. As large as this goddamn mansion is, as well built and well insulated, you'd think it would lessen the noise and keep the heavier gusts from shivering the glass in the windows. But it doesn't. I've been on edge ever since the blow began.

It might not be so bad if Moira hadn't gone to L.A. for the weekend with her sister, if the servants didn't have the night off, if I weren't alone in the house. I thought about inviting Marty or Jack or Terence to come over and share the scotch, but I don't want company badly enough to endure business discussions and small talk. I thought about going out somewhere, but where would I go? You can't outrun the elements.

The wind has never been this hellish bad, this disturbing. And it shows no signs of letting up. It'll go on raging and hammering for hours, probably all night. Won't let me sleep. Won't give me any peace.

Won't let me stop thinking about Pat, reliving that terrible night on the cliff at Anchor Bay.

Howling wind up there too that night as we walked along the path, the sudden gust that caused her to lose her balance. Her hand pulling free of mine when she stumbled sideways, her voice crying "Tommy!" as the sandstone crumbled under her feet. I couldn't catch hold of her, couldn't keep her from toppling over the edge and plunging to the ocean rocks below. Couldn't save her. Couldn't save her.

I still hear her screaming.

Damn that wind! The noises it's making now are replicas of Pat's screams.

Stuff earplugs or cotton in your ears, Hughes. No, I tried that before, it doesn't work. Just have to endure it.

Another drink, that's what I need. How many scotches have I already had? Four, five? But I barely feel them. I doubt I could get drunk tonight if I wanted to. It wouldn't help anyway. Even if I drank enough to pass out, this devil wind would still be blowing when I woke up.

Went to pour another scotch, and when I came back with it I read what I wrote before. Babblings. Why? What's the point? I don't know but I can't seem to stop doing it. Doesn't matter. No one will ever read it. Once this compulsion or whatever it is has run its course I'll hit the delete key.

Another moan, another wail, another scream.

Pat. Falling.

No, dammit, think about something else. Think about the rise of Thomas Hughes, the realization of the long sought objective. Write about that if you have to keep on writing.

The early struggles. Growing up poor in San Jose, never having decent clothes, a decent car, any of the things other kids took for granted. The burning need to be somebody people looked up to instead of down on. Good at building things, good in math and science, analytical, detail-oriented, all the necessary qualities for a career as a mechanical engineer. More struggles toward that end. The series of menial jobs to pay my way through college. The mostly average grades no matter how hard I studied. Made it through, earned the engineering degree, but what did it get me after graduation? Just the entry level job in Montgomery Polymer's mechanical design and prototyping department.

Worked my ass off there and all that got me was one rung up the corporate ladder in two years, a second rung after another three. Climbing too slow to ever reach the executive level and a six-figure salary. Highest I could hope for if I stayed with Montgomery Polymer were Design Manager at forty, Assistant Engineer at fifty, and no guarantee I'd have either one. Applied for positions with other plastics companies, put out feelers, cultivated connections—no takers, no luck. Still working long hours for too little money at MP when I met Pat.

Not the sort of woman I yearned to have a lasting relationship with. Newly hired secretary in the company's sales department, same sort of poor blue-collar background as mine. But the attraction was immediate, undeniable. Just physical, I thought, but it was more than that for both of us. Marriage? No way, only there we were in front of a justice of the peace after three months. And for the most part we were good together. Compatible in bed and most other ways. Not a harsh word between us in two years of budgeted living on our combined salaries. Satisfaction enough for Pat but not for me. I still craved money, position, respect, the kind of life I'd dreamed of. The prospect of never having them was like an inflammation that wouldn't heal—

Enough. That's enough. What's the matter with me? Why don't I just delete this crap, have another scotch, crawl into bed with a pillow over my head?

Sudden loud banging noise. That last gust must have been fierce enough to rip one of the shutters loose upstairs. As if the wind were trying to invade the house. As if it were trying to get at me.

Stupid notion. Go up and close the shutter, lock it down. No, the hell with it. Why bother? Shutting the shutter won't shut out the wind or muffle the screams.

I'm not sorry Moira went to L.A. I couldn't talk to her about the wind if she were here, she wouldn't understand, she'd ridicule me for being childish. Insensitive woman. Self-indulgent. Always going off somewhere with her sister, her friends, by herself—clubs, meetings, charity events, parties, gallery openings. Marriage to her isn't anything like I thought it would be. She's tight-fisted, she orders me around in public, she questions every decision I make here and at the factory. We don't communicate about anything meaningful, we don't laugh, we have sex two or three times a month and she's never more than lukewarm. We're more like strangers than husband and wife.

I wish now I'd never met Moira Henderson, unmarried daughter of the late founder of West Coast Plastics. I wish she hadn't been so obviously attracted to me at the industry conference in Chicago. I wish to God I was still with Pat.

Pat.

I remember that night at Anchor Bay as clearly as if it happened yesterday, not five years ago. Her reluctance to leave the rented cottage, only doing it as a favor to me. The walk along the clifftop path close to the edge. The gust that made her stumble off balance. Her hand pulling loose from mine, the sandstone crumbling, her body toppling sideways. Her voice crying my name in the instant before she fell.

Crying "Tommy, why?"

No. Just my name—

"Tommy, *why?*"

Stop pretending, damn you, stop lying! You've told and retold the lie for so long you almost made yourself believe it. Almost. Face the truth, admit the truth. Pat wasn't blown off balance, she didn't stumble, her hand didn't pull loose from yours. You let go of her hand and then you pushed her.

You pushed her over the edge.

You murdered the only person you ever really loved.

Thomas Hughes, conniving opportunist. Tommy Hughes, murderer.

I'm sorry, Pat. I'm so sorry!

The wind, screaming. Pat, screaming.

The wind—

"I have felt the wind of the wing of madness pass over me."

Baudelaire. Quote read in a college class and lodged in my memory. Why should I remember it now, type it out? I'm not mad.

Or am I? Maybe I am.

Thrust over the edge, falling as Pat fell.

Confession. That's what I've been writing here, a long overdue confession. Oh, but it's something else too. I understand that now, I know why I was compelled to sit down here, I know what this really is.

The wind. And the gun in the desk drawer.

Delete delete—

Save.

Print.

Tommy Hughes, murderer, logging out.

SUCH THINGS AS NIGHTMARES ARE MADE OF

Dark place, warm, safe. Sleeping.
Not sleeping anymore. Listening.
Noises outside. Loud, weird.
Thump. Grunt, slurp, crunch.
Something's out there.
Something ... terrible.
Grunt. Crunch.
Stay here, stay safe, don't get up.
No. I have to find out what it is—
Dark place, cold. Walking.
Long hallway, shadows crawling on the walls, faint glow from someplace that lets me see where I'm going. Cold floor beneath my bare feet, as if it's made of ice. Shivering as I walk straight on, then turn right, turn left—
Door ahead, closed. The noises come from behind it outside—thump, slurp, grunt, crunch. I keep walking toward the door. I can't stop.
Closer.
Close.
I reach out for the knob, touch it, start to turn it.
No!
Predator out there.
And what it's doing—
Crunch, slurp, crunch.
It's feeding!
It wants to eat me next!

"Does the dream, the nightmare always end there, Mr. Lubeck? Or is there more to it?"

"There's more, I think, but I don't know for sure. I wake up at the same point every time."

"Then your dream self never opens the door?"

"No. Never."

"What sort of predator do you suppose it is?"

"I have no idea. I'm terrified of finding out."

"You're convinced that it will devour your dream self if you open the door?"

"Yes. Feed on me. Yes."

"How often do you have this dream?"

"Not often until recently. Now … almost every night."

"When did it first begin?"

"A long time ago. Twenty years or more."

"In your childhood."

"Yes. When I was nine or ten."

"A product of childhood terrors, perhaps. The bogeyman, the monster under the bed or in the closet. Such things as nightmares are made of."

"I never had those kind of fears when I was a kid."

"Every child has some sort of fear. Surely there was something that frightened you. The dark, for instance. The unknown. Images in horror films, comic books, video games."

"None of that. I dislike violence and I'm not an imaginative man."

"Hurtful conflicts with parents, siblings?"

"No. I had no problems with any member of my family."

"School mates, bullies? Teachers, other adults?"

"No conflict with anyone."

"Have you any idea of what precipitated the dream?"

"None. It just came one night and kept on coming. Well … I did see a wild dog kill and eat a rabbit, but I think that was after the dream started."

"But you're not positive?"

"Not absolutely positive, no."

"Such an experience can be traumatizing. How did it affect you?"

"It was upsetting at the time, but that's all. I wasn't haunted by it or made afraid of dogs, nothing like that. My only fear then and now is the dream, the nightmare. And that it isn't—"

"Yes, Mr. Lubeck?"

"Isn't just a nightmare. That it might actually happen someday. A premonition that …"

"You will be devoured by some sort of beast."

"If I let my guard down, yes."

"Have you had this fear from the dream's inception?"

"No, not until recently, when I began having it more and more often."

"Surely you understand that monsters are products of the mind, not the real world."

"Of course I do. I know how delusional, how paranoid the fear sounds, but I can't rid myself of it. It gets stronger, more terrifying every time I have the dream. I can't cope with it any longer. You have to help me, Doctor Pruett."

"Have you sought psychiatric help before?"

"No. You're the first I've consulted."

"… I see from your personal information sheet that you're divorced and have no children, and that you reside on Pinecrest Road. In a private house, I presume?"

"Yes."

"How long have you lived there?"

"Eight years."

"Do you live alone?"

"Since the divorce last year, yes."

"Pinecrest Road, if memory serves, is located in a wooded, somewhat isolated area on the outer edge of the city. Correct?"

"More or less. There are neighbors not far away."

"Do the woods harbor predators? Bears? Wild dogs?"

"Not that I'm aware of. But ... there *could* be something there."

"Yet you continue to live in such surroundings. Your profession is systems analyst and you work from home; you could just as easily live in an apartment in the middle of the city."

"I could, but I won't be driven from my home by fear, irrational or otherwise. I refuse to give in to it."

"Very good. Such attitude underscores your determination to overcome your anxieties."

"How do we accomplish that?"

"By establishing a means, such as identifying the source of both dream and delusion, that will allow you to face them for exactly what they are. Confronting one's fears, Mr. Lubeck, is the only certain method of banishing them."

Dark place, warm, safe. Sleeping.
Not sleeping anymore. Listening.
Noises outside. Loud, weird.
Thump. Grunt, slurp, crunch.
Something's out there.
Something ... terrible.
Grunt. Crunch.
Stay here, stay safe, don't get up.
No. I have to find out what it is—
Dark place, cold. Walking.
Long hallway, shadows crawling on the walls, faint glow from someplace that lets me see where I'm going. Cold floor beneath my bare feet, as if it's made of ice. Shivering as I walk straight on, then turn right, turn left—
Door ahead, closed. The noises come from behind it outside—thump, slurp, grunt, crunch. I keep walking toward the door. I can't stop.
Closer.
Close.

I reach out for the knob, touch it, start to turn it.
No!
Predator out there.
And what it's doing—
Crunch, slurp, crunch.
It's feeding!
It wants to eat me next!
Don't open the door, don't let it in!

In my mind's eye I see what will happen if I do. I see it rise up from the carcass of whatever it's feeding on, I see its open mouth and yellow-spike teeth dripping crimson, I see it leap forward and rush in. I see myself down on all fours trying to crawl back into the dark place, trying to make myself smaller, squirming like a worm into a hole.

But the thing has hold of me now, clutching my arm, yanking me upward. I feel pain erupt, then wild panic as it drags me close and shakes me so hard my teeth rattle like bones. I smell the hot stink of its breath as it shakes me harder, and then it—

—rips my arm off and hurls it on the floor—

—and rips my head off and hurls it on the floor—

—and my head rolls into the wall, wobbles and stops, and my eyes stare up, stare up—

—and in horror I watch my headless body being stuffed inside the red gaping mouth—

"So you did not open the door. Your dream self imagined that the beast burst in and attacked you."

"Saw it happen in my mind's eye, yes."

"A dream within the dream. For the first time."

"But will it be the last."

"Perhaps not. Describe the imaginary creature."

"I told you ... red gaping mouth, sharp yellow-spike teeth."

"Its size and shape? Claws, fur, scales? Demonic eyes?"

"I ... don't remember. I didn't see it clearly."

"It must have been large and quite powerful to have handled you as it did, torn off your arms and head."

"Powerful. Savage."

"How would you classify your reaction to the experience?"

"Classify? I don't—"

"How terrifying was this dream compared to the previous ones?"

"Well, I didn't wake up screaming. Or hyperventilate."

"So it was not substantially more frightening."

"It should have been, but ... no, it wasn't."

"Would you say that indicates a certain detachment? Psychological detachment, that is. No pun intended."

"I don't know what you mean."

"Your dream self imagined the attack rather than experiencing it directly. Observed your head being torn off, thrown to the floor and wobbling into a corner from where you watched your body being devoured. There is an element of macabre humor in such a lurid fantasy, wouldn't you agree?"

"There's nothing funny in having your head ripped off."

"Of course not. But the perceptions and distortions of the subconscious mind are sometimes quite revealing. Instead of opening the door, your dream self imagined what might be termed a *reductio ad absurdum* confrontation. What does that suggest?"

"I don't know. What?"

"That our sessions are beginning to have the desired effect. The dream is lengthening, evolving—an indication that your subconscious is coming to terms with the reality delusion, preparing you to consciously reject it. Bringing you to the crisis point, in a subsequent dream, where the confrontation will be direct and rational."

"Crisis point. You mean …"

"Yes. To complete the rejection, Mr. Lubeck, you must open the door."

Dark place, warm, safe. Sleeping.
Not sleeping anymore. Listening.
Noises outside. Loud, weird.
Thump. Grunt, slurp, crunch.
Something's out there.
Something … terrible.
Stay here, stay safe, don't move.
No. I have to find out—
Dark place, cold. Walking.
Long hallway, shadows crawling on the walls, faint glow from the nightlight that lets me see where I'm going. Cold floor beneath my bare feet, as if it's made of ice. Shivering as I walk straight on, then turn right, turn left into the kitchen—
Back door ahead, closed, locked. The noises come from behind it outside.
Stop! Wake up! Wake up!
I am awake. Not dreaming this time. Living the dream.
I keep walking toward the door. I can't stop.
Closer.
Close.
I reach out for the knob, touch it, start to unlock it.

No! Predator out there. Feeding.

Nothing out there. Delusion, paranoid fantasy. Such things as nightmares are made of.

No, it's there, it's real. The premonition coming true—

Monsters dwell in the mind, not the real world.

Listen. Listen. *Something* is making those feeding sounds.

Animal, just a harmless animal.

Not harmless. Too loud, too violent. Something big, savage, with a gaping red mouth and yellow-spike teeth—

No. Confront the fear, reject it, banish it once and for all.

I take a deep shuddery breath.

And then I open the door—

Thump. Thump. Grunt, slurp, crunch crunch crunch.

A MATTER Of JUSTICE
(with Barry N. Malzberg)

Computer-typed letter dated March 11, 2008, and signed by James B. Darnell:

TO WHOM IT MAY CONCERN:

I killed a man tonight.

It was a willful and premeditated act. I waited outside his house in the Fairview section of the city, hidden behind a hedge, and when he came home late, as was his custom, I stepped out and pressed the barrel of my .22 caliber revolver against his temple. I told him why he was about to die and then I shot him. No one saw me. The police have no reason to suspect me. Perhaps they think it was a domestic crime, or a botched robbery attempt, or a random act of violence—in any case, a cold-blooded murder. But it was no such thing.

It was a matter of justice.

Please don't misunderstand me. I did not commit this act rashly, nor do I make these statements lightly. I am not a murderer, even though I have taken a human life. On the contrary, I am a man with a highly developed moral sense, a man who has lived righteously for all of my thirty-seven years. Until last night I had never knowingly broken the law, nor raised a hand against another person. I believe in the basic sanctity of life. Why, then, did I kill this man?

I did it because he deserved to die.

I did it because if I hadn't, he would have gone unpunished for an unconscionable—a capital—offense.

I did it because he killed my wife.

A willful and premeditated act, yes, but in the same sense that a state-sanctioned execution is a willful and premeditated act. I was his executioner, no more than that. For I also believe in the biblical precept of an eye for an eye. A capital offense must be paid for by capital punishment.

His name was Marvin Peterson. An innocuous name for a seemingly innocuous individual. He was a pharmacist, an honorable profession for a dishonorable man, employed by one of the large chain drugstores. I knew him slightly from the not infrequent visits Caroline and I made to Consolidated Drugs, where he was employed—just well enough so that the three of us were on a first-name basis. Caroline suffered from heart trouble and hypertension and I have a thyroid condition, both of which required prescribed medication renewable on a monthly basis. We also did other shopping at the drugstore. On the average, one or both of us had occasion to go there perhaps once a week.

This frequency increased as Caroline's heart condition gradually worsened. She had always been somewhat frail and prone to physical ailments, which she bore without undue complaint—she was a good wife, if a little too placid, dramatic, and intellectually weak. She'd had a serious arrhythmia for many years and it had led to congestive heart failure, which, her doctor told her, needed to be carefully controlled with medication. In conjunction with other meds, he prescribed enalapril for treatment of her high blood pressure, in 5mg tablets to be taken twice daily—though she preferred to take them both at once with her morning coffee, as she did with most of her medications. Naturally she had the prescription filled at Consolidated Drugs. By Marvin Peterson. He attended to it with evident care, as he had all of our prior prescriptions, until the fourth refill, one week ago.

On that occasion he was not careful, he was criminally, unpardonably negligent. Instead of enalapril, he somehow managed to substitute Armour Thyroid, the drug I take in a 60mg daily dosage to replace my thyroid hormone. Enalapril and Armour Thyroid are both round and similar in size, though of very subtly different shades of white. Caroline hadn't noticed the difference; she paid too little attention to any of her medications when she took them. She trusted Peterson to have provided her with the proper ones.

A large dosage of Armour Thyroid can be lethal to a person with a serious arrhythmia and congestive heart failure, particularly when taken with a stimulant such as coffee. The combination jolted Caroline's heart, increasing its beat to the point where she suffered cardiac arrest and died almost immediately. The date of her death was six days shy of her forty-fifth birthday.

Marvin Peterson killed her. He killed her as surely as if he had done what I did to him, pressed the barrel of a handgun against her temple and pulled the trigger. He killed her with his gross criminal negligence, and a cheerful smile, as he slid the fatal prescription across the counter and said to her, in my hearing, "Here you are, Mrs. Darnell. A pleasure to serve you, as always."

There can be no doubt that he was guilty. He always filled our prescriptions "as a personal service," and he was the only pharmacist working at Consolidated Drugs that day. No one had access to the prescription in our home; no one but Caroline touched the vial after it passed from Peterson's hands to hers.

Caroline's doctor did not discover the Armour Thyroid substitute. There was no compelling reason for him to check her medication, nor did I permit an autopsy; he assumed the cause of death was a sudden heart attack. I was the one who discovered the truth, purely by accident, as I was about to dispose of the vial. It slipped from my hand, the loose top came off, the tablets spilled on the floor, and when I retrieved them I realized that they were Armour Thyroid, not enalapril as marked on the label. She could not have gotten the vials mixed up. The only person who could have been responsible was Marvin Peterson.

I could have informed the police, but to what end? In the eyes of the law, Peterson had made a monstrous but not a felonious mistake. It might have cost him his pharmacist's license, but nothing more. Even if criminal charges could have been brought against him, the worst punishment he would have faced was a short prison term; there is no capital punishment in this state. A wrongful death suit? I do not care about money, or civil satisfaction—I cared only about Caroline, I cared only about justice.

Once Peterson had been judged guilty by the evidence, my only recourse was to mete out his punishment myself.

I do not expect the police to question me, unless they decide to question every one of Peterson's customers. I am a model citizen, a respected tax accountant, and there is nothing to connect the two of us except for Caroline's and my regular patronage of Consolidated Drugs. The vial of mislabeled Armour Thyroid tablets no longer exists; I destroyed it completely after deciding that Peterson must be executed.

I do not believe that I should be punished in any way for what I've done. I have not, despite the letter of the law, committed a crime. If I believed otherwise, I would take appropriate steps; as I've stated, I live by a strict moral and ethical code. But my conscience is clear. Should an executioner be made to suffer for pulling a switch or making a lethal injection? No, of course not.

This document, therefore, is not intended as a confession but an explanatory statement of fact. I will place it in my safe-deposit box, among my other papers, to be read by interested parties long after my own death. I abhor loose ends, unexplained happenings. The world should know, even if it no longer cares by the time the truth be known, of Peterson's offense and the price he paid for it.

Handwritten letter dated March 2, 2008, five days before Caroline Darnell's death, and signed by her:

Dear James,

This is a very difficult letter to write. I've tried very hard not to write it, but there is an overwhelming need in me to confess. You have the right to know the truth.

For the past six months I have been having an affair. You don't know the man and his name isn't important. At first, I loved him madly. He was charming, attentive, passionate—all the things I've always ached for you to be. But then I learned the truth about him. He was only using me for his own amusement and satisfaction. He doesn't really care anything about me. Or about anyone, including his wife. Your ways may sometimes be cold and rigid, James, but I know that you do care about me and always have.

I've been such a fool. I feel terribly guilty, and with the guilt has come a deeper depression than ever before. I've tried to fight it with increased amounts of antidepressants, but the drugs no longer work. The guilt and the depression have become unbearable.

I must put an end to my misery. Soon.

I don't know yet how I'll do it. Pills, probably, perhaps something to counteract my heart medicines.

My first thought, once I made my decision, was not to reveal the truth to you or to anyone else. It would be a mercy to you, I know, if I kept quiet and let you believe my death was either accidental or of natural causes. But the desire to confess is too strong and I'm too weak and cowardly to resist. I won't add to your burden by putting this letter where you'll find it immediately after I'm gone. Instead I'll place it among the papers in my desk. You're such a meticulous man, James—I'm sure you'll find it eventually.

I'm so sorry. Please forgive me.

Barely legible handwritten note, undated, signed by James B. Darnell:

Marvin Peterson was innocent! I murdered ... not executed, murdered ... an innocent man!

How can I live with the terrible mistake I've made? I can't. My conscience, my moral code ... no. I am guilty and the guilty *must* be punished. Prison is not an option, I couldn't stand to be locked up. The punishment must fit the crime. There is no other choice.

The executioner must now execute himself.

Handwritten letter, dated March 5, 2008, two days before Caroline Darnell's death, and signed by her:

Darling—

I don't know why I should still call you "darling" after the way you've treated me. Habit, I suppose. A small, a very small part of me still cares for you. But you've destroyed all the deep love I felt with your cruel and vicious words. You may be an expert lover, and you certainly know how to *pretend* to care for a woman, but underneath you're selfish and cold.

James is a saint compared to you.

I've been so depressed since you told me you didn't want me in your life anymore that I actually planned to do away with myself. I even wrote a letter to James telling him I was going to. But I've changed my mind. I can't let you drive me to self-destruction, or get away with what you've done to me. I'm going to make you suffer as I've suffered these past few days. You've used me, now you'll pay for it.

In the next day or two or three, or maybe a week from now, I'll call your wife and tell her about us. Every sordid detail. And all the terrible things you said about her and about me. I'll call your friends and business associates and tell them too.

Don't think this is an idle threat because it isn't. And don't try to make amends, it's too late for that. You can't talk me out of it. All you can do is wait for it to happen and then suffer the consequences.

From the report of Police Inspector Evan Norris, Homicide Division:

The four documents in this file, together with the other evidence we've gathered, clearly outline the odd series of circumstances linking the deaths of Caroline Darnell, Marvin Peterson, and James B. Darnell.

It amounts to this: The husband committed murder because at the time he believed the pharmacist had made a fatal error which caused his wife's death. He then discovered the wife's letter to him, in which she admitted to her affair and stated that she planned to take her own life. This convinced him that he'd murdered an innocent man, and his guilt and strict moral code prompted him to shoot himself with the same gun. Unknown to him, however, his wife had changed her mind and written an angry and threatening letter to her lover. The lover's reaction was to do away with her to protect himself.

The final irony here is that the lover, the man who substituted the Armour Thyroid for Caroline Darnell's heart medication, was the pharmacist, Marvin Peterson. He neglected to destroy her last letter to him; we found it in the trash at Consolidated Drugs, where we also learned that two dozen 60mg tablets of Armour Thyroid were missing and could not be accounted for. James Darnell had been right after all: The man he executed was guilty, not of gross negligence but of premeditated homicide.

A tragedy of errors, the whole business.

But if you want to look at it another way, what happened to Peterson and Darnell, if not to Mrs. Darnell, was fitting and proper punishment for their crimes. In Darnell's own words:

It was a matter of justice.

I DIDN'T DO IT

Well, I keep telling you I didn't do it. I don't care how much evidence there is. You got to believe me. I didn't do it.

Sure, I was out there that night. I already admitted that, didn't I? I went out there to see Mr. Mason about a job. He gave me a dollar in town that day. I told him I was homeless, down on my luck, and he gave me a dollar and said come out and see him and maybe he could put me to work doing something on his farm. He told me his name and where he lived, said it was only about half a mile outside of town. So I walked out there that night. It was a hot night and I didn't have nothing to do in town, nowhere to go, no place to sleep, so I figured why not go out there and see Mr. Mason instead of waiting until the next day. I figured maybe he'd give me something to eat and a place to sleep. So I went out there. How was I to know he'd gone off to Springville on business and wouldn't be home until after midnight?

Well, I come onto his property about nine o'clock. Just after dark, so it must have been about nine. Wasn't nobody around, but lights was on in the house. It was a hot night, quiet, and when I got up near the porch I heard them sounds plain as day. Did I know right off what they was? Well, not right off. They was just moaning sounds to me at first, like maybe somebody was hurt. So I went around the side of the house, through the garden, to see if that was what it was, somebody hurt. That's how come you found my footprint over by the bedroom window, where I stepped in the mud from the sprinklers. I never said I wasn't in the garden, did I? But I never went up close to that window. No, sir. I'll swear it on a Bible. I never went close to that window and I never looked inside that bedroom.

I recognized them sounds, that's why. I knowed then what was going on. Him and her in there, making all that moaning noise, making them bedsprings squeak and squeal like a soul in torment. I knowed what they was doing. So I beat it right out of there, you bet I did. Fast.

Did I know it wasn't Mr. Mason in there with Mrs. Mason? Well, I guess I did. I guess I knowed it, all right. I heard the fellow's voice plain, some of the things he was saying to her ... no, I ain't going to say what them things was. I don't even want to repeat them things in my own mind, let alone out loud. But I heard his voice plain and it wasn't Mr. Mason's voice so I guess I knowed it wasn't Mr. Mason in there. But I didn't know who it *was*. She didn't call him by his name. No, sir, not by his *name*.

No, I didn't go back to town right away. I told you that. It was a hot night and I didn't feel like going back to town right away, on account of what was I going to do once I got there? I didn't have no money or no place to go. What I did, I walked down by the river. River runs close to Mr. Mason's farm—runs right through a corner of it, didn't you say? Well, it was a hot night and I thought maybe I'd go for a swim.

But before I got there I seen this car parked in amongst the trees betwixt the river and Mr. Mason's house. Big fancy car, parked right in there under the trees, off the road so you couldn't see it unless you was walking by like I was. Well, I knowed it was his car, the fellow in the house with Mrs. Mason. Who else's car was it likely to be?

Sure, I looked inside. Door was unlocked, so I figured I might's well. But it wasn't my intention to steal nothing, even if there'd been something to steal. Which there wasn't. Big fancy car like that and not a thing in it that anybody'd want to steal. Not a thing you could of got fifty cents for at a hock shop, let alone a few dollars to buy you a decent meal and some new shoes and maybe a room to sleep in for a few nights.

I sure *didn't* wait there for him to show up. No, sir, you're wrong about that. I went on down to the river just like I said before. I went on down to the river and took off my clothes, all except my underpants, and I went for a nice cool swim. Then I laid on the bank a while and dried off. It was peaceful there on the bank, and I thought I'd stay right there the whole night. No point in going back to town, I says to myself. Might's well just stay right there for the night and then in the morning go and see if Mr. Mason had come home from wherever he was and ask him for that job he promised. I didn't have no intention of telling him about his wife fornicating with some other man. Not if he give me a job like he promised, and a place to sleep. I wouldn't hurt a good man that way. No, not a *good* man, I wouldn't.

Why didn't I spend the night there? Why'd I go on back to town instead? Well, I told you—I found that money. Eighty-nine dollars. Lying right there on the river bank. Way I found it was, I decided to take a walk along the bank, after I dried off from my swim, and see could I find some soft grass for a bed. And there that money was, in a little cloth purse that somebody must of dropped. Some fisherman or somebody. Dropped it right there on the bank and never realized it. There was a bright moon that night, you remember? That's how I seen the purse with the money in it lying there in the grass.

After I took the money out I throwed the bag in the river. I told you about that too. What did I want to keep an empty purse for? It didn't have no identification or nothing in it. Finders keepers, losers weepers. So I walked back into town with that found money. I figured I might's well spend some of it. I figured I was entitled, being as how I'd been down on my luck so long. So I bought myself a good meal and a bottle of bourbon whiskey and a room for the night, where you fellows found me the next morning.

What's that? No, sir, I sure didn't steal that money from Thomas Harper's wallet. I told you where I got that money. I found that money in a cloth purse lying on the river bank

No, sir, I didn't hit Thomas Harper over the head with no chunk of willow limb. I didn't kill Thomas Harper. I never even knowed his name until you told me, or that he was a bigshot lawyer, or nothing about him except he was sinning with Mr. Mason's wife.

My fingerprints? Not just on his car but on one of them little window things in his wallet? Well, I don't know how they could have got *there*. You sure them fingerprints is mine too? Well, I don't know how they could of got there.

No, sir, I didn't rob and kill Thomas Harper.

No, sir, I didn't.

I tell you, I didn't do it ...

All right. All right, all right. I guess it's no use. I guess I might's as well tell you.

I done it.

But I didn't mean to kill him, nor even to rob him. I come walking back from the river, back toward that fancy car of his, and I had that chunk of willow limb in my hand. I don't know why I picked it up down on the river bank. I just did, that's all. And here he comes from Mr. Mason's house where he'd been fornicating with Mr. Mason's wife, all cheerful and whistling, real pleased with himself, and I don't know ... I don't know, I just stepped up behind him and let him have it. I didn't mean to hit him so hard. I truly didn't.

Sure, I took the money afterwards. Eighty-nine dollars is a lot of money to a fellow down on his luck. But that ain't why I hit him. I don't know why I hit him.

Yes I do. He had it coming, that's why. Sinning with Mr. Mason's wife like that, saying all them things to her right there in Mr. Mason's bed in Mr. Mason's own house. That Thomas Harper had it coming, all right.

But I *didn't* do that other thing. I swear I didn't.

I never looked through the bedroom window when I was in the garden, I never watched them two in Mr. Mason's bed. It's a mortal sin for a man to fornicate with another man's wife, and only a person with lust in his heart would gaze upon what he's moral certain is a act of fornication. God knows I don't have no lust in my heart and He knows I didn't watch them two committing their mortal sin. You got to know it too. You got to believe me.

I didn't do it!

HOME

Rennert unlocked the door to his apartment, thinking that it was good to be home. It had been a long day at the office and he was eager for a dry martini and a quiet dinner. He walked in, shut and relatched the door. The hall, five steps long, led into the living room; when he reached the end of it he stopped suddenly and stood gawping.

A man was sitting on his couch.

Just sitting there, completely at ease, one leg crossed over the other. Middle-aged, nondescript, wearing shabby clothing. And thin, so thin you could see the bones of his skull beneath sparse brown hair and a papery layer of skin and flesh.

It took Rennert a few seconds to recover from his shock. Then he demanded, "Who the hell are you?"

"My name is Dain. Raymond Dain."

"What're you doing in my apartment?"

"Waiting for you."

"For Christ's sake," Rennert said. "I don't know you. I've never seen you before in my life." Which wasn't quite true. There was something vaguely familiar about the man. "How did you get in here?"

"The same way you just came in."

"The door was locked. I locked it this morning—"

"I'm good with locks."

A thread of fear had begun to unwind in Rennert. He was a quiet, timid man who took pains to avoid any potentially dangerous situation. He had no experience with anything like this; he didn't know how to handle it.

"What's the idea?" he said. "What do you want?"

Dain was looking around the room. "This is a nice apartment. Really nice."

"I asked what you want."

"Comfortable. Warm. Everything in good taste."

"None of the furnishings is worth stealing," Rennert said. "There's nothing here worth stealing—you must know that by now. I have twenty dollars in my wallet and about two hundred in my checking account. I work for an insurance company, my salary isn't—"

"I'm not after your money, Mr. Rennert."

"... So you know my name."

"From the mailbox downstairs."

"If you're not a thief, then what are you?"

"A salesman. That is, I used to be a salesman. Sporting goods. At one time

I was the company's top man in California."

"I don't—"

"But then one of the bigger outfits bought us out and right away they began downsizing. They said my salary was too high and my commissions too low, so I was one of the first to be booted out."

"I'm sorry to hear that, but—"

"I couldn't get another job," Dain said. "Everywhere I went they said I was too old. Eventually I lost everything. My wife and I had been living high and on the edge and it didn't take long, less than a year. House, car, all my possessions of any value—everything went. Then my wife went too. I ended up with nothing."

Rennert couldn't think of anything to say. He felt as though he'd walked into the middle of somebody else's nightmare.

"You can't imagine how bad it was," Dain said. "The first year I tried twice to do away with myself. But gradually I came to terms with my situation. Developed a new outlook and started to put my life back together. A long, slow process, but it's going to work out. It's definitely going to work out."

"Well, I'm glad to hear it, but that doesn't explain what you're doing in my apartment. Or give you any right to be here."

Dain got slowly to his feet. Rennert stiffened, but Dain didn't come his way; instead he moved to the undraped picture window and stood peering out.

"Quite a view from here," he said. "You can see a lot of the park. On clear days I'll bet you can see the ocean, too."

Rennert said, "That's it, the park."

"What about the park?"

"That's where I've seen you before. Panhandling in the park."

"I don't do that," Dain said in an offended tone. "I've never once resorted to panhandling."

"All right. Wandering around over there then."

"I've seen you in the park too. Several times."

"How did you find out where I live?"

"I followed you the last time. Yesterday."

"Why? Why *me?*"

"You were always alone, whenever I saw you, and I wanted to find out if you lived alone."

"Well, now you know," Rennert said shakily. "I live alone and you live in one of the homeless camps in the park. So what? What's the idea if you don't intend to rob me?"

"I've been existing in one of the camps, yes. I hate it. I hate being homeless."

"I'm sure you do. It has to be rough—"

"You have no idea how rough, Mr. Rennert. Only those of us who've been through it really know."

"I believe that. And I'm sympathetic, I truly am. But I think you'd better leave now."

"Why?"

"Why? Because I don't want you here. Because you're trespassing. Because you won't tell me why you broke in or what it is you want."

"I did tell you," Dain said. "You weren't listening."

"All you told me is that you've started to put your life back together, and I can't help you with that."

"But you can."

"How? How can I?"

"Isn't it obvious?"

"Not to me. Do you want me to call the police?"

"No."

"Then leave. Just leave, right now. I don't want any trouble with you."

Dain looked at him in silence. A sad, waiting look. No, not sad—hungry.

"Go away," Rennert said desperately, "leave me alone. Don't you understand? I can't do anything for you!"

Dain said, "You're the one who doesn't understand, Mr. Rennert. I told you I hate being homeless and I meant just that. A decent job, possessions, even a wife and family—I can manage without those. But I can't go on, I can't have any kind of life, without a home."

"For God's sake, what does that have to do with me? This is my apartment, my home—"

"Not anymore," Dain said.

Understanding came to Rennert in a thunderous jolt. Even before he recognized the object Dain took from his pocket, heard the faint snicking sound, and saw the shine of steel, he understood everything. Panic sent him running into the hall, his mouth coming open and a scream rising in his throat.

He didn't quite make it to the door. And the scream didn't quite make it all the way out.

Dain sighed, a deep and heartfelt sigh. "It's good to be home," he said, and went into his bathroom to wash the blood off his hands.

THE CRACK OF DOOM
(with Barry N. Malzberg)

Not yet the climactic figure he soon will be, Elias sits huddled on a bench in the empty park, his threadbare coat wrapped tight around his thin body. The November day is cold, wind warped, forlorn. Leaves and litter scurry like small dead things along the deserted paths. Swollen, black-veined clouds bulk thickly overhead. He hopes the rain will hold off so he can remain here another hour or two but senses that it won't.

He could leave now, a little in advance. After all, he is free to go when and where he chooses until the time comes. Except, of course, for the shadowy figures, agents of the Conspirators, who follow him everywhere. Watchers assigned to make sure he does nothing to betray his mandate, he supposes.

He is here today, as on most days, because he has nowhere else to go. He is a man alone. No family left (except for Gloria, he thinks bitterly), or friends, or even casual acquaintances—entirely alone. His once unlimited world has been reduced to a single room, too small to occupy all day as well as all night, and the Westside Café where he eats his meager breakfast and his equally meager dinner, the city streets he wanders aimlessly, and this park where he sits and tries not to think too much, tries not to worry. He has no money; his food and lodging are paid for. He cannot even spend an hour or two in the warm, dark anonymity of a second-run movie house.

A pigeon flaps down near him. Sits flexing its wings and eyeing him for a time, waiting. He ignores it; he has nothing to give to pigeons or any other creature. And wouldn't if he did, with so little time left. Finally, the bird makes a derisive sound, the avian equivalent of an obscenity, and flaps away again into the afternoon gloom.

Elias's life was not always like this. There was another time, a happier if not a better time. Before he was selected. Before the Conspirators seized control of him. He was a man of some influence then, a vital cog in the machinery that runs the world. Now he is nothing. They have taken everything away from him, not piece by piece but in one thunderous appropriation.

Now, in his disgrace and his terrible responsibility, he is at the focal point of the known world. He is the man who, in one way or another, will strike the match to spark the paper to light the fuse that will bring on the raining fire of annihilation, the final crack of doom. He does not want to be the instrument. His goal was always to be one of the saviors. But the forces who now control him have selected him for the dreadful task for reasons he cannot imagine, and sometime soon they will give him the definitive order. Until then it is his fate to wade through the days, bringing no attention to himself, giving to the Conspiracy an unwitting gift of patience.

He wonders again who the Conspirators are. Figures as shadowy as their agents, with motives he now—too late—realizes must be evil. Rich, powerful, ruthless, soulless men. Monsters in the guise of saviors. Why has he been chosen by them? The question haunts him. Why?

To drive it from his mind, he thinks of his son and daughter. He has not seen either of them since the Conspirators toppled him. For all he knows, both were so shattered that they have changed their names by now. It is painful to realize that they, too, will soon be destroyed along with so many others. He would save them if he could. But he has no authority now to save anyone, not even himself.

The one person he would not save if he could is Gloria. She is still a significant force in his life, more so than ever. Not because she has stood by him; oh, no, just the opposite. She is one of Them now. How the Conspirators convinced her to betray him is beyond his comprehension. Her betrayal is even more heinous because she takes sadistic pleasure in stopping by his room at ridiculous hours, suddenly appearing while he is here in the park. To torment him, to make sure he remains available to complete his mission when the time arrives. She is the one who will tell him when. She is the Judas.

Oh, Gloria. It almost makes the coming apocalypse joyous: She will be among the millions he will remove from the world.

Elias sighs on the bench, stretches his legs, slowly rises. It was all a lie, wasn't it, Gloria? The love you professed for me, the compassion, the kindness. It was nothing more than capitulation, bought and paid for. And all along, hidden away beneath the false facade of faithful tenderness, there were vast resources of resentment and hatred. Why else would you exult in my fall from grace?

He tells himself he must not dwell on her or any part of the past. Such thinking leads nowhere, means nothing. He will walk now to the Westside Café, sit there drinking coffee and reading an abandoned newspaper, if there is one, until he is told to buy something else or vacate the premises. Then he will prowl his way north and end this day, as so many others, in his ugly little room.

Elias leaves the park, hurrying. The wind has sharpened and the first drops of rain begin to slant down, teeth of ice that bite into his bare cheeks, his exposed neck, his gloveless hands. He half stumbles in his haste, his head lowered, his eyes cast downward. Brakes squeal as he starts blindly across the street against the light, a taxi swerves and just misses him. The driver shouts invective, but Elias pays no attention to him or any of the gaping pedestrians that clog the sidewalk. They're of no importance, bereft as they are of knowledge of what is in store for them. Nothing is of any importance, Elias thinks, except the present, for there is no future.

He reaches the cafe, enters. Familiar, almost pleasantly so, the place is not crowded. He starts toward his customary stool at the counter, but a voice halts him—a familiar voice from one of the booths. He stops, turns, the cafe's warmth vanishing into a chill colder than the wind-flung rain outside.

The voice is Gloria's.

Alone in the booth, smiling her pale Judas smile, she beckons to him. He hesitates. He does not want to see her, talk to her, yet he knows he must. She may have brought word from the Conspirators that the time has come. Slowly, on tremulous legs, he crosses to the booth and joins her.

She looks at him in the old way, her round face a mask concealing the contempt, the disdain, the darkness within. Yet she seems somehow different today, faintly distorted, as if he is seeing her through thick glass.

"How are you feeling, my dear?" she asks.

"Don't call me that. I'm not your dear, not anymore, not ever."

She pretends to wince at the harshness of his words. "As you wish."

"Why do you want to know how I feel? I'm well enough to do what's expected of me, if that's worrying you."

"It's not. I'm sure you'll do what you must."

"Is it time? Is that why you're here?"

"Not yet, no. Soon. It will all be over soon."

"How soon?"

She doesn't answer. Instead she says sadly, almost as if speaking to herself "I used to admire you so much. Before all of this, before I found out what you are."

"And what am I, besides a tool of the Conspirators?"

"I still don't know you," she says. "I never did."

"Who are They?" Elias says impulsively. "You know, don't you? Tell me who *They* are."

"You already have the answer to that."

"I don't, damn you." He leans forward. "Why won't you tell me?"

"Lower your voice, Elias. Calm yourself."

"I am calm," he says, "I am very calm. But I can't go on like this, waiting, not knowing. If you won't reveal who the Conspirators are, at least have the decency to give me some idea of when the end will come."

There is a long moment of silence. Nearby voices murmur, crockery rattles, gusts of rain spatter against the windows. Gloria sighs.

"Tomorrow," she says. "It's to be tomorrow morning."

Elias sits back with a mixed feeling of exhaustion and relief. "And what do I do then, how do I proceed?"

"When the time comes, you'll know." She reaches out as if to touch him, then draws her hand back. Good. Her fingers would surely have seared his flesh. She sighs again. "I'd better go now."

"You're sure it's to be tomorrow? You're not just tormenting me again?"

"I'm sure." Gloria slides out of the booth, stands. "Goodbye for now, Elias," she says, and leaves him mercifully alone.

Elias continues to sit in the booth. No one has left a newspaper; he drinks coffee and watches the rain, glimpses through the streaked glass one of the shadowy followers waiting outside. The cafe becomes more crowded as the dinner hour approaches. A waitress stops by several times to ask if he wants food, but he has no appetite. Finally, predictably, the owner comes and tells him to order something besides coffee or leave so other customers can occupy the booth.

He doesn't protest. The rain has slackened to a light drizzle; he would have left soon anyway. Outside, he hurries through the wet streets and closes himself inside his small, cramped room.

The cold park bench, the rain, the meeting with Gloria, the long walk, the watchers, the constant waiting have combined to fill him with a deep weariness. As early as it is, he crawls into bed. And sleeps. And dreams of fire, and thunder, and the silent screams of millions all through the long night.

When he wakes in the morning he is not refreshed. He feels even worse today. Oh, Gloria, you better have told the truth that this is the day. His patience is rapidly eroding, is now as thin as membrane.

Elias is dressed and pacing the room when the knock comes on the door. He opens it quickly. Several men stand in the hallway. The followers, the watchers, like shadows in the background. And three others, apparently also Conspirators, all of them dressed in dark business suits and hats and carrying briefcases—precise, poised, relaxed, yet somehow menacing. Like the trio in the surrealist painting by Magritte, the one entitled ... What is the title? He can't remember.

"Why are so many of you here?" he demands. "I thought I was supposed to do the job alone."

"You're not alone, Elias," one of the three men says. "We're all going with you."

"Where's Gloria? Why isn't she here too?"

"She's waiting for us. Come along, now."

"Where?"

"You know where."

"No, I don't. Tell me."

The man shakes head. Elias looks from one of their grim faces to another, and remembers the title of the Magritte painting then. *The Threatened Assassin*.

They take him in hand, lead him ... somewhere, he's not sure where. Soon they emerge into a massive, high-ceilinged room filled with people, one of them a black-robed figure seated behind a high bench. Nothing here is familiar, except for Gloria who occupies a seat in a long row. Elias thinks this must be a gathering of still more of the Conspirators, but he feels confused now, light headed.

He is guided to a table, made to sit. Voices rise and fall around him; he tries not to listen. Tries to keep his mind closed, to cast himself back to the safety of the park, the cafe, his tiny room.

Tries and fails.

He realizes where he is now. Knows everything now. No longer can he hide from the truth, temporarily escape into fantasy and self-delusion. With awe and horror, he faces it once again.

The park bench, the pigeons, the Westside Café, the aimlessly wandered streets ... old memories, mechanisms of denial. The small enclosure he has been living in—not a room but a cell. Yesterday's meeting with his wife—not in the cafe but in the prison visitors' room. The followers, the watchers—prison guards. The three men in dark suits and hats—lawyers, his lawyers. And Gloria, standing by him after all, the only one who has done so throughout his ordeal, looking at him now not with hatred but with the pity and sorrow and shame he couldn't face. She is not the betrayer, the Judas—he is. He, Elias, the once highly placed government official, he is the only Conspirator in the courtroom.

"Elias Philip Deane. How do you plead to the crime of conspiracy to commit treason?"

One of the lawyers starts to speak, but Elias silences him with a gesture.

I never wanted to destroy the world, he thinks. "Guilty," he says.

And the judge's gavel comes down with a sound like the crack of doom.

DO IT YOURSELF

Roland was at it again as usual when I got home on Friday evening. His garage workshop was insulated, but as close as our properties were, you couldn't help hearing the whirr and whine of his saws, drills, lathes, the pounding of nails, the thump and clatter of lumber. And of course the noise he made was even louder and more intrusive when he was working outside with hammer, chainsaw, electric clippers, yard vac.

Not that he was a bad neighbor; he wasn't. Easy going, friendly in a reserved sort of way, always willing to lend a helping hand. But he was an inveterate do-it-yourselfer. Every suburban or small-town neighborhood has one, I guess—individuals who aren't happy unless they're making or repairing or painting something, mowing lawns, trimming trees and shrubbery, tending flowerbeds, poisoning weeds, washing and polishing cars, even scrubbing garage floors and driveways.

Roland's house and property were in never less than immaculate condition. In the eight years he had lived next door to Peg and me, he'd never once made use of a gardener, plumber, electrician, roofer, or any other type of service person. His motto was, "If you want something done and done right, do it yourself."

His mania had been tolerable while his wife Ellen was alive—she'd kept it within reasonable bounds—but in the four months since her accidental death, it had grown into what amounted to an obsession. They had no children, no relatives except for Ellen's mother who lived ninety miles away. Friends and neighbors like us were supportive, but Roland had always been an introvert and grief and loneliness had caused him to withdraw even more, to devote most of his time to his home-improvement projects. There couldn't be much left to do over there, as spic and span as everything was, except maybe to build more furniture for an already overstuffed house.

Another piercing whine sounded as I got out of my car. The July day had been sweltering; even this late, after six, it must be like an oven in his workshop. But then, the heat didn't seem to bother him the way it did most people. As for me, I was tired, sticky, and in dire need of a cold beer. I trudged into the house, deposited my briefcase on the living room couch.

Peg was in the kitchen, putting together what appeared to be a Waldorf salad for dinner. I stepped up behind her, brushed aside strands of damp sandy hair, and nibbled her slim neck just under an ear.

"You taste good," I said, "if a little on the moist side."

"Moist is right. What I need is a shower."

"Me, too. How about we take one together?"

"Uh-uh. That always ends up the same way, and it's too hot for bed games."

"Poor Hank," I said in mock pique. "He never gets to have any fun."

"Hah."

I liberated a bottle of pale ale from the fridge, opened it, swallowed about a third at a gulp, and then rolled the icy bottle across my forehead. Ah, better. But then the screech of Roland's big table saw cut through the evening stillness, loud because Peg had opened the kitchen windows in response to the heat.

She sighed. "I was hoping we could eat out on the patio."

"Maybe he'll be done by the time we've had our showers."

"That would be nice. He's been working over there all day again. I feel so sorry for him, losing Ellen the way he did, but I can't help wishing he'd find another way to deal with his bereavement."

"Same here." Another shriek came, prompting me to say, "I wonder what he's building this time."

"Whatever it is, he's been at it pretty much nonstop for three days now."

We found out what his latest project was on Saturday morning. Or rather I did. The sawing and banging had started again while we were having breakfast, and after we finished I closeted myself in the den to do some homework on the Harper account. But the den is on the side of our house nearest the Osborns' garage, and even with all the windows shut and the drapes drawn, the noise intruded and played hell with my concentration. After an hour or so I gave it up, and driven by a combination of mild annoyance and curiosity, I went over to see Roland.

And wouldn't you know that as I started up his driveway, the racket stopped. Silence still prevailed when I reached the outside door to his workshop. I rapped on it, then opened it and stuck my head inside.

"Morning, Roland. Mind if I come in?"

He was standing next to a long, rectangular redwood box laid across a pair of sawhorses, in the process of shedding the leather apron he wore while working in the shop. Muscles rippled beneath his shirt from all the home maintenance work and his construction job before smart investments allowed him to take an early retirement. He'd always kept fit, and until his wife's death he'd looked years younger than fifty-six. Now he looked years older.

"Sure, come ahead," he said. Then as I approached him, "I guess you've come about the noise."

I temporized on that. "Well, not really. Just wondering what you've been making. What is that, another planter box?"

"Yes. I just finished it."

"Where are you going to put it?" His front porch and back deck were already jam-packed with planter boxes.

"This one's not for me. It's for Ellen's mother."

"Oh, I see." That explained its somewhat decorative design. Beveled edges, interior slots along two sides and on one end, the other end built slightly shorter. Expert workmanship, as with everything he constructed.

"I'm taking it up to her today, as a matter of fact," Roland said, "and I'll probably stay in Westvale for two or three days. After I get back I'll try not to bother you and Peg so much."

"You're not a bother," I said automatically. "Want me to help you load it into your pickup?"

"No thanks, Hank. I can manage. It's not that heavy."

We chatted a little longer, but he seemed anxious to get moving now that the planter was finished and ready for delivery. So I wished him a good trip and went back home and told Peg about the present for Mrs. Peterson and the fact that we were due for two or three days of blessed silence while Roland was gone. Now if only the hot spell would break.

Roland was true to his word. He stayed in Westvale three full days, and when he got back, he didn't start another do-it-yourself project that required a lot of sawing and hammering. Of course, we weren't completely noise-spared; wind-blown leaves and such had collected on his property during his absence, which necessitated liberal use of the yard vac. But that was only a one-afternoon activity.

Another CPA's work-week vanished busily, unlike the hot spell which continued unabated. And when I got home on this Friday night, Peg had news for me.

"Poor Roland," she said. "As if he hasn't had enough heartache already."

"What's happened now?"

"You know Joan Goldman, her husband's an attorney? Well, I ran into her today and she told me Louis Sherman was acquitted of vehicular manslaughter. All he got from a soft-hearted judge was a fine and two years' probation."

"Well, that's a damn shame." Sherman, a salesman with a poor driving record, had caused the accident that killed Ellen Osborn while she was in Westvale visiting her mother. He had recklessly swerved past a slow-moving truck, forcing Ellen's car off the road and into a concrete abutment.

"A miscarriage of justice, if you ask me," Peg said.

"When was the verdict handed down?"

"Ten days ago. Roland must have been too bitter to talk about it."

I opened a beer, showered, and we had a light dinner on the patio. Afterward I went into the den, ostensibly to do some work. But all I did was sit and think unpleasant thoughts. Finally I got up and went looking for Peg.

She was outside on one of the chaise lounges, reading a novel. "Do me a favor," I said. "You're on good terms with Mrs. Peterson. Give her a call, see how she's doing. And ask her how she likes the planter box."

"Planter box? You mean the one Roland made for her?"

"That one, yes."

"What on earth for?"

"Just do it, okay? Humor me. I'll be in the den."

I did some more brooding at my desk in there, waiting. It was ten minutes or so before Peg came in.

"Mrs. Peterson was glad to hear from me," she said. "She's holding up fairly well, but she still needs moral support."

"What did she say about the planter box?"

"Well … she said, 'What planter box?' She didn't know anything about it."

"I was afraid of that."

"Afraid of what? You must have misunderstood Roland—he made it for somebody else. That's what I told Mrs. Peterson."

"I didn't misunderstand him," I said. Then, "Funny thing about that planter. I had a good look at it in his workshop. There were slots on both sides and one end, about an inch below the upper edges, and the other end was built slightly lower without a slot. At the time I thought it was just decorative woodworking. But it could be those slots were meant to contain a lid that would slide in tight over the low end."

"A lid? Why would a planter need a lid?"

"I don't think it was a planter. At least not the conventional kind."

"What are you talking about?"

"A box intended to seal something inside."

"Such as what?"

"Such as a dead body. Or worse, a live one."

Peg jerked upright, staring at me with her mouth open. "My God, what are you suggesting?"

"Remember what Roland said after the funeral, the only thing we've ever heard him say about the accident? 'The bastard who did this to Ellen belongs in the ground, too.'"

"Hank, no! You can't seriously believe Roland would commit cold-blooded murder!"

"Just about anybody is capable of it in the right circumstances. He loved Ellen more than anything in this world, and the law didn't punish the man who took her from him. He started building that box right after getting the news of Louis Sherman's acquittal. And don't forget his motto: If you want something done and done right, do it yourself."

She shook her head, hard.

"Another thing," I said. "He seems less depressed since he came back from that three-day trip. And where did he go on that trip? Not to visit Ellen's mother, or she'd have mentioned it to you."

"It's his business where he went, not ours," Peg said, angrily defensive now, "and if he's less depressed, it's because he's finally coming to terms with his loss."

"What if Sherman has suddenly and inexplicably disappeared? Would you admit the possibility then?"

"No, I would not. People leave their homes and jobs all the time, for all sorts of reasons… Don't tell me you're thinking of going up to Westvale to find out?"

The thought had crossed my mind, but what definite purpose would it serve?

"Or of going to the police?" Peg said. "Or accusing Roland to his face?"

"No. None of those things." Not without more than just circumstantial evidence. Besides, I'm an accountant, not a detective or a moral crusader.

"Well, thank God for that. Now you listen to me, Hank Foster. I don't ever again want to hear you even hint that that poor suffering man next door is a murderer. It's an absurd notion. Forget it."

There's no point in arguing with Peg when her mind's made up. "All right. I'll forget it."

But I knew I wouldn't. And that I would never again feel the same about Roland Osborn, the inveterate do-it-yourselfer.

THE NIGHT, THE RIVER

The night, the river.
And the girl he loved.
Janine.

He sat waiting for her on the sloping bank, as he always did on warm nights like this one. Soft grass, soft breeze, soft darkness all around. The river like black glass, wide here, wide and deep and fringed with reeds. The moon painting its surface with bands of shimmery light. Thrum of crickets, a nighthawk whickering in one of the willows farther down. Sweet scents—clover, wildflowers. Even the slow-moving water, the reeds, smelled sweet on nights like this.

His home, his world. The river, the little town beyond the railroad bridge, the countryside, the solitude. Most people his age who'd grown up here couldn't wait to get out. That was how Janine felt, always talking about going away to San Francisco or Los Angeles, New York, London. Not him. He didn't like cities, he didn't drink much or do drugs, he didn't want anything to do with wild parties or any of the crazy stuff that went on in cities. There were enough pleasures right here. Weekend dances and socials at the rec center. Boat rides, fishing trips. Hikes in the hills and valleys. And warm nights on the grassy riverbank. Janine hardly ever talked about going away when they were here, in this secret spot where they'd first vowed their love and lost their virginity together.

He thought of how she would look when she came tonight. Skin like finely veined alabaster—white. Wearing her favorite swimsuit, one piece—black. Lean, coltish body, those wonderful long legs. Shoulder-length dark hair that was silk-smooth beneath his fingers. That shy-bold smile just for him. Whispered words just for him.

"Janine," he said aloud.

Night whispers answered him. But it wouldn't be long now. He felt her nearness, out there in the dark. It was as if all he had to do to summon her was say her name.

Five minutes, maybe less. Beyond the reeds, the black glass fragmented into faint ripples that glistened in the moonshine. He sat forward, watching for the ebon shape of her head to break the surface. He would see her before he heard her. She swam so well, so quietly and effortlessly. A mile upriver from her home beyond the ruins of Miller's Ferry, a mile back down—all that distance, two or three nights a week, and not once had the swim tired her or left her winded. Born to the river, that was Janine. She'd said so herself, before all that nonsense about big cities had come into her head. "I'd much rather swim than walk, much rather be in the water than on dry land. Except when I'm with you."

There. Coming now.

Excitement built in him, drying his mouth. His gaze was avid as she floated in toward the bank. She came straight through the reeds, not avoiding them as most swimmers would, rising up out of them, dripping, like a black-and-white water sprite. When she reached the shore, she stood for a moment as if posing for him, shaking herself, tossing the wet hair from her eyes. Then, in that slow, shy way of hers, she came to him through the sweet-smelling grass.

"Janine."

The special smile, the whisper of his name, and she sat down beside him. "Have you been waiting long this time?"

"No. Just a few minutes."

"I don't like to keep you waiting."

"I know. I know you don't."

"But I'm here now. I always come, don't I, when I know you're waiting."

"You always do."

Her smile turned mischievous. "And you're always glad to see me."

"Always."

"So you can make love to me."

"That's not the only reason."

"Isn't it?"

"I just ... I love you, you know that."

"Then say it. Tell me."

"I love you."

"Say it's a beautiful night and you're beautiful."

"It's a beautiful night and you're beautiful and I love you."

"Warm night, too."

"Yes."

"But the river is cold. Even on warm nights it's very cold."

"I know."

"I'm cold," she said.

"Not for long."

"Wet-cold, and I want to be warm."

"I'll make you warm, Janine. I will."

"Promise?"

"I promise."

She moved closer. "Kiss me."

He kissed her. Butter mouth. Soft. The feel and taste of her made him ache inside and out.

"Touch me. Here."

He touched her.

"And here."

"Oh, yes."

"Take off my suit."

His fingers trembled. She had to help him. White alabaster in the moonlight.

"Now you. All your clothes."

Again she helped him. And when he was naked, she moved into his arms. Entwining him. Touching him with electric fingers.

"So big," she said.

"Yes."

"So hard."

"Yes."

"All for me?"

"Yes!"

Her arms tightened around him. He pressed her back into the grass, stroked her, kissed her nipples, her mouth, tasted her tongue, her tongue—

"Love me," she whispered.

"Yes."

"Make me warm."

"Yes."

"Hurry, hurry! Make me warm!"

Easing into the wet hollow of her. Deep. Soft moans, hers and his both. Slow movements, faster, too fast—slowing to make it last.

"Don't wait, hurry!"

Fast again, fast, faster, fastfastfast—

Long moments of ecstasy.

But only for him.

"I'm still cold," she said.

The feathery night wind was warm on his skin, but it did nothing to take the chill from hers. She was like ice covered with goosebumps. He held her tightly, still trying to infuse her body with the heat from his own.

"Janine, I'm sorry, I'm so sorry."

"You promised you'd make me warm again."

"I tried, I won't stop trying ..."

"Why?" she said.

He stiffened, drew back from her.

"Why?"

"You always ask me that. Don't."

"Why?"

"Please, Janine, please don't keep asking me that."

"Why?"

"I don't *know* why, I don't know."
"You don't love me. You never loved me."
"I do. I swear I do, I love you."
"I don't believe you."
"Would I have asked you to marry me if I didn't love you?"
"You didn't mean it."
"I did! I'd marry you tonight, right now—"
"It's too late."
"Don't say that. I know you still love me."
"Do I?"
"You're here, you keep coming here ..."
"Too late."
"Keep letting me make love to you."
"Too late, too late."
"Stop saying that!"
"What will you do if I don't stop?"
"Oh God, Janine ..."
"You're so big, so strong. What will you do?"
"Nothing, nothing ... you have to believe that I'm sorry!"
She sat up. "Why?" she said.
"No, don't."
"Why?"
"Please!"
"Why?"
"I don't know I don't know I'm sorry I don't know!"
"Look at me," she said.

A chill swept over him, through him, made him as icy as she was. His hands began to shake. "No," he said. "Look at me."

"I can't, I won't, not again ..."

"Look. Look. Take a close look at me."

He looked because he had to, he had no choice. He saw her face, her body change. White alabaster dissolving, layers peeling away slowly, then quickly, until bone showed beneath the nibbled strips of flesh. Both eyes vanished, leaving empty skeletal sockets that dripped water, mud, furry green moss. Something crawled out of her mouth, something like a huge swollen tongue, purple and black in the talcumy moonlight. He screamed.

She made a different sound, a choking sound. He covered his face, and moaned, and then wept.

When he lifted his head, she was Janine again. White alabaster covered by the black bathing suit, smiling her special smile over her shoulder— young and beautiful like a water sprite. Walking away. Leaving him again.

"No! Janine, don't go!"

"It's time," she said. "I can't stay any longer tonight."

Down the slope. Into the river. Not swimming this time, just walking slow and then slowly sinking. The water closed over her head, but he could still see her as if lie were there with her, drifting down into the mud, the tangle of reeds, the darkness. Gone. As if she'd never been here at all.

Until the next time.

The surface smoothed, reformed into black glass. He kept on sitting there, naked, in the soft grass, soft warm breeze. Shivering. Crying.

The night, the river.

And the girl he loved. The girl he'd strangled when she first told him it was time for her to go away. The cold dead girl who kept coming back to beg him to make her warm again, and to ask him why.

All that was left of Janine.

ALWAYS HER EYES
(with Barry N. Malzberg)

A reckless and hateful man, my brother Carl. Spurned in childhood, mocked as a teenager, friendless as an adult; failure as sibling, husband, businessman, human being. And yet, as much as I despised him, I envied his aggressiveness, his ability to charge through circumstance. I am a passive man by nature, in my personal life if not where my profession is concerned. A man who "lets things happen to him," as Evelyn said to me once, "and then wonders why they don't turn out the way he wants them to."

Carl and I had not spoken since the debacle with Evelyn four years ago. And yet now, when he was teetering on the brink of bankruptcy, it was me he turned to in his time of need. He simply walked into West Valley Semiconductor one afternoon, bullied his way past the receptionist, barged into my office unannounced, offered up one of his charming smiles, and made his outrageous request.

"Well, Lawrence," he said, "it's been a long time. I can't blame you if you haven't forgiven me for what happened with Evelyn, but really, it's all water under the bridge. You're the only person who can save me from going under."

"I haven't forgiven you, and I never will. Why should I save you?"

"We're still brothers, after all."

"An accident of birth. You won't get a dime out of me."

He pretended not to have heard. I watched him sit down, cross one leg over the other, adjust the knifelike crease in his slacks. Immaculately dressed as always; the same suave manner and glib self-assurance. Facade, all of it. On occasion it had worked with his ex-wife, with Evelyn, and a few other women, with the original investors in his sports-promotion business. But now the pretense had worn thin. Underneath he was as desperate as a man can be. He would not have come to me if he weren't.

"A hundred thousand ought to bring me even," he said. "I'll give you a two-year promissory note."

The nerve and ego of the man! "You've already left worthless promissories all over the city."

"So you've been following my unfortunate series of setbacks. With relish, I suppose."

"I'm not that petty. I don't take pleasure in the misfortunes of others."

"No? Not even Evelyn?"

"What do you mean?"

"Her ill-advised marriage to Roger Frederickson last year. You know about that, of course."

Of course. I also knew why she'd married Frederickson, and it had nothing to do with love. He was fifteen years her senior, a mean-spirited, unattractive man whose first wife had divorced him for mental and physical cruelty. He was also wealthy, very wealthy. And highly competitive. He had built Frederickson Electronics to twice the size of West Valley, and made it three times as successful.

I said, "It doesn't matter to me who Evelyn sleeps with anymore, legally or otherwise."

"All over her now, are you? Not still carrying the torch?"

"... No."

Carl laughed. "Always her eyes," he said.

"What?"

"You used to say that about her, remember? Your favorite phrase."

Yes, I remembered. They were her most striking feature and her greatest vanity—large, pale gray, luminous. The most perfect eyes I had ever seen. Evelyn was a beautiful woman by anyone's standards, with golden hair and a sleek body, but it was always her eyes that you noticed first, that captivated you.

"I thought so," Carl said. "Still carrying the torch. You wouldn't be so bitter if you weren't."

"Of course I'm bitter," I said. "You knew how much I loved her, how much I wanted our marriage to work. But that didn't stop you from seducing her—"

"Seducing *her*?" He laughed. "It really was the other way around, you know."

"You've thrown that lie at me before."

"It's not a lie. Actually, I made an effort to resist her charms, and whether you believe it or not, I'm sorry I didn't succeed. Unfortunately, beautiful women are a weakness of mine."

More images, ugly ones, crawled out of my memory. Following Evelyn to the hotel in Hadleyville, suspicious of her fidelity and yet desperately hoping my fears would prove groundless. Catching her and Carl together in flagrante and the terrible shock that the man she was cheating with was my own brother. The rage and hatred I had felt rendered impotent by my passivity, so that I had done nothing except stand sputtering and helpless in front of them. The wild grief afterward, the long months of deep depression. Gradually the depression had lifted, but my self-confidence had never quite recovered.

I was no longer looking at Carl; I could not stand the sight of him. But even as I turned my head away, I could see his reflection in the mirror over the portable bar. How composed he seemed, far more composed than I. No matter what the situation, he seemed to feel he had the upper hand in his dealings with me.

"I wasn't the first, you know," he said. "While you were married to her, I mean."

"That's another damn lie."

"We both know it isn't."

I knew it, yes, but I would not admit it to Carl. It had taken me long enough to admit it to myself. He hadn't been the first, nor even the second or third. But Evelyn's betrayal with him, and his with her, were by far the worst.

"You won't admit this to yourself, Lawrence," he said, "but you're better off without her. She would have made your life miserable eventually, just as she has with Frederickson."

"What do you know about her marriage to Frederickson?"

"That she's as much to blame for their troubles as he is. More, in fact. She's cheated on him any number of times."

"With you?"

"No, not with me. I haven't been near her in four years."

"I don't believe you."

"If I were seeing her," he said, "you'd have heard about it, wouldn't you?"

"Not necessarily. You could be discreet when you felt like it."

He shrugged elaborately. "Poor Frederickson. He can't afford to divorce her because he made the mistake of not insisting on a prenuptial agreement."

"How do you know that?"

"He told me. He's a friend of mine."

"Is he? Then why don't you ask him for the money you need?"

"I already have."

"And he turned you down."

"He turned me down. He's tight-fisted as hell, even makes Evelyn do with a monthly allowance. But you won't turn me down, will you, Lawrence." It was neither a question nor a plea; Carl's voice was as casually composed as his reflection in the mirror. Nonetheless, I could detect cracks in the facade now, the simmering desperation like glimmers of light shining through them. "You'll let me have the hundred thousand."

"Not a dime," I said. "Not one single penny!"

"Come on, be reasonable," he said, and now there was an edge to his voice. "The past is dead. Ancient history. Can't we just bury the hatchet and move on?"

I had heard enough, seen enough. I stood so that I was looking down on him. "The past isn't dead. It isn't even past."

"Quoting Faulkner now, are we?"

"Get out of here, Carl. Get out of my sight."

He stood, too. "For God's sake, we're brothers. You can't turn me away at a time like this—"

"I can and I am. I want nothing more to do with you."

The facade cracked completely, his control crumbling with it. "Damn you, I need that money! I'll lose everything if you don't give it to me!"

"Out," I said, "or I'll call building security. And don't ever come back."

He left, but not without a stare of black hatred. The real Carl Bennett, the mask of urbanity stripped away to show him as he really was. I could have given him five times the amount of money he'd asked for, and it would not have saved him. He was beyond saving by anyone, including himself.

Carl's visit brought Evelyn back to the forefront of my mind, kept her there in spite of myself. God help me, I *was* still carrying the torch for her. Had "let her happen to me" once, in her words, and was still letting her happen to me. For how long? For the rest of my life?

I kept seeing her eyes, always her eyes, haunting me, mocking me. And hearing her voice, with its underlay of what I now knew to have been secret amusement. "Carl? Your silly brother? I can't stand to be alone in the same room with him." And when I caught them together: "I don't see why you're so upset, Lawrence. This is the first time anything like this has happened—a momentary lapse in judgment. It will never happen again, I promise you." And the last time I'd seen her, the day I moved out of the house, when I couldn't resist asking the question that had been uppermost in my mind: "Marry Carl? Don't be ridiculous. He's a loser, he has nothing to offer me except a little harmless fun. Not like you, darling. Are you sure you won't change your mind about a divorce?"

I *had* almost changed my mind. It was only on the strong advice of my attorney that I went through with it. He negotiated a settlement that favored me as the aggrieved party, though I still lost the house to Evelyn along with a not insignificant amount of cash.

I kept telling myself I was so much better off without her, and as time went by I knew it to be true. My life was calmer, quieter without all the parties and social events and expensive trips I had indulged in with Evelyn to keep her happy and feed her vanity. I was able to focus on my work, the kinds of engineering projects that had made West Valley into a small force in the electronics industry.

And yet, as much as I wanted nothing more to do with her, as much as I preferred to be alone, there were seconds here, minutes there, when I yearned almost uncontrollably to hold her in my arms and gaze again into those perfect eyes. If I had been Carl, I would have given in to those impulses. Was it strength or weakness that I hadn't?

Was I a better man than my brother, or just as much of a loser?

Carl did not come to see me again, at West Valley or my home. Didn't call or e-mail or text message. His silence surprised me a little; I expected that he would make at least one last effort to change my mind. But he must have realized how futile such an effort would be.

Certainly he still needed the hundred thousand dollars. I would have heard if he had found someone else to loan him the money. He might even have trumpeted the fact to me himself.

Strangely, I had no word at all about him or his actions. It was not like my brother to maintain a low profile at any time, and especially not when he was on the verge of bankruptcy. I couldn't help wondering why.

Two and a half weeks had passed when I found out.

The phone call came as I was about to go to bed after a long, tiring day. The caller was not Carl, but the last person I expected to hear from.

"Lawrence, thank God you're home. This is Evelyn."

Her voice had a shrill, near-hysterical pitch. It tightened my throat, put a band of coldness on my shoulders.

"What do you want, Evelyn?"

"I need your help. Please, you have to help me."

"To do what after all this time?"

"Something's happened ... an accident, a terrible accident."

"What kind of accident? What're you talking about?"

"It's Carl. He ... oh God, he's dead."

I had difficulty grasping the words. "Carl? Dead?"

"Right here in my living room. He came here to try to get Roger to loan him money, so frantic he brought a gun with him. He lost his head when Roger turned him down, threatened him with the gun ... they struggled and it went off. Carl was shot, but before he fell he managed to grab the gun and shoot Roger. He's dead too, they're both dead ..."

My brother dead, her husband dead. Killed with a weapon carried by Carl, who had always been afraid of firearms. The news was shocking, nightmarish. But I felt no sense of loss; Carl had been dead to me for four years.

"Lawrence, I don't know what to do. I don't have any right to ask after the way I've treated you, but there's no one else I can turn to."

"Have you called the police?"

"No. Not yet." Her voice rose another octave. "What if they think I had something to do with it?"

"Why would they think that?"

"I told you, they're both dead and there's no other witness to what happened. Roger and I have been having trouble, Carl was once my lover

... they could blame me, put me in jail. You have to come help me!"

"Why should I?"

"Carl was *your* brother."

As if that were a valid reason. She seemed to feel nothing for Frederickson or for Carl. Or for me, for that matter. Her only concern was for herself. "Just what do you expect me to do?"

"You could say you were here when it happened, you saw the whole thing. Or you could take Carl's body away and I could say an intruder shot Roger. We can decide when you get here."

My God.

"You will come, won't you? You won't regret it if you do. I know you still love me and whether you believe it or not, part of me still loves you. I'll make things right between us again, I promise I will."

So sure of herself, so sure of me, but I was not fooled. Lies. Deception. False promises. Evelyn had used men all her life—me, Carl, Frederickson, no telling how many others. Now she wanted to use me again.

The torch flame flared bright for an instant. And then guttered. And then died. "Please, Lawrence." Begging now. "Please, please, please!"

"No," I said, and broke the connection.

And then I called the police.

It was from the homicide lieutenant in charge of the case, a man named Robb, that I learned what actually happened to my brother and Roger Frederickson. And I was not surprised.

Almost everything Evelyn had told me was a lie. They had not shot each other during and after a struggle for Carl's handgun. She had killed them both—Carl by accident and her husband in a panic a few seconds later. After my refusal to become an accessory, she had attempted to rearrange the crime scene and badly botched the job. Her story and her nerve both collapsed under intensive police questioning and finally she confessed the truth.

Carl had lied to me about not seeing her anymore (so many lies); they had become lovers again during the past year. Together they had planned to murder Roger Frederickson in order to gain control of his assets and allow Carl to pay off his creditors. The plan, rash and foolish, had been to make Frederickson's death appear to be the work of an intruder. Carl was to have done the shooting as soon as Frederickson entered the house, but at the last minute he was unable to go through with it. Evelyn had grabbed the gun from him and fired, but the shot missed her husband and killed Carl instead. It was her second shot, at close range, when Frederickson rushed at her, that ended his life.

Two men destroyed by greed, desperation, panic, and vanity. And if I had agreed to help her, if I had not quit letting things happen to me, letting her happen to me, I would have been the third.

Why vanity? That was the final irony. Evelyn had accidentally shot Carl instead of her husband because the hallway had been in semidarkness, the two men had been standing close together, and her vision was too poor for her to distinguish between them. Her perfect eyes were not perfect after all, you see. She had developed cataracts in both—cataracts that could have been removed if she had not been so terrified of disfigurement that she refused to have corrective laser surgery.

Always those eyes.

But not anymore.

I KNOW A WAY

Summerville Sheriff Mike Cameron finished locking the cell door after the seven drunks he and his deputy, Jack Hannigan, had taken into custody at the Gandydancer roadhouse on the outskirts of town.

It was a lucky thing, he told himself wearily, turning deaf ears to the slurred grumblings from within the cell, that none of the seven had suffered anything worse than a bloody nose. If there'd been serious injuries, he and Hannigan would have had to wait around until the hospital in Kennerton sent over an EMT unit. As it was, they'd had a difficult time getting the drunks calmed down enough to transport them to jail. And one of them had thrown up messily in his patrol car on the way.

As he followed the corridor back to the jail office, Cameron thought it would've been easier to have forgotten the entire incident and sent the lot of them home. But damn it, he didn't like public brawling and it served them right to have to cool their heels in a cell overnight. When old Judge Lee fined them each fifty dollars on Monday, maybe they'd think twice about getting into a ruckus again.

Hannigan was at his desk with his feet propped on an opened drawer, massaging the back of his neck. Across the room, Goofy Henry, the handyman, sat reading a comic book at one of the utility tables. Cameron went to his desk, catty-corner to Hannigan's, and sat heavily—a big, solid man with a deeply lined face and tired gray eyes.

He said, "Well, another jolly Saturday night."

"Yeah," Hannigan said. His normally good-humored features had a dour look. "You know, Mike, I get damned sick of this job sometimes. Seems the only thing it entails is pulling in weekend drunks or breaking up barroom brawls—or both, like tonight."

"No argument from me."

"Summerville is such a damned quiet town. Nothing ever happens here. We get maybe two felonies a year, if you want to call some kids stealing a car to go joyriding or a transient breaking into Havemeyer's Grocery to raid the liquor felonies. The rest of the time, it's drunks. Damn lousy drunks."

"Well," Cameron said, "there're quite a few lawmen who'd like to change places with us."

"Oh, I suppose. But haven't you ever wished for something big to break? Something really big? Something to put Summerville on the map, get our names in the big city papers?"

"Like what?"

"Hell, I don't know. Maybe the bank getting robbed. Or a couple of escaped murderers holed up over at the Summerville Hotel, and we take 'em after a shootout. Something like that."

"I guess I wouldn't mind capturing escaped murderers or bank robbers," Cameron said wryly, "but you can leave out the shootout, thanks."

"You know what I mean."

"Sure, I know. But things like that aren't going to happen here. Nothing of state-wide interest, or even county interest, has happened in Summerville since the old man founded it in 1884."

"Well, I still wouldn't mind being famous for a while."

"Neither would I. But we might as well face it, Jack. We're doomed to anonymity and that's that."

Goofy Henry looked up from his comic book. "I know a way," he said.

He was smiling, his wide blue eyes shining. Evidently he'd been listening to their conversation; he didn't have much of an attention span even for a comic book. He was a tall, lanky man with a moss-like tangle of brown hair and long, powerfully muscled arms, dressed in his habitual outfit of blue denim shirt and worn dungarees. It was his job to sweep up and do general odd-job chores in and around the jailhouse. He wasn't officially on the city payroll, but Cameron gave him ten dollars a week for food and essentials, and let him sleep on a cot in the woodshed out back.

"I know a way," he said again, his gaze flicking back and forth between Cameron and Hannigan.

He was always saying little cryptic things like that that didn't have any meaning. Maybe he got them from the violent comics he liked, not that it mattered. Nothing ever came of anything he said.

Cameron humored him by saying, "Well, that's fine, Henry."

"A real good way."

"I'll bet," Hannigan said under his breath.

"You and the sheriff been real good to me," Goofy Henry said. "I want to do something for you. Something for Summerville, too."

"Such as?"

"I can't tell you now. It's my secret."

"Uh-huh."

Cameron yawned and stretched. It was quiet back in the cellblock; the drunks were docile now, probably already starting to sleep it off. He said, "All right, Henry. Tell you what you can do right now. First clean up the back seat in my patrol car, then watch things here while Jack and me go over to Elsie's for some coffee. Run and fetch us if the phone rings."

"Okay, Sheriff."

"I'll bring you back some pie, how's that?"

"Blueberry?"

"Sure."

"That's my favorite."

"Mine, too."

Goofy Henry grinned and nodded. Cameron and Hannigan got on their feet and put their hats on. "Another hour and a half, and Bert comes in to relieve, thank God," Cameron said on their way out.

When they were gone, Goofy Henry got a bucket and some rags and soap and went out and cleaned up the patrol car, cleaned it quick but real good. Then he went to the woodshed for a couple of minutes before returning to the jail office. The ring of keys was on the sheriff's desk; he picked them up and crossed to the cellblock door.

"I know a way," he said with a secret smile.

And with the keys in his left hand and the big sharp woodsman's axe in his right, Goofy Henry walked quietly down the corridor to the cell with the seven drunks...

NEIGHBORS

It was one of those rare late-summer evenings just past dusk, a light breeze blowing to soften the day's heat, the air so clear the town lights spread across the shallow valley below had an unwinking, crystal clarity. Lorraine and I were sitting on the back deck with coffee and after-dinner brandy, enjoying the view and the quiet. At least I was. The neighborhood we live in, spread across the brow of the western hillside, is a haven of home and property improvement; the daylight hours, especially on weekends at this time of year, are filled with the racket of leaf blowers, chain saws, circular saws, electric hedge clippers, banging hammers.

But Lorraine had other things on her mind than the peaceful night. "Harry," she said abruptly, breaking the long, mellow silence, "there's something wrong with the Gundersons."

"The Gundersons? What do you mean?"

"They're not what they seem to be."

I sighed. Here we go again, I thought.

"They struck me as a nice enough couple the one time we met them."

"Well, I don't think they are. They don't fit into a neighborhood like this. Everyone else here is a homeowner. They're transients."

"A one-year lease doesn't make them transients."

"They're standoffish. And secretive. Not our kind of neighbors."

I happened to think the Gundersons, who had lived in the house slightly below and to the left of ours for over a month now, were exactly our kind of neighbors. Exactly my kind, anyway. They may have preferred keeping to themselves, but they were pleasant enough and, a major plus in my book, they were quiet—no home-improvement projects, no loud parties.

Lorraine leaned forward in her chair to look over the low deck railing. From here, unfortunately, she had a clear view of the near side of the Gundersons' house and most of their front yard. "I don't suppose you'll believe me," she said, "but there's something very strange going on with those people. No, not just strange ... sinister."

"Such as what?"

"I don't know yet. But I'm going to find out."

We've been married thirty years, Lorraine and I, and in most ways she's been a good wife, mother, and companion. But she has two incurable flaws. She's a busybody, poking her nose into other people's business at every opportunity. And she has an overheated imagination that she fuels constantly with lurid novels, soap operas, and bad TV movies.

I made no comment, in the slim hope that she would drop the subject.

No such luck. She said, "Their drapes and curtains are always closed, day and night, even the ones overlooking their patio. As if they're trying to hide something. And Paul Gunderson, if that's his real name ... well, I don't think he's the architect he claims to be."

"What makes you say that?"

"Architects keep regular hours, for one thing, and he doesn't. Some weekdays he doesn't leave the house at all."

"Maybe he works at home part of the time. Some architects do."

"And for another thing, he doesn't know anything about Le Corbusier or Peter Eisenman."

"Neither do I. Who are they?"

"Famous architects. I looked them up on the Internet so I could have an informed conversation with him about architecture if the opportunity came up. He knew Frank Lloyd Wright's name, but not theirs."

"When did you find this out?"

"Three days ago. I happened to be outside when he came home from ... wherever, and I went over and tried to be neighborly. He didn't want to talk to me. He was almost rude, in fact."

"Well, maybe he had something important to do."

"He also sneaks around in the middle of the night," Lorraine said.

"Now how do you know that?"

"I got up to use the bathroom last night and happened to look out the bedroom window, and there he was leaving the house all by himself. At three A.M., and without any lights on. Don't you think that's odd behavior?"

"Not if he had a good reason for leaving home at that hour."

"That's not all," she said. "Strange men keep coming and going over there during the day and sometimes in the evening, did you know that?"

"What do you mean by strange?"

"Different ages, different types. Half a dozen of them. For all we know Fran Gunderson could be prostituting herself."

I managed not to laugh. "Or selling drugs."

"Yes, or selling drugs."

"Like what you thought Marguerite's Mexican neighbor was doing to high-school students last year," I said. Marguerite, our married daughter, lives in a development on the other side of town. "When what the woman was really doing was tutoring them in Spanish."

"You don't have to remind me of that," she said stiffly. "We all make mistakes."

Yes, and she'd made more than her share with her prying and spying. The time she convinced herself Tom Anderson had done away with his wife because Mary hadn't been seen for three weeks and Tom was "acting suspiciously," when the truth was Mary had gone off to a fat farm and Tom was too embarrassed to talk about it. And the time she was sure she'd seen the Brewsters' sixteen-year-old daughter shoplifting perfume at Kohl's and told the girl's mother, only to be confronted with a sales slip. There were other incidents I could have reminded her of too. But all I said was, "Yes, dear."

"But I'm right about the Gundersons," she said. "I *know* I am. They're not ordinary people who just want to be left alone, they're criminals. Thieves planning a robbery, or fugitives hiding out from the law." Then, ominously, "Or something even worse."

"And what would that be?"

"Spies. Terrorists. One of those strange men I told you about looked Middle Eastern."

I made an effort to hang onto my patience. "You're getting yourself worked up over nothing," I said. "Those men could be friends or relatives who were invited to see the Gundersons' new house. They also could be salesmen like me."

Lorraine made an exasperated noise. "The trouble with you, Harry, is that you look at the world through rose-colored glasses. You think everyone is basically good and honest and it's just not so. There are a lot of bad people out there."

"Yes, dear."

"Well, then? Can't you conceive of the fact that your new neighbors, living right next door, could be two of the bad ones?"

"Yes, dear."

"You don't mean it, I can hear it in your voice. You're so mild-mannered about everything, it drives me crazy sometimes. I wish you had more gumption."

"Yes, dear. So do I."

She subsided, which meant she felt that she'd made her point. I sipped brandy and resumed my enjoyment of the cool breeze, the stationary light show, the quiet. But not for long.

"Harry."

"Mmm?"

"Do you *have* to go away on Monday?"

"Unfortunately, yes. It's that time again."

"How long will you be gone?"

"Depends on how long the sales meetings last. No more than a week."

"A week," she said. Then, "I really wish you didn't have to travel so much."

"But I don't travel much," I said. "Just one week, two at the most, a couple of times a year."

"Couldn't you get another salesman to cover for you this time? Or call and tell the company you're ill?"

"You know I can't do that. I might lose my job. Why would you even ask?"

"I hate the idea of being here alone. Especially now, with the Gundersons in the neighborhood."

The Gundersons again. "If you're so nervous, why don't you ask Marguerite to come and stay with you? Or stay with her and Neal in their guest room?"

"I don't want to impose on them. Besides ..."

Lorraine let the rest trail off, but from past experience I knew what she'd been about to say. She may not have liked the idea of being here alone, but she was determined to keep a close watch on the Gundersons.

I didn't try to argue with her; it wouldn't have done any good. All I said was, "Do what you think is best. And try not to worry so much."

On Monday morning I flew down to L.A. as scheduled. I was gone six days, and too busy to call home more than twice. Lorraine hadn't seen any more "strange men" coming and going at the Gunderson house, or conjured up any more fantasies about the new neighbors, but this didn't mean that her latest teapot tempest was ready to go away like all the others.

When I got home, she met me at the door all red-faced and breathless, and the first thing she said was, "Harry, the police were at the Gundersons last night. Two officers, just before midnight."

"The police? Why? What happened?"

"Fran Gunderson *claimed* they had a prowler, but that's ridiculous. A prowler, in this neighborhood!"

"How do you know about the prowler?"

"I went over there this morning and spoke to her. Tried to speak to her, I should say. She was very short with me. Covering up."

"Covering up what?"

"The real reason the police were there so late."

"Which was?"

"To question them about their illegal activities, whatever they are. You mark my words—they'll be arrested before long and then it will all come out."

I went into the kitchen, made myself a drink, and took it out onto the back deck. Lorraine followed me, talking the entire time, but I was no longer listening. I was thinking, defensively, about the assignment in L.A.

It had gone smoothly, as always. A dark street, a casual approach, the usual single shot behind the right ear. No witnesses, nothing overlooked or unaccounted for. How many did that make now? An even dozen? Three or four more, and I'd have enough saved to retire from the Company and live out the rest of my life in relative peace and quiet. If Lorraine would let me. And if Zagetti would keep his promise in the first place. "I'd hate to lose you, Harry," he'd said to me once. "You're the best shooter we got on account of you look and act just like what you are most of the time, a timid little salesman...."

Lorraine's voice, raised querulously, penetrated again. "Harry? What's the matter with you? You're not paying attention!"

"Sorry. I was thinking about business."

"Well, for heaven's sake listen to what I'm trying to get through to you about the Gundersons. I told you all along they're not *normal* people like us. Now will you believe me?"

"Yes, dear," I said. "Not like us at all."

FINAL EXAM
(with Barry N. Malzberg)

For his final exam I take the Kid to Candlestick Park.

It is a bright and brisk fall Sunday, typical football weather in San Francisco. The 49ers are playing the Colts and the game is a sellout—fifty thousand fans, at least half of whom will soon be half drunk on beer and all of whom will be deeply involved with the game and such matters as the point spread. It is an ideal location and the one where I always hold my finals.

"I want to start getting the money right now, Old Man," the Kid says to me after we pass through the turnstiles. He calls me the Old Man and I call him the Kid. This is part of our professional relationship, although I like to think that there are undertones of genuine affection between us. The Kid is my most recent and greatest student and every now and then, watching him operate, I see the 24-year-old me when the world was mine for the taking. But I sometimes suspect he pictures me as being over the hill and himself as the new king of the hill, which is why I am putting him through a final exam. I have had such brash and eager students before and some have not, it has turned out, properly learned their lessons; I am hoping the Kid is not one of these and that I will not be forced to fail him as a result.

I say in answer to his question, "Remember what I've taught you, Kid. No more than two marks pre-game and no more than two during the half-time ceremonies. Save your major operations for the post-game exodus."

"Sure," the Kid says. "Whatever you say."

When we approach the tunnel to our section I nudge him and gesture to where a big man in a grey suit is lounging against the wall pretending to read a program. "See that fellow over there?" I say.

"What about him?"

"His name is Harrahan. He is one of Candlestick's security chiefs and also very difficult on people in our profession. Avoid him and anyone who looks like him—anyone who seems to be an easy mark. Easy-looking marks often turn out to be security officers or undercover cops."

"Right," the Kid says. "Nothing comes easy in this business, right? You always got to work hard for the money."

"Good," I say, and nod my approval.

I steer him away from Harrahan and the tunnel and over toward the crowded concession stands. The Kid eyes a fat man who is paying for a hot dog with money from an equally fat wallet, but I shake my head. The fat man is not a good mark because he is with a fat woman who has eyes like a television camera: they see everything and record it in detail. The Kid looks half annoyed and half disappointed, but says nothing.

After five minutes I select his first mark—a moustachioed gentleman with a preoccupied expression and an expensive camel's-hair coat folded across one arm. The Kid dips him deftly, so deftly that I almost miss the operation even though I am watching each of the Kid's moves. He has the greatest left-hand snag hook I have ever seen, and in his right thumb and forefinger there is magic. I once saw him lift a lady's pocketbook on a crowded bus while at the same time tipping his hat to a clergyman.

I allow him a second score, from a white-haired man with a hip flask, and give him a fatherly smile after he executes another perfect dip. He grins. "A piece of cake, Old Man," he says. "Let's go count up the swag."

"Patience, Kid," I say. "The game will be starting pretty soon. It's time to take our seats."

We go through our tunnel and come out into the seats near the thirty-yard line, midway up. The 49ers and the Colts are already on the field and the referees are about to reenact the coin flip. The Kid and I sit down, after which I unfold the blanket I am carrying and spread it over our laps. The wind at Candlestick Park is always cool and blustery on fall days and I have to be careful of my rheumatism. It is the rheumatism, of course, which has necessitated my retirement from active service and my new profession as teacher of young hopefuls.

The 49ers lose the coin toss and prepare to kick off to the Colts. While the teams are lining up, the Kid takes out the two wallets he has dipped and opens them under the blanket. His face quirks in disgust. "Forty-six dollars, total," he mutters to me. "Damn lousy take so far."

"Not to worry," I tell him. "We have a long afternoon ahead of us."

"Yeah, I guess so. But hell, Old Man, I want to get the money—the *real* money. That fat dude at the concession stand must have had two, three hundred in his wallet."

I give him a reproachful look. "The most important thing at this point in your career," I say, "is artistry. Haven't I explained that often enough? The act is its own reward; even in a rain forest Jean-Pierre Rampal would still play the flute."

"What's a rain forest?" the Kid says. "Who the hell is Jean-Pierre Rampal?"

Brilliant in many ways, he is ignorant of matters cultural. But this does not bother me; like wine and age, the command of the intellect will develop. Still, I seem to have detected a note of belligerence in his voice. Belligerence, ofttimes, is a sign of ingratitude; this will have to be watched more carefully as the day progresses.

The game has already begun and I give my attention to the conflict below. The 49ers intercept a pass, cannot move the ball, and settle for a 37-yard field goal. The Colts score a touchdown on a fifty-yard pass play to their wide receiver. The 49ers score a touchdown on a 22-yard pass play to their tight end. The first quarter ends with San Francisco leading 10-7.

The Kid, I have noticed, is uninterested in the game. He fidgets in his seat and his eyes roam the crowd in a restless way. "Relax," I say to him. "Enjoy the contest. Half-time will arrive soon enough."

"I don't like football," the Kid says. "I don't give a damn for it. All I want is to get the money."

"That is all any of us want," I agree. "Nevertheless, too much anticipation can lead to mistakes. You're an artist, Kid, and there is no need for an artist to be overeager. The money will be there when the time comes."

"Okay, okay." But I detect the note of belligerence in his voice again, along with something which sounds like annoyance. This makes me wonder if the Kid is no longer listening to my advice, if he feels he knows more than I do about the business. An unhappy prospect. I have never had such a brilliant student and to have to fail him would depress me a great deal.

Little happens in the second quarter of the game. The Colts manage to make a field goal to tie the score at 10-10 with three minutes remaining, and that is the tally when the teams leave the field for half time. As soon as the gun sounds, the Kid pushes the blanket aside and stands. His eyes are bright and determined and I watch his nimble fingers flex eagerly, as if they are already plucking wallets from the pockets of marks.

"I'm going to work, Old Man," he says.

I have already informed him that on this second part of his final exam—the half-time score, as it were—he will be on his own; I will wait here and he will choose his own marks. I nod. "Remember," I say, "no more than two. And make sure to watch out for—"

"Yeah, yeah, I know," the Kid says shortly. "Watch out for Harrahan and his boys, and watch out for pickings that look too easy. You think I'm stupid, Old Man? I don't need to be told things a hundred times." He pushes past me and hurries up the stairs to the tunnel.

I sigh, rearrange the blanket, and place my once-great hands beneath it to keep them warm. The half-time ceremonies at 49er games are usually interesting, but today I am unable to enjoy the marching bands and the dancing girls. My mind is occupied with the Kid and how he is doing on his exam.

He is gone for twenty minutes; the teams are already back on the field when he returns. He does not look at me as he slides past, sits down, and sips at a cup of beer.

I say, "All went well?"

"So-so. No sweat with the operations, but this is a goddamn cheap crowd, let me tell you. A hundred and six bucks and that's it."

This makes me frown. "Then you've already made an accounting," I say.

"Yeah. In one of the johns."

"Your instructions were to bring everything straight back here to me—"

"The hell with my instructions. I did it my own way for a change."

I say, tight-lipped, "What else did you do your own way, Kid? How many operations? It wasn't just two, was it?"

"No, and the hell with that too. I told you, it's a cheap crowd. Five scores and barely more than a C-note."

The belligerence is unveiled in his voice now and it is accompanied by a certain contempt. I feel sadness inside me, for there seems to be little doubt that I am going to have to fail the Kid. It is not too late for him to redeem himself—he may yet pass—but in my heart I sense that he is beyond redemption.

Neither of us has anything to say during the second half. I have lost my taste for football and I am not even cheered when the 49ers score a last-second touchdown to win the game 24-23. As before, the Kid is on his feet the instant the gun sounds. I watch him as he moves quickly up the aisle and see he has forgotten or chosen to ignore everything I have taught him. He does not even wait until he is inside the tunnel before he makes his first dip. But he is good, very good, and no one is aware of the operation, least of all the mark.

I follow him through the tunnel and around to the concession area. He works fast, with utter confidence and utter carelessness: four marks, five, six, seven. Wallets disappear into his pockets, along with a folder of traveler's checks, a money clip, and a digital calendar watch. It is a virtuoso performance, begun and completed within the space of eight minutes, and in one sense I am awed by the artistry of it. But in the last analysis, of course, I feel even more saddened and depressed because, for all its brilliance, it is the performance of a failure.

The Kid has hopelessly failed the exam.

But I determine to give him one last chance. Despite all his shortcomings, I am still impressed by his talents and am not quite able to shed the remnants of my fatherly affection for him. I approach him near the main turnstiles and place my hand on his arm. He tries to shrug me away, scowling, but I say, "We're going to have a talk, Kid, right here and now. If you make a scene, it will only call attention to you."

He accepts the wisdom of that, and allows me to lead him over to one of the concession stands, out of the flow of departing fans. "You've done everything wrong today," I tell him, "ignored everything I tried to teach you. Why, Kid? Why?"

"Because you're an old fool," he says, "you're small potatoes. I want the big money, and I sure as hell can't get it doing things your way."

I wince at this; it hurts to hear him say these things to me. "You could have been caught," I say. "Then neither of us would have gotten the money."

"I'm too good to get caught," he says cockily. "I'm the best there is, Old Man."

"The fact remains that you jeopardized the entire operation. I'm going to have to penalize you for that."

"Penalize? What the hell you talking about?"

"Our arrangement was for an even split of the proceeds," I say. "Instead, I intend to take sixty percent."

His lip curls. "Is that so? Well, I've got another idea. How about if I take a *hundred* percent?"

I look at him sadly. "You'd do that to me, Kid? After all I've done for you?"

"You ain't done nothing for me," he says. "You gave me a few pointers, that's all—maybe smoothed off a couple of rough edges. I been giving you half my scores for three months now and that's plenty. I'm in the big time now; I'm an artist, just like you said. You want any more money, Old Man, go out and work for it just like I been doing."

"You have to pay your dues in this business," I say. "Don't you understand that? Nothing comes easy, nothing comes free. You've got to pay off, Kid, one way or another. There's plenty of money to be had, more than enough for everybody, but you've got to learn to honor your commitments and make your splits."

"I ain't making no splits with you or anybody else," the Kid says. "Now get out of my way, Old Man. I want to make another score or two while there's still a crowd around."

He shoves past me roughly and heads toward the nearest tunnel, out of which people are still emptying. I shake my head. I had thought that the Kid was different from most, but it was not so—he was my greatest student, but now he is my greatest disappointment. Sad, very sad—but what is to be done? The final exam is over and he has failed, and as his teacher I have no choice except to flunk him out of school.

I drift over to where Harrahan is waiting and watching the Kid from his position by the bathrooms, and I give him the high sign. He nods and moves in quickly, just as the Kid is about to dip an elderly gentleman in sunglasses and straw hat. Harrahan, who is as good at his job as I used to be at mine, has him handcuffed and is leading him away before the Kid quite realizes what has happened.

If only the Kid had listened to me. If only he had listened and if only I could have trusted him from the beginning.

Because then there would not have been any need for a final exam; trust would have superseded such a hard necessity. And because then I would have been able to tell him about my long-standing working arrangement with Harrahan, a humble crook like myself who knows that one must always pay the price—here in Candlestick Park if not to all of the world.

As it is, the Kid will bother me. He had all of the tools, all of the genius; he could have continued my life's work and granted me a kind of immortality.

He will bother me for a long, long time.

FUNERAL DAY

It was a nice funeral. And easier to get through than he'd imagined it would be, thanks to Margo and Reverend Baxter. They had kept it small, just a few friends; Katy had had no siblings other than Margo, no other living relatives. And the casket had been closed, of course. A fall from a two-hundred-foot cliff ... it made him shudder to think what poor Katy must have looked like when they found her. He hadn't had to view the body, thank God. Margo had attended to the formal identification.

The flowers were the worst part of the service. Gardenias, Katy's favorite. Dozens and dozens of gardenias, their petals like dead white flesh, their cloyingly sweet perfume filling the chapel and making him a little dizzy after a while, so that he couldn't concentrate on Reverend Baxter's mercifully brief eulogy.

At least he hadn't been pressed to stand up next to the bier and speak. He couldn't have done it. And besides, what could he have said about a woman he had been married to for six years and stopped loving—if he had ever really loved her—after two? It wasn't that he'd grown to hate or even dislike her. No, it was just that he had stopped caring, that she had become a stranger. Because she was so weak ... that was the crux of it. A weak, helpless stranger.

Afterward, he couldn't remember much of the ride to the cemetery. Tearful words of comfort from Jane Riley, who had been Katy's closest friend; someone patting his hand—Margo?—and urging him to bear up. And later, at the gravesite ... "We therefore commit her body to the ground, earth to earth, ashes to ashes, dust to dust ..." and Reverend Baxter sprinkling a handful of dirt onto the coffin while intoning something about subduing all things unto Himself, amen. He had cried then, not for the first time, surely not for the last.

The ride home, to the small two-story house he had shared with Katy a half mile from the college, was a complete blank to him. One moment he was at the gravesite, crying; the next, it seemed, he was in his living room, surrounded by his books and the specimen cases full of the insects he had collected during his entomological researches. Odd, he realized then, how little of Katy had gone into this room, into any of the rooms in the house. Even the furniture was to his taste. The only contributions of hers that he could remember were frilly bits of lace and a bright seascape she had bought at a crafts fair. And those were gone now, along with her clothing and personal effects; Margo had already boxed them up so that he wouldn't have to suffer the task, and had had them taken away for charity.

Nine or ten people were there, Katy's and his friends, mostly from the college. Mourners who had attended the funeral and also been to the cemetery. Jane Riley and Evelyn Something—Dawson? Rawson? a woman he didn't know well that Katy had met at some benefit or other—had provided food, and there were liquor and wine and hot beverages. Margo and the Reverend had referred to the gathering as a "final tribute"; he called it a wake. But Katy wouldn't have minded. Knowing that, he hadn't objected.

Katy. Poor, weak, sentimental Katy ...

The mourners ate and drank, they talked, they comforted and consoled. He ate and drank nothing; his stomach would have disgorged it immediately. And he talked little, and listened only when it seemed an answer was required.

"You *are* taking a few more days off, aren't you, George?" Alvin Corliss, another professor at the college. English Lit.

"Yes."

"Take a couple of weeks. Longer, if you need it. Go on a trip, someplace you've always wanted to visit. It'll do you a world of good."

"Yes. I think I might ..."

"Is Margo staying on awhile longer, George?" Helen Vernon, another of Katy's friends. They had gone walking together often, along the cliffs and elsewhere. But she hadn't been with Katy on the day of her fall. No, not on that day.

"Yes, Helen, she is."

"Good. You shouldn't be alone at a time like this."

"I don't mind being alone."

"A man needs a woman to do for him in his time of grief. Believe me, I know ..."

On and on, on and on. Why didn't they leave? Couldn't they see how much he wanted them to go? He felt that if they stayed much longer he would break down—but of course he didn't break down. He endured. When his legs grew weak and his head began to throb, he sank into a chair and stared out through a window at his garden. And waited. And endured.

Dusk came, then full dark. And finally—but slowly, so damned slowly—they began to leave by ones and twos. It was necessary that he stand by the door and see them out. Somehow, he managed it.

"You've held up so well, George ..."

"You're so brave, George ..."

"If you need anything, George, don't hesitate to call ..."

An interminable time later, the door closed behind the last of them. Not a moment too soon; he was quite literally on the verge of collapse.

Margo sensed it. She said, "Why don't you go upstairs and get into bed? I'll clean up here."

"Are you sure? I can help—"

"No, I don't need any help. Go on upstairs."

He obeyed, holding onto the bannister for support. He and Katy had not shared a bedroom for the past three years; there had been no physical side to their marriage in almost four, and he had liked to read at night, and she had liked to listen to her radio. He was grateful, now that she was gone, that he did not have to occupy a bed he had shared with her. That would have been intolerable.

He undressed, avoided looking at himself in the mirror while he brushed his teeth, and crawled into bed in the dark. His heart was pounding. Downstairs in the kitchen, Margo made small sounds as she cleaned up after the mourners.

You're so brave, George ...

No, he thought, I'm not. I'm weak—much weaker than poor Katy. Much, much weaker.

He forced himself to stop thinking, willed his mind blank.

Time passed; he had no idea how many minutes. The house was still now. Margo had finished her chores.

He lay rigidly, listening. Waiting.

A long while later, he heard Margo's steps in the hall. They approached, grew louder ... and went on past. The door of her room opened, shut again with a soft click.

He released the breath he had been holding in a ragged sigh. Not tonight, then. He hadn't expected it to be tonight, not this night. Tomorrow? The need in him was so strong it was an exquisite torture. How he yearned to feel her arms around him, to be drawn fiercely, possessively against the hard nakedness of her body, to succumb to the strength of her, the overpowering dominant *strength* of her! She had killed Katy for him; he had no doubt of it. When would she come to claim her prize?

Tomorrow?

Please, he thought as he began to masturbate, please let it be tomorrow....

CAIUS
(with Barry N. Malzberg)

Caius watches the lights on the board, red, red, red, red, with eager eyes (not that he could be seen) and fast-beating heart (not that he could be monitored). Elbows on the table, headphones tight against his ears. Throat cleared to allow his mellifluous voice to draw slowly, exquisitely, the pulp of his listeners' desires.

Jeremy, his engineer, picks one red light at random. No screening except for the FCC mandated seven-second delay—Caius does not need to have his calls screened. There is no listener, no heckler, no type of problem or question that he cannot address with knowledge, wit, perfect aplomb.

This caller, as usual, is one of the faithful. Stan in Cheyenne. How're they screwing you, Stan, he asks, up there in the cold, cold Rockies? Stan mumbles, grumbles, spews harsh and bitter words into his ears. One and a half minutes of Stan is sufficient. Caius deftly cuts him short, waves to Jeremy to put on another caller.

Georgiana in Seattle. Yes, of course, he says to her, let's talk about the rule of the gun and the rule of law, not that there's any difference in these United States. He draws her out slowly, inexorably, tugging on and loosening the strangling rope of her consciousness.

"Now do you understand, Georgiana?" Caius says when her three minutes are up. "Do you know what must be done?"

"Oh, yes, Caius," she says. Her voice is breathless, as if his words have brought her to orgasm. "Oh, yes!"

In the glistening glass wall of the engineer's booth, he sees reflected the outlines of his own face. Strong jaw, ears like miniature radar scanners, eyes huge and glowing with testimony to his incontestable vision, his indomitable spirit. Caius, nomad of the Space Age airwaves. Caius, the man with the answers, the man with the power to strip away falsehoods and false fronts, to unburden and provide direction to so many in this age of inanition. Caius, the oracle of his times. How he has suffered for his art, his genius! How he suffers as confessor for these fools who know nothing of the gravity of his heart.

He feels their pain radiating through the headphones. He hears their murmuring voices, millions of voices, echoing through the corridors of his mind. He has come to give them what they need, not what they want, the difference accomplished through his own inextinguishable judgment.

We live in perilous times, he tells them again and again. Times in which the bad has been masked as good, in which destruction has been masked as compassion. Times which have taken from us what we might have had, what we should have received. Are they listening? Are you listening, Georgiana in Seattle, Stan in Cheyenne, Karl in Saginaw, Benjamin in Coeur d'Alene, all the rest of you?

Sometimes he thinks they ask too much of him, they ask more than he can give—he is, after all, only one man, one frail stanchion standing against the enormities of the present and the future. Sometimes he despises them, the puny, stupid ones unworthy of his benevolence. Sometimes he thinks it doesn't matter what he does, for his power, always, is in what he *could* do if he wanted to.

Jeremy signals that another caller is on the line. Caius waves him off, indicates that it is time to cut to the usual recorded commercial messages. Sighs, removes his headphones. Enough for now. Enough. He needs a few minutes to regenerate himself before he once again takes the fools through the inconstancy of this world and points them in the right direction. One day he might even lead them, all of them, all his faithful, into the promised land.

Dazzled by the images of himself reflected from the glass walls, he stands, stretches. Caius, cloned and magnified, larger than life.

The door to the control booth opens and Jeremy comes in. Caius favors him, as he does all his minions, with a beneficent smile. "Going well tonight," he says.

Jeremy nods. Jeremy nods at everything. A fawning youth, nothing like what Caius was at his age, no ambition for one thing, but he does his job and that is sufficient. If Caius needed more, he could have more. But he doesn't. Why should he? Jeremy is no different than Stan in Cheyenne or Gail in Indianapolis, but Caius is kind to him nonetheless. He is kind to all the members of his flock. One of the obligations of power.

"As always," Jeremy says. "You the man."

"Caius, nomadic interpreter of all their secrets."

"Absolutely right, that's what you are. Not even Limbaugh can keep them coming back the way you do."

"How many calls so far tonight?" Caius asks.

"Ninety-six."

"Grand total to date?"

"Nearly a million since you've been on the air."

"Six million listeners, one million calls."

"Amazing record," Jeremy says. "Amazing. It's an honor to work with a great man like you, a real honor."

An honor. That is what so many of them say when Caius releases them from the coffins of their unnecessary, irrelevant lives. What an honor to speak with you! What a thrill! Been listening to you for years, you taught me a lot, you make such good sense. Their praise, their unction coursing through him like the fever heat of his own blood.

"We need some sound bytes," he says to Jeremy. "You have them ready on the roll, of course?"

"Yes, sir. Always. Ready when you are."

"Numbers forty-two and fifty-seven," Caius says. "Those are the ones I want tonight. First the one where the Pope attacks me personally, by name, then my clip at the Correspondents Dinner."

"Forty-two and fifty-seven. Right." Jeremy chuckles. "I remember that dinner clip. Pretty funny stuff."

"Yes, very amusing."

"You nailed the bastards in that one," Jeremy says. "Nailed 'em right up there on the cross, just like Jesus."

Just like Jesus.

And just like Jesus, Caius thinks, I have my disciples. My Caiusites. My Causations. My Causators. The groveling faithful that pour through all the tangled and whizzing lines of the nation directly into me, Caiusites drawing from the power which is mine.

In the early years he had traveled everywhere, spoke from the trenches and the front lines in all the gleaming, devastated parts of the nation, advancing to this destination in stages, in movements as careful and well planned as those on a chess board. He has a history, he sometimes likes to remind his listeners, his disciples, he didn't get to this point without years of study, questing, humility, honor, suffering.

He heard their pleas then, the same ones he hears now: Tell us, Caius. Lead us, Caius. But he also heard, sometimes still hears, their bitterness and their spite. Why are you where you are, Caius, and we're trapped down here in the swamps of human existence? How did you get the power instead of us? When he is confronted with such apostasy he thinks of sucking out their brains, the gray and spongy material which surrounds their tiny thoughts, and draping them on a line to wave in the breeze before he puts the torch to them. Blinding fire against the sky. Caius remembers John Lennon. First they ask for an autograph and then they come back and kill you. That Spider's Kiss.

But Lennon's fate will not be his. No, never. He is above such an absurd end to his life and his life's work. He is destined to continue his mission for many more years to come. Caius, the invincible.

Jeremy gestures at the clock. "Almost airtime again," he says.

"Yes, I see."

The engineer leaves the booth quickly and quietly, and Caius sits again in his comfortable chair. Headphones on. Microphone on. Green light on. And here I am again, listeners, disciples, Caiusites, he thinks but doesn't say. Go ahead, Ronald in Little Rock, he says. What's on your mind this evening, Ronald? How can I help? How can I bring you the wisdom of Caius?

The board continues to light up with incoming calls, red, red, red, red, red. Jeremy makes his selection, Caius presses the button that opens the line. The voice of Elaine in Charleston drones in his ear. Tormented Elaine, until Caius's words elevate her to new heights of consciousness and perception.

Another green light. Marvin in San Antonio. Another. Big Dave in Biloxi. Another. Linda and Jolene, mother and daughter, suffering in Corpus Christi. Help us, Caius. Lead us, Caius. Save us, Caius.

One after another he takes the calls, listens to the voices of the faithful and, now and then, the unfaithful. So many voices. Night after night. And after a while they begin to blend and flow together, to rise to a roar that pours through the headphones, through his ears, into the center of him. The voices of admiration, of love and approbation, these are what he lives for.

And yet—

And yet, the voices grow decibel by painful decibel until they fill him, swell him to the bursting point. Frantically he signals to Jeremy to cut off the new caller—Darlene in Thousand Oaks? Andrew in Sheboygan?—but the engineer ignores him. Caius rips off the headphones, claps his hands over his ears. The roar of the million voices continues to increase, louder, louder, louder, until it reaches a thunderous crescendo.

Caius's vision dims when this happens, shifts, and the glass walls shimmer, Jeremy shimmers in the control booth, everything shimmers, blurs, fades, and then re-emerges as something other than the familiar surroundings of the studio, as white cushioned walls, white cushioned floor, bare cot, screens and bars, Jeremy in a white attendant's uniform. The voices cease their babel; all at once he finds himself wrapped in a deep trembling silence. He cries out, but there is no one to hear him, he is alone. Alone. He understands then, the monstrous knowledge descends upon him with the force of a blow, and he screams, he screams—

—and the white room shifts, shimmers, fades, and then re-emerges as the interior of his booth at the studio, where he is once again sprawled in his comfortable chair, headphones on, microphone on, his mind as clear as the glistening glass walls. He looks at the board, red, red, red, red. Sees Jeremy signal from the control booth, then turn one flashing red to green. Smiles, winks, gives the thumbs up. And safe, secure, supremely confident as always in the efficacy of his genius, he takes a call from Eric in Council Bluffs.

Caius, nomad of the Space Age airwaves. Caius, oracle of his times.

Caius, the man with the answers, the man with the power, the man who will one day show them all the way into the light, finally and forever into the light.

THE SPACE KILLERS

The door to Rnfibl's Outpost Grattl Shop opened and two Terrans came inside. They sat at the counter.

"What'll you have?" sPfzl asked them.

"I don't know," one of the Terrans said. "What kind of grattl do you want, Big Ernie?"

"I don't know," Big Ernie said. "I don't know what kind of grattl I want."

It was dark outside. There were no street lights. That was because there were no streets. The robot labor crews hadn't got around to building them yet.

The two Terrans at the counter read the menu scanner. Down at the other end, Nikkk watched them. He was drinking a Lyran yerfulmus latte. It was early in the evening so he was still sober.

"I'll have the Rigelian wild rrfim *au jus* with a side order of grrib," the first Terran said.

"We don't have any Rigelian wild rrfim," sPfzl said.

"What the hell do you put it on the scanner for?"

"It isn't on the scanner."

"So you think it isn't on the scanner?"

"Well, it wasn't on the scanner this afternoon."

"Oh, fleek the scanner," Big Ernie said. "What kind of grattl have you got?"

"I can give you Beta Hydran, Low Brmian, Sigma Draconan—"

"Give me Titanian yatz, medium rare, with fragm sauce and candied summitan."

"We don't have any Titanian yatz," sPfzl said.

"Everything we want you don't have, eh? That the way you work it?"

"I can give you Beta Hydran, Low Brmian—"

"I'll take Low Brmian," the Terran called Big Ernie said. He wore a dark green loose-fitting oxy suit with a bulge under the right arm of his tunic. One of his ears looked like a bas relief of the surface of Mars.

"Give me Sigma Draconan," the other Terran said. He was nine inches shorter than Big Ernie, seventy-three pounds lighter, and had a long red beard and a bronze Gork ring dangling from one nostril. The bulge under his tunic was on the left side. The two Terrans didn't look like twins at all.

"This is some crappy little hunk of rock," Big Ernie said. "What do they call it?"

"Outpost Fourteen."

"Ever hear of it?" Big Ernie asked his friend.

"No," the friend said.

"Must be out in the middle of the asteroid belt."

"It is," sPfzl said.

"You think we don't know that?" the friend said. "How could we be here if we didn't know that?"

"So what do you do here nights?" Big Ernie asked sPfzl.

"They eat and drink," the other Terran said. "They all come here and eat the grattl and drink the fleeking yerfulmus."

"That's right," sPfzl said.

"So you think that's right?" Big Ernie asked.

"Sure."

"You're a shiny freeb, aren't you?"

"Sure."

"Well, you're not," Big Ernie said. "Is he, Bruno?"

"He's as stupid as an Acheiportyx zirp," Bruno said. He turned to Nikkk. "What's your name?"

"Nikkk. With three k's."

"What kind of name is Nikkk with three k's?"

"It's a Terran name with a Martian spelling."

"Another shiny freeb," Big Ernie said. "Ain't he a shiny freeb, Bruno?"

"This crappy little outpost is full of shiny freebs," Bruno said.

sPfzl put two platters, one of Low Brmian zullf, the other of Sigma Draconan hado xthan, on the counter. He didn't set down any side dishes. Low Brmian zullf and Sigma Draconan hado xthan didn't come with side dishes.

"Which is yours?" he asked Big Ernie.

"Don't you remember?"

"The Low Brmian."

"Some shiny freeb," Big Ernie said. He leaned forward and took the dish of Low Brmian zullf. Both Terrans began eating.

"What are *you* looking at?" Bruno asked sPfzl.

"I was looking at your beard," sPfzl said. "It's longer on the left side than on the right."

"So you think my beard's longer on the left side than on the right. You hear that, Big Ernie? The shiny freeb here thinks my beard's longer on the left side than on the right."

"It is," Big Ernie said, and went on eating his Low Brmian zullf.

"This is lousy hado xthan," Bruno said.

"I know it," sPfzl said.

"Then what the hell do you serve it for?"

"On account of Rnfibl can make it cheap," sPfzl said.

"Oh, so Rnfibl can make it cheap. He's another shiny freeb."

"What's the shiny freeb's name down at the end of the counter?" Big Ernie asked Bruno.

"He says it's Nikkk with three k's."

"Hey, Nikkk with three k's," Big Ernie said. "You go around on the other side of the counter with your friend here."

"Why?" Nikkk asked.

"Because I told you to."

"You better go around," Bruno said.

Nikkk went on around the counter.

"Who's out in the kitchen?" Big Ernie asked sPfzl.

"Nobody," sPfzl said.

"Where's the Melnusian?"

"What Melnusian is that?"

"The Melnusian that cooks."

"There isn't any Melnusian that cooks."

"Every grattl shop on crappy little outposts like this has a Melnusian that cooks."

"We don't," sPfzl said. "We had a Rhyx dishwasher for a while, but he quit to take a mining job on Altair IV."

"Just a shiny freeb," Big Ernie said.

Bruno got off his stool and went around behind the counter and looked into the kitchen. "Nobody there," he said.

"Say," sPfzl said, "what would you have done to the Melnusian if we'd had one?"

"Zirp stupid, all right," Big Ernie said. "What would we do to a Melnusian?"

sPfzl looked at the wall. If there had been a clock there, it would have said a quarter past six. But there wasn't any clock on the wall. The only thing on the wall was a dried spot of Lyran yerfulmus.

"Well," Bruno said, "why don't you shiny freebs say something?"

"What's it all about?" Nikkk asked.

"You hear that, Big Ernie? Nikkk with three k's wants to know what it's all about."

"Why don't you tell him?"

"What do you think it's all about?" Bruno asked Nikkk.

"I don't know," Nikkk said.

"What do you think?"

"I don't like to think too much. It hurts my head."

"You hear that, Big Ernie? He says he don't like to think too much because it hurts his head."

"You don't have to repeat every fleeking thing," Big Ernie said. "I'm right here and I got ears."

"Talk to me, Nikkk with three k's," Bruno said. "What do you think's going to happen?"

Nikkk did not answer.

"I'll tell you," Bruno said. "We're going to skrank a Terran spacer. Do you know a Terran spacer named Otoo Andersson?"

sPfzl and Nikkk looked at each other. "Yes," sPfzl said.

"He comes here for grattl whenever his ship vectors in, don't he?"

"Sometimes he does."

"He's due in tonight, ain't he?"

"I suppose he is."

"We know all that," Bruno said. "You think we don't know all that?"

"What are you going to skrank Otoo Andersson for? What did he ever do to you?"

"He never had a chance to do anything to us. He never even seen us."

"And he's only going to see us once," Big Ernie said.

"How come you're going to skrank him then?" Nikkk asked.

"We're skranking him for a friend of ours. He's paying us ten thousand credits for the job."

"Ten thousand credits?"

"That's right."

"You know how we're going to do it?" Bruno asked sPfzl.

"No," sPfzl said.

"Well, I'll tell you. We're going to do it with the lasers we got hidden under our tunics. What do you shiny freebs think of that?"

"Oh, skrut," Nikkk said, and he took the Orgellian blaster out from under *his* tunic. He shot the Terran named Big Ernie through the head, and then he shot the Terran named Bruno through his off-center red beard. Then he put the blaster back under his tunic and went around and sat down at the counter again.

"Bring me another yerfulmus," he said to sPfzl.

sPfzl was looking down at Bruno and Big Ernie lying dead on the floor. After a while he made another Lyran yerfulmus latte and took it to Nikkk.

"That was some nice shooting you did there," sPfzl said. "But you took quite a chance, didn't you?"

"Well, all that talk about skranking Otoo Andersson for ten thousand credits made me mad."

"I know what you mean," sPfzl said. "It made me mad, too. You know, I can't help wondering what he did."

"Who?"

"Otoo Andersson."

"Got fleeked up with some corrupt politician in the Federation. That's how come contracts get put out nowadays."

"He must have got fleeked up with more than one corrupt politician," sPfzl said. "He must have got fleeked up with a whole bunch of them."

"I guess he must have."

"It's a hell of a thing."

"It sure is," Nikkk said. "I'm going to get out of this business pretty soon."

"Yes," sPfzl said. "That's a good idea."

"I can't stand to think about those two Terrans getting ten thousand credits for skranking Otoo Andersson. It's too damned awful. All we're getting to skrank Otoo Andersson is five thousand credits."

"Well," sPfzl said, "you better not think about it."

FREE DURT

They were out for a Saturday drive on the county's back roads when they saw the sign. It was angled into the ground next to a rutted access lane that wound back into the hills—crudely made from a square of weathered plywood nailed to a post. The two words on it had been hand-drawn, none too neatly, with black paint.

FREE DURT

Ramage laughed out loud. "Look at that, will you? Proof positive of the dumbing-down of America."

"Oh, don't be so superior," Carolyn said. "Lots of people can't spell. That doesn't mean they're illiterate."

"D-u-r-t? A five-year-old kid can spell *dirt* correctly."

"Not everyone's had the benefits of a college education, you know. Or a cushy white-collar job."

"Cushy? Any time you want to trade, you let me know. I'd damn well rather be a school administrator than an ad-agency copywriter any day."

"Sure. At half the salary."

"Beside the point, anyway," Ramage said. "We were talking about that sign. Whoever made it couldn't've got past the first grade—that's the point."

"You can be such a snob sometimes," she said. Then: "I wonder why they're giving it away?"

"Giving what away? You mean dirt?"

"Well, out here in the country like this. Why don't they just spread it over the fields or something?"

"That's a good question."

"And where did they get so much that they have to give it away for nothing? Some kind of construction project?"

"Could be." He slowed the BMW, began looking for a place to turn around. "Let's go find out."

"Oh, now, Sam ..."

"Why not? I'd like to know the answer myself. And I'd like to meet somebody who doesn't know how to spell *dirt*."

She put up an argument, but he didn't pay any attention. He drove back to the rutted lane, turned into it. It meandered through a grassy meadow, up over the brow of a hill and down the other side. From the crest they could see the farm below, nestled in a wide hollow flanked on one side by a willow-banked creek and on the other by a small orchard of some kind. The layout surprised Ramage. He'd expected a little place, run-down or close to it, something out of Appalachia West. He couldn't have been more wrong.

It wasn't just that the farm was large—farmhouse, big barn, smaller barn, chicken coop, two other outbuildings, a vegetable garden, the rows of fruit trees, fences around the house and along the lane farther down and marching across the nearby fields. It was that everything was pristine. The buildings, the fences gleamed with fresh coats of white paint. The wire in the chicken run looked new. There wasn't anything in sight that seemed old or worn or out of place.

"Whoever owns this may not know how to spell," Carolyn said, "but they certainly know how to keep things in apple-pie order."

Ramage drove down between the fences and into the farmyard. A dog began to bark somewhere in the house as he nosed the BMW up near the front gate. Once he shut off the engine, the noise of the dog and the clucking of chickens and the murmur of an afternoon breeze were the only sounds.

They got out of the car. The front door of the house opened just then and a man came out with a dog on a chain leash. When Ramage got a good look at the man, he thought wryly: *Now that's more like it.* Farmer from top to bottom, like the one in the Grant Wood painting. In his sixties, tall, stringy, with a prominent Adam's apple and a face like an old, seamed baseball glove. He was even wearing overalls.

As he brought the dog out through the gate, Carolyn moved close to Ramage and a little behind him. Big dogs made her edgy. This one was pretty big, all right, some kind of Rottweiler mix, probably, but it didn't look very fierce. Just a shaggy farm dog, the only difference being that its coat was better groomed than most and it didn't make a sound now that it was leashed.

"Howdy, old-timer," Ramage said to the farmer. "How you doing?"

"Howdy yourself."

"We were driving by and saw your sign down by the road."

"Figured as much. Brings visitors up every now and then."

"I'll bet it does."

"Interested in free dirt, are you?"

"Might be."

"Can't get but a couple of sacks in that little car of yours."

"We couldn't use any more than that. You the owner here?"

"That's right. Name's Peete. Last name, three e's."

"Sam Ramage. This is my girlfriend, Carolyn White."

Carolyn gave him a look. She didn't like the word girlfriend. Ms. Feminist. But hell, that was what she was, wasn't it?

"What's the dog's name?"

"Buck."

"He doesn't bite, does he?" Carolyn asked.

"Not unless I tell him to. Or unless you try to bite him."

That made her smile. "You have a nice place here, Mr. Peete."

"Suits me."

"Must take a lot of work to keep everything so spic-and-span."

"Does. Always something that needs tending to."

"Keeps you and your hired hands busy, I'll bet."

"Don't have any hired hands," Peete said.

"Really? Just you and your family, then."

"No family, neither."

"You mean you live here alone?"

"Me and Buck."

"Must be kind of a lonely life, way out here, if you don't mind my saying so."

"I like it. Don't like people much." Peete was looking at Ramage's right hand. "Some trick you got there, young fella," he said.

Ramage grinned. He'd been knuckle-rolling his lucky coin back and forth across the tops of his fingers, making it disappear into his palm and then reappear again on the other side.

"That's his only trick," Carolyn said. "He's so proud of it he has to show it off to everybody he meets."

"Don't pay any attention to her. *Her* only trick is running her mouth."

"Never seen a coin like that," Peete said. "What kind is it?"

"Spanish doubloon. I picked it up in the Caribbean a couple of years ago."

"Genuine?"

"Absolutely." Ramage did three more quick finger rolls, made the coin disappear into his hand and then into his pocket. "I don't see this free dirt of yours, old-timer. Where have you got it?"

"Barn yonder."

"Let's have a look."

Peete led them across the farmyard to the smaller of the two gleaming white barns, the big dog trotting silently at his side. On the way Ramage asked conversationally, "What do you keep in the big barn? Cows?"

"Don't have any cows."

"Sheep? Goats?"

"No livestock except chickens. Big barn's for storage."

"Farm equipment?"

"Among other things."

When they reached the smaller barn, Peete unlatched the double doors and swung one of the halves open. Ramage could smell the dirt before he saw it, a kind of heavy, loamy odor in the gloom. It was piled high between a pair of tall wood partitions, not as much as he'd expected, but a pretty large hunk of real estate just the same—ten feet long, maybe twenty feet deep, by seven or eight feet high. He moved closer. Mixture of clods and loose earth, all dark brown with reddish highlights. Some of it toward the bottom had a crusty look, as if it had been there for a while; the rest seemed more or less fresh.

"What makes this dirt so special?" he asked the farmer.

"Special?"

"Well, there's a lot of it, and you keep it in here instead of outside, and you give it away free. How come?"

"Best there is. Rich. Good for gardens, lawns."

"So why don't you use it yourself, on that vegetable garden behind the house?"

"I do. Got more than I need."

"Where does it come from?" Carolyn asked. "Someplace on your property?"

"Yep. Truck it in from the cemetery."

She blinked. "From the ... did you say cemetery?"

"That's right. It's graveyard dirt."

There was a little silence before Ramage said, "You're kidding."

"No, sir. Gospel truth."

"Graveyard dirt."

"Yep."

"From a cemetery on your property."

"Yep. Old Indian burial ground."

"Never heard of any Indian tribes around here."

"Long time ago. Miwoks."

Carolyn asked, "You don't desecrate the graves, do you? Just so you can carry off a lot of rich soil?"

"Nope. Do my digging in the cemetery, but not where the graves are."

"How can you be sure?"

"I'm sure. You would be, too, if you saw the place."

"Miwoks?" Ramage said. "I didn't think they ranged this far south."

"Nomadic bunch, must've been."

"Nomads don't build cemeteries for their dead."

Peete fixed him with a squinty look. "Don't believe there's a burial ground close-by, that it?"

"Let's just say I'm skeptical."

"Prove it to you, if you want," Peete said. "Take you over and show it to you."

"Yeah? How far away is it?"

"Not far. Won't take long."

Ramage looked at Carolyn. "Oh, no," she said, "count me out."

"Real interesting spot," Peete said. "Artifacts and things."

"What kind of artifacts?" Ramage asked.

"Arrowheads, bowls, pots. Just lying around."

"Uh-huh."

"Fact. See for yourself."

"Not me," Carolyn said. "I don't like cemeteries. And I've seen all the Native American artifacts I care to see."

"No damn spirit of adventure," Ramage said.

"You go ahead if you want. I'm staying right here."

She meant it. And when she got stubborn about something, you couldn't change her mind for love or money.

Ramage said disgustedly, "All right, the hell with it. I guess we'll have to take your word for it, old-timer. About the dirt and the burial ground, both."

"Some do, some don't. Suit yourself."

"For now, anyway," he added. "Maybe some other time."

"Any time you want to see it." Peete gestured at the pile of free dirt. "How many sacks you want?"

"None right now. Some other time on that, too."

Peete shrugged, led them out of the barn into the sunshine. He closed the doors, set the latch, and started to move off.

"Hold on a second," Ramage said. And when the farmer stopped and glanced back at him, "About that sign of yours, down by the road."

"What about it?"

"Don't take offense, but you misspelled *dirt*."

"That a fact?"

"It's with an 'i,' not a 'u.' D-i-r-t. You might want to correct it."

"Then again," Peete said, "I might not."

He took the dog away to the house without a backward glance.

Carolyn said, "Did you have to bring up that sign?"

Ramage ignored her until they were in the car, bouncing down the rutted lane. Then he said, more to himself than to her, "Some character, that Peete."

"You think he's just a dumb hick, I suppose."

"Don't you?"

"No. I think he's a lot smarter than you give him credit for."

"Because of that business with the dirt and the Indian burial ground? I didn't believe it for a minute."

"Well, neither did I," she said. "That's the real reason I didn't want to go along with him. The whole thing's a hoax, a game he plays with gullible tourists. I wouldn't be surprised if he misspelled *dirt* on that sign just to draw people like us up here."

"Might have at that."

"If we'd gone along with him, what he'd have shown us is some spot he faked up with Native American artifacts and phony graves."

"Just to get a good laugh at our expense?"

"Some people have a warped sense of humor."

"Didn't look like Peete had any sense of humor."

"You can't tell what a person's like inside from the face they wear in public. You ought to know that."

"I'd still like to've seen the place," Ramage said.

"Why, for heaven's sake?"

"Satisfy my curiosity."

"You'd've been playing right into his hand."

"Still. I can't help being curious, can I?"

He stayed curious all that day, and the next, and the next after that. About the fake Miwok burial ground, and about Peete, too. How could the old buzzard afford to pay for all the upkeep on that farm of his, and give away good rich soil, when he had no help and no livestock except for a few chickens? Crops like alfalfa, fruit from that small orchard? Maybe he ought to drive back out there, alone this time, and have a look at the "cemetery" and see what else he could find out.

On Friday afternoon, Ramage decided that that was just what he was going to do.

The snotty young fella named Coolidge said, "I don't believe it."

"Gospel truth."

"Graveyard dirt from some old Indian cemetery?"

"Every inch of it."

"And you truck it in here and hoard it so you can give it away free. You think I was born yesterday, Pop?"

"Prove it to you, if you want."

"How you going to do that?"

"Burial ground's not far from here," Peete said. "Other side of that hill yonder."

"And you want me to go see it with you."

"Up to you. Only take a few minutes."

Coolidge thought about it. Then he grinned crookedly and said, "All right, for free d-u-r-t, why not? What have I got to lose?"

"That's right," Peete said. He tightened his grip on Buck's chain, tossed his new lucky piece into the air with his other hand. Sunlight struck golden glints from the doubloon before he caught it with a quick downward swipe. "What have you got to lose?"

ZERO TOLERANCE
(A "Nameless Detective" Story)

The little girl in the polka-dot playsuit was a holy terror. So was her mother. In fact, the kid wasn't all that bad—just spoiled and rambunctious—compared to the mom-thing that had spawned her.

The whole sorry business was the mother's fault. You couldn't lay any blame on the child; she hadn't been taught any better. You could lay a little of the blame on me, I suppose, but not much if you looked at it in perspective. In some ways the mother was an even nastier villain than the pudgy guy in the leather jacket.

It started with the little girl. She kept finding me out of all the other shoppers crowding the Safeway aisles, like some sort of pint-sized heat-seeking missile. First she charged out from behind a bin full of corn in the produce section, accidentally banged my shin with one of her cute red shoes, and then charged off without so much as a glance. Next she showed up in the meat department, standing directly behind me when I turned with a loosely wrapped package of ground round in my hand. I had to do a juking sidestep to avoid tripping over her, which caused me to drop the package; the wrapping split and bloody spatters decorated the right leg of my trousers. And finally there was the collision in the pet-food aisle.

I was pushing my cart near the end of the aisle, grumbling to myself, when she came flying around the corner with her arms outflung at her sides—playing airplane or some damn thing. Neither of us saw the other in time; she banged into the cart with a startled yelp. Just as this happened, the mother—a doe-eyed blond in her twenties—pushed her cart around the corner. She let out a yelp of her own when the kid bounced off and flopped down on her chubby little backside. She wasn't hurt; her face scrunched up but she didn't cry or even whimper. But the way the mother reacted you'd have thought her daughter had been mortally wounded. She rushed over, picked the child up, brushed her off, examined her with a probing eye, clutched her possessively, and then glared at me.

"What's the matter with you?" she said accusingly. "Why don't you watch where you're going?

Under ordinary circumstances I would have diffused the situation by smiling, muttering a polite comment, and sidling off to continue my shopping. But the circumstances here were not ordinary. There was my sore shin, and my soiled pantleg, and the facts that I'd had a long tiring day and Kerry was working late and it was my turn to do the shopping, and the additional fact that I have zero tolerance for parents who allow their children to run wild in supermarkets and other public places. I managed the smile all right, a tight little one, but not the polite comment or the sidling off.

"And why don't you curb your kid," I said, "before she really gets hurt."

"What?" It came out more like a squawk than a word.

"Just what I said, lady. This is the third time she's run into me—"

"How dare you!"

"How dare I what?"

"Talk to me that way. Accuse Amy of attacking you."

I wasn't smiling any more. "I didn't say she attacked me—"

"Of all the insane things. A six-year-old child and an old brute like you."

"Old brute?" I said. "Listen—"

"You practically run Amy down and then you…" Words failed her. She sputtered and said, "Oh!" and then realized that we'd drawn a small group of onlookers. This spurred her on; she was the type that would always play to a crowd. "Did any of you see it?" she asked the gawkers. "He almost ran my little girl down with his cart."

Nobody admitted to having seen anything, but there were angry mumbles and a couple of hostile looks thrown my way.

"She lets the kid run loose," I said, "play games in the aisles—"

"I never runned loose!" cute little Amy said. "I never did."

"Nice family like this," a henna-rinsed woman said, glowering at me. "You ought to be ashamed of yourself."

The nice family stood hating me with their bright blue eyes. The baby holy terror stuck her tongue out at me.

Some guy said, "Apologize, why don't you?"

"Apologize? I'm the one who—"

I stopped because I didn't have a sympathetic ear in the bunch. A no-win situation if ever I'd found myself in one. Let it go on much longer and it would turn ugly and escalate into an incident. So I took a tight grip on my offended pride and lied and dissembled.

"Okay," I said, "I'm sorry, it was all my fault. The child's not hurt. Let's just forget the whole thing."

That satisfied the gawkers. Within ten seconds they were gone. The mother set the little girl down—as soon as Amy's feet touched the floor she was off again—and turned back to her cart. She tried to jockey it past mine at the same time I tried to jockey past hers. This produced a mutter on my part, an exasperated sigh and another angry glare on hers.

I finished loading my cart in a dark funk, wheeled it to the checkout stands and into the shortest line. I had just transferred the last item onto the conveyor thing when something banged hard into the backs of my legs. I swung around.

The blond with her cart, naturally. "Oh," she said in a voice like maple syrup over arsenic, "I'm so sorry, I didn't mean to bump into you like that."

I swallowed eight or nine choice words. Sweet young Amy was clutching mommy's skirt; she showed me her tongue again. I put my back to them and kept it there the entire time my purchases were being rung up and paid for. And I didn't look their way as I left the store.

The parking lot at the Diamond Heights Safeway is almost always full in the evening, and tonight was no exception; I'd had to park toward the back of the lot, near the exit onto Diamond Heights Boulevard. All I could see over that way, through swirls and eddies of San Francisco's famous fog, were shapes and outlines.

I spotted the pudgy guy in the leather jacket at about the same time I located my car. He was wandering around in the general vicinity, about three cars north of mine. He stopped when he saw me, turned his head partway as I neared with my rattling cart. When I was close enough for him to get a good look at me, his head turned again and he moved away. Not far, though, just over to a backed-in Ford Econoline van new enough to still be wearing dealer plates. He bent and peered at the van's front end.

There was a furtiveness about him that I didn't like. I kept watching him when I put the groceries away in the trunk. He straightened after about ten seconds, went around on the far side of the van without looking my way again. I shut the trunk and approached the driver's door. The van was bulky enough and the fog thick enough so that I couldn't tell where the pudgy guy had gone.

I got into the car. The fog had laid thick films of wetness over the windows; I couldn't see through them. I scooted over on the passenger side, rolled the window down about two inches. The van was visible again through the narrow opening, as was the empty asphalt lane in front of it. There was no sign of the pudgy guy.

Nothing happened for about three minutes. I was still trying to decide if something dicey was going down when somebody materialized over that way.

It was the blond woman pushing her grocery cart, little Amy skipping along beside her.

And where they went was straight to the Ford van.

The woman unlocked the rear door and began shoving sacks inside while the holy terror hopped back and forth. Still no sign of the pudgy guy. Tension built in me, made me crack open my door.

The woman finished loading her groceries. As she unlocked the driver's door I heard her call, "Amy, you come here this instant—"

That was as far as she got. The pudgy guy appeared around the front of the van, something dark and pointy in one hand that could only be a gun, moving with such suddenness that Amy shrieked and ran to her mother. He got there at the same time she did, yanked the keys out of the woman's hand and then slugged her hard enough to pitch her backward into the grocery cart.

I was out of the car by then, running. The guy was half inside the van when he saw me; he tried to squirm back out instead of going all the way in and locking the door, and that was his mistake. I hit the half-open door with my shoulder, knocked him back against the side of the van. He struggled to get the gun up on me, but I pinned his arm with my left hand, slammed him in the belly with my right. He made a thin squealing noise that blended right in with the shrieking of the woman and the child. I smacked him in the belly again, twisting the gun out of his fingers, then punched him on the jaw as he was starting to sag. It was a solid, satisfying punch; he went all the way down and lay twitching at my feet.

Things stayed somewhat chaotic for the next couple of minutes. Some people came running up out of the fog, asking alarmed questions. The woman had quit yowling and was on her feet again, clutching Amy who was still going off in up-and-down riffs like a busted fire siren. She stared at me with one eye round as a half-dollar; the other, where she'd been slugged, was already puffy and half closed.

I stuffed the gun in my coat pocket, then gave my attention to the pudgy guy. He was lying on his side, moaning a little, his hands folded across his bruised midsection. I was almost sorry that he wasn't going to give me any more trouble.

Carjackers are something else I have zero tolerance for.

The cops came pretty quick, asked questions, finally handcuffed the pudgy guy and took him and his gun away. The crowd that had gathered gradually dispersed. And I was alone once more with a calmed-down Amy and her calmed-down mother.

The woman hadn't said a direct word to me the whole time, and she didn't say anything to me now. She pushed the kid into the van, hoisted herself in behind the wheel. Well, that figures, I thought.

I walked away to my car, but before I could get in, the woman was out of the van again and hurrying my way. She stopped with about four feet separating us. Changed her mind, I thought. Thanks or an apology coming up after all.

Wrong. All she said was, "I just want you to know—I still think you're a jerk." After which she did an about-face and back to the van she went.

I stood there while she fired it up, switched on the headlights, swung around in my direction. The driver's window was down; I saw her face and the little girl's face clearly as they passed by.

Amy stuck out her tongue.

And the mom-thing gave me the finger.

Right, I thought with more sadness than anger as I watched the taillights bleed away into the fog.

Zero tolerance night in what was fast becoming a zero tolerance world.

THE FELICITIES OF FICTION OR THE HEART OF THE ARTICHOKE
By Barry N. Malzberg

1) *Every work of fiction is one of crime fiction.* Like the proposal "All fiction is science fiction," seemingly ridiculous when shouted in an empty room it is clearly defensible...all stories, novelettes, novels, take place with characters, background, situation which to some degree must represent an altered reality; even the most doggedly researched or searing of historical novels create an imagined interior for their characters and historical events, however faithfully transcribed, must by definition veer from reality because neither the audience nor the author were there and never will be. Fiction is a transcription of *transgression*; one character or more or all of them resist the situation in which they have been placed; they struggle to change that situation, they must do so in a way which goes beyond the norms of the culture to which they have been assigned. Killers, plagiarists, unreasonably ambitious politicians, faithless lovers, all the apparatus of stories long and short are involved in someone's struggle to change circumstance and that struggle is going to cross taboos, iron laws, formulated social systems. The protagonist of almost every novel from *Huckleberry Finn* to *Madame Bovary* to the Jack Reacher novels is struggling against a circumstance, bestowed or forced, which must somehow be changed; the process of change must threaten to destroy the original situation or at least alter it dramatically. "Society" does not like this; "society" resists entropy even as it struggles against it and the meanest short-short for *Alfred Hitchcock's Mystery Magazine* or the most sprawling of novels like *Bonfire of the Vanities* depicts a protagonist and subsidiary characters who are either in a series of naked attempts to change the original situation or they are, however unwillingly or ineptly resisting those attempts; each of the party or parties of combatants are convinced that the opposition are both misguided and destructive and transgression for their own cause inevitable.

Just as the argument over the legitimacy or comparative importance of genre vs. "mainstream" fiction is a construct, not a reality—*all fiction is genre fiction when seen through the lens of its essential*—so is the dismissal (or acceptance) of crime fiction, the deductive mystery, the suspense novel to be seen as assuming a barrier which is artificial. Classifying fiction by genre is a publishers' rather than a writers' invention and although it may make life seemingly a little easier for the reader (or for the publishers) it is an artificial process enacted in an artificial fashion. "This isn't just science fiction/suspense/mystery/ western fiction," the paperback covers may testify, "It transcends the category." No it does not. The work at issue *enacts* the category and if it does so well it is exceptional. *The Shootist* is a splendid Western novel, *Canticle For Leibowitz* is both more penetrating and disturbing as post-apocalypse religious speculation than any earlier science fiction novel but science fiction it is and insistent denial merely displaces the work from its centrality to science fiction, and to the novel of the criminous which Walter Miller's renegade and apostate characters are forced to be.

2) *The short-short story* is the core of fiction; it is where the wheels and gears and movement necessitated for successful fiction can be observed in their starkest form; in their most penetrable function. Henry James described the short story as a narrative of one event which shakes the life of one person (and can be read in a sitting) but what James forgot, possibly because the works of Jack Ritchie or Roald Dahl did not exist in his time, is that this occurs in its purest form (and may be so observed) in the short-short story where the cleverness of the author must triumph over the inherent obviousness of a compressed story. The collection at issue—by one of the most notable practitioners of the form to have emerged in the last half century—is among its other qualities a schoolperson's text of process as story after story here gleam with the ability of the writer to both advance a narrative openly and fuse with that advance an indirection which only fuses in the final paragraph when all comes together. (Or, as in the works of Saki, Roald Dahl, Jack Ritchie or Bill Pronzini plunges toward a surprising but inevitable disarray.)

3) *Collaboration may be the heart of the artichoke*—the short-short story and the literary collaboration are both survivors of a series of creative necessities which may be anomalous; stories which apparently head in one direction are suddenly and often stunningly shifted to another; two disparate sensibilities fuse in the creation of such works while simultaneously finding a single, central, credible voice. Not all writers can do this and some of the most admired and famous don't even understand how it is done (Mailer, Nabokov, Hemingway, Fitzgerald), but collaboration is both an honored and successful (although sparing) form which "mainstream" writers mostly find bewildering and "genre writers", whether they practice it or not, understand instinctively because form and function can be synchronous. Several stories in this collection are collaborative, all with myself as collaborator; the author and I found ourselves almost from the beginning of our acquaintance capable of this and there are a few stories within so wicked ("What Kind Of A Person Are You?") of which I would clearly have been incapable alone. We have done

this intermittently over more than half a century and have produced half again more stories of which I am right pleased. Furthermore, in the short story we have never produced anything which did not sell *somewhere*, a claim I can certainly not make of my own singular body of work. This Afterword is a difficult but necessary honor upon which I insisted. What kind of person am I? Not too pontifical I hope. All credit to Bill Pronzini who showed me the way.

May 2021: New Jersey

BILL PRONZINI BIBLIOGRAPHY
(1943-)

Crime Fiction:

The Stalker (Random House, 1971)
Panic! (Random House, 1972)
Snowbound (Putnam's, 1974)
Games (Putnam's, 1976)
Masques (Arbor House, 1981)
The Cambodia File (with Jack Anderson; Doubleday, 1981; mainstream)
Day of the Moon (with Jeffrey Wallmann; Robert Hale, 1983)
The Eye (with John Lutz; Mysterious Press, 1984)
The Lighthouse (with Marcia Muller; St. Martin's, 1987)
With an Extreme Burning (Carroll & Graf, 1994; reprinted as *The Tormentor*, Leisure, 2000)
Blue Lonesome (Walker, 1995)
A Wasteland of Strangers (Walker, 1997)
Nothing But the Night (Walker, 1999)
In an Evil Time (Walker, 2001)
Step to the Graveyard Easy (Walker, 2002)
The Alias Man (Walker, 2004)
The Crimes of Jordan Wise (Walker, 2006)
The Other Side of Silence (Walker, 2008)
The Hidden (Walker, 2010)
The Violated (Bloomsbury, 2017)
The Peaceful Valley Crime Wave (Tor/Forge, 2019; western mystery)

"Nameless Detective" Series:

The Snatch (Random House, 1972)
The Vanished (Random House, 1973)
Undercurrent (Random House, 1973)
Blowback (Random House, 1977)
Twospot (with Colin Wilcox; Putnam's, 1978)
Labyrinth (St. Martin's, 1980)
Hoodwink (St. Martin's, 1981)
Scattershot (St. Martin's, 1982)
Dragonfire (St. Martin's, 1982)
Casefile: The Best of the "Nameless Detective" Stories (St. Martin's, 1983; stories)
Bindlestiff (St. Martin's, 1983)
Quicksilver (St. Martin's, 1984)
Double (with Marcia Muller; St. Martin's, 1984)
Nighshades (St. Martin's, 1984)
Bones (St. Martin's, 1985)
Deadfall (St. Martin's, 1986)
Shackles (St. Martin's, 1988)
Jackpot (Delacorte, 1990)
Breakdown (Delacorte, 1991)
Quarry (Delacorte, 1992)
Epitaphs (Delacorte, 1992)
Demons (Delacorte, 1993)
Hardcase (Delacorte, 1995)
Sentinels (Carroll & Graf, 1996)
Spadework: "Nameless Detective" Stories (Crippen & Landru, 1996; stories)
Illusions (Carroll & Graf, 1997)
Boobytrap (Carroll & Graf, 1998)
Crazybone (Carroll & Graf, 2000)
Bleeders (Carroll & Graf, 2002)
Spook (Carroll & Graf, 2003)
Scenarios: A "Nameless Detective" Casebook (Five-Star, 2003; stories)
Nightcrawlers (Tor/Forge, 2005)
Mourners (Tor/Forge, 2006)
Savages (Tor/Forge, 2007)
Fever (Tor/Forge, 2008)
Schemers (Tor/Forge, 2009)
Betrayers (Tor/Forge, 2010)
Camouflage (Tor/Forge, 2011)
Hellbox (Tor/Forge, 2012)

Kinsmen (Cemetery Dance, 2012; novella)
Femme (Cemetery Dance, 2012; novella)
Nemesis (Tor/Forge, 2013)
Strangers (Tor/Forge, 2014)
Vixen (Tor/Forge, 2015)
Zigzag (Tor/Forge, 2016; stories)
Endgame (Tor/Forge, 2017)

Carpenter and Quincannon Series:

Quincannon (Walker, 1985)
Beyond the Grave (with Marcia Muller; Walker, 1986)
Carpenter and Quincannon (Crippen & Landru, 1998; stories)
Burgade's Crossing (Five-Star, 2003)
Quincannon's Game (Five-Star, 2005)
The Bughouse Affair (with Marcia Muller; Tor/Forge, 2013)
The Spook Lights Affair (with Marcia Muller; Tor/Forge, 2013)
The Body Snatchers Affair (with Marcia Muller; Tor/Forge, 2015)
The Plague of Thieves Affair (with Marcia Muller; Tor/Forge, 2016)
The Dangerous Ladies Affair (with Marcia Muller; Tor/Forge, 2017)
The Bags of Tricks Affair (Tor/Forge, 2018)
The Flimflam Affair (Tor/Forge, 2019)
The Stolen Gold Affair (Tor/Forge, 2020)
The Paradise Affair (Tor/Forge, 2021)

As by Robert Hart Davis
The Pillars of Salt Affair (*The Man from U.N.C.L.E. Magazine*, 1967; novella)
Charlie Chan in The Pawns of Death (with Jeffrey Wallmann; *Charlie Chan's Mystery Magazine*, 1974; reprinted as by Bill Pronzini & Jeffrey Wallman, Wildside Press, 2002)

As by Jack Foxx
The Jade Figurine (Bobbs-Merrill, 1972)
Dead Run (Bobbs-Merrill, 1975)
Freebooty (Bobbs-Merrill, 1976)
Wildfire (Bobbs-Merrill, 1978)

As by Alex Saxon
A Run in Diamonds (Pocket, 1973)

In Collaboration with Barry N. Malzberg
The Running of Beasts (Putnam's, 1976)
Acts of Mercy (Putnam's, 1977)
Night Screams (Playboy Press, 1979)
Prose Bowl (St. Martin's, 1980)
Problems Solved (Crippen & Landru, 2003; stories)
On Account of Darkness and Other SF Stories (2004; stories)

Mystery Short-Story Collections:

Graveyard Plots (St. Martin's, 1985)
Small Felonies (St. Martin's, 1988)
Stacked Deck (Pulphouse, 1991)
Carmody's Run (Dark Harvest, 1992)
Duo (with Marcia Muller; Five-Star, 1998)
Sleuths (Five-Star, 1999)
Night Freight (Leisure, 2000)
Oddments (Five-Star, 2000)
More Oddments (Five-Star, 2001)
Dago Red (Ramble House, 2010)
The Cemetery Man (Perfect Crime, 2014)
A Little Red Book of Murder Stories (Borderlands Press, 2016)

Western Novels:

The Gallows Land (Walker, 1983)
Starvation Camp (Doubleday, 1984)
The Last Days of Horse-Shy Halloran (M. Evans, 1987)
The Hangings (Walker, 1989)
Firewind (M. Evans, 1989)
Give-A-Damn Jones (Tor/Forge, 2018)

As by William Jeffrey
Duel at Gold Buttes (with Jeffrey Wallmann; Tower, 1981)
Border Fever (with Jeffrey Wallmann; Leisure, 1983)

Western Short-Story Collections:

The Best Western Stories of Bill Pronzini (Ohio University Press, 1990)
All the Long Years: Western Stories (Five-Star, 2001)
Coyote and Quarter-Moon (Five-Star, 2006)
Crucifixion River (with Marcia Muller; Five-Star, 2007)

Non-Fiction Books:

Gun in Cheek (Coward McCann, 1982)
1001 Midnights: The Aficionado's Guide to Mystery and Detective Fiction (with Marcia Muller; Arbor House, 1986)
Son of a Gun in Cheek (Mysterious Press, 1987)
Sixgun in Cheek (Crossover Press, 1997)

Wicked satires from the master of black humor.....

Barry N. Malzberg

Underlay $15.95
"A brilliant novel, wildly funny and surprisingly poignant in its deeply knowledgeable portrait of the obsessed world of the compulsive bettor."
— Robert Silverberg

Lady of a Thousand Sorrows/ Confessions of Westchester County $19.95
"Both novels are told through first person narration and effectively display Malzberg's uncanny insight into character and motivation."—Alan Cranis, *Bookgasm*

The Spread/Horizontal Woman $15.95
"Blackly comic... *The Spread* centres on pornography and its effect on people, *Horizontal Woman* on sexual liberation... they get under your skin."—Paul Burke, *NB*

Screen/Cinema $15.95
"...the language of erotic literature repurposed for rather more disturbing ends—this is no paean to film, this is a lamentation..."—Joachim Boaz

Each book includes a new afterword by the author.

Overlay/A Bed of Money/Underlay $19.95
The Horseplayer Trilogy in one volume.
"Barry Malzberg is a comic genius."
—Michael Hurd, *Review*.

Oracle of a Thousand Hands/ In My Parents' Bedroom $15.95
"Very strange but at the same time, very interesting..."—Ralph Carlson

Fire/Machine $15.95
"As a 'Vietnam novel,' it does comment on PTSD and what soldiers coming back home from an unpopular war have to endure."—Michael Hemmingson

The Man Who Loved the Midnight Lady/In the Stone House $21.95
"... displays the exuberance, wit, and, above all, the terrific ear that distinguish his best work."—*Kirkus Reviews*

A Way With All Maidens/ A Satyr's Romance $15.95
"I wish I could see the face of the poor soul who bought this in 1968, hoping for some pornography, and instead getting a lecture in existentialism."—*GoodReads*

"Mr. Malzberg writes with cold stylishness about hot subjects."
—*Detroit Free Press*

Stark House Press, 1315 H Street, Eureka, CA 95501
griffinskye3@sbcglobal.net / www.StarkHousePress.com
Available from your local bookstore, or order direct via our website.

www.ingramcontent.com/pod-product-compliance
Lightning Source LLC
LaVergne TN
LVHW011932070526
838202LV00054B/4606